Please return/renew this item by the
last date shown to avoid a charge.
Books may also be renewed by phone
and Internet. May not be renewed if
required by another reader.

www.libraries.barnet.gov.uk

BARNET
LONDON BOROUGH

Invisible Women

Sarah Long is a London-based author of two previously published commercial fiction novels and one hilarious memoir about her ten years living in Paris. She is a married mother of three.

Invisible Women

Sarah Long

ZAFFRE

First published in Great Britain in 2017 by

ZAFFRE PUBLISHING
80–81 Wimpole St, London W1G 9RE
www.zaffrebooks.co.uk

A CIP catalogue record for this book is available from the British Library.

Paperback ISBN: 978-1-78576-265-9

Also available as an ebook
1 3 5 7 9 10 8 6 4 2

Typeset by IDSUK (Data Connection) Ltd
Printed and bound by Clays Ltd, St Ives Plc

Zaffre Publishing is an imprint of Bonnier Zaffre,
a Bonnier Publishing company
www.bonnierzaffre.co.uk
www.bonnierpublishing.co.uk

For all the visible women in my life.

'Art is a hard mistress, and there is no art quite so hard as that of being a wife.'

Blanche Ebbutt, *Don'ts for Wives*, 1913

PROLOGUE

She watched the passengers coming through the glass doors, pulling their suitcases and looking around expectantly. Smiles of recognition for loved ones, business-like nods if it was just a man holding a placard. How often she had done this before, waiting at airports for one of the children to fly back, safe, into the nest. Even, in the early days, coming to surprise Matt on his return from a business trip, when his face would light up at the sight of her and she'd be glad to have braved the traffic for his sake.

Today was different. She had no idea who she was waiting for. Not really. The last time she'd seen him, he was at that exquisite stage of late boyhood when they're all graceful limbs, slim hips and effortless beauty. They were dancing under the trees in his garden, the music was cranked up and she'd finally come to believe what he had been telling her for years. They belonged together. Then he'd led her into the house, upstairs into the playground of his single bed.

That was thirty-two years ago but she could feel it still, his hand on her teenage waist, the heat of his kiss and the urgent sense that he was most definitely The One, as defined by *Jackie* magazine. You'll know, they had all solemnly agreed as they flicked through the pages at break time in their school uniform with regulation two-inch heels and skirts hitched up to the limit, you'll just know when it happens that you've found The One.

She glanced at her watch, she was early as usual, plenty of time for a reality check as she tried to marry up the boy she remembered with the portly figure revealed in his Facebook photos. They weren't what they were, either of them, but she knew from the way they had spoken that it was still there. The longing that disregarded the years in between and demanded to be rediscovered right now, just as soon as his flight touched down and he'd worked his way through the alien passport queue. He'd gone American now, she'd seen the picture of him waving the little flag after the citizenship ceremony, claiming the right to bear arms and swagger around in a pair of big shorts. 'Oh my America, my new-found-land!' as John Donne proclaimed in that sexy poem they'd studied at school.

He wasn't big on poetry, she didn't think, unless he'd acquired a taste for it during the intervening decades. He had been more of an action type, he'd be the one pushing someone down the street in a hijacked shopping trolley or deconstructing the engine of his motorbike or smashing someone on the squash courts. During a Boy Discussion between lessons, Harriet had said he was like a Labrador, in need of constant fuelling and exercise, but then she was always keen on dog analogies. Sandra had found him too sporty, she preferred moody Bryan Ferry lookalikes who hung around in linen suits, smoking cigarettes in pencil-shaped holders, which was why she had ended up with miserable Nigel. You got what you were looking for, on the whole.

Harriet and Sandra were still her best friends, standing together in the murky chaos of middle age. All three married, just about, and wondering how to make sense of the rest of their lives now that their children no longer needed them. You go for it, Sandra had told her, when Tessa had expressed her doubts about this illicit meeting with her teenage heartthrob, you'll regret it if you don't, when you're dribbling next to me in an old people's home.

The arrivals board announced that his flight had landed.

Tessa felt a tightening in her stomach and her hands were sweating. There was surely time to freshen up, she didn't want to meet him with a shiny forehead. Abandoning her prime position by the barrier, she went to inspect herself in the mirror of the nearest washroom, dabbing at her face with a powder puff and wondering how she would appear to him now, in the flesh, as opposed to the enhanced version offered online through carefully edited photographs. The hair, at least, was visibly unchanged, still chestnut brown thanks to Clairol, she wasn't of the go-grey school, why would you do that to yourself? Face: not too saggy, wrinkles commensurate only with age and experience, and no random beard hairs. If she screwed her eyes up to fake the myopia that her lenses corrected, she could passably say that she still looked *exactly* the same, the way people always shrieked to each other at reunions, with varying degrees of sincerity. She stepped back to get a full-length perspective. The trusty waterfall cardigan was doing its job, rippling over the lumpy bits, but maybe black was a little funereal, especially here at the airport where people were mostly dressed in bland leisurewear.

Too late now, she thought, as she flicked back her hair, you are where you are and you're wearing what you're wearing. Matt was safely away at a conference, he had no idea where she was, she'd told him she might catch a film with the girls. A big fat lie, but to her surprise she no longer felt the slightest bit guilty. Instead she was getting a delirious sense of excitement and freedom and possibility.

The announcement board now said Baggage in Transit. She slowly worked her way to the front of the crowd by the barrier and waited.

CHAPTER ONE

Six weeks earlier

'Don't forget the anniversary of your wedding. Keep it up. The little celebration will draw you closer together, year by year.'

Blanche Ebbutt, *Don'ts for Wives*, 1913

On the morning of her silver wedding anniversary, Tessa Draper put on her make-up, took off her nightie and stood in front of the mirror. Did she look good naked? No, she looked like a fat fifty-year-old with a bit of lipstick on.

This was a shame because she planned to put in a few lengths this evening before dinner. Even in her tummy-control swimsuit, she'd be a godsend to the other women in the hotel pool, a hefty piece of meat tossed to the lions. On second thoughts, maybe she'd go for the privacy of the spa treatment room. Nobody could watch her there except the beauty therapist, who was paid to be nice to her, just as Tessa was paid, essentially, to be nice to her husband. It sounded crude but that is what it boiled down to. Twenty-five years together and she hadn't contributed a penny for most of them.

She turned sideways and tried looking over her shoulder in a winsome *Calendar Girls* pose. Slightly better, but let's not kid ourselves. Her naked days were over. As they should have been for Celia Imrie and all those other old birds. There comes a time when you should do everyone a favour and cover up.

Slipping on her dressing gown, Tessa turned her attention to the clothes laid out on her side of the bed. Floating panels for dinner, with a bold fake pearl necklace to draw the eye to the upper chest; leggings for cliff walks with loose-cut shirts and a forgiving cardigan; a Drizabone mac to confer the swagger of a New World pioneer. Definitely not a boring old Barbour.

Matt had pulled out his clothes earlier, before rushing out for a chemistry meeting with a potential client. Don't forget your Bunsen burner, she'd said but he hadn't laughed. It was alright for her to mock modern business jargon; she no longer needed to stay ahead of the game, thanks to him. Let's face it, she wasn't even *in* the game.

She turned on the taps and poured a generous slug of Grumpy Cow uplifting oil into the egg-shaped marble bath installed at the height of their renovation folly. The builders had reinforced the floor to support its giant weight, but Tessa still expected it to go crashing through the sitting room ceiling whenever she climbed in. Lined up alongside Grumpy Cow were Lazy Cow and Horny Cow from the gift set Matt had given her. Who on earth had come up with the idea that women would enjoy the cattle analogy? Mooing round the shed in mindless subservience to their moods.

Taking care not to streak the mascara, she dropped her head back into the water and rubbed in shampoo that promised to deliver gleaming highlights. Why bother? Matt wouldn't notice, just as he wouldn't notice her back fat – they slept together every night without him mentioning it – but the artifice of the weekend away required you to raise your game. You had to imagine yourself featured in the snooty hotel brochure: a successful couple enjoying a well-earned break.

Feeling the warm water swirling round her ears, Tessa thought back to their first weekend away together, a thousand years ago when they were young and poor and happy. A bed and breakfast in Bath, they couldn't afford a car in those days, and had sent away for free train tickets using coupons saved from soap powder packets. She remembered them setting off from their grotty basement flat in Brixton on Friday morning with their weekend bags, then counting down the hours until 5.30 on the dot, when she had raced off to the tube, ignoring the disapproving look from her boss who shouted after her about being a part-timer. There were delays on the line so she only just made it to Paddington on time, and Matt was waiting, agitated they would miss the train. He took her by the hand and pulled her, running, down the platform until they found their carriage and fell, laughing, into their seats. As soon as the train pulled out, Matt took his tie off and they splashed out on a gin and tonic from the bar, enjoying the views as they journeyed away from the unlovely city outskirts and into the gentle fields. 'I could live here,' said Matt, negotiating the map as they walked from the station to their bed and breakfast in a perfect Regency terrace, 'everything is so beautiful. When we're grown up we should definitely move here to raise our kids.' and Tessa agreed. They were only twenty-four, everything was safely in the rosy future, fuzzy and unpredictable but there was no doubt they were in this together. The landlady opened the door and you could tell from the way she looked at them that she didn't believe for a moment they were married. Tessa was glad she had taken the precaution of putting a curtain ring on her finger, she had guessed from the woman's voice on the phone when she made the booking that unmarried couples would not be welcome. Upstairs, they had whispered and giggled as they slipped under the flouncy bed linen, imagining the landlady might knock on the wall if she heard any action.

Tessa stepped out on to the bath mat and squeezed her hair dry in front of the mirror that covered an entire wall. Her basin up one end, his up the other, each accessorised by its respective grooming products. A harbinger of separate beds, perhaps, if unwillingness to spit into a shared sink was the first symptom of mutual physical distaste.

Her phone beeped, and she smiled when she saw it was a text from Max, wishing her a *gr8 weekend* and to say he would be dropping off some washing soon, hope that was OK. She texted back: *Fine, lol, mum xx*. It was a joke between them that she still pretended to think lol stood for lots of love. Silly old woman, Luddite fool, with her anachronistic fondness for remaining a domestic slave to her children. In a post-modern way, which meant she volunteered to do it, unlike her mother's generation who had it foisted upon them. She was exercising a woman's right to choose, which was where we were now, in terms of sexual politics.

Right now the choice she was exercising was in favour of Big Hair, to offset the ballast that lay below. She rubbed in some volume-enhancing mousse and walked through to the bedroom, plugging in the drier and hanging her head upside down, fixing her tinted roots in a gravity-defying upward whoosh. Take that, nature! She glanced sideways in the mirror and was intrigued to see how it wasn't just her hair that was falling down, it was also her entire face. Her cheeks and her lips were hanging down, as if melting towards her eyes, like a facelift gone wrong.

Her phone rang, and Tessa righted herself to take the call. Get over it, she thought, you're fifty, not twenty-five so why wouldn't your face show a bit of slack?

'Sandra!'

Her best friend, confidante and fellow under-employed homebird.

'Congratulations on your silver wedding. May it long remain untarnished.'

'Thank you. Are you standing near a mirror?'

'Of course.'

'Can you do something? Hold your head upside down, look in the mirror and tell me what you see.'

'That's a funny request, I ring to wish you a happy anniversary and now you've got me . . . urrgh!'

Tessa smiled down the phone at the thought of her friend confronting another unwelcome sign of inelasticity.

'Weird, isn't it? Do you think it's time for the knife?'

'Too painful. And anti-feminist.'

'Ha!'

'So, all packed up and ready to show Matt how lucky is he is to have you?'

'Don't depress me.'

'What's depressing about it? A quarter century of fidelity to the man you love. Your meal-ticket and partner in the three-legged race of marriage.'

'Or a failure of nerve and fear of the unknown.'

'Oh dear.'

'Not really, of course I'm looking forward to it. Just can't believe I'm old enough to be doing this. I remember my parents' silver wedding party and everyone seemed so ancient.'

'Well you can tell us all about it next week. Enjoy!'

Tessa returned to her packing and thought about the finger buffet party her parents had given all those years ago. Egg and cress sandwiches, cubes of cheese and pineapple piled on to the table, and rising above it all, the tacky silver-plated candelabra she and her sister had pooled resources to buy as a present. The best Wedgwood was brought out for the occasion, with friends and family pouring their goodwill into the swirly patterned Clementine tea cups. That was before the white plate generation, before it became desirable to celebrate your nuclear couplehood in the restrained chic of a boutique hotel.

It had been a challenge for her to come up with a suitable gift for Matt. He already had everything he needed and would buy most other things that took his fancy. She'd settled on an electric photo frame that displayed two hundred heartwarming snaps of their life together in relaxed rotation. He could have it on his desk at work, though she found it hard to imagine it there as she'd never been to his office. He liked to keep things separate.

The suitcase packed, she smoothed down the bedcovers – Egyptian cotton, 600-thread count, bought from the White Company after exhaustive research through linen suppliers – and wondered how to fill the rest of her day. She wanted to ring Lola, to find out how Freshers' Week was going, but she didn't like to intrude. The last thing she wanted to be was that needy, fretful mother left behind.

Eight hours later, Matt and Tessa were heading out of town in the stop-start traffic of the Friday exodus.

'Too many people, that's the problem.'

Matt slapped his hand on the steering wheel. 'I mean, what's the point of having a fast car when the roads are so clogged up? And the minute you're out of traffic, you hit a bloody speed trap. Who ARE all these people, where are they all going, in their horrible Ford Fiestas and Nissan bloody Micras and eco pansy people carriers?'

He shouldn't have made that remark to the client this morning. He'd caught Richard looking at him like he was a complete dick, but it was true. That boy didn't look old enough to be an intern, never mind the marketing director. They had to convert this piece of business or he'd soon be out on his ear, then there'd be trouble. They weren't exactly queuing up for him, not any more.

'Pull over and let me drive,' said Tessa, in her best soothing voice, 'then you can have a nap, you look like you need it.'

Sleep did not figure high on Matt's priority list. She sometimes woke in the night to find him lying on his back like an entombed archbishop, eyes open to heaven, hands pressed together as if in prayer as he pondered his next assault on the corporate ladder.

He dismissed her offer, as she expected.

'What, and get there at midnight? I don't think so. Let's listen to the CD, shall we? What did you get?'

Matt's busy life left little time for reading, so journeys were an opportunity to catch up. Tessa took two CDs out of her handbag.

'Gory thriller or coming-of-age Arab thing?'

'Gory thriller, of course.'

She loaded the discs and settled back to enjoy the story, which involved detailed descriptions of butchered corpses that might have been upsetting to someone with a less strong stomach. It was odd how much pleasure could be found in vicarious depravity.

Matt was edging up behind a grubby white van, flashing him to get out the way. Someone who couldn't spell had traced a message in the film of dust on the back door:

I WISH MY WIFE WAS THIS DURTY

Tessa pointed it out to Matt. 'Do you wish I was that dirty?'

He ignored her and leaned across her seat, shaking his head at the van driver as they finally overtook.

'Thank you!! Idiot!!!'

The road ahead was opening up now and he started to relax, absorbing the grisly details of the story through the four-speaker Bose best-in-class surround sound system.

She tried to answer the question herself. Did her husband, the C suite executive-in-waiting, find her sufficiently dirty? 'You've got to be a C suite executive at my age,' he'd told her recently, 'otherwise you're just a liability waiting to be fired.'

'What's a C suite executive?' she'd asked him, 'is it like en suite, where you get your own bathroom?'

He'd looked at her with that mixture of amusement and exasperation.

'Chief. As in Chief Executive Officer – I can forget that one – or Chief Operating Officer – more feasible.'

'Chief cook and bottle washer?' she'd suggested. 'Big Chief Sitting Bull? Chief Brown Noser?'

'It's alright for you to take the piss,' he'd said, 'you won't find it so funny when I'm pushed off the gravy train and the money runs out.'

Tessa focused again on the question. How dirty could you be at fifty, anyway? How dirty should you be? Not at all, was the correct answer. Appropriate was what you had to be. Behave and dress in a manner appropriate to your age, or risk being ridiculous. With this in mind, she had bought new nightwear for the weekend, to make a change from the shapeless T-shirt she normally wore. Not a negligee, not – God help us – a baby doll, but an appropriate and elegant pair of silk pyjamas. She pictured herself wearing them, sitting up in the king-size bed of the Enodoc suite while Matt brought her a cup of tea from the in-room facilities.

According to the website, their particular room boasted far-reaching views across the bay.

'How come rooms are always described as boasting views?' she said to Matt, 'As if they're in competition with each other. Hey, my view's better than yours.'

'What are you on about now?'

'Our room in the hotel. It boasts a view.'

It was the sort of room they would have been thrilled to stay in twenty-five years ago – a silver age away – when it was far beyond their budget. Now they could afford it, it was less thrilling. Just as it was less thrilling for Matt to get this low-slung car in his fifties, when it was too late to jump out of it without his knees creaking. He'd gone for the four-litre engine in spite of Tessa's objections. Three litres was for ordinary people, he said, almost without irony, though Tessa pointed out that ordinary people, however you defined it, didn't tend to buy Maseratis.

The weekend was a present from their children. 'Obviously you don't need any more *stuff*,' Max had said, grinning at her as she'd opened the card on Christmas Day. 'Experiences are what you want at your age. We thought Cornwall would be best.' He knew he'd been conceived in Cornwall, and had been indoctrinated by enough bucket-and-spade holidays to believe they held the secret of family happiness. As though his parents could be pushed back to the time when they still looked good in the photo album, playing French cricket on a windswept beach in swimsuits and waterproofs. How conservative the young were, in their belief that everything was better in the good old days of their childhood. 'It's a bit expensive, so we're only paying for one night but we've booked two and Dad can fork for the other one. Though you could say he's paying for it all indirectly, seeing as he finances us.'

She wished that Max and Lola were with them now, back in the big old car instead of this silly toy that Matt referred to, semi tongue-in-cheek, as the 'mazza'. They used to set off at dawn, the sleeping children strapped in the back seat of the Ford Galaxy, surrounded by paraphernalia to entertain them when they woke up, usually around Yeovil. The car was a messy playpen, littered with books and teddy bears and Playmobil figures along with crumbling crackers and beakers spilling juice. The Maserati, in contrast, was as cold and clean as a showroom model, it was Matt's gift to himself to celebrate the children reaching the age of adulthood. 'They can clean up after themselves now' he said, 'finally we are safe from sticky fingers.'

They still took family holidays, most recently in Greece to celebrate Lola's *graduation* from school, right after her *prom*. Tessa didn't disapprove of the Americanisation of the young, why shouldn't they whoop it up, and take any opportunity to celebrate, however ersatz? You have to enjoy it while you can, that was the one truth you could glean from this uncertain, god-less world. And she was determined to enjoy this weekend with her husband of twenty-five years who was now swearing into his wing mirror at some jumped-up motorist who was thinking of overtaking. Her life partner, to use the modern phrase. Life partner, life sentence. But stop. Cheerfulness was a duty, that much she believed, and she had plenty to be cheerful about it.

Lola seemed to be enjoying Freshers' Week, judging from the photos she'd posted on Facebook that afternoon. Personally, Tessa wouldn't dream of wearing an oversized T shirt and inviting strangers to write crude slogans all over it. Yet Lola and her new friends clearly found it hilarious, offering up exaggerated expressions of pleasure to the camera: rictus grins, thumbs-up signs and, in one case, a young man's hairy bare bottom, exposed by lowering the flap of his giant baby-gro.

She must have dozed off after the second corpse had been discovered in wet leaves. When she came round, the narrator's actorly delivery had been replaced by the robotic tone of the satnav. Matt called it Samantha the Stepford Wife. She never got cross or dithered about unmarked roads, and always gave adequate warning.

'At the next junction, turn half left,'

It saved a lot of arguments. After years of frowning over a map and annoying her husband by failing to identify key landmarks, Tessa could now sit beside him, hands folded in her lap, absolved of this responsibility as of so many. It was another example of how she was more and more redundant.

It was getting dark now, and exciting to be on the small country roads.

'I've missed Stonehenge,' she said, 'you should have woken me.'

'Ah, your fantasy!'

Matt put his hand out to squeeze her leg. Tessa used to talk about moving to Cornwall, imagining a removal van packed with all their things driving past the primitive monument, while they followed behind, on their way to a sure and happy new life. It was a snapshot from the virtual album of their past, as real as the actual photos of holidays and birthdays that made up the official record of their years together. Matt considered it a pedestrian dream; there were too many people with estuary accents in Cornwall, lured by the annual fortnight's holiday and now condemned to a retirement of walking the cliffs in Marks & Spencer anoraks and growing fat on cream teas.

She opened her window and breathed in the cold air.

'I love it when you get to the wild bit. I can smell the sea! We must be nearly there.'

They were coming into the outskirts of a village, lined with tidy rows of bungalows with optimistic names: Bella Vista, Cosy Nook, Belle Vue.

'Ouch!' said Matt. It was his stock response to the sight of buildings that displeased him, as if modest new houses were erected for the sole purpose of causing him pain. She pulled a packet of sweets out of her bag.

'Have a Werther's Original, take your mind off it.'

She unwrapped one and put it in his mouth.

'Betjeman was right about Cornwall. An ugly picture in a beautiful frame. Let's hope our hotel isn't blighted by bungalow eczema.'

He didn't know that Tessa had taken the precaution of checking it out on Google Earth. Max and Lola would not have been concerned by such details when they chose the hotel, but Tessa had zoomed out behind the harbour looking for eyesores. She didn't want to spend two days hearing him drone on about lax planning laws in areas of outstanding beauty.

The descent to the cove was steep, with high banks of foliage defining the narrow lane leading down to a tiny harbour littered with fishing pots and scruffy boats. A tight clutch of cottages, built close against storms, made up the hotel, harmonious in its surroundings.

'It's lovely!' said Tessa, looking out over the dark sea as Matt took their bag from the boot, pleased to find he had the best car on the parking terrace that had been hacked out of the cliff.

They were shown to their room by an eager young man called Justin who looked as though he'd just put on his first-ever suit and reminded Tessa of their son. She made appreciative noises as he pointed out the fresh milk jug and showed them the sea view. Above the harbour she saw the cliff path they would be taking tomorrow. 'Just to remind you, we stop serving dinner at nine,' he said on his way out. He knew you had to warn London types.

'A bit beige,' said Matt, stretching out on the bed and running his hand over the parchment lampshade. 'God, I wouldn't want to do that drive every weekend.'

'But you do like it? You must!'

'Course I do. Come here.' He patted the bed and she lay down beside him, kicking off her shoes.

'I'd say off-white, rather than beige,' she said, looking round the room, drawing on the Farrow and Ball colour card that was still imprinted on her memory. 'Dimity and Pointing at a guess, a neutral organic palette.'

He laughed. 'That's because you're a glass half full person. I'm sticking to beige. Or magnolia.'

'Ah, that reminds me.'

She went over to their suitcase and produced a bottle of champagne, ready-chilled in a freezer sleeve, together with a pair of Veuve Clicquot glasses. 'No point in paying minibar prices.'

'Your careful husbandry amazes me.'

'And that's not all.' She rummaged again in the bag and came up with a Tupperware box.

'Homemade cheese straws?'

She arranged them on a plate, then opened the bottle and poured two generous glasses.

'Cheers!' She was back on the bed now, the plate balanced between them.

'Do you think you're obsessed with food?' Matt asked, as he bit into the buttery pastry, careful to catch the crumbs.

'Not obsessed. It's a hobby. Obsessed is when you take a coolbox of home-made food on your honeymoon, like Nigella did, if you remember, on the private plane. Not that it saved the marriage from strangulation of course.'

'Oddly enough, I don't remember. At least her obsession paid off. Big time. I just wish your own interest in food had led to something so profitable. You've got the same buxom figure as Nigella, but not her vast fortune, more's the pity.'

He could never resist his little digs and Tessa was getting a bit sick of it. She snatched the plate away from him.

'You won't be wanting any more of these then! May I say you've done pretty well out of me over the years, all those delicious dinners I've made for you. I'll stop cooking now if you want, see how you like it!' She curled into her side of the bed.

'Only joking!' Matt cajoled, snuggling up behind her. 'You are a domestic goddess and I like your curves, you know that.'

Tessa softened slightly. No point in arguing, she was determined to enjoy this weekend, with all the pampering treats on offer in the hotel.

'I was thinking of having a full-body seaweed wrap in the spa before dinner, but it's a bit late now. Don't want to miss our table. We have been warned.'

He looked at his watch.

'There's always tomorrow for your me-time. I've got some work to do – I could get on with that after breakfast while you work on yourself. As per. Top up?'

He fetched the bottle and refilled their glasses.

'Happy anniversary, Mrs Draper. Now, we've got some time to kill. What say you we address the business in hand? Get it out the way before dinner. Controversially.'

He was unbuckling his belt.

She hadn't unpacked yet. And what about the silk pyjamas? Oh well, she thought, as she felt the familiar weight of him, they'd always do for watching the late-night film in. On the television screen that Justin had shown them, artfully concealed in a painted-beige cabinet at the foot of the bed.

Couples, she thought, as they were shown into the dining room. There was no escape from the deadly hush of a roomful of couples with nothing to say to each other.

'I'm including myself in that category, by the way,' she explained to Matt in a church whisper. 'I mean, no offence, but when you've spent the whole day together, you kind of run out of things to say. Never mind twenty-five years.'

'At least *you've* got something to say for yourself.' Matt spoke at his normal volume. 'Even if it's just to say you've got nothing to say.'

He smiled at her, and caught the eye of the woman at the next table who had looked up to see who had raised the sound level. She wore a floral dress and a heart-sinking haircut, the short-back-and-sides inexplicably favoured by so many women over a certain age.

'I tell you what, Tessa.' He lowered the volume. 'I reckon you're the best-looking woman here.'

She looked round the room.

'I'm not sure that's much of a compliment, but thanks anyway. Though she's quite hot.'

She gestured towards a younger couple who had been allocated the window seat, in deference to their relative youth and beauty.

'Short legs,' said Matt, 'I clocked her on the way in. I couldn't be with a woman who's got short legs, just as I couldn't be married to a woman who couldn't cook. Glad to say you pass on both counts.'

Justin came over to take their order.

'Ah, Justin, man of many parts I see, acting as both front of house and *maitre d*'! All part of the charm of the boutique hotel I suppose. We'll have the seafood platter, I think. When in Rome. And a bottle of Chablis, I'm assuming you also double as the sommelier. Now, which of these sparkling waters is closest to Badoit? I want sparkle, but not fizz, if you're with me. Don't want it going up my nose, but just enough to give it a fillip, if you know what I mean.'

As Justin talked him through the relative sparkliness of the mineral waters on offer, Tessa noticed the sensible-haired woman looking over in disbelief. She and her silent husband were making do with tap. They seemed untroubled by the need to make conversation. But perhaps that was it, Tessa thought, maybe a perfect complicity meant you didn't need to talk incessantly, exchanging inanities just to make the point that you were 'communicating'. Silence, after all, was a normal and agreeable condition. Tessa knew all about that; she could sometimes go perfectly contentedly all day without speaking. Matt could not.

'Clever choice, the seafood platter,' he said as Justin left them, 'low-cal, to offset the egg and bacon you know we're going to have tomorrow.'

He was keen on offsetting: the offset mortgage, the offset expenses, even the offsetting of his catastrophic carbon footprint by getting his secretary to tick the box to buy a tree whenever she booked him a flight. All charged to the company of course.

'And we'll walk it off anyway,' she said, 'let's go for a really long hike.'

She wanted to go to all their old places; the wide beaches, the discreet coves where they used to have sex when no one was watching. She wanted to revisit the rock pools where they would spend hours crouched with the children, poking fluorescent plastic nets on sticks through green weed to bring out wiggling brown bits of pond life that bore no resemblance to fish. Tomorrow they'd relive it all again, they'd take the sandy cliff path lined with gorse and thrift right out to the headland, then down to the wild grey sea, maybe even go paddling if it was warm enough, they were always happy in Cornwall and this weekend would be no exception.

Matt was wearing his stern black spectacles this evening and as he turned his head she could read the silver letters P-R-A-D-A written up the side. Max had given him a hard time about that; 'might as well spell out A-R-S-E' he said, and Matt had looked hurt. He had chosen them for the design, and if that came with some branding, that was okay by him, you had to remain on trend in his business. The spectacles were part of his armour, along with the understated Hogan shoes and dark shirts, the expensive casualness that carried him into the battleground of his mysterious office world.

'It was sweet of the children, wasn't it, to do this for us?' said Tessa. 'I was just thinking how lovely it would be if they walked in right now to have dinner with us.'

'What, am I too boring for you?'

'Of course not,' she said quickly, 'I just meant, wouldn't it be nice . . . I wonder what Lola's up to tonight.'

She thought of her daughter in her functional student bed-room. Something of the prison cell about it on first sight, with its mean dimensions and small bed fitted with standard-issue mattress protector. At least she'd have put up her posters up by now, which would cheer it up, and those empty shelves would be filled with books and photos to take away the bleakness. Maybe she was getting ready for a night out, trying on the leopard-skin top from New Look or the strappy one from Topshop they had chosen together that was just the right shade of tawny rose to set off her beautiful complexion. She'd said something about a bar crawl this evening, ending up in a club. Hopefully she would be out with a good crowd and wouldn't get left behind somewhere or have her drink spiked. There was that case recently where a girl hadn't realised her drink had been spiked and had collapsed on her way home. After all, it could happen to anyone, and what if Lola was on her own?

'I hope she's not lying unconscious in a ditch,' she said to Matt, who reacted as she knew he would, by letting her know she was being ridiculous.

'Stop worrying! You know how sensible she is.'

'You do hear terrible stories, though, don't you? It's often the sensible ones who go wild and drink two bottles of vodka and fall in the river.'

'It's not going to happen.'

'I know, but I can't help imagining it. I think it's because she's a girl, or maybe because she's the last one to leave.'

'Sad old empty nester.'

'No I'm not. Anyway, they haven't really left, have they?'

'Not with those slack university terms. Wait till they emigrate to Australia or something. Then you'll just have me. It'll be a permanent second honeymoon.'

He reached for her hand and pulled a cheesy romantic face.

It wasn't something she cared to think about. She laughed and pushed her chair back.

'We can become an active older couple. Go on cruises like in the Saga ads. Gaze dreamily out to sea before having dinner with the captain. Get sunstroke round the pool with all the other beached old whales.'

'Shoot me now.' He put an imaginary gun to his head.

'Let's eat first. Look, here it comes.'

Justin was approaching with a large and sizzling platter which he placed with a flourish on their table.

'Enjoy!'

They stared at the mussels and langoustines, whelks and crab, bubbling in buttery sauce.

Matt was frowning in disbelief.

'But it's . . . HOT.'

Justin nodded.

'Yes, that's right, please be careful not to touch the plate! We used to serve a classic seafood platter, on a bed of ice, but people complained. As it's a main course, they don't expect it to be cold.'

'It looks delicious,' said Tessa quickly, anxious to avoid a scene.

'Who complained?' asked Matt, 'I wouldn't complain if it was presented on a bed of ice as it is supposed to be. As it is, I *am* complaining. If you'd put on the menu, "platter of seafood done to death beneath a blanket of sauce", I would have chosen something else. Obviously.'

The silent couple were both looking at them now and, beyond them, in the window seat, the short-legged blonde was giggling with her boyfriend, enjoying the spectacle. Tessa felt a stab of envy, remembering how insufferable the middle-aged were when you were young, with their boring concerns and fussing about things that weren't important.

Justin was doing his best to smooth things over.

'I can bring you something else, sir, if you'd prefer.'

'No, no,' said Tessa, 'it's fine, really.'

'Yes, please, I'd like to see the menu again,' said Matt, then to Tessa: 'What? Don't look at me like that. It's alright to complain, you know, you don't have to sit back and take whatever's dumped in front of you.'

'I'll stick with the seafood, thanks,' said Tessa.

'Don't do that! This is supposed to be our anniversary dinner, let's try and eat it together, not me watching you eat warm seafood, then you waiting for mine to arrive.'

'Alright!'

She turned to Justin, all appetite gone.

'I'll order something else as well. So sorry.'

Justin went to fetch the menus and the other diners settled back into their couples.

'Don't say you're sorry,' said Matt. 'Don't tell the waiter you're sorry because you've got to re-order because they put misleading information on their menu.'

'Stop it, please! Please can we just not talk about it any more.'

'Fine!'

Matt put his hands up, as though making a huge concession.

By the time their steaks arrived Tessa was beyond hunger, but she ate it anyway, good companion that she was. Companion was a word they once used to define each other, before they were married. They'd had a list of them, revelling in the clichés: Better Half, Significant Other, but Companion was their favourite, with its overtones of shabbiness and financial obligation: the drab spinster of limited means taking breakfast with a *grande dame* who couldn't get anyone else to go on holiday with her; the single gent shuffling round the cruise ship ballroom with a wealthy widow.

And here she was now, the official silver wife of this slick businessman in Prada specs who was tapping his index finger on his front teeth across the table at her.

'Bit of parsley,' he explained, 'no, right a bit, yes, gone.'

She wiped her finger on the napkin, 'I always wondered why they bothered to put toothpicks on the table,' she said, 'but that was before we hit the reality of receding gums.'

'Lovely conversation.'

'It's often what ends a marriage, apparently. You can't bear to watch the other person eat. It happened to Kirsten; her husband suddenly turned round and said he couldn't stand the noise she made when she chewed her food.'

'It's true, it's the little things that get to you. Like Jerry, who ditched his wife because she always took her jeans and knickers off in one go, it drove him mad. And Anne, who divorced her husband because he couldn't go to sleep at night unless her shoes were lined up straight in her wardrobe. He used to go over and inspect them before coming to bed.'

'Lunatic.'

'Bonkers.'

They took comfort in these scenes from other people's failed relationships which offered gratifying contrast to their own stability.

'Not like us,' said Matt, 'still going strong.'

'Don't say what I know you're going to say.'

'The secret of our successful marriage?'

He was fond of repeating it, usually at dinner parties to amuse their friends. She should have guessed he'd come out with it tonight.

He raised his glass in a toast.

'Don't expect too much! Set the bar too high and you're bound to run into trouble.'

She agreed that people demanded too much of their relationships. But did he have to imply that the only reason they were still together was because they'd decided to settle for less?

'You romantic fool,' she said, clinking glasses with him. It would be nice to feel a bit more passion but they'd been together for decades, you had to be realistic. 'Shall we have pudding?'

Upstairs, Tessa changed into her new pyjamas while Matt flicked through the sports channels.

She slipped into bed beside him with a copy of the *Daily Mail*. Not her usual reading matter, but she'd treated herself at the service station and nobody would judge her here.

Matt patted a companionable hand on the bulge of her tummy.

'All paid for,' he said, without taking his eyes off the screen, 'Still, not bad for your age. Twenty-five years, eh? OOH, REF!!'

She self-consciously pushed his hand away and flicked through the paper until a headline caught her eye: '*Women feel "invisible" by the age of 51*'. Beneath it was a photo of a sad-looking woman with a lined face. The article was the usual litany of laments: plummeting confidence, middle-aged women judged negatively, left on the shelf, blah blah blah.

'Honestly, you've got to ask yourself where they get these figures from,' she said. 'It says here that two-thirds of women in their fifties feel completely unnoticed by men.'

Matt ignored her and carried on staring at the match. She kicked him under the duvet.

'Did you hear what I said?'

He looked round briefly and frowned at her choice of newspaper.

'As if we need another bloody survey of women bleating on about what they feel,' he said, turning back to the TV. 'Too much time spent navel-gazing if you ask me.'

'But what do you reckon? According to this, I'm well over the hill. Do you think I've become invisible?'

Matt patted her tummy again.

'Hardly! You look pretty visible to me. All eleven stone of you.'

'Oi!'

Tessa pinched him on the arm.

'Ow! Only joking. I've already said you look good for your age, what more do you want?'

Tessa sank back and thought about not being noticed. She remembered her indignation the first time she'd walked past builders and they'd stepped aside for her, instead of wolf whistling. The cheek! Then she'd rationalised it; here was a breakthrough for feminism, at last the sexual objectification of women was over. Who was she kidding? In one simple, middle-aged step, she had gone from possible sex object to invisible woman. She had joined the ranks of the great unseen.

'Also,' Matt added, 'there are loads of good-looking older women. I caught Peter at work the other day looking at this website called Hot Women over 50 Years You Would Bang.'

'You are so low.'

'Wasn't me, it was Peter! But then he made me have a look. Jane Seymour, Kim Basinger, Sharon Stone, loads of them in their sixties. And of course there's always Helen Mirren. The ultimate GILF.'

'Ah, yes, Helen Mirren. If only we could all look like her. Pity most of us aren't stunning Hollywood actresses. Actually, when I think about it, I *am* always being ignored. Even at the deli queue at the supermarket, you can see the girl's more interested in serving the yummy mummy behind me, while I'm dismissed along with the other apologetic middle-aged bags.'

'Sorry, did you say something?'

'Haha!'

She snatched the remote from him and turned the TV off.

'Hey, what are you doing, I was watching that!'

'It's our silver wedding anniversary, you're supposed to be giving me attention.'

'Fair enough.'

He snuggled up to her under the covers.

'But only if you turn off the light and stop reading out depressing statistics.'

'Deal.'

'And admit that actually you're quite lucky to have me. Because, let's face it, if we were both single again, I'd easily get somebody else. Whereas you would be just another invisible woman wringing your hands about the hell of midlife dating.'

Tessa looked at him with distaste.

'Who says I'd be dating? Maybe I've had my fill of men. Also, I'm not a hand-wringer. And don't kid yourself, you're not George Clooney.'

'Just saying the odds are stacked against you,' said Matt. 'Apparently a woman over fifty has more chance of being hit by a bus than of finding a partner.'

'Thanks for that.'

Tessa turned her back on him and helped herself to her usual drug cocktail – cod liver oil and glucosamine with chondroitin, washed down with a sip of Evian. The menopause shelf in Boots was so irritating with its Wellwoman bullshit products flogging evening primrose with photos of laughing middle-aged women. What the hell had they got to laugh about? She reached to turn out the light and was pleased to see there was a text from Sandra, which always cheered her up.

So did you give him one?

She texted back.

Yes. An invisible woman must hang on to what she's got.

CHAPTER TWO

'Don't be surprised, if you have married for money, or position, or fame, that you get *only* money, or position, or fame; love cannot be bought.'

Blanche Ebbutt, *Don'ts for Wives*, 1913

Alone in her kitchen, Sandra swung open the door of her industrial-sized stainless-steel fridge. It looked like it belonged in a restaurant, but mostly fed just three careful eaters. She took out the skimmed milk and mixed it into a bowl of porridge, then into the microwave. She wasn't bothered about breakfast, but everyone said you shouldn't skip it, and porridge was supposed to give the right kind of slow-release energy to see you through your busy day. 'Busy day my arse,' Nigel had said when she had discussed this with him. 'I wish I had your life.'

Her daughter's empty bowl was in the sink, traces of cereal already crisping up after her early departure to the ice rink. Sandra often wondered how she'd managed to produce a child of such efficiency that she laid her place for breakfast before going to bed. She'd watched her at it last night, lining up the box of Special K, putting the teabag in the mug, glass ready for the juice. 'You're marvellous, Poppy, you know that,' she'd said, and Poppy had given her a patronising smile. 'It's just a question of being organised, Mum,' she'd replied, tightening the belt of her dressing gown round her hard little body and twirling off upstairs to put the final touches to her history essay.

As well as being a total babe, Poppy served the useful function of providing Sandra with an excuse for her life of idleness. Unlike her friends Tessa and Harriet, whose children had turned into adults, Sandra still had a reason to be home in the afternoon; she didn't want her daughter to be a latch-key kid. Not much risk of that, she thought, stretching herself out on the daybed with her porridge, a copy of *The Week* and a couple of hours to kill before meeting the others for what they ironically termed a 'catch-up coffee'.

The Week was ideal because it saved you having to trawl through all the newspapers and offered the best bits in nugget form, ideal for her gnat-like concentration span. Sometimes it was hard to remember what a massive big-shot she had been. Her own PR company with thirty employees who all thought she was It. She *was* It, let's face it; every big fashion house wanted to work with her and she was at the absolute top of her game when she sold the business. Nigel had begged her to give up work; she was pregnant with Poppy and didn't take much persuading. It would be a life of luxury at his expense, she would reinvent matriarchy by becoming the glamorous head of a family of tousle-headed beauties. She wasn't to know that her first child would also be her last. It should have been obvious she'd have an early menopause; she had passed every milestone ahead of

Chipping Barnet Library
Tel: 020 8359 4040
Email: chippingbarnet.library@barnet.gov.uk

Customer ID: 8089

Items that you have checked out

Title: Invisible women
ID: 30151056513403 1
Due: 30 December 2023

Total items: 1
Account balance: £0.00
09/12/2023 13:19
Checked out: 1
Overdue: 0
Hold requests: 0
Ready for collection: 0

her contemporaries and in a way it was a blessing. Bad enough clearing up the litter of plastic toys that one child scattered across her minimalist home, never mind the damage inflicted by a horde of them.

So here she was. Sometimes she thought it might be amusing to have a job, but who would hire a woman who hadn't darkened the doorstep of an office since the new millennium? And it would be too humiliating to start again from the bottom. If there were two words that depressed her, they were 'entry level'. The world had moved on without her.

Nevertheless, she was bang up-to-date with modern technology. Her home was awash with gadgets and when her phone rang, she could immediately silence the music flowing through the ceiling speakers with the lightest touch of one of the sleek silver controls lined up beside her.

'Hello, Sandra, good morning!'

'Mariusz! How are you?'

Suddenly her morning had become more interesting. She swung her legs round and put her bowl down on the table, listening to his reply.

'Physically I am in my house.'

'That's WHERE you are, I asked HOW you were.'

'Sandra! I know my English is no good!'

He sounded so down-hearted, she shouldn't be hard on him.

'No, no, Mariusz, you've made very good progress.'

'Thank you!' He was like a child, instantly brightening under her praise.

'I'm leaving soon my house for big job in the letterhead.'

'What letterhead?'

'In the Surrey. And maybe I call by for small coffee.'

'Aah, you mean Leatherhead.'

'Yes. And if you like see my person, I call by?'

'If you like.' She hoped he did like. The thought of it gave her an unexpected fillip of pleasure. 'In fact I need you to look at the bathroom tap so that would be good.'

'Small problem with tap?'

'It drips.'

'No problem, I fix him.'

'Good.'

'And maybe, Sandra, it is possible you give me today one thousand pounds?'

Of course, it all came down to the money. She shouldn't flatter herself.

'When you've finished the snagging list.'

'Sandra, always you kill my person with this list!'

'See you later, Mariusz. I'm going out at eleven so come before then.'

She went through to the office to open the snagging list on the computer. Every couple of weeks Mariusz called by for small coffee, and to address the unfinished business of the building project they'd both rather lost interest in. She glanced through it on the screen, added the dripping tap, then printed it out and went upstairs to check her make-up. It wasn't that she needed to seduce him – that was all in the past – but it was a matter of pride. She changed into a pair of tight jeans to accentuate her slim hips, and applied an extra coat of mascara and a touch of concealer to hide the shadows below her blue eyes. Not bad, she thought, fluffing up her hair in front of the mirror, that shade of blonde was definitely an improvement on her natural colour which had always been verging on mouse. Her heart-shaped face was nourished with expensive creams and did not yet require surgical intervention.

Sandra didn't regret her fling with the builder, though she knew her friends had been shocked. It was uncomplicated. And liberating, when the curtain poles were down in the bedroom and a dozen workers were prowling around outside on the scaffolding and Mariusz had asked her in a panicked whisper, 'Sandra, quick, you have TOWELS?' She smiled now at the memory of him jumping on to a chair and hammering her Conran Shop bath sheets up at the newly painted window to preserve their privacy, and then diving back into bed. It was fun, spontaneous, the complete opposite to everything else in her grown-up life.

The bedroom was possibly her greatest decorating triumph. Here she had abandoned the prevailing off-white palette in favour of mauve walls and chartreuse-green silk curtains, interlined for luxurious bulk and combined with blackout blinds in a belt-and-braces solution to her husband's insomnia. She ran her fingers down the fabric, recalling the market in Hong Kong where she had spent the morning choosing from a dazzling selection while Nigel was at his meeting. It was before they bought the house but she knew that wherever they moved to, she wanted this silk at her windows. Poppy was ten years old and it was her Easter holidays so they'd been able to fly out with Nigel on his business trip. Looking back, it was one of their happiest times as a family. She had taken Poppy to buy a Hello Kitty handbag, then they ate lunch overlooking the harbour where Poppy ordered a luridly coloured ice cream topped with a paper umbrella that she carried around for the rest of the day and arranged carefully on her pillow before going to sleep in the little bed that had been set up in the deluxe suite at the Peninsula.

Through the window now she could see Mariusz arriving in his bashed-up van. He was always driving into other cars though he claimed it was the other way round, with a bravado that Sandra found attractive. She watched him jump out and run up to the front door, in a hurry as usual.

When she opened the door he was in his favourite position, leaning with his arm raised against the wall, showing off a physique that you got from doing proper man work, as opposed to sitting on an office chair. He beamed at her from behind his incongruous wire-framed spectacles – somehow you didn't expect builders to be short-sighted – and stepped inside, casting a proprietorial eye around the freshly painted interior.

'Lime White, Sandra, very good choice,' he said, touching her lightly on the shoulder and sitting down on the window seat while she prepared his coffee. Thick and cloudy with grounds, she knew the Poles believed that filters were for pussies.

He sighed and launched into the usual gloomy assessment of his health.

'Still I have big pain in my back and the huge migraine. Next weekend I go see doctor in my country for tests, doctors better in my country.' And then, with mercurial charm, he smiled again, and passed her his phone to show her a photo of a blonde baby, 'Look, my son is walking!'

It was an odd family life. His girlfriend and child lived back home in his village while Mariusz lodged on the outskirts of London, sitting down to an all-male dinner every night with his 'boys' as he affectionately called his co-workers. Then again, wasn't every form of family life odd? There was no normal, least of all Sandra and her husband, isolated in their separate thoughts within a shared bed. Everyone had all come a long way since the Ladybird picture books of Mummy and Daddy sweeping up the leaves with their rosy-cheeked children before sitting down together for a conventional six o'clock supper.

'I move to very nice house in new street, Sandra, very good area. Only white people.'

'You can't say that, Mariusz, it's racist.'

'I share bedroom with Gregor, we have forty-eight-inch plasma on wall.'

She pictured him sitting up in bed with his electrician, watching a movie and sharing a box of popcorn, a comic sexless duo, like a latter-day Morecambe and Wise. It was a heroic bachelor existence, like being in the army, toiling on the front line of rich people's houses and sending home all their money for their families.

'How lovely, I'm pleased for you. Now, shall I show you this tap?'

Upstairs in the bathroom Mariusz dropped to his knees and leaned forward in the cupboard to fiddle with the hidden workings of the Vola mixer. She stood behind him, enjoying the view of his lower back, the boyish smooth skin above the waistband of his jeans, listening to him express disbelief at what the rich were prepared to spend on brassware.

'You crazy, Sandra, in my country I no need me spend huge money for tap.'

She could see his point but when your life is temporarily subsumed by browsing bathroom brochures, you inevitably choose the most expensive. She had spent days poring over those images, comparing the angles and proportions of the Vola with lesser models and, in the end, there was no other possible decision. They could afford it, so why not? Although it did put her on the back foot when it came to Mariusz's frequent demands for another payment of small money.

He stood up, brushing his hands on his jeans and looked at her with real concern.

'Tell me, Sandra, how is your husband? Is he still crazy?'

That was the thing about intimacy. Once you'd slept with someone there was no place for small talk. You couldn't just chat about the weather, or revert to a professional relationship.

'We don't say crazy, Mariusz. He's depressed.'

'Ah yes, I too am very depressed. Yesterday I pay me £360 to get car back from pound. Very, very depressed.'

'It's not the same thing, though I do sympathise. Getting done by a parking attendant is completely infuriating. But when you're depressed like Nigel you can't even feel infuriated, you just feel blank. Like nothing's worth it.'

'He take medicine for this?'

'Yes, but I'm not sure it's helping.'

The happy pills were stacked in the bathroom cabinet. Cetalopram, or Silly Pram as they called it in an attempt at levity. He was also undergoing Cognitive Behavioural Therapy with a South American woman who was good-looking as well as kind, according to Sandra's Google image search. She'd love to sit in on those sessions. Surely it was every man's dream, talking about himself to a beautiful woman with no risk of her yawning or leaving the room.

'Maybe he sad because he pay too much for this Vola tap?' Mariusz suggested.

Sandra laughed. 'There's probably a lot of truth in that. But it's what he wanted. Anyway, he'll get better. But thanks for asking.'

He stepped forward and gave her a warm hug, then gestured to the bedroom.

'If you like, I cheer you up?'

She felt his strong, competent arms around her and for a moment was tempted, it wouldn't be the first time after all. And you had to admire his gall; if you don't ask, you don't get. She gently released herself from his embrace.

'I think not, that's all behind us now.'

He nodded his acceptance.

'As you like. You are very nice person, Sandra. So now, maybe we go through rest of this list.'

They walked through the house; elegant empty rooms, showcasing their owners' understated good taste. Sandra paused to point out a botched door handle, some loose grouting, a wonky shelf, small failings in what Nigel referred to as the Eastern Bloc finish. It didn't matter to her, but Nigel had made it clear he couldn't handle these imperfections, not in his condition. She was pleased with a money-saving idea she'd had; to install Ikea shelves in the laundry room, it was chic now to be a little bit thrifty. The inspection over, she accompanied Mariusz back to his van, stuffed to the roof with the paraphernalia of home improvement: planks of wood, ladders, heavy dusty tools. Tatiana across the road was coming out of her house and waved to Sandra who returned the greeting. She was a stick-thin blonde like Sandra, they mostly were in this street which was known with false modesty as The Little Boltons. Every house had a boastful piece of art displayed in the front window, bought at eye-watering cost to impress the neighbours.

'I come for sure next week, Sandra, I believe me.'

She did love his use of English.

'You may believe you, Mariusz, but should I believe you?'

'Sandra, Sandra! Yes! You know you like my person!'

It was true, she did like his person, especially the athletic way he jumped up into the driving seat.

'I come Thursday,' he shouted through the window. 'I go Ikea first, get your shelf, I like very much Ikea cafe. I have me hot dog and small cock, then I come to you.'

'WHAT did you say?'

'Hot dog and small cock!'

'You mean COKE.'

'Yes, I believe me!'

She waved him off and turned back to the house, letting herself in through the side gate to the garden. Against the wall, zinc boxes were lined up with geometric precision, filled with plants chosen for the architectural value of their leaf-shape. Above all, no flowers unless they were white. Colour in the garden was a no-no, far too vulgar. She unchained her bicycle from a Victorian railing that had somehow escaped the ruthless purge of all things old – she had ripped out the charming shed covered with a rambling rose in a fit of modernist zeal – then lit a cigarette and rode off down the street, steering with one hand as she inhaled from the other in an effortless piece of multitasking. As she turned into the Fulham Road, she thought of Mariusz in his van and how nice it would be to join him, to put on some messy overalls and drive off to help him on his next job.

Harriet double-locked her front door – you couldn't be too careful – and set off down Ladbroke Grove towards the park. She'd have to be quick, she was meeting the girls for coffee soon. Girls, of course, was a ridiculous misnomer: she, Sandra and Tessa were all the wrong side of fifty, but when the three of them got together, it was straight back to the school canteen, even if their topics of conversation had moved on. Instead of Latin homework and boys, it was art exhibitions and mothers-in-law, but the bond was still there. She was looking forward to hearing about Tessa's weekend in Cornwall, it had been so long since she and Sam had been away *à deux* that she'd forgotten the protocol of a rekindle-the-magic minibreak.

Hyde Park was quiet at this time, just a few joggers and dog people, and tourists looking out for Kensington Palace, hoping to catch a whiff of the royal magic. Two young women with perfectly toned bottoms encased in black Lycra were laughing together as they pushed their padded triangular prams. Harriet let the dogs off their leads and strolled after them, adopting the half-smile worn by dog-walkers. A half-smile for a half-purpose as they followed their pets, the way a senior aide walks a few respectful steps behind a dignitary. Having the dogs got her out of the house and gave a rhythm to her day, which could otherwise be alarmingly unstructured. Not like her time practising at the bar, when her timetable was tightly constructed, or her subsequent life as full-time mum (those words!) with the weekly diary stuck on the fridge, reminding her exactly when the boys had to be delivered to their various CV-enhancing classes, a pair of adults-in-waiting, honed and polished for the good of their future careers. Walking the dogs made her feel useful, could even be seen as a form of household economy. Many of her neighbours spent a fortune employing professional dog-walkers, so that was one expense that Harriet was defraying by making herself available to Benson and Hedges. And of course, she loved them to bits; the way they jumped on her bed, wagging their silly tails, offering the unconditional devotion it was hard to find elsewhere.

Two dogs were better than one, not least for the opportunity it presented for amusing twin names. Castor and Pollux, Terry and June, Benson and Hedges. In a similar spirit, the people next door made a point of parking their cars side by side on their drive, displaying their personalised number plates: 2 BE and NOT 2B. An expensive joke, though neither of them appeared to be of a merry disposition from Harriet's occasional exchanges with them, mostly about burglaries and the case for establishing CCTV cameras. She hadn't expressed her opinion that they were asking for it, flaunting their wealth like that.

She took a well-chewed rubber ball out of her bag and threw it for the dogs, who went yapping after it, panting on their short legs. Pugs weren't really designed for exercise, being better suited to their original purpose of bed-warmers to the Emperor of China. Had they moved to the country, she would have gone for Labradors or some other breed with long legs, but it wasn't fair in London.

Benson was squatting by a tree and with practised ease Harriet sheathed her hand in a scented orange plastic bag and stooped to pick up the warm faeces. Like many mothers, she had acquired the dogs when her sons left home, filling the empty nest with a more amenable type of small animal, the sort that didn't answer back and make unreasonable demands. The nappy sack evoked distant days of soft babies and breastfeeding, the smell of Kamillosan smoothed on cracked nipples. At least it was only the dogs she was now on toilet duty for. So far.

She thought of their new tenant in the basement, the large and garrulous cuckoo triumphantly installed in the nest. It had seemed the decent thing to do, inviting Sam's mother to live with them; they got on well enough and, anyway, the flat was self-contained. What she hadn't counted on was Celia falling ill the moment her last box of winter clothes had been unpacked.

Seventy-five years of perfect health, and now THIS, as she liked to remind them at the hospital, while Harriet sat beside her, wearing her best carer's expression, anticipating the years and years to come, for it was clear Celia would outlive them all, with her ox-like constitution only temporarily diminished by a few mutant cells.

Weakened by the thought, she sat down on a bench and pulled out *The Times*. Doing the crossword brought a sense of achievement, although it was a monumental waste of time. And surely a dying art; none of her children understood the contorted logic of cryptic clues and nor did anyone else of the younger generation as far as she could work out. Chewing on her pen to contemplate possible anagrams, she let her gaze wander to the bench opposite where a young man in a duffel coat was sitting, looking across at her, his long legs extended in front of him. She averted her gaze and scribbled down the letters randomly, hoping to pull them into a pattern. Of course. Intuition. She filled in the column, then looked up again. He was still staring at her. And now he was getting up and walking over towards her. Quick, eyes down.

'Excuse me.'

She looked up, his expression was anxious and entreating.

'I hope you don't think I'm being cheeky, but I just wondered if you fancied going for a coffee or something.'

He was in his thirties, she guessed, a kind face and the kind of beard that managed to look unfashionable, in spite of the current trend.

'That's very nice of you,' she said, 'but I'm quite busy with my crossword.'

He nodded. 'I see, of course. Hope you don't mind me asking, but you've got to try, haven't you?' He smiled agreeably and strolled off.

Only then did she smile to herself. She wasn't exactly a romantic target, a middle-aged woman in a sensible Barbour and scuffed flat shoes. Even her husband didn't want to have sex with her any more, so why a good-looking stranger would hit on her, she had no idea. He can't have been that desperate. Still, it would give her something to laugh about with the girls.

She called to the dogs and fastened their leads, calculating there would just be time to hang out the washing. She preferred to focus her mind on small, achievable tasks. Making sure to hang the heaviest clothes on the highest part of the rack – because heat rises, remember your Physics O Level. It was less daunting than the big imponderables. Like: what was the purpose of her life? And how on earth had she let herself morph from top-dog lawyer into a provider of maternal services, now surplus to requirements? She was so proud of how her two sons had turned out, and of course she wanted them to spread their wings and have their own lives, but now they were both on the other side of the world she had only her pets and her mother-in-law to look after. And her husband, but who knew where that was heading. Was he slipping away?

Tessa was feeling particularly empty this morning. The weekend in Cornwall was already a distant memory, Matt was at work and the house was silent as the grave. She unpacked their bags, placing the electric photo frame in the study – as predicted, Matt hadn't wanted to take it to the office; too naff and sentimental, he'd said. As she looked through the photos now, she recalled the last time she'd seen Lola when they'd left her standing outside her halls of residence, looking fragile in her leggings and favourite blue jumper as she waved them off. Matt had driven all the way home because she couldn't see through her tears to take the wheel. Feeble beyond belief, but she could tell he felt it too, from the set of his mouth and the restless tuning between radio stations.

She opened her daughter's bedroom door. It was chilly in there; the radiator had been turned off, no point in heating an empty room. The bed was still rumpled, and she sat on the Cath Kidston covers, sprigs of pink flowers on a baby-blue background. She leaned over to pick up the debris that had fallen down by the bedside table: tissues, hair elastics, cereal bar wrappers. In the drawer she found birthday cards, topless pens and an old school ID card, with Lola's face staring solemnly out, rounder than it was now. An unwashed mug with a corny slogan, 'you're my cup of tea', sat congealing next to the lamp. Tessa had told Maria not to bother with Lola's room, she wanted to keep it as it was.

Discarded pairs of knickers were strewn across the floor, neat and small, unlike Tessa's inelegant undergarments, along with a number of T-shirts that had not made the final cut of the uni selection. Putting them away in the wardrobe, Tessa remembered exactly when each one had been chosen, mother and daughter squeezed into a changing booth while Lola put her lovely young limbs through the sleeves and Tessa had given her verdict. It was so much more enjoyable than choosing her own clothes; an exercise in aesthetic appreciation informed by maternal love.

Beneath the bed, the storage drawers held a gruesome tangle of mutilated Bratz dolls, with unscrewed oversized feet welded to platform shoes. Exercise books with wobbly writing, the pages stiff with glue from stuck-on stars and collaged picture patchworks; the witch's outfit she'd worn for Halloween, with purple straw hair sprouting out from a conical hat; a fencing mask with breeches and jacket, now abandoned and forgotten.

Tessa sat back on the bed, overcome by a sense of loss. She usually made a point of not calling Lola: the tacit understanding was that it should be the other way round, but there was no harm in sending a text.

Just found your fencing stuff, sure you don't want me to send it up, now you've got all those lovely FACILITIES? How are you?

She thought back to the time when she used to drive Lola round to the fencing competitions. Little fake warriors in their white outfits, each one accompanied by a willing mother, a packhorse-cum-servant, her life put on hold for the sake of her children's extra-curricular accomplishments. It was a good thing to put on the UCAS form, that's what they agreed as they chatted over coffee poured from Thermos flasks they had prepared at daybreak, before setting off in their people carriers, children riding in the back like minor royalty. What had it all been for?

Her phone buzzed with a reply.

No, don't bother, my fencing days are over. Yeah, great thanks, major bar crawl last night!

It was enough! Lola was fine and everything was going to be alright. Tessa quickly plumped up the pillows and shook out the duvet. It was time to meet her friends.

She stepped out into the fine autumn day, it was a brisk ten-minute walk to the Bluebird Cafe. They used to meet at the Picasso before it closed down, and still lamented its raffish old Chelsea charm, but the seats were comfortable at the Bluebird, and it was still in the right location. A long way from Orpington High Street, that was for sure, where the three of them would saunter after school, treating themselves to soggy jam dough-nuts at the bakers shop where Tessa had her Saturday job, before heading back for some telly and homework followed by a Vespa curry presented on a ring of rice, or beef stew with dumplings.

Harriet was already installed at the cafe, where they always met for coffee, never for lunch. They were so absolutely not Ladies Who Lunch, with those terrible overtones of wasted tal-ent and idleness.

This did not prevent Sandra from quoting Sondheim's song at every opportunity.

'Another long, exhausting day, another thousand dollars,' she said, arriving just after Tessa and sinking into the sofa alongside her friends. 'Sorry I'm late, had to deal with Mariusz. Not in that way, Harriet, so you can take that disapproving look off your face.'

Harriet turned up her empty hands like one unfairly accused.

'I said nothing, I'm not judging you, it's your affair.'

'Ex-affair.'

'Ah, the reformed sinner.'

'Can you please keep sin out of it,' said Sandra, 'we're not in the Garden of Eden. We have evolved.'

'Up to a point,' said Tessa, 'though, of course, we are the dinosaurs.'

It was Sandra who had come up with the term. 'Housewives like us are an anachronism,' she claimed, 'in fact we're practically extinct. The dependent wife should have died out with our mothers' generation, yet here we are.'

'I think it's time we dropped that term,' said Harriet. 'I don't like being compared to those huge skeletons in the Natural History Museum.'

'Oh I don't know,' said Sandra from the safety of her tiny physique, 'I think that's what we are. Quaint reminders of the prehistoric world. Funny old things who have ended up on the side-lines of the modern world. Hats off to us, I say. Frankly, I can't think of anything more boring than spending all day at the office. Let the men go out and earn the money.'

'Anyway it's become fashionable now,' said Harriet. 'Look at those gorgeous young things who are only too pleased to give up their glittering careers and live off their banker husbands. Homemakers, they prefer to call themselves now, it sounds better in American.'

'Young and gorgeous now,' said Tessa. 'Just wait till they hit fifty, then they might think again.'

'Speaking of old fashioned wives, you'll love this book I picked up in a second-hand bookshop.'

Harriet took out a book the size of a cigarette packet, clearly a facsimile of its original, the date 1913 printed below the title *Don'ts for Wives*.

'Blanche Ebbutt,' said Sandra, reading the author's name, 'she sounds like a porn star.'

'It's hilarious and full of instruction,' said Harriet. 'Listen to this: "Don't forget to feed the brute well, as much depends on the state of his digestion." Or what about this: "Don't think it beneath you to put your husband's slippers ready for him." I reckon that all women should be handed this on their wedding day.'

Sandra took it from her and flicked through. 'Here's a good one, "Don't think your husband horrid if he seems a bit irritable; probably he has had a very trying day and his nerves are overwrought." That sounds just like Nigel. Oh, and here's one for me: "Don't try to excite your husband's jealousy by flirting with other men."'

'That reminds me,' said Harriet. 'I was chatted up in the park this morning by a very attractive young man who invited me for coffee.'

Sandra's eyes widened.

'Really? Did you accept?'

'You needn't sound quite so surprised. And no, I didn't. I am a respectable married woman, I would never do such a thing, I leave that to you, Sandra. Though of course it's good to know I've still got it. I think he was attracted to my reassuringly conventional clothes, or maybe because he saw me doing the crossword. He looked like an academic type.'

'The same way you wowed Sam with your tweed skirt, back in the day,' said Sandra.

Harriet had always been the clever one, a shoo-in for Cambridge while Sandra and Tessa went red-brick. Sandra liked to tease Harriet that she'd only managed to pull Sam in the first term because of the imbalance between the sexes. One woman to nine men in those days, it gave you a massive head start.

'Well it's not wowing him now,' said Harriet.

'Do you remember that time we all went up to London to buy something for the school disco?' said Tessa. 'Sandra and I bought miniskirts in Chelsea Girl, but you insisted on dragging us into Laura Ashley so you could buy a high-necked modesty gown?'

'To be fair, there was nothing very modest about her behaviour when she was wearing it and got off with Paul Davies,' said Sandra. 'Respect to her.'

'It's the appeal of the demure,' said Harriet, 'you need to hold something back.'

She thought back to her early days with Sam in her room in Corpus; it made her blush to think of it, their hot entangled limbs, no position untried. During one particularly acrobatic session, she'd looked out of her window at the dreaming spires and knew that they had found the centre of things, the whole point of life. Hard to equate with their present relationship of polite evasion.

'Anyway, that's my news,' said Harriet, 'apart from the fact that I've just had to rearrange the furniture in Celia's room as she didn't like the layout. What we really need to hear about is Tessa's weekend. Were the flames rekindled?'

'Actually, it was lovely,' said Tessa. 'You can't go wrong with Cornwall, can you?'

'Don't be anodyne.' Sandra wasn't interested in the official version.

'Alright. It was fine, really, but he was a bit of an arse at dinner, making a fuss about the food. As if you have to complain to show how macho you are.'

'And plenty of sex?' asked Harriet.

'Yes, that too.' Tessa did not care to give bedroom details. 'Oh, but he did say something that really annoyed me.'

This was more like it. The women perked up, ready to become indignant. Tessa felt a pang of disloyalty to Matt. She doubted he would find time to sit in a cafe with his friends to share details of annoying things that she had said. But then again, he didn't really have friends, only colleagues. And anyway, he wouldn't want to discuss such minutiae.

'He said, basically, that I was lucky to have him—'

'Lucky, lucky girl!' said Harriet.

'Because, at my age, that is at OUR age—'

'We are in our PRIME,' Sandra interrupted, pushing up her cheeks in a grotesque approximation of a facelift.

'Once you're over fifty,' Tessa resumed, 'as a woman, you become invisible. Actually, it was me who told him that, I read it in the paper but he didn't disagree. Unless you're Sharon Stone or Helen Mirren of course.'

They thought about it for a moment.

'I actually don't mind being invisible,' said Harriet. 'Don't you remember as a child wishing you could wear an invisibility cloak and go around where no one could see you and listen to what everyone was saying? Well now we can. We'd all make brilliant spies.'

'Speak for yourself,' said Sandra, 'I am completely and fabulously visible.'

'It's true, the builders still whistle at you,' said Tessa. 'Or at least one builder does.'

'Whistling's not the half of it,' said Sandra.

'How is the snagging going?' asked Tessa. 'Or whatever you call it.'

'Oh, you know, one thing crossed off, three more added.'

They all nodded knowingly.

'I must say though that Mariusz was looking particularly hot this morning,' said Sandra.

'You're so *inappropriate,* that's why we love you,' said Tessa, 'but I couldn't do what you do, even in the unlikely event of an opportunity presenting itself. I'd just feel so guilty.'

'Guilt is wasteful emotion, said Sandra. 'As you've just pointed out, we've got a small window of opportunity here, a few precious years before we become completely invisible to men. Anyway, it's all over with Mariusz.'

'Cougar!' Harriet couldn't help herself.

'Nasty, sexist term. And inaccurate. I don't rule out older men, and your sons would certainly be out of bounds, Harriet, on the grounds that young men are boring. But you must admit there is nothing as fabulous as that spark of connection, that *frisson . . .*'

She exaggerated the accent, it sounded so much better in French.

' . . . that is the whole point of being alive. You don't have to take it any further, but if you can't get that buzz, you're just . . . dead, aren't you?'

She flicked back her blonde hair, expensively cut by Ben in Brompton Cross, and stretched her arms out in front of her, interlocking her manicured fingers, enjoying their envious stares. It was the Chelsea Girl changing room all over again, when she was the only one who really looked any good in the sparkly white trouser suit.

'That's so *reductive,* Sandra.' Harriet was put out. 'You're saying that sex is all there is, that a woman must seduce, or else – nothing. What about everything else in our lives? Our children, our husbands—'

'Your dogs?'

'Yes, alright, my dogs. Don't mock it.'

'I'm not mocking. I'm just saying that's what makes me feel alive. You have other criteria.'

They all fell silent. It was no secret that Harriet was no longer having sex with her husband.

'How are things between you?' Tessa asked gently.

'Oh, you know. OK. He's got a housekeeper, and now a carer for his mother. I've got a handyman and generous provider. We function, but I'm not sure how long we can go on like this.'

'You're a saint,' said Sandra. 'Having that woman in your basement. I don't know how you put up with it.'

'It would certainly cramp your style.'

'It would certainly never happen.'

Harriet tried, and failed, to imagine Sandra escorting a frail old person into the passenger seat of her primrose-yellow Mini.

'That's enough about me,' she said, not wanting to think about Celia any more than she already did. 'Let's get back to Tessa and her supposed invisibility.'

'Oh yes,' said Tessa, 'the other thing he said was I had more chance of being hit by a bus than finding a new partner. Statistically proven, apparently, for the over-fifties.'

'Bollocks,' said Sandra. 'You're a great-looking woman. I'd do you myself if I was a bloke.'

'If you were a bloke,' said Tessa, 'you wouldn't be spending the morning gossiping with your old school friends. You'd be hard at work earning money for your family, like our poor husbands. As Matt never fails to remind me.'

'Not if I was a young man. They're all on three years paternity leave these days or else primary carers, can you imagine more of a turn-off? Nothing less sexy than the sight of a man pushing a pram.'

'Anyway, that statistic doesn't apply to us, we've already got husbands,' said Harriet. 'I prefer the theory that a woman over fifty who gave up her career to raise a family has more chance of being hit by a bus than getting a job that won't see her being patronised.'

'Oh yawnsville, Harriet, get off your hobby horse,' said Sandra. 'Now, anyone fancy a facial? I've got a voucher for that beauty salon that's just opened round the corner. Make a change from the nail bar.'

As they were leaving, Sandra saw she had a message from Mariusz.

I am in the Ikea and you miss me. ❤ ❤ ❤

She corrected his grammar.

I miss you, is what you mean

YES SANDRA!!! I MISS YOU TOO XXXX

CHAPTER THREE

'Don't be out if you can help it when your husband gets
home after his day's work.'

Blanche Ebbutt, *Don'ts for Wives*, 1913

Tessa was hard at work in the kitchen, chopping celery and
green olives. It was a relief to be occupied; she'd wasted an hour
earlier today at the beauty salon, a den of vacuous women with
time on their hands. True, she had emerged feeling cleansed and
refreshed, but she could never become one of those high-main-
tenance types who were always having themselves prodded and
rubbed like oven-ready birds.

The chicken was marinating and she had time to kill before
Matt came home, so she made a cup of herbal tea and settled
down on the sofa to indulge in her secret pleasure. She knew it
was an addiction. The reassuring blue homepage, the licence to
snoop, Facebook was endlessly fascinating. It was also a buffer
against her loneliness: if she was feeling a little low, she could
just lose herself in the stream of updates of other people's lives,
invariably more fabulous than her own.

Her son Max wasn't a Facebook user, he considered it an invasion of privacy and a vehicle for boasting. He was right on both counts, she thought as she opened her laptop, especially the boasting, and the worst offenders were the middle-aged. Too old to compete in photogenic terms, they instead bragged about their families and careers. Here we go, Cal Thompson could always be relied on to share the details of his dynamic schedule: 'five days, three continents, four happy clients and a great webcast on entrepreneurship'. Oh do fuck off. Eighteen people claimed to like this, no doubt his sycophantic junior colleagues. Tessa especially enjoyed the social braggers. William X, a successful man of letters, is 'wondering in which order he should attend the three parties he's invited to tonight'. Tosser.

She reached for a sip of tea, it was all entertaining fun, but she wasn't sure how many people used it the way she did, to find out who her most ghastly 'friend' was. She scrolled down to a magnificent torso shot of a young gay man, stripped to the buff and glowering into the lens, provoking appreciative comments from his friends: 'miao!' and 'woof!' So it was OK to make sex objects of young men the way you weren't supposed to with girls any more. Tessa had a lot of gay friends on Facebook, sharing the details of their glamorous lives. Lucky them: untrammelled by children and bourgeois expectations, here were men of her age whooping it up, making the most of each day. Why didn't we all live like that? Ah, but here there was trouble in paradise. Her friend Alan Doulton was bristling with indignation at a critic who had failed to appreciate the genius of his novel. Huffy old queen, she thought.

And then she turned to the chief object of her obsession. Lola now had 1,245 friends and 3,680 photos of herself, though sometimes it was hard to distinguish her in the crowd of slick-haired good-timers huddled together. She looked happy though, and gorgeous as ever. Tessa clicked through the photos, looking for evidence of any special relationship she should know about. Lola hadn't mentioned anyone, but sometimes a picture could speak a thousand words. Who was that tall boy looking down into her face as though she were the most fascinating person in the world? She clicked on his profile to find out more.

Her research was cut short by the sound of Matt's key in the lock. She guiltily closed her browser and returned to the reality of her dinner preparations.

While Tessa was enjoying a leisurely afternoon at home, Matt was having a horrible day at the office. Not for the first time, he was being chastised for inappropriate behaviour by the woman he liked to term the Chief Behaviour Officer or Little Miss Spoilsport.

'Obviously I was JOKING!'

He raised his hands in the manner of a man delivering a joke and stared at the plain face of the HR woman. Why were people in Human Resources always so unattractive? No chance of anyone sexually harassing her, that was for sure.

'I was being IRONIC' he continued.

'So you don't deny you sent this email?'

She pulled out a paper from the file of evidence on the desk in front of her and began to read it out.

> I've got a hot new temp (raising standards!) Feel free to help yourself.

'That's the way I talk with Roger, it's an in-joke between us that we talk like a couple of blokes from a 1970s sitcom. We're not SERIOUS!'

'I'm afraid the temp doesn't see it that way, she's too young to remember seventies sitcoms.'

'She wasn't supposed to see it, this was a private email to Roger. Not my fault if she read it over his shoulder, she should have minded her own business. Anyway, she should be flattered. It's the other girls who should take offence, the ones I imply are less hot. If anyone was going to get upset, it should be them . . .'

Human Resources was scowling at him now. Felicity, he remembered her name now, as in Felicity Shagwell in *Austin Powers*, how mightily inappropriate.

They were sitting in one of the meeting rooms dropped into the open-plan offices, a goldfish bowl where everyone could look in and wonder what was being said. Through the soundproof glass Matt caught sight of the temp in question, the little minx, carrying her coffee on an unnecessary detour so she could watch his discomfort as Felicity continued her assault.

'I'm talking to you off the record here, Matt, I'm trying to guide you. Call it re-education if you like, but you'd better listen to me. You can't go around referring to colleagues as being "hot" and talk about "helping yourself" like she's a piece of meat.'

She'd got the wrong end of the stick, as usual.

Matt took a deep breath and tried to explain.

'I meant helping yourself in the work sense, obviously! No point in paying for a temp I'm not using full time. And you tell me why women come to work in tight little mini-skirts and stilettoes if it's not to look hot? They might also be clever and great and efficient and lovely, but those clothes are chosen to look HOT because that's how women want to look!'

He took in her brown knitted jacket and mannish trousers.

'If they can,' he added, unwisely.

She looked at him in contempt.

'This may be impossible for you to understand, Matt, but there are some women in the twenty-first century whose self-esteem is not rooted in how they look.'

'And good for them! I wouldn't be making jokes about some-one dressed in drab, sensible clothes. As it is, I am acknowledging the efforts of a pretty girl to . . . showcase her talents!'

Felicity slipped the paper back into the file.

'As I said, we're not taking it any further at this stage, this is strictly off the record. But if I were you, I'd show a bit more contrition and think seriously about changing your attitude.'

I'm not having it, thought Matt, I'm not having this ghastly woman haul me over the coals for a throwaway private remark. Human bloody Resources. He remembered when they were called Personnel, just glorified secretaries who wrote down when everyone was on holiday.

'Here's another joke for you, Felicity,' he said, as he stood up to leave. 'Or rather, a maxim, from the good old days of how we used to do things. What's the first rule for running a successful business? Sack the personnel department.'

By the time he got down to the car park, Matt was starting to feel better. The sight of his Maserati, parked in a prime spot reserved for directors, reminded him that things could be worse. That woman Felicity cycled to work, he had seen her arriving in her fluorescent-green jacket and hair-flattening helmet. She probably went home to her cat and her sustainably farmed soya bean supper, prepared with equal division of labour between her and her partner, poor sod. Whereas he could look forward to one of Tessa's indulgent dinners and not even think about washing up.

There were definite advantages to having a stay-at-home wife, though it was a pity she didn't bring in any money. Moving up through the gears on the Marylebone Road, Matt made a mental list of them. Not having to do the boring stuff like put out the bins or shop for food. Someone to deal with electricians, etc. A sympathetic ear for his trials at work. Sex on demand, if you felt like it. Not much point having a wife who went off on her own business trips, where was the fun in that? He had a female colleague who travelled a lot, and was always complaining she needed a wife. 'Like you've got, Matt,' she'd said. He wondered if it had been a bit of dig, suggesting he was old school.

He parked a few doors down from his house and walked back past a flashy line-up of cars to his own front steps. At his age he should be able to park outside his own home, damn it, but everyone seemed to have two cars these days: an armoured tank for the lithe young wives to take their kids to school and a sports car for the hedgies to get into the office and make more millions, the bastards. He often flicked through the property magazines that came through the door in spite of their 'no junk mail' sticker – and looked at what they could get in the country. A proper house with room to park a fleet of cars in the in-and-out drive. He'd go for it in a heartbeat – with a pied-à-terre in London of course – but Tessa was reluctant. She was worried about being lonely, though you could hardly say she led a giddy social life here in the city. It was unclear how she filled her time but, as far as he could tell, she was usually on her own.

Throwing his keys on to the hall table, he could smell she'd been at it again. Middle-Eastern spices, saffron, a tang of ginger, it must be Ottolenghi. He wasn't complaining, he liked those big flavours, bringing the warmth of the souk incongruously into the sleek modernism of their kitchen-dining room.

'Smells good!'

He picked his way carefully down the cantilevered stairs that stuck out from the wall with no apparent means of support. You wouldn't want to slip on those, with the perilous open spaces between the treads and only thin wires for banisters.

Tessa was standing behind the huge granite-topped island, not so much an island as a continent, as the builders had pointed out, eight of them staggering beneath its weight when they brought it in from the garden through the tall glass doors.

'Hi!' Smiling up at him, she wiped her hands on her apron, its olde worlde rose pattern at odds with the cutting-edge interior design. 'Red or white?'

'What are we having?'

'Chicken with saffron and hazelnuts, with mackerel and raisin salsa to start.'

'White in that case.'

She pulled a bottle out from the chiller beneath the hob and poured two generous glasses.

'That's what I thought. Here you go, mineral overtones. From northern Italy.'

'*Chin-chin*,' said Matt. 'Tell you what, I really need this after the day I've had.'

He picked up his drink and went to stretch out on the Italian sofa, bought at vast expense, after months of deliberation, to make an impact in the glass box of their extension. He kicked off his shoes and admired the evening light streaming in through the high windows. He looked back at Tessa, absorbed in her preparations, her dark hair messily pushed back, the swell of her breasts and tummy clearly visible from this angle.

'Ready!' Tessa whipped off the apron and beckoned him to the table. 'Now, come and tell me about your horrible day.'

He sat down facing her, just two places laid at one end of the large table. When the children were at home, the conversation would always focus on the mini dramas of their lives, with Tessa fostering their self-centredness, eager to know every detail, greedy for involvement while it was still on offer. Now they had gone, Matt had Tessa's full attention, which was really rather nice. He told her about his outrageous treatment at the hands of the PC brigade, how you couldn't say anything these days, how the fun had gone out of it all. As he spoke, she made sympathetic noises, laughing at po-faced Felicity's disapproval, and he felt the tension drain away. By this time they were on to the second bottle and everything seemed alright.

'So, that's enough about me,' he said. 'How was your day?'

Tessa got up to clear the table.

'Oh, you know . . .'

She picked up their plates and bustled over to the sink.

'No, I don't know. Come on, fill me in.'

'It's not interesting.'

She was rinsing the dishes now, ready to go in one of the dishwashers. They had installed a pair of them, so you could put dirty plates into one while the other would always hold clean crockery. Or that was the idea, the reality was more chaotic.

'Try me.'

'Alright then. Random household tasks, unpacked our bags, accepted a fiftieth birthday party invitation from Ben and Eva. Sorry, make that a hundredth birthday party. Fifty years each, so a hundred altogether, geddit?'

'Nauseating. I really can't bear fiftieth birthday parties, it's all about people showing off how well they've done.'

'Don't be miserable just because you didn't want one. Anyway, to continue the precis of my interesting day, I renewed the car insurance and cut back the wisteria. Then I had coffee with Sandra and Harriet.'

'Ah, what's naughty Sandra up to these days?'

'Nothing! I wish I'd never told you about that.'

He was glad she had, they'd had a good laugh about it. Shagging the builder in broad daylight while her husband was at work, it was straight out of Readers' Wives, you couldn't make it up. She was pretty hot, too, Sandra, always had been. And she'd kept her figure.

'What about Harriet, still playing the martyr?'

'She has a lot on her plate, poor thing, with the live-in mother-in-law, she spent a whole day on the phone trying to rearrange her hospital appointments. We don't how lucky we are, having healthy parents who can look after themselves. My parents, I mean, but at least yours were healthy right up until the end.'

That was Tessa all over, counting her blessings, constantly reminding him of their good fortune. Her good fortune, actually, he wasn't sure his own life was the breezy pleasurefest that hers seemed to be.

She was taking something out of the freezer.

'Aha! Do I sense pudding?'

'Blackberry ice cream parfait. But made with yoghurt so it's really healthy.'

'Give me a big slice then.'

She cut two generous portions and brought them over to the table.

'And how about a glass of vin santo to wash it down?' said Tessa.

'Why ever not?'

Several reasons why not, he thought as she poured out the sweet liquor. They both drank way above the guidelines and neither of them needed the extra calories. On the other hand, what the hell. You had to have some compensation to tide you over the hell of early middle age.

'What do you think of my face?' Tessa asked, wiping away the crumbs.

'Funny question. I've grown accustomed to it.'

'I had a facial today, Sandra had a voucher so I got it half price. Look, smooth as a baby's bottom.'

She traced her fingers over her cheeks, as though gauging the quality of a fine fabric. He looked at her critically. She still had a good complexion, lightly tanned from the memory of summer, but the lines had deepened, brackets etched around her mouth, a downward line between her eyebrows that could make her look severe.

'Not bad for your age. Though of course you can't polish a turd.'

'You certainly know how to make me feel good about myself.'

She felt her self-esteem lurch down another notch. Make your own dinner, she thought.

'It's big business, beauty for the ageing lady. I wish I'd got into that, licence to print money.'

He glanced at his watch. 'So, should I depress myself by watching *Newsnight*, or take a look at the match highlights?'

It wasn't a question that required an answer. He made his way back up the precarious staircase and into the through lounge, or double reception room as the estate agents called it, settling himself into his favourite chair, placed at optimum distance from a large TV screen mounted above the mantelpiece. Barcelona by Mies van der Rohe, an original, not the cheap fake, upholstered in tan leather, which made him think happily of a gentlemen's club. A far cry from the neat Barratt home in a cul-de-sac where he'd grown up, whose only advantage was that it was cheap to heat, as his mother would tartly remind him when he asked why they didn't live in one of the old houses he passed on the way to school, which looked such fun with their ramshackle front gardens. All he needed now was a cigar but that was something else that had been outlawed by the health police. He flicked on the TV and sat back to enjoy the sight of muscled men in much better shape than him chasing each other round the high-definition pitch.

Downstairs, Tessa cleared up the plates. She couldn't finish the pudding tomorrow as she'd planned a fast day. When the children were at home, there were never any leftovers; everything she put on the table would be cheerfully dispatched by Max and Lola and any random friends they brought in for dinner. Still, not long now, they'd be home for the Christmas holidays before she knew it, cluttering the house with all their stuff, clothes and toasted sandwich-makers piled up in the corners of their bedrooms, bringing in the bright chaos of their complicated social lives. She stopped herself right there. It was weeks off. Don't wish your life away.

She took her laptop and went over to lie on the sofa. The garden was softly illuminated by uplighters, the newly pruned wisteria covering the back wall, ready for another season. She must get the bulbs in tomorrow, fritillaries and lambada tulips that had been delivered from the nursery. They usually had a party in May, when the garden was at its best, for Matt's birthday – apart from when he turned fifty, which he had preferred to keep quiet about.

She opened her computer and went straight into Facebook. No further update from Lola on the possible boyfriend, so she scrolled back through the photos of the Freshers' fancy-dress bar crawl. Just as she was about to log out, she noticed there was one friend request and one message. She opened the message first.

Oh. My. God.

OMG.

Bugger me sideways and fuck my old boots.

There he was. John Ormonde.

After all these years.

Sandra pulled the pillow up around her ears in an attempt to block the sound of Nigel snoring. She had tried earplugs but they made her feel claustrophobic, as if she were drowning. Some women made their partners wear snore guards, but she thought that was mean. As if Nigel didn't have enough on his plate, without shoving a bit of plastic into his mouth every time he went to bed. He was really going for it now, though, thunderous noises echoing round the room. He'd wake Poppy at this rate, even one floor up it was hard to see how that racket wouldn't be heard through the dead quiet of the night.

She reached across with one hand and squeezed his nose, blocking out the air. Two seconds of silence, a small and welcome death, then a sudden violent snort as he spasmed back into life, greedily sucking the oxygen back in and humping away from her, pulling the duvet protectively around him.

It did the trick, his breathing was quiet now. She stroked his head gratefully, her fingers running over the smooth forehead to the spiky hairline. It had been a godsend to him, this fashion for bald heads. Even young men with a full head of hair were shaving it off in order to appear macho. So if you were fifty and receding you'd be silly not to, even if it did make you look like a bit of a skull-face. She continued to stroke him, listening to his steady breathing, matching his slow pulse.

He was proud of his low pulse rate. Before they bought the house, a nurse had come round to check him over, to make sure he was wasn't going to fall sick and default on the repayments. He had to give a urine sample on the spot – to prove it was really his – and the nurse weighed and assessed him, as if buying a horse at the market. 'Aren't you going to inspect his teeth?' Sandra had joked as she came in with the coffee, an accessory before the fact, colluding in the need to keep the old beast working. Nurse Adams had laughed, hand on the restraining rubber arm wrap, as she took the reading. 'Lovely low pulse,' she said, 'you're lucky, you've got a strong heart.' And Nigel had looked really chuffed.

She snuggled up to him, folding her body into his back, feeling the strong heart beating. She liked him most when he was sleeping, as long as he wasn't snoring of course. She could imagine him then as he used to be, before he went mad and started finding fault with everything. Before he lost the appetite for life and forced her to sleep with the builder. Oh God, the shame. In spite of her bravado she still couldn't really believe she'd done it. And now Mariusz was making it very clear he wanted more. As if reading her thoughts, Nigel shuddered, and she smoothed his head again. Steady boy. Good dog. Good Boy Choc Drops, she should get some for him, along with the blueberries and muesli with low-fat milk which ensured that his arteries remained unfurred, enabling him to continue to function as a top-drawer breadwinner.

She was wide awake now, but it wouldn't be fair to put the light on to read. She thought of creeping downstairs to the computer, but dismissed it as a bad idea, it would only lead to compulsive surfing of medical websites speaking in resolutely positive terms that fooled no one about terrible diseases crouching in the shadows and ready to pounce on the over-fifties.

Instead, she stared into the darkness and smoothed her hands over the linen sheets. She was glad she'd insisted on one-thousand-thread count from Josephine Home, you should always get the best you could afford, that was her mantra. She remembered the cheap nylon sheets of her child-hood, supposed to save on ironing, and how she had sweated into them during hot summer nights and promised that she would get a better life for herself, one with crystal glasses and Caribbean holidays and the fine bed linen she used to run her fingers over in Liberty during her dreamy window shop-ping expeditions up West. She'd finally got what she wanted, the house was a complete triumph. My finest achievement to date, she thought. When a celebrity was asked what their finest achievement was, they always said 'my children', but you could only get away with that if you were famous. If a normal person said 'my children', everyone would yawn and roll their eyes. Far better to say, 'my beautiful home'. Mind you, if someone had told her in her twenties that one day she'd spend all her time running a home, she'd have laughed in their faces. Homes ran themselves, unless you had nothing better to do. Which she didn't.

Her reverie was interrupted by the shrill ringtone of her phone. She quickly reached for it in the darkness, anxious not to wake Nigel. It was Tessa, what the hell did she want?

'What's up?' she whispered, hunching away from her sleeping husband.

'Sorry, did I wake you? Listen, you'll never guess who's just messaged me on Facebook!'

'I have no idea, and frankly I couldn't care less,' Sandra hissed. 'You know what Nigel's like about sleeping. Why don't you tell me tomorrow!'

'Sorry, sorry, really thoughtless of me. I'll tell you tomorrow, go back to sleep.'

'Hang on, you might as well tell me now! The damage is done.'

Nigel was still snoring, she was safe.

'Alright then! John Ormonde!'

'DONNY ORMONDE!'

'The same! Can you believe it?'

Sandra was thrown straight back to their girlhood. John Ormonde, or Donny Ormonde as they called him, because he looked a bit like the heart-throb pop singer Donny Osmond with his wavy dark hair and American white smile. They all adored The Osmonds: hunky squeaky-clean Mormon brothers who were rumoured to wear all-in-one chastity suits beneath their blingy stage outfits, what could be sexier to teenage virgin girls? Everyone fancied John but he only ever had eyes for Tessa.

'No way!' said Sandra, remembering the aftermath of his great betrayal.

'I can't believe it,' she said. 'What brought him crawling out of the woodwork? Did he say why he walked out on you all those years ago?'

'He didn't walk out on me!'

'If you say so.'

'It wasn't like that.'

'OK, whatever. Tell you what, let's discuss it in the morning at the rink.'

'Yes. Sorry to wake you, I just needed to tell someone.'

'I know. Goodnight.'

''Night. Thanks for listening.'

Sandra settled back on to her pillows. She could tell from the rigid silence across the bed that Nigel was awake.

'Who the fuck was that?' he grumbled.

'Tessa.'

'Christ sake, couldn't it wait? It's not as if you don't live in each other's pockets.'

'Never mind. Go back to sleep.'

Easier said than done for her highly strung husband. She waited until his breathing became slower, heavier. Good, no need to recourse to the sleeping tablets; you could become addicted to them if you weren't careful. Time to go to sleep herself, Poppy was preparing for a skating competition and

Sandra had promised to take her up to the rink tomorrow. She was trying to be supportive even though she couldn't tell the difference between an axel and a Salkow. Tessa was planning to join them, she liked spending time with Poppy now her own children weren't around. At least they'd have plenty to talk about. You really never knew what was round the corner.

Tessa put down her phone and reread the message on the screen.

> Hey Tessa! I was just browsing and stumbled on your name! How are you? Still gorgeous, if that picture's anything to go by!! Sure would love to hear from you! I've sent you a friend request. Do be my friend!! John.

Too many exclamation marks, as usual. She had once counted five of them on a Valentine's card. He used to speak in them, too, his enthusiasm for life had to be exclaimed at full volume, and the thing he was always most enthusiastic about was Tessa.

She stood up and walked over to the window, gazing out into the garden. The sight of the carefully structured line-up of pots did nothing to calm her churned-up thoughts. She was seventeen, it was a steamy summer night at his party where they were playing 'I'm Not In Love' by 10ccs, and he was pushing her gently up against the apple tree and explaining that it was her and nobody else who could make him happy. She could feel his hand slipping inside the back of her waistband, stroking the rift between the top of her buttocks, making his point. He was wearing a cheesecloth shirt that gaped between the buttons with a packet of soft top Camels parked in the top pocket, and he tasted of tobacco and Watney's Party Seven.

Tessa went back to her computer, her fingers hovering over the keyboard. She shouldn't reply. Not yet. But she wanted to look at his wall so she'd have to accept his friend request, then he'd know she'd seen his message. She typed quickly. *Hey John!* Those exclamation marks were catching. *Lovely to hear from you. I'm good, thanks.* She corrected herself, no need to sound like a teenager. *I'm fine, thanks. Fancy you tracking me down after all this time!* She deleted the last sentence, mustn't sound too keen and grateful, and wrote instead, '*Still smoking Camels?*'

He was replying already, she could see the squiggly lines going, it was too much to take in. In a blind panic she turned off her computer. Cut the connection, get back to the here and now.

She sat back on the sofa and stared at the black screen, now safely extinguished. From upstairs came the distant roar of the football game. Matt was probably asleep in front of it. She let her mind return to the morning after the party, when she had woken up with a dry mouth and a thick head, to find herself alone in John's bed. He had gone. She knew he was planning a gap year in Australia, but he hadn't said exactly when he was going. It certainly wasn't discussed that night when he was telling her how they were meant to be together for ever and this was just the beginning. Why had she never heard from him again?

CHAPTER FOUR

'Don't grudge the years you spend on child-bearing and child-rearing. Remember you are training future citizens, and it is the most important mission in the world.'

Blanche Ebbutt, *Don'ts for Wives*, 1913

Early starts were not a regular feature in Tessa's life and the rink at seven-thirty was a bleak place. She'd been here several times in the evening, with crowds of rowdy teenagers clattering off the ice in clumsy hire skates to treat themselves to burgers and ice creams. Now the cafe was closed and a solitary cleaner was pushing a mop across the floor while a handful of mothers sat behind the glass, following their daughters' progress, willing them to make the sacrifice worthwhile.

She sat down beside Sandra and took a sip of the vanilla latte brought in from Starbucks, trying to focus on the action through her lenses that were usually resting safely in their case at this ungodly hour.

'What's that she's doing?'

Dressed in a tiny black skirt and T-shirt emblazoned with diamanté skates, Poppy was leaping off her back foot and spinning round in the air before landing with a flourish.

'Don't ask me,' said Sandra, putting down her magazine, 'I never know what anything's called, I just sit back and admire.'

She turned to face her friend.

'So come on then! Spill the beans on John Ormonde, why has he suddenly decided to get in touch?'

Before Tessa had a chance to reply, they were interrupted by the woman at the next table, who had looked up from her embroidery hoop.

'It's a double toe loop cherry flip.'

Oh Christ, thought Sandra. It's that goody two-shoes Megan showing off again. Sitting there with her bloody tapestry, making the worst cushion cover ever. She gave her a cold stare.

'Cherry flip, my arse,' she said. 'What kind of a name is that? Sounds like the sort of disgusting drink my friend here likes to order. Honestly, Tessa, I don't know how you can drink that stuff at this time in the morning. I'm practically gagging just looking at you.'

'That's because you've got issues around food,' said Tessa. 'Anyway, you need to keep up calcium levels at our age, otherwise your bones will crumble away and you'll collapse.'

'Like Cousin Boneless in *Cow and Chicken*.'

'Exactly.'

Their long friendship provided shared references from every phase of their lives, in this case a TV cartoon series once enjoyed by their children.

'Wow, that's a fabulous camel spin!'

Megan was leaning forward now, intently focusing on Poppy who was rotating on one leg with the other extended behind her.

'Is that what they call it? She looks like the Duke of Edinburgh to me,' said Sandra. 'The way he folds his hands behind the small of his back when he's following the Queen.'

Megan frowned.

'I'm surprised you don't follow more closely, Sandra. Your daughter's really good, she could go all the way you know.'

Sandra pulled a face.

'I hope not, she's only fifteen.'

Megan gave her a disapproving look. She had a fresh complexion and wore no make-up, her sandy eyelashes untouched by mascara. Even her hair looked self-righteous, a single plait falling neatly in front of one shoulder.

'I'm here, aren't I?' said Sandra. 'She's got a competition coming up so I'm willing to cheer her on. But you need to keep perspective, it's her life and I'm not going to pile on the pressure. You can't live through your children.'

'I'm not living through my children,' said Megan. 'I'm just giving them the best possible start. Which is also why I opted for homeschooling.'

Sandra and Tessa looked at her incredulously.

'That's amazing,' said Tessa. 'Aren't you worried about them not having any friends?'

'Of course they have friends. I make it my business to ensure they have friends. And this way I get to check them out. School is such an aggressive, bullying environment, you don't know what damage it's inflicting on your children. I'm a Libra, so I'm very concerned about balance.'

'And I'm a Capricorn so I smell of goat,' said Sandra.

'Take no notice of her,' said Tessa. 'I'm Tessa by the way, an old friend of Sandra's and nowhere near as rude.'

'Nice to meet you. I'm Megan, I'm new to this rink. Do your kids skate?'

'No! Maybe hobble round the Christmas ice patch outside the Natural History museum from time to time. But they're away at university now.'

'Oh you poor thing! So you're at a bit of a loss I guess.'

'Not at all!' said Tessa quickly, 'it's great to have some time to myself at last. Are you American?'

'Is it that obvious?'

'Well the homeschool was a clue, we don't go in for it much here. And the accent.'

'Oh my God, did you see that?' said Megan, 'Double loop, double cherry, gallop, axel! Your daughter's something else, Sandra! It's so great for my kids to work alongside her, it gives them something to skate up to – especially since Kim lost her flying camel in the summer.'

'I haven't the faintest idea what you're talking about, Megan,' said Sandra.

Megan wasn't listening, she had left her table and was standing close to the glass wall, gesticulating to her daughter, urging her to give it another go as the poor child stood shivering on the ice.

'So, what did he say?' Sandra asked, now they were on their own.

'Nothing really, just asked me to be his "friend", which always reminds me of the Quakers. I messaged back and he's replied. I haven't dared to read it yet.'

'Intriguing. Maybe he wants to explain why he ditched you the moment you gave in to his smarmy charms.'

'He wasn't smarmy, and I didn't give in!'

'Maybe not technically.'

'Technically! You sound so forensic.'

'You know what I mean. He didn't TAKE you, did he? Remember how we loved that bodice-ripper language, about men HAVING and TAKING women?'

'We didn't do it, no.'

'But you were so upset when he disappeared. It was like you were engaged or something, the way he'd been talking, and then just to bugger off without a word.'

'That's why I can't bring myself to read his latest message. I'm still trying to get my head round it, which is pretty pathetic when you think about it. Fifty-year-old housewife in dizzy spin at news of old boyfriend!'

'Homemaker, please.'

'Fifty-year-old homemaker all of a tizz!'

'Well, let me know what he says when you've plucked up the courage to read it. I'm going out for a ciggy but don't tell Poppy. Meet me outside.'

Ten minutes later Poppy came through from the changing room, groomed and plaited in her school uniform. Her face lit up at the sight of her mother's friend.

'Hello, Tessa, what are you doing here?' she said, kissing her on the cheek.

'Watching you, lovely girl, what a treat!'

'Thanks. Did you get up specially early just for that?'

'I've been meaning to come for ages. I loved it, I'll definitely come again!'

'Will you?'

Poppy gave her a sharp look. Oh God, thought Tessa, she thinks I'm a complete loser.

'Where's Mum?'

'She's just gone out to check on the car.'

'You mean to smoke a cigarette.'

''Course not! Come on, let's go, Sandra said to meet her outside.'

Together they walked up the stairs. Tessa caught sight of their reflection in the mirrored walls, a plump middle-aged woman and a beautiful, lissom teenager.

'Do you come here every day?' she asked. 'You must be so fit.'

'Most days. I usually get the tube but Mum drove me in today, she's trying to show an interest in this competition I'm doing and it's not like she's got anything else to do.'

'Well . . . she's like me, we're both very lucky—'

'Kept women,' said Poppy with a smile, 'you're both kept women, we were learning about it in gender studies. It's cute really, kind of old fashioned.'

Sandra came up behind them on the pavement.

'Old fashioned? *Moi?*' she said, striking a pose in her tight leather jacket and high-heeled boots.

Tessa laughed. 'It's true, you really are the ultimate MILF.'

'Gross,' said Poppy. 'I'm not talking about your clothes, I mean it's really old fashioned of you not to work or anything.'

'At least it means I'm free to drive you to school,' said Sandra, opening the door of her yellow Mini Cooper. 'Now get in, before I change my mind and make you take the tube.'

Tessa watched them drive off, then walked down Queensway, past the shops selling London souvenirs and elaborate eastern smoking equipment, with snake-like pipes attached to giant Aladdin's lamps. At Bayswater station, she went briskly down the stairs to the platform, matching her pace to the men and women in their busy city suits, and crammed herself into the train, pressed against a boy plugged into his iPod, his eyes glazed away from her. She'd forgotten how ghastly it was in the rush hour, how sensible of her to usually remain safely at home until the mid-morning lull.

She got off at Fulham Broadway, intending to visit the street market to shop for tomorrow's dinner party. It gave her a thrill to get so much for so little and she saw it as a modest way in which she could contribute to the household budget. Coming out through the precinct, she avoided the temptation of the Krispy Kreme doughnut stand, though just the smell of it gave her a taste of that sugar rush, the odd metallic aftertaste that came after biting through the sweet crust to the insubstantial interior. Should she buy a box, just in case Max dropped by later on? No. She was on a fruit and vegetable mission.

'Hello! How are *you* today!'

Out on the street, a young man with a clipboard was demanding eye contact, waving his arms in an attempt to block her path.

'Fine, thank you,' she said, moving sideways like a crab to get round him.

He, too, moved sideways, as though partnering her in a dance.

'Can you spare me two moments?'

'Sorry, terribly busy.'

Poor thing, she thought, as she made her escape, he was only trying to earn a living, it could be Max next year, once he graduated. The way things were now, there was no guarantee he'd get a proper job even with a psychology degree, unless he could become one of those bearded experts who comment on the antics of participants in reality shows.

Walking up the North End Road, Tessa enjoyed the immersion in multicultural London. Working-class white stallholders selling fruit to women in veils who spoke little English but knew how to choose the best on offer, while Middle-eastern food shops displayed baskets of exotic vegetables, strange-shaped roots and lush bunches of herbs. She joined the queue at her favourite fruit-seller. She knew it was a bit sad to take pleasure in his outrageous flirting, but it always made her laugh. He was showing off a tan acquired on a Canary Island, as he was explaining to the woman he was serving.

'Beautiful it was, no trouble at all, people good as gold. Then I get back to Gatwick, queuing at Immigration, bloke taps me on the shoulder.'

He dropped his voice to a stage whisper.

'*Black.*'

Then resumed his normal tone.

'Says "'ere, mate, can you lend me a quid?" I thought; here we go, welcome home.'

He handed over the fruit.

'There you go, girlfriend, that's five pounds for you, and I'll see you tonight as usual.'

His 'girlfriend' was well over seventy and made no response as she put the bags of fruit into her basket on wheels. Then he was on to the next customer, a stout matron in tweed, who was speaking into her phone while passing him a bowl of apples.

'You phoning me? I wish you were. There you go, darling, give us your bag, let me slip it in for you, if you'll pardon the expression, that's for you for being a good-looking young lady.'

Then it was Tessa's turn. She handed him bowls of oranges and lemons, three pomegranates and a large bunch of Italia grapes, and he turned to his son to order further supplies.

'Luke, more oranges please! I'm serving this little girl here.'

'Don't you love your dad's banter?' Tessa asked the boy.

'Oh I love it,' he said, swinging a box of oranges on to the stall, 'all day long. I never get sick of it.'

His father was still on the patter.

'I see you're getting your five a day, love,' he winked at Tessa, 'you're looking good on it.' He threw in an extra pomegranate.

'That's for being a good girl, not like you were last week, I heard all about it. What time are you expecting me this evening?'

His fruit really was good, it wasn't just his sitcom repartee that she came back for, though the entertainment was a bonus. It took her back to a simpler time when people didn't have to watch what they said, when men considered it their duty to crack cheery jokes, before everyone become so damned earnest. A simpler time, when you were seventeen and believed John

Ormonde when he told you he loved you and wanted to spend the rest of his life with you.

She was in a hurry now to read his message, but first she must complete her shopping for tomorrow's dinner party. Boudin blanc – she'd have to get that in Harrods – pan-fried with the grapes and chestnuts that she'd pick up from the French greengrocer near her house. Then a classic rack of lamb with celeriac purée and Heston's orange and almond cake, gluten-free to accommodate Alan who fancied he could no longer tolerate flour.

She stopped off at her favourite Lebanese store to buy some pomegranate molasses and fresh mint. The old-fashioned stall-holders disapproved of these shops, there won't be a market soon, one of them had told her, they would be driven out by 'them people'; immigrant shopkeepers who had dared to bring their rich food culture into a society that used to make do with meat and two veg.

Swinging her bag of provisions, she decided to walk home through the Brompton Cemetery, which always raised her spirits. It made her feel part of the exciting fusion of new and old in the city, with the football stadium rearing up behind the Victorian mausoleum and the gravestones, surrounded by artfully wild vegetation, with Michaelmas daisies and long grasses left to whisper memories of the departed. Beatrix Potter used to walk here and took the names of her characters from the tombstones: Jeremiah Fisher, Peter Rabbett, Mr Brock and Mr Nutkins.

As she opened her front door, Tessa was greeted by the distant roar of the vacuum cleaner. She put away her shopping, ignoring the lure of her computer, then made two cups of coffee, carrying one up the stairs for Maria, who jumped as she came up behind her in the bedroom, removed her earphones, then nodded her gratitude. Tessa liked having a cleaner who spoke little English, it kept a distance and didn't oblige you to share your life stories. She remembered old Mrs Evans, short-sighted and talkative, who used to 'do' for them in Orpington. Her mother would sit her down at the kitchen table with a pot of tea and Rich Tea biscuits and listen to tales of sun-baked package holidays to Spain and the dangers of being spat on by camels in Tunisia. Tessa and her sister would pass round the photos of Mrs Evans spilling out of her bikini and wonder why they only got to go to rainy Wales in a caravan.

Alone in her kitchen, Tessa compared her own life to her mother's. Not so different, after all. 'Find a job that keeps your mind sharp,' her mother had urged her, harassed and bored in her apron, sweeping away the debris of another family meal, the grey perm and pleated dirndl skirt confirming that her life as a vibrant woman was over. Tessa's hair was carefully maintained at a constant chestnut brown and she was better than her mother at disguising middle-aged spread beneath layers of black cashmere. She had achieved what her mother had wanted for her: a university education and a career where she was taken almost as seriously as a man. If she had subsequently found that sitting at a City trading desk was less appealing than bringing up her children, then good for her. Her mother couldn't argue with that, it was a rational and human decision, and hadn't Tessa learned from her example that a mother's hands-on love was the richest gift you could offer? Anyway, Matt could earn enough for them all and she'd loved those afternoons in the park and calm days at home, watching Max and Lola putting their enthusiastic little hands into the mixing bowl to pull out fistfuls of cookie dough.

Keeping busy, now they'd gone, that was the key. Tessa pulled a cookbook down from the shelf and opened it at the page she had bookmarked earlier. She could get ahead now with the caramelised oranges, they'd keep in the fridge, then Maria could clear up the mess before she left. She selected a Japanese knife with a lethal blade from the block recently reinstated on the countertop. They were burgled a couple of years back and the police had found the carving knife abandoned on the study floor. Matt and Tessa were seriously freaked out, though they didn't tell the children, and took to hiding anything sharp in a cupboard. But you soon forgot, and the Global eleven-piece kitchen set was now back in pride of place, challenging the next intruder to do his worst.

Tessa removed the skin from the oranges, then painstakingly cut away the pith between each segment, producing a dish of perfect crescents ready to be steeped in the sugar melting slowly on the hob. You could just slice them across but that wasn't good enough, not when she had time to do things properly. The sugar had turned brown now and she took the pan to the sink to add a splash of water, watching it spit and hiss, then poured the caramel over the oranges. There, that was ready, one thing less to do tomorrow, getting ahead was the secret of being a successful hostess. When she was in the Girl Guides, she had been awarded her hostess badge, proudly sewing it on to the sleeve of her uniform. A kind woman had quizzed her about the steps the hostess should take when receiving guests, which mostly involved opening the window to air the spare bedroom and offering cups of tea. These days the stakes were higher, she had her reputation to think of, everyone agreed she was the most marvellous cook and she clung to this with almost comic pride, as though her *raison d'être* depended on the quality of her menus. I cook therefore I am.

Right, that's enough cooking, she thought. Now it was time for her to read John's message. She switched on he laptop and went straight into her Facebook, trying to ignore a new photo of Lola looking a little the worse for wear. You'd sometimes rather not see it; she was glad her mother had been spared the evidence of her own youthful indiscretions in the pre-internet age.

She took a deep breath and opened the message. It was disappointingly short. One word, followed by the sad face emoticon that Tessa herself had only recently mastered.

married ☹

What was that supposed to mean? He was sad about her being married? Or sad because he was married? He gave nothing away about his own situation, maybe she'd missed the clues. It was time for some serious stalking. She settled in for an in-depth trawl through his photographs, to get the measure of this man who was already becoming her obsession.

Was that his wife, standing beside him in the Grand Canyon? She peered closely at the slim woman in sensible hiking gear, grinning at the camera. Hang on, weren't all American women supposed to be fat, once you got away from the two coastlines? John himself had certainly gained some weight, she was hard pressed to see the skinny teenager in the solid figure he now presented, with hat pulled down over his sunglasses as he wrapped a protective arm around the woman. Who was she? Tessa clicked through more photos, trying to get a fuller picture of this life she knew nothing of. A barbecue in someone's backyard, John slapping the steak down on to a massive grill. Boating on a lake, he's holding on to a rope, wearing a baseball cap, not a look she favoured. Did anyone look good in a baseball cap? Certainly not that woman who is on board with him again, sexless in shorts and polo shirt, neutered by the unflattering headgear.

Ridiculous, that's what I am, thought Tessa, drawing back from her laptop. Already jealous of the possible partner of someone she hadn't seen for thirty years. Mooning around like a teenager. Ridiculous.

She got up to make herself a coffee. No milk, today was a fasting day and she'd got off to a bad start with that vanilla latte earlier. Fasting used to be a religious thing, now it was what everyone did to make themselves more fabulous. She was already looking forward to her lunch, a single slice of smoked salmon with cucumber, making up half of the five hundred calories she was allowed before bedtime.

She clicked on a different album, entitled Conquering Colorado! Still loving those exclamation marks. He was definitely chunkier than he had been, but it suited him, it gave him solidity, gravitas even. And he was obviously fit, you couldn't climb up that rock face unless you were in pretty good shape . . .

She was so intent on Johnny Ormonde's strong thighs that she failed to hear footsteps on the stairs until someone came up behind her and clapped their hands over her eyes, pulling off the headphones to whisper in her ear in a horror movie voice.

'Sur-prise!!!'

Tessa jumped as she felt his hands, smelling faintly of smoke, pressing against her eyelids. She spun round and there was her son.

'Hello, darling, what a lovely, lovely surprise!'

She sat back for the pleasure of taking him in, absurdly good-looking in his slovenly jeans.

He bent down to give her a hug.

'I thought I'd look in and check up on the old woman. What's this, whiling away the day on Facebook? Who's that old bloke?'

He leaned over to get a better look and frowned at the photo. 'Terrible clothes!'

'Oh, nobody,' said Tessa, quickly logging out, 'just someone I was at school with.'

She was annoyed with herself for blushing.

Max looked at her with his father's amused brown eyes. He was so like Matt, or like Matt used to be.

'You know you can tell everything about someone by going through their browsing history,' he said. 'Do you think I should take a look, check out your favourite websites and discover your secret vices?'

'Go ahead!' she replied, 'I can assure you there's nothing there to get excited about.'

'No, I'll be alright. I'm not really interested, to be honest. Just saying.'

Of course he wouldn't be interested, she knew that. It was one-way traffic with your children, you were passionately curious about their lives, but they really couldn't care less how you filled your days. As long as you were still there to provide laundry and food services and unconditional love.

Max was moving towards the utility room with a large sports bag.

'I'll get these on, shall I? Or are you still possessive about the washing machine?'

'Not possessive. Just keen to ensure you select the right programme and don't overload.'

He grinned and dropped the bag on the floor. 'Probably best if I leave it to you then. What's for dinner? I thought I'd stay the night if that's OK.'

'Of course it's OK. Always a treat.'

'Indeed.'

He patted her on the shoulder, then went to stretch out on the sofa, heavy boots plonked disrespectfully on the cream cushions.

'Feet down, please!'

She was already thinking about what to make for dinner, Chinese duck maybe, with pancakes and hoisin sauce. Never mind the 5-2 diet, it was so good to be needed again. She pushed his feet off the sofa and sat down beside him, making the most of him.

'Come on then, fill me in. What have you learned this week?'

It was a game that dated back to their first separation: reunited as they walked home from school, his hand in hers, when he would earnestly divulge the information he had acquired that day. How the stars emit their own light, how a seed swells beneath the soil, the naming of parts of a castle: portcullis and drawbridge, barbican and buttress.

Max clearly decided to humour her. 'Well, I was reminded that Freud believed that love is an overestimation of the object. As opposed to the Ancient Greeks, who likened it to fire.'

'I see. And what do you think?'

He shrugged. 'Both views are viable.'

Max was non-committal about his love life. He was a Facebook refuser but Tessa had seen plenty of contenders on his friends' timelines: glossy-haired girls, arms entwined with his as they confided to the camera that it was all SO FUN!, which was irritating to those who deplore poor grammar. But there was no one special at the moment, he said. Nobody for her to meet and assess as a possible provider of grandchildren.

'I think it sounds fascinating,' she said, 'I wish I'd done psychology.'

'Never too late, Mum. You could enrol for a second degree. Go on that Open University summer camp where all the old people shag each other.'

'No chance. I doubt I'd be capable of sitting another exam. Anyway, I struggled with motivation with my first degree so I'd be hard pushed to see the point of doing another one.'

'I know the feeling,' said Max.

'No, come on, you've got your whole life ahead of you, every motivation I'd have thought!'

'Whatever. How's Dad? Oh, wait, how was your Cornwall weekend? I forgot to ask. Did you love it?'

'Of course, have I not spoken to you since? It was lovely.'

'Did you go in the sea?'

'No! We got an ice cream though. Coated in clotted cream with a flake, the way you like it.'

'Nice.'

He nodded, evidently pleased to find them freeze-framed in his idea of their simple contentment. Mum and Dad in the hazy Cornish sunshine, smiling into the camera over their ninety-nines.

He jumped up. 'Right, I'm going to crash out for a couple of hours. What time's dinner?'

'Eight o'clock, when else? I'd better get out to the shops. I'll just text Dad, let him know you're here.'

'Sick.'

Max winked and held out his fist to exchange their mock street gesture, palms brushing then hands clasping in brother-hood. It was like the old days, thought Tessa, as she watched him leave the room, almost a full house again, another mouth to feed, busy busy busy.

What time was it in Wyoming? Six hours behind. John might be having his breakfast now, cinnamon toast maybe, or driving to work in his Cadillac or a Buick, kicking up the dust of the Midwest plain stretching out before him, like in the *Wizard of Oz*. She listened to make sure Max was safely upstairs, then opened her computer. There it was, another message.

> Camels? I wish!!! They'd sooner you shoot to kill than smoke a cigarette in this goddam country!! Another pleasure lost to the mists of time! Tell me your news! I'm all ears!! Xx

Xx. Kiss kiss. Two kisses.

She hadn't smoked a cigarette in twenty-four years. Not since she'd seen that blue line on the home pregnancy kit and thrown the remains of the packet of Marlboro into the bin. Now, suddenly, she felt that nothing would give her more pleasure. Pulling the tiny thread on the cellophane wrapper, flipping open the packet to remove the foil, then pulling out the slim pencil form of what they laughingly referred to as coffin nails or cancer sticks when they were young enough to believe themselves immortal. 'Cancer stick? One for you, one for me,' then heads bent over the lighter, the hit of that first inhalation, the best feeling in the world. Why had she ever stopped?

She wrote her reply.

> You know the headlines. Married. Two kids.

The wiggly line started, showing he was typing his response. Oh my God, they were on Facebook chat!

> Gutted. You already saw my ☹. Who's the lucky man?

So he was gutted, was he? Tessa sat back angrily and frowned at the screen. If he was so gutted, why had he walked out on her like that? Alright, not exactly walked out, she knew he was going to work on a farm in Australia for a year, but still. Humiliating to think how she'd watched the post, waiting for a letter, making excuses for him about the unreliability of airmail. But nothing, not even a postcard.

She typed her slightly chilly reply.

No one you know. He's called Matt. We just had our silver wedding.

Happy ever after then. It's been a long time, Tessa.

It has. For all I know, you're still herding sheep in Adelaide.

No chance! It was a great experience but I stuck to the plan. Came back to study engineering at Manchester.

So he *had* come back. Without telling her. Manchester was two hours by train from Nottingham. Tessa had checked out the journey after he'd gone, already thinking about the weekends they would spend together when she arrived at her hoped-for university. She'd always been a planner and even though everyone said that school romances never survived, she honestly believed they were in it for the long term. Although John clearly hadn't seen it that way.

Hello? Are you still there? Talk to me, Tessa!!

I'm here.

This is so amazing, talking to you again. I'm picturing that scar you had on your fingertip.

Tessa inspected the forefinger of her left hand, it still had the silvery line where the surgeon had stitched it up after her misadventure with the food mixer. She had been making coffee butterfly cakes when her hand slipped and her mother's face turned white before she sprang into action, binding up the finger and rushing her to A & E. John said it was endearing when she showed him, he said it was like the mark on Action Man's cheek, she was a kitchen hero.

Why hadn't he contacted her? What was she supposed to think when he disappeared from her life? It was too big a question, she mustn't show how much he'd hurt her. Get over it, this was ancient history. She should stick to the finger detail.

Scar still there. Added a few more over the years, occupational hazard.

I'd like to see them ☺. I'd love to see you again.

Would you now?!

Of course I would.

Don't you think you owe me an explanation?

Yes and when we meet, I'll make you understand. But right now, I've got this picture of you in my head, we're on that camping trip and you're wearing a tight pair of jeans and it's started to rain and all we've got for dinner are two cans of chunky chicken, and that jerk Tom forgot the tin opener, and you're laughing and I just want to kiss you so much. I think that was when I realised.

She hadn't thought about it for years but it came back to her, clear as day. They had taken the train the first day of the holidays, pitching their tents in the field above the wild Cornish coast, trying to pin down the flaps that were blowing in the gale. She rushed out her reply.

We had to smash them open with a rock! What did you realise?

That you were my dream girl! Especially in those jeans, have you still got them?

Dream girl. It was unexpectedly painful to read those words. When you found your dream girl, you married her and lived happily ever after, you didn't vanish for thirty years without saying a word. She remembered the jeans, though. FUs, the provocatively named brand of choice for those who fancied themselves a little bit daring. She'd noticed him eying her up when she was wearing them, following her up the hill as they laboured beneath the weight of their rucksacks until they reached the chosen spot along the cliff from Tintagel. The sun came out the following day and they'd gone skinny dipping, plunging through the waves then running back up the beach to wrap themselves in towels and cook sausages on a barbeque.

> No I don't still have those jeans.

> Shame.

> Anyway, what about you, are you married?

> Divorced.

In spite of everything, her heart leaped.

> Sorry to hear that, what happened? If you don't mind me asking.

> I don't mind you asking. Why does anyone divorce? I guess I married the wrong person ☹. How about you, Tessa, did you marry the right person?

What a question, of course she had married the right person! Or maybe that was something you never asked yourself if you wanted to stay together. Anyway, John had sacrificed any right to ask such a thing.

> In the words of Garrison Keillor, We Are Still Married. So I suppose I did.

> Too bad. I bet you'd still look great in those jeans.

Tessa was thinking about her reply when Max came crashing back down the stairs.

'Mum! Have you seen my earphones? I think I must have left them here a couple of weeks ago.'

There was just time for her to hastily sign off.

Got to go! Speak soon x

She closed her computer and set about looking for the earphones. Max and Lola both lost them with alarming regularity, usually down the back of the sofa. They were eventually located in a drawer along with other technical accessories and assorted rubber bands. She handed them over to Max who returned to his lie-down.

Alone again, Tessa was free to daydream about that first evening when they were all gathered around the camp fire, huddled together for warmth. They've had their first swim and are giddy with cider and John is licking her arm to taste the salt from the sea, then he's pulling her into the tent and she's slipping into his sleeping bag for several delicious minutes until she realises this is not what she should be doing and she must stop right now.

When she returned from the rink, Sandra was surprised to find Nigel hunched over his computer at the breakfast table, pinging an elastic band against his wrist. Beside him, the seasonal affective disorder lightbox was emitting a ghostly glare designed to replicate cheerful summer sun.

'Oh, still here?' she said, unzipping her jacket and throwing it on the back of a chair.

He looked up at her briefly then turned back to his screen.

'Sorry to disappoint you. I've got an appointment with Paola this morning.'

She curbed her irritation at the way he pronounced her name, with full Latin American inflection. He'd always been good at languages; it was one of the things that had impressed her when they first met at a French country themed wedding. She was placed next to him at a long table covered with a cheerful chequered tablecloth, set out in a rustic tent decorated with hay bales. Nigel had read out the menu to her, and the way he had pronounced '*côtes d'agneau*', with the perfect accent acquired during his international education, had completely won her over. His father was a diplomat so he had grown up in many exotic places. As opposed to Orpington, which he had never had the pleasure of visiting, he told her, as he led her on to the dance floor.

'That's good.' she said, watching him now, completely absorbed in himself. 'You seem quite pleased with her.'

He nodded.

'She's really helping me. And there's more good news. I've been doing some research and I'm pretty sure I'm not clinically depressed. I'd say I'm somewhere between moderately and severely afflicted on the scale, so it could be worse.'

'Indeed it could, and at least you're fully embracing your condition, which is important. You're not one of those ostriches who struggle on in denial.'

'Yes, I'm pretty confident that the course of treatment I'm following will cure me.'

'Rising like Lazarus from your sick bed.'

He flashed her an angry look. 'There you go again, taking the piss!'

'I'm not!'

She pulled off her boots, leaving them in the middle of the kitchen floor.

'Put them away, can't you?' said Nigel. 'It's not helping me, the way you're incapable of putting things back in their place!'

'Don't be anal, I'll be wearing them again later, so what's the point.'

'I'm surprised you're even out and about at this early hour, it's not like you.'

'I took Poppy skating, but I forgot how many boring mothers you get up there. I had to talk to this unbelievably dreary American woman who homeschools her daughter. At least Tessa came along to watch. Did you remember we're having dinner there tomorrow?'

'I remembered. Anyway, I'm off now, mustn't keep Paola waiting.'

He unplugged the SAD lightbox and packed it carefully back in the cupboard, then picked up his laptop, sweeping it into an expensive-looking leather bag which coordinated with a soft-charcoal jacket Sandra hadn't seen before.

'You look nice,' she said. 'New jacket?'

'Thanks. I bought it a while back, but forgot all about it, what with everything else. Still, might as well put my best face forward for Paola.'

'Or Paula, as I prefer to call her.'

'Wrong. It's spelt with an "o" in the middle. Anyway, see you later. I'll try not to be too late.'

Don't rush back on my account, thought Sandra. She kissed him goodbye, running a finger down the back of his head.

'Getting a bit spiky, you long-haired layabout.'

'Didn't have time to shave this morning, I'll do it later.'

She waved him off. He worked as a consultant in a boutique financial outfit which looked after the money of a few extremely rich clients. It was supposed to be less stressful than his previous job in charge of a hedge fund but the change had not produced the desired effect. If anything, he was more unhappy now that he had more time to think about his unhappiness. He'd tried to explain it to Sandra: you climb off the hamster wheel but still have to watch it spinning round without you, propelled by younger men who made you feel inadequate. It was hard for her to understand that feeling, he said, because she'd never been an alpha male. No, she said, I'm a beta female, nothing wrong with that.

What she needed now was a little downtime to recover from her early morning start. A leisurely trawl through the repeats of *Location, Location* was calling, so she made her way downstairs to the home cinema, arguably the flashiest room in the house with its monster screen and surround sound and vintage cinema seats upholstered in blood-red leather. Sandra and her brother

Peter used to squeeze up on the Dralon settee in their Orpington semi to watch *Blue Peter* on the black and white rental set.
On Saturdays she'd go with her dad to get fish and chips so mum
didn't have to cook, and the four of them would eat off their laps
in front of *The Generation Game*. When her dad died, her mum
moved to Scotland to be near Peter's growing family. The first
time she visited Sandra after the renovations, she had sunk into
the maroon leather seat and marvelled at the size of the screen.
'You've done so well, Sandra,' she said, 'I can't believe how far
you've come.' Her visits were infrequent; it was a long journey
and Peter's children took up much of her time.

The cat jumped up beside her and she stroked his silky grey
coat, admiring the way he matched the plush velour of the
ottoman. It was no accident; she had researched every breed
before settling on a British Blue. His name on the pedigree
certificate was Heathrose Steely Dan – they always sounded
like porn stars – but she had renamed him Leo. Proper cat-
lovers would disapprove of choosing a pet to match the furniture, but she thought it was perfectly sensible. A cat's role
is to look decorative, you didn't get much else from them. If
you wanted personality and noisy love, get a dog and enslave
yourself to daily walks like poor old Harriet.

Kirsty was showing a young couple round a dream cottage
with outbuildings and some land which would enable them to
develop an unspecified business venture to get them out of the
rat race. Lucky them, still young enough to think there was a
wonderful new life waiting for them if they only found the right
house. She followed them round, from room to room, watching

their eyes light up as they contemplated the way they would decorate the attic rooms for their children, planning their golden family years.

She looked round her own room and felt as alienated as a guest in a five-star hotel. There was nothing there to suggest it was her house; no personal photos, just valuable abstract paintings which Nigel had bought at the Frieze fair on the recommendation of his art advisor who was paid to know about these things. They'd spent so much on creating this giant TV lounge that it would probably be cheaper to move into a hotel for the rest of their lives and go to the cinema every night.

A stash of DVDs was neatly stored in a shiny low cupboard that ran the length of the room, they usually watched one in the evening to help Nigel relax, as recommended by Paola. Focusing on the film meant they didn't need to talk to each other, so that was a bonus. Currently they were three series into *Breaking Bad*. Sandra had worried that a cancer-stricken middle-aged teacher turned drug baron was not a suitable role model for someone in Nigel's condition, but at least it let him feel that someone had it worse than him. She fancied Walt's sidekick and former pupil Jesse Pinkman so there was something for both of them as they stretched out their legs in competition for the B & B Italia ottoman.

Yes of course, that's what she needed to do! It had struck her last night that it was hopeless having only one ottoman, they needed another one, in a toning shade of grey, but definitely not matchy-matchy.

Energised by the project, Sandra leaped up and switched the TV off, zipping herself into her boots. She pulled on her jacket, wound a scarf round her neck and grabbed her bag. She was a woman on a mission.

Unlocking her bike, she cycled towards the park, whizzing past the joggers and the yummy mummies strolling aimlessly behind their buggies, poor things. They might be younger than her but she would soon be free from the shackles of parenthood. Lucky me, she thought as she braked to a halt at the bottom of the hill, then crossed over into Gloucester Road. This was what I was born for, this is what I've always wanted. The spontaneity that money bought, the possibility of buying exactly the right piece of furniture to complete the perfect home.

Just being in Brompton Cross made you feel part of the new European elite to which she naturally belonged, a tidal wave of successful people enriching London with their style and lovely foreign money. Pushing open the door to B & B Italia, she was welcomed by the throbbing ambient music and sense of emptiness associated with the most expensive furniture shops. She nodded at the girl on the desk and walked past the arrangements of floating armchairs and corner seating units, wide beds with built-in side tables, suggestions of rooms that could be yours if your pockets were deep enough. She smiled at one of the assistants and was soon seated beside a hanging file of fabric swatches, feeling through the velours and the wools, imagining each of the colours into her room, moving from deep amber to burnt orange, then on to bitter purple chocolate.

'Sandra! I thought it was you!'

Sandra looked up and saw a woman with a plain, wholesome face that she vaguely recognised but couldn't place.

'Megan,' said the woman, 'from the ice rink?'

She sat down beside Sandra, who clocked her functional training shoes and sensible anorak, so wildly out of place in this temple to style.

'Megan, of course! Sorry, it just didn't click, seeing you out of context—'

'I know, it's not exactly my milieu! Which is why I've just had this great idea, seeing you sitting there looking so much at ease.'

'Oh I love B & B Italia, don't you?'

'I guess I do, but what do I know? This is where you come in. Let me explain. My husband often needs to entertain his clients at our apartment but our furniture just isn't right. We shipped it over from home but he wants to send it back and get a modern European style. You know, I'm a very committed needlewoman, but somehow my patchwork quilts and woven cushion covers don't look right here . . .'

Sandra suddenly felt sorry for her. Cruelly snatched away from her loom and banished to the unforgiving chic of Chelsea.

'They'd look great in the country,' she said. 'You know, if you ever decided to live out of town.'

Megan looked wistful. 'I wish! But my husband didn't want to commute, and we both agreed that with the homeschooling we needed to be in the centre of things, so our daughter could get the best cultural exposure out of our time here.'

Sandra nodded.

'Of course. You don't need to sell the city to me, I wouldn't live anywhere else.'

'Someone told me this was the store to come to,' said Megan, 'but you know what, I'm kind of out of my depth here. We're looking for an expensive Italian vibe, like this store. You look as if you know what you're doing. Look. I know this sounds mad, but . . . I'd like to take you on as my interior designer.'

Sandra was taken aback.

'Me? I don't know what gave you that idea, I'm not an interior designer . . .'

'You've done your own home, right?'

'Well yes . . .'

'And I bet it's beautiful, I can tell just from looking at you.'

'Well yes, it is really, even though I say so myself . . .'

'The thing is,' Megan went on, 'interior design is just not my area of expertise. I mean I can weave rugs and make a beautiful *homely* home, if you know what I'm saying. My house in Connecticut is full of ornaments we've collected on our travels, I remodelled our bathroom with the most beautiful Victorian bathtub and faucets, I just loved putting that house together . . .'

She suddenly looked close to tears.

'I'm sorry,' she went on, pulling herself together, 'But I guess I just don't have the eye for this sort of . . . European penthouse look, I suppose you'd call it, where everything has to look so . . . empty.'

'I can see that,' said Sandra, then realised it sounded rather rude.

'I mean,' she added quickly, 'I can tell you're more interested in your child's education than fussing around fabric swatches. Whereas I am entirely shallow and exactly suited to the job of interior designer, in fact I can't believe I haven't thought of it before! Thank you, I'd absolutely love to take in on. And honestly, it shouldn't look empty if you do it properly, it's a question of making the right choices. A signature piece in a bay window, an original sculpture to arrest your attention as you walk in the door, above all it's about attention to texture and space and light.'

She had read so many design magazines over the years, she could do it standing on her head.

'Great, that's settled then.' Megan looked so happy and relieved that Sandra felt as if she had already done her the most massive favour.

She exchanged details with Megan, then placed her order for the ottoman, confidently settling on the deepest shade of puce. On the cycle ride home, her mind was full of Megan's exciting project and Tessa's reconnection with Donny Ormonde. It was also entirely possible that Mariusz might drop in later on; he was making it quite obvious that his frequent recent visits were not exclusively work-related.

CHAPTER FIVE

'Don't sneer at your mother-in-law's old fashioned ways'
Blanche Ebbutt, *Don'ts for Wives*, 1913

In the hospital waiting room, Celia was getting impatient.

'How much longer?'

Harriet wondered why she cared, it wasn't as if she had anything else to do. They had been sitting there for two hours already because Celia liked to be early and Harriet liked to oblige. She turned round to look at the board.

'It says they're running ninety minutes late, so I reckon another half an hour. At least you've had your blood test done.'

Celia sighed theatrically. She looked stunning, in spite of her illness, in a turquoise silk dress and elaborate make-up applied for the benefit of her consultant oncologist, whom she always referred to as 'The Professor'.

'Just as well you don't have a job, Harriet. Can't see how I'd get to all these appointments otherwise. It's not as if Sam could spare the time, jetting off here, there and everywhere. He woke me up at five o'clock this morning, I could hear him rattling around in the kitchen, right above my room, I thought it was a burglar at first, then I remembered he was getting the plane to New York.'

'That's right,' said Harriet. 'He's having dinner with Alex after the meeting and Alex is bringing his new girlfriend. She's called Nadia. I've seen the photos and she looks very glam.'

Her eldest son had been working on Wall Street for three years, long enough for her to get used to it, but she still missed him terribly, especially since her younger son James had moved to Shanghai last year where he was marketing luxury goods to the Chinese. Both boys were born in this hospital, it only seemed like yesterday that Sam had brought her into the ward, clutching a packet of frozen peas because the NCT teacher said that massaging them against her back would relieve labour pains. Lunatic woman. When it was over, she held Alex's tiny hand as he lay beside her with what seemed almost supernatural stillness. Sandra and Tessa were her first visitors, once Sam had slipped off to wet the baby's head with his friends. They had arrived together in a giddy after-work whirl of perfume and short skirts, producing expensively wrapped baby clothes from Petit Bateau and marvelling at this perfect new addition to all their lives. 'Such beautiful flat ears,' Tessa had said, running a reverential hand over his head, he's going to be an absolute looker.

'I don't know why everyone has to go abroad all the time,' said Celia. 'Plenty of banks in England with jobs if that's what you want to do.'

'It's exciting to live somewhere else, though,' said Harriet, wishing right now that she was somewhere more exotic than the oncology clinic. 'Life is short, after all.'

She looked round the room. Women of all ages and back-grounds, randomly brought together by their rogue cells. Black women, white women, some of them expensively dressed, others in shapeless joggers; the disease was ruthlessly indiscriminate. On the way up, they'd passed the wig shop, but many of the patients had opted for more creative options, wearing turbans or the arty headscarves favoured by National Trust volunteers as they sat reading the paper, waiting their turn. The atmosphere was business-like, almost upbeat, not at all like you might expect. Some were accompanied by their husbands, others by their entire extended families.

'I should think I'll get to see The Professor today, don't you?' said Celia. 'I imagine he'll want to see me himself.'

Celia took it as a slight when she was allocated anyone other than the main man.

'I've no idea, Celia, we'll just have to wait and see.'

'Mrs Watson?'

Harriet jumped as her name was called, before remembering that it was also Celia's.

A lanky schoolboy figure had appeared at the door, reading out from the file he was holding. He looked expectantly round the crowd of patients, all of them under his care, all hoping they would be the one to buck the trend. How on earth could he remember them all, Harriet wondered.

'Yes!' said Celia, a note of triumph in her voice. No under-ling for her. She gave The Professor her most radiant smile. In a gallant gesture, he swept up behind her and took charge of the wheelchair, steering her at speed past admiring nurses and patients into his consulting room. Harriet followed behind, the loyal foot soldier.

He settled them in, and then leaned forward, chin cupped in his hand, head on one side.

'So, tell me,' he said, as Celia smoothed down her hair, slightly flustered by the attention. 'How are you feeling? Honest answer.'

Harriet admired his charm, the way Celia opened up beneath his questioning, so that as she was describing her symptoms, they became trivial details compared to the massive good fortune that her welfare was entrusted to this handsome, capable man.

'So, we have a plan, don't we?' he said eventually, putting a conspiratorial hand on his patient's shoulder. 'We'll see how that goes, and if that doesn't do the trick, I've got plenty of other things up my sleeve.'

He shook his shirt above his cufflinks to demonstrate just how many options he had up there.

'He's such a lovely man,' said Celia, still basking in the glow of his charisma, as Harriet wheeled her into the lift, on the way back to the car.

'Now, I'm not going to want to sit through those chemotherapy sessions on my own. I'll need someone to be with me and I suppose it will have to be you. At least there's one member of the family who's not busy.'

Don't rub it in, thought Harriet, as she opened the car door to help Mrs Watson senior into the passenger seat. She folded up the wheelchair and packed it into the boot. Busy. If only. In a world where busyness was the measure of your worth, she was down there with the bottom feeders.

The first time she'd driven away from this hospital, Sam was at the wheel and she'd sat in the back, fragile and strong at the same time, holding her precious boy wrapped in her grandmother's knitted shawl. Sam had looked at her in the rear-view mirror and she could read the pride and happiness in his eyes.

She glanced across at his mother now. Celia had dropped her flirtatious bravado, she looked pale beneath the make-up and was struggling with her seat belt.

'It'll be alright, Celia,' she said, reaching over to attach it for her. 'Don't you worry, I'll look after you.'

Tessa was writing out the place names for her dinner party with a calligraphy pen, dipping it into a pot of deep-purple ink, when Sandra called to announce her distressing news.

'You've got a JOB!!!'

Tessa felt so betrayed that she knocked over the ink in shock and made Sandra wait until she'd cleared it up. As long as the three of them were in the same position, there'd always be someone to hang out doing nothing with while most of the world was at work. And now Sandra was threatening to end that cosy arrangement.

'Chillax, let me explain.'

By the time Sandra had finished outlining the exact nature of her employment, Tessa had calmed down.

'So basically, you're just doing what you always do. Buying lots of expensive stuff for the home, but in this case you're spending someone else's husband's money.'

'Exactly. Genius, isn't it? And then I'm setting up my company so I can be properly businesslike about it. As I said to

Megan, who's my absolute new best friend by the way, I can't believe I didn't think of it before.'

'Well, good for you, you need something to keep you occupied. And so do I, to be honest, which is why I may have overreacted just now. Although I'm just wondering whether interior design might be a a little less . . . cerebral than befits your mighty intellect.'

'Don't be a snob, and anyway my brilliant career in PR wasn't exactly challenging. Design uses a different side of my brain, all that creativity, darling.'

'It's true you've got a flair for it, I could never have done my house without your help. You can talk about it with Alan's boy bride tonight, just his cup of tea.'

'Will do. Anyway, must fly, I've got mood boards to consult. Laters.'

Tessa went back to her name cards, then carefully folded each one to stand at the head of the relevant place setting around the table, according to her seating plan. It was amazing how you could spend all day getting ready for a dinner party; it was a perfect example of Parkinson's Law, where the task expands to fill the time available. When she had a job, she could rustle up dinner in twenty minutes on returning from the office. During the child-rearing years, she would prepare the food in stages, in between attending to Max and Lola, making sure they were in bed before the guests arrived. Now she had all day in the echoing silence of her home, to ensure that everything was just perfect. She'd swap this perfection any day for the messy rough and tumble of their old family life. Clearing away the children's tea, sending them off upstairs to have a bath while she restored some kind of order to the kitchen before their friends arrived, although really who cared what it looked like, they'd have fun and that was what mattered, as she Matt would agree when they fell into the unmade bed at the end of the evening.

When Matt arrived home, she was putting the final touches to her candle arrangements. Nigella said you couldn't have too many of them, so she had dozens of nightlights dropped into coloured glass holders, displayed on the dining table and every surface around the room.

'Blimey, *Arabian Nights* or what,' said Matt, coming carefully down the stairs into the dining arena. 'Don't you think we should at least have one electric light on? Don't want any gays falling to their death, they're terribly litigious.'

'Don't say that, you sound like a raving old homophobe. Alan is very sensitive to ambience, last time they came he made us eat in the dark because he said it was killing to sit in unflattering direct light at our age. Do you mind putting the glasses out, while I go upstairs to get ready?'

In the bathroom, Tessa stared critically in the mirror. Alan was quite right about harsh light, it was alright to see every line and wrinkle in private but you certainly wouldn't want them accentuated over the dining table. She ran an exploratory finger along her jawline, stopping at a short, hard bristle. Unbelievable, how these beard hairs just appeared from nowhere, nasty reminders that time was running out, that she was a breath away from becoming an old witch. She administered the tweezers, expertly gripping the hair at the root and tweaking it out for inspection. A white one! That was a first. She flicked it into the basin and reached for her lipstick. Putting lipstick on the pig, that was the expression, wasn't it, for disguising a bad thing with a glossy veneer.

The doorbell rang. She ran down to open the door to Sandra, whippet-thin in suede trousers, and Nigel, two steps behind, arms folded in the stance of a man who would much rather not be there.

'Come in!'

'Chocs,' said Sandra, handing over an extravagantly wrapped package. 'L'Artisan du Chocolat, the box is made of rosewood so you can keep it. In fact, knowing you, I expect you'll make your own homemade truffles and regift it.'

'Excellent plan,' said Tessa, 'Oh look, here are the others, you've all arrived together.'

Alan and his boy bride were climbing out of a taxi behind a large bunch of white flowers. Tessa and Sandra had been friends with Alan since schooldays, when he had been the stand-out intellectual, given to smoking a pipe and wearing knitted waistcoats. He was in the same year as John Ormonde but while John was keen on throwing himself around the football pitch, Alan could usually be found indoors reading Proust. He didn't come out until he was at Oxford, where he had flourished in every sense. Tessa had been fond of his previous partner, a self-deprecating professor of linguistics, but Nathan had been ditched last year in favour of twenty-two-year-old Stefan, following a coup de foudre on a club dance floor. They were now married.

'Hello, my darling. God, you're looking gorgeous,' said Alan, coming towards her in his heavy velvet suit.

Tessa surrendered to his flattery as he crushed her to his bear-like chest.

'You too,' she said. 'Though obviously not as gorgeous as Stefan.'

Alan turned to admire his protégé, whose T-shirt was straining tightly over his biceps, jeans slung low beneath Calvin Klein underpants, hair whooshed up into an insolent tousled mop.

'Tessa, I am so happy to see you,' said Stefan, 'I say to Alan always I am happy to come to Tessa's house because she is very good cook.'

'And I thought it was my wit and sparkling conversation,' said Tessa, 'but thank you, that's very nice of you. Come in, all of you.'

It was a contract, of course, she thought as she led them down the stairs, a modern take on the trophy wife. The adoring older man with his boy-child, a delicious fusion of son and lover, the only child he'd never had. Alan was putting him through university, funding a lifestyle giddily beyond student expectations, and was rewarded by a dewy young thing installed in his bed, giving Alan the glow that comes with love and the joy of giving. Tessa found it enviably romantic.

'Oh, oh, oh!' said Stefan gazing round the low-lit dining arena, 'This is fantastic! Have you been featured? You MUST have been featured.'

He had ambitions in interior design and had done marvellous things with Alan's apartment, scoring a five-page accolade in *House and Garden*.

'Oh no,' said Tessa, 'I can't be bothered with all that.'

'Oh but you should,' said Sandra, tossing one suede-clad leg over the other as she perched on the edge of the sofa. 'Get the publicity shots, put together in a portfolio, then you can sign up with a location agency, like I did. Don't you remember, Tessa, when I had that film crew in, when we were still in Lonsdale Road? Never had such a rich supply of hunky men under my roof. Got paid a fortune, as well. Handy little earner, should our husbands ever get laid off.'

'You don't work either then?' asked Stefan. He had only met Sandra briefly at his wedding.

'Only on myself, love, and that's a full-time job. No, hang on, I've just remembered! As of today, I actually run my own business. I'm an interior designer.'

Stefan was delighted by this news and they immediately locked into an intense conversation about LED lighting and the relative merits of granite and limestone, as Matt popped the champagne cork and set the party underway.

Three hours later and four courses heavier, Tessa was sitting in the garden watching Sandra smoke. Matt and Nigel were indoors, exchanging gloomy tales from the workplace, while Alan and Stefan had gone on to dance at the club where Princess Diana had once got in unnoticed, disguised as a police officer.

'Well they couldn't wait to get away,' said Sandra. 'I loved the story of Alan dislocating his leg while striking a sexual position. Do you remember when they used to call him Dartboard Doulton? Everyone had a pop at him apparently.'

'He's settled down now, though,' said Tessa. 'With that beautiful boy. Although I can't help thinking that Nathan might have been a more comfortable companion for later life.'

'Listen to you! You sound about ninety. I'm just sorry I didn't take them up on the offer to go dancing, it's been years since I went to a nightclub.'

'They pack it in, don't they?' Tessa agreed. 'How come gays have all the fun while we stay home with our husbands?'

'Because we're boring old breeders. You might get Matt on the dance floor though, he's pretty lively. Not like Nigel.'

'He did well this evening, I thought.'

Sandra flicked ash on to a hosta.

'Puts on a good show. He announced this morning that he didn't think he was clinically depressed. Hold the front page.'

'Well, that's good news.'

'Not really. If it was clinical he'd be carted off to the funny farm and I wouldn't have to put up with him.'

'Sandra! You don't mean that.'

'No, I don't, I'm just being nasty. But I am sick of the sight of his SAD lightbox.'

'He'll get through it.'

Sandra shrugged.

'The awful thing is, I'm not sure I care. At least, I want him to get better, of course I do, but I'm not sure I'm interested in what comes out the other side. To be honest, I can't remember why we're still together. Apart from Poppy.'

'They say the best gift you can give your child is to love her father.'

'Staying together for the sake of the children? So fifties housewife, excuse me while I slip into my Playtex girdle and fix my husband's suet pudding.'

'Ginger Rogers said when two people love each other, they don't look at each other, they look in the same direction.'

'You're full of homilies this evening. Nigel and I aren't looking in the same direction, we're standing back-to-back with our arms crossed.'

'But you both want the best for Poppy. How's his therapy going? Is he still having CBT?'

Sandra pulled a face. 'Talking therapy.'

'But everyone says it's really effective.'

'They say that talking is cheap. Not when he's talking to her, it's not. Still, he can afford it. Money talks!'

'Must admit I share your scepticism about shrinks,' said Tessa. 'At the end of the day, we're all a bit mental, aren't we? It's called being human.'

Sandra shook her head. 'No, I'm being mean. I'm sure it's helping him, and at least she's qualified. At least she's not a bloody life coach.'

Tessa smirked. Life coaches were one of their *bêtes noires*.

'Redefining his goals and boundaries. Bollocky bollocks.'

They sat silent for a moment in the Italianate gardens and Sandra lit another cigarette.

'It's not big and it's not clever,' said Tessa.

Sandra inhaled deeply. 'Neither am I, so that's OK. Anyway, what's the latest from Donny heart-throb Ormonde?'

At last. Tessa had been dying to talk about him. She made sure Matt wasn't about to eavesdrop. No worries on that score; through the glass doors she could see him and Nigel facing each other across the table, like a couple of hanging judges.

She leaned forward in confidential mode, pulling her cardigan tight against the evening chill.

'We messaged last night and he told me I was his dream girl.'

'Player! But seriously, he was crazy about you,' said Sandra, 'I never understood why it took you so long to get together.'

'Oh you know, other fish to fry. I thought I was madly in love with Gavin Jones.'

'Wasteman!'

Tessa smiled.

'I do love your teenspeak. He came back, you know, after his gap year. He went to Manchester, but never let me know. His family moved away from Orpington, so I was never going to bump into him in the holidays or anything.'

She had never told Sandra how often she'd walked past his house in the hope of seeing him, until one day when there were new curtains at the window and a different car in the drive and she knew he was gone.

'Weird he broke off contact like that. So are you going to see him?'

'Of course not. Anyway, he lives in America.'

'Don't tell me, Utah. Along with his Osmond brothers and all the other Mormons.'

'Haha! Wyoming, I think, wherever that is.'

'You think, or you know? That sounds fairly precise to me.'

'I was looking through his profile, of course I was.'

They both looked up as Nigel stepped out on the terrace.

'Sandra, we need to go. Some of us have to go to work in the morning.'

Tessa made herself wait until she had cleared the kitchen. She loaded the dishwasher, stored the leftovers into the fridge, lined up the empty bottles for recycling and blew out all the candles. Only then did she allow herself to open the laptop. There it was, the little red number 1 telling her she had a message. She knew it would be from him. She listened for a moment, making sure that all was quiet.

He had sent a photo of the camping trip, five of them gathered round the fire, with Tessa stirring the pan. She was wearing her hair in a coupe sauvage, the shaggy mop favoured at the time, and was very slim. You never realise at the time, beset by teenage anxiety, how gorgeous you are, but she'd give anything to look like that now. He'd written a caption:

hottie with a pot, look what I found in my memory chest x

Bottles of Bulmers cider were scattered around them, and Sandra was raising one to her lips, striking a pose in a pair of tiny white shorts. Harriet was in the background, clearing up, nothing had changed there. Alan Doulton was stretched out, reading a French novel with an understated cream Gallimard cover, he had an entire collection of them which nobody was allowed to borrow. John was nowhere to be seen, he was behind the camera. She'd like to see a picture of him, she thought, as she typed her reply.

Seems like yesterday! And would you believe it, I've just had Sandra and Alan to dinner. Didn't drink cider though, only lots of WINE. But where are you? SHOW YOURSELF!

His immediate response confirmed her suspicion that he spent his days crouched over his computer, watching and waiting for her.

Nobody photographs the photographer! But I have found this one.

There he was, lying on his back by the entrance to the tent. Bell-bottom jeans, a skimpy shirt, wavy dark hair, she'd forgotten how good-looking he was.

Nice! You look really tasty. As we used to say.

Let's Skype, Tessa. You can check out the updated model!

She'd never tried Skype, but Matt used it sometimes; she'd seen him wearing his business face, making assertive statements into the screen. It was all a bit conference-like.

Not now, I'm going to bed.

That's OK, I'd love to see you in your nightie ☺ xx

No you wouldn't. I've changed a bit since that photo.

You haven't, I've already checked you out. Come on!

Maybe tomorrow. It's late.

It's a date! Let's say six o'clock, your time. I'm no good at typing and I want to hear your voice.

Tessa could hear Matt coming down the stairs.

Got to go now.

She closed her laptop in a mild panic as Matt came in to fill a glass of water from the fridge.

'Still up, you night owl?' he said. 'Stop stalking Lola! I keep telling you, she's fine, come to bed now.'

Tessa followed him up the stairs.

'Fancy a shag?' asked Matt, as he extended a friendly hand towards her when they were beneath the sheets, 'or do you think we've had enough excitement for one evening?'

'Let's just digest, shall we,' said Tessa, giving his hand a dismissive pat. 'It's late and you've got work in the morning.'

'Thanks for reminding me.'

As Matt started to snore, she let her mind wander to another scene, it must have been the October half-term and John had taken her on a spontaneous expedition to pick apples on his uncle's farm in Somerset, just as a friend. They climbed a ladder and used a stick to knock down the fruits they couldn't reach, filling several sacks, then drank so much scrumpy that John declared himself incapable of driving home, so they spent the night giggling under a blanket in the eaves, listening to the mice running around in the roof, it was incredible how noisy they were. She must ask him if he remembered next time they spoke, or messaged or Skyped or whatever they were supposed to be doing. Nothing happened between them that night, she made that perfectly clear to her curious friends once they were home. Or at least nothing to challenge her status as *virgo intacta*, they were all into Latin terminology at the time. She could smell the apples now, and feel the rough, rosy skin, the memory was as sharply defined as if it all happened last week.

CHAPTER SIX

'Don't forget to wish your husband good-morning when he
sets off to the office. He will feel the lack of your good-bye
kiss all day.'

Blanche Ebbutt, *Don'ts for Wives*, 1913

'That cat contributes nothing,' said Nigel, staring at Leo as he
sat curled up on the cashmere jacket he had placed on the chair
beside him.

It was the morning after the dinner party and neither he nor
Sandra were in the best of moods.

'He's a cat, he's not supposed to contribute.'

'Except for shedding his coat all over my clothes.'

He pushed Leo off the chair and reclaimed his jacket, then
took a lint roller from the drawer, running it over the fabric to
remove the offending hairs.

'This house is a pigsty,' he said, putting on the jacket. 'Covered
with dust. What's the point of paying for a cleaner if I end up
living in a dust bowl? Look at these skirting boards!'

He crouched down and traced a long, slim finger along the
top, with the delicacy he once used on her when they were still
on loving terms, and thrust the evidence in her face.

'Don't worry,' said Sandra, 'I'll take care of it. A quick flick of the duster and Bob's your uncle.'

'You always say that, but nothing ever happens. Anyway, I've got to go.'

He walked into the hall. 'WHAT THE HELL?! Come out here!'

She followed him out to where he was pointing to a small mark on the carpet.

'It's nothing,' she said, 'I can deal with it.'

'Bring a cloth.'

'You'll be late. I told you, I'll do it.'

But he was already back in the kitchen, returning with a cloth and a bowl of water. He knelt down and started dabbing the offending spot.

'Nigel, just leave it.'

'You have to dab, never rub . . . That's the mistake you make, I've seen you do it, you always RUB instead of DAB.'

She watched as he carried on jabbing at the floor, matching his words to the action.

'Drives. Me. Mad.'

Count to ten, Sandra thought. Don't react. Be sympathetic, it's his condition, it's not him. She waited until he had finished, then took the bowl from him.

'That's fine now, off you go.'

Sandra closed the door with the sense of relief that always accompanied his departure and thought how she could really murder a bacon sandwich. Slathered with ketchup, the way she and Nigel used to like them after a heavy night, sitting up in bed, never mind the crumbs, recovering together in happy intimacy. She couldn't remember the last time they'd had breakfast in bed, maybe a thin bowl of muesli, nothing that might stain those pre-mium sheets. Anyway, there was no bacon in the fridge; it gave you cancer so that was off. A Bloody Mary would sort her out, but you couldn't start drinking in the morning, that was a slip-pery slope, she'd have to find another way of dealing with her hangover and the ugly morning episode with Nigel. Something to sweeten her day. Of course! She'd make herself feel better by playing the goody-goody mum and baking a batch of cupcakes.

Unlike everyone else in the country, Sandra wasn't a *Bake Off* fan. The show reminded her of a damp village fete, Union Jack bunting hanging from the tent, bubbly commentary from that bespectacled school prefect and the hunky sex pest with blue eyes flirting with a woman his mother's age whose ancient fin-gernails made her feel quite nauseous, frankly. But the thought of cracking out the butter and sugar was definitely something she could handle.

An hour later, she was looking at a tray of flat little discs sit-ting despondently in their pleated paper cups. She hoped the butter cream icing would cheer them up. This was supposed to be the fun part, according to the Hummingbird Bakery Cook-book; you could let your creativity and imagination run wild as you spread a thick carpet of calorific nightmare over the dull-brown tops, then add playful decorations to give that personal touch. It said in the introduction that the authors – a couple of Stepford Wives staring out of the photo with their identikit faces – had been round the world, to Australia, America and the Philippines, if you please, in search of suitable bits of coloured sugar for the purpose.

Fairy cakes, that's what they used to be called when she was growing up. A grudging smear of watery icing if you were lucky, certainly not the thumb-deep layer of coloured butter demanded by modern cupcakes. But then again, nobody went to the gym in those days, nobody felt they had *earned* it, the way they did now. Me, me, me, work hard, play hard, then stuff your face on a cupcake topped with amusing crystallised flowers. In Sandra's case, white stars and popping candy which exploded in your mouth, a toned-down Ecstasy for all the family.

It really wasn't her thing, she thought, scooping up a dollop that had run down the side and pushing it back with her finger. Even as a child, she'd found it a bore, humouring her mother by pretending she enjoyed getting messy with a wooden spoon and a mixing bowl. Her mother used margarine because it was cheaper than butter, and drinking chocolate powder instead of rich dark foil-wrapped tablets. It gave a wartime feel to the results; in retrospect, Sandra fancied she could almost smell the powdered eggs. Then when she was pregnant with Poppy and had given up work to become an earth mother, she decided to go huge on home baking. She drove down to Divertimento on the Fulham Road and stocked up on every cake tin you could imagine, a state-of-the-art food-mixer and some hand-painted rustic Italian bowls so she could become a Tuscan matriarch in the middle of her open kitchen with a scrubbed pine surface the size of a snooker table where she would hand-make pasta ribbons with Tipo 00 flour imported from Italy. It was a passing phase, most of the tins had never been used and she soon realised only a fool would roll out their own sheets of pasta when it was so easy to buy.

She'd got the stuff all down her Zadig and Voltaire jumper; it was a good thing Ivana was coming later to clear up. She just hoped that Poppy would appreciate her efforts to show that she was a proper mum, the sort of mum who expressed her love through baking cakes, even though sugar was now public enemy number one. She'd left it a bit late; when Poppy was little, she always hired professionals to do the food, along with the clown and magician, the party bags and all that nonsense. Thank God those days were over.

Abandoning the cupcakes, she made herself another coffee, pressing the button to set the machine whirring into action, grinding the beans, reminding her of her extreme good fortune. It was payback time, these quiet mornings, the just reward for a hardworking mother who has seen her child off to school and was now free to face the empty day at her own pace. She lay down on the daybed to count her blessings, Leo sleeping at her feet. He slept for at least twenty hours a day, leaving little time for anything else, but then again his interests were few: eating rubble food and clawing the carpet pretty much summed it up. She could maybe get going on Megan's project this afternoon, but not before she'd had a little nap to refresh her creative juices.

She was just nodding off when her phone rang.

'Sandra!'

Here was a tonic she could do with. She sat up.

'Mariusz, how nice to hear from you!'

'I am in the Jewson near to your place.'

'Good for you.'

'So if you like, I come for small coffee.'

'Yes, I like. Very much. You can have a cupcake, I've just made some.'

'You make cake!'

'Don't sound so surprised. I can actually cook, you know.'

'I believe you, I believe me!'

'With sparkly sprinkles on top and popping candy.'

His silence indicated this was beyond the limits of his vocabulary.

'I'll show you when you get here,' she said. 'See you later!'

There was no denying he still put a spring in her step. She took three cupcakes from the rack, two for him, one for her, and placed them on a cake stand in the middle of the table. A few more confetti sprinkles and edible stars, and there they were, all ready. Sexy little sweeteners for her and Mariusz, and still plenty left for Poppy when she got home.

It was quite thrilling how the past could now just reach out and claim you. She had to admit she was slightly jealous that Tessa had been tracked down by a long-lost lover, though of course he was bound to have run to fat and she never fancied him anyway. And what was the point of harking back to your school days when you had your strong young admirer here and now, in the flesh?

These were Sandra's thoughts as she opened the door to Mariusz, and took in the pleasing curves of his body, strong and slim beneath his dusty shirt, his paint-spattered jeans tapering down to the solid workman boots.

'I need me big coffee today, Sandra,' he announced, touching her lightly on the shoulder on his way in.

'Why is that?' She banged the coffee waste container to release the dregs into the pull-out bin, a miracle of ergonomic design. Mariusz picked up the cat and nuzzled him under his chin and Sandra noticed how Leo threw his head back to stare adoringly into his eyes, the little tart.

'That cat loves you,' she said.

'All animals love me, Sandra. And now I must have big coffee because last night I have me too much vodka and ape juice.'

'Ape juice?'

'From apes. Grow on tree.'

'Ah, apple juice.'

'Yes! Lucky I have driver. Because I no pass breathalyser test this morning.'

He had told her how every morning, he made his 'boys' breathe into the apparatus on their way into the van. If they failed, they didn't get to work. Sandra imagined them lining up, like the seven dwarves in the Disney film, whistling with their shovels, hey-ho, hey-ho, only to be turned back if they'd over-done the vodka the night before.

'Me too, Mariusz,' said Sandra. 'I also overdid the wine last night. Not feeling too good this morning, and I look like shit.'

'No, Sandra, always you look beautiful to me.'

He let go of the cat so he could put his arms round her.

'*And* I had a horrible scene with my husband this morning,' she added, relaxing into his warmth. 'He was having a go at me about the state of the house.'

Marius drew her closer.

'Your house very clean, Sandra. It is your husband who is crazy, but it is not his fault.'

How succinctly he expressed it, he made her feel so much better.

'You're right as usual. I love how you're always so positive.'

She broke away to fetch his double espresso, heavily sweetened the way he liked it.

'It's from the machine, I'm afraid, I've run out of the ready ground stuff. And here's a cupcake, tell me what you think of the popping candy.'

She watched him bite into it, enjoying his surprise at the fizzing sensation.

'Very good cake,' he said, reaching for another. 'Tell me, Sandra, my other client in the letterhead, who like my person, she say I look like Huge Grant, what do you think?'

'Hugh Grant, you mean. But I like Huge.'

'Yes.'

'Well, there is a passing resemblance. Although you're more handsome. And a much better physique.'

Mariusz beamed with gratitude and flexed his arms in a muscle-man pose.

'Thank you, Sandra! I am a very lucky man, to be here drinking the coffee with delicious cakes and a beautiful woman, and a big business where I am every day an urgent person.'

Watching him drink his coffee, knocking it back in one powerful gulp, so happy in his skin – *bien dans sa peau*, what a lovely expression – she wanted to lean over and kiss him on the throat.

'So, where's your driver?' she asked.

'He go to other job.'

'Oh.'

'So you see, we on our own.'

He brushed the cake crumbs from his mouth and opened his arms to her. Why not, she thought, as she slipped on to his lap. My husband thinks only of himself and it's good to be appreciated. Carpe Diem, before the final curtain falls.

'Thanks, Hayley, very kind of you.'

Matt nodded his appreciation to the temp who had just brought him a cup of coffee. He had made a point of learning her name and being especially courteous, as part of his self re-education. Even though he was still furious with her for complaining about his harmless little joke.

'That's alright,' said Hayley, watching him pop out a couple of Paracetamols. 'Heavy night, was it?'

'You could say that. We had some friends over for dinner. I'm afraid I fall into that new category of problem drinker, middle-aged professionals who binge on wine in the privacy of their own homes.'

She gave him a sympathetic smile and went back to her desk. She was alright really, he thought, it was just the way the young were now, touchy and politically correct. She wasn't much older than Lola who could be equally spiky, hauling him up for what she called his casual racism, just because he talked about ordering in a ching chong from the local Thai restaurant.

He stared at his screen and tried to focus on the presentation he was putting together for next week's pitch. It was his great strength; getting up in front of the client and delivering punchy, persuasive arguments. He was a right little show pony, they all loved him. Or at least they used to. He was reordering his bullet points when Tessa rang.

'Hi, just a quickie to say Lola's coming home this weekend. Feeling a bit homesick, she said, so thought she'd join us for lunch with my parents on Saturday, isn't that lovely?'

'Oh yes!'

His spirits lifted at the prospect. He didn't miss her the way Tessa did, he had more on his plate to think about. But how great that she was coming, that would cheer up the outing with the in-laws.

'Is she OK, though? It's a bit soon to get homesick, isn't it?'

'No, she's fine, loving it all. Just fancied a little dose of home comfort I think.'

'Well you're the expert in that department. Brilliant news. Anyway, better get on, see you later.'

He returned to his work with renewed vigour. If it all sometimes seemed a little pointless, he was always able to remind himself that he was a good father, a reliable provider for his family. He loved everything about being a dad. He had friends who confessed they found it a strain, that sometimes they wished it could be a bit less full-on, that they could dip back into their bachelor life on occasion. Not him. The happiest moments of his life had been spent with his children. Kicking a football around in the park, teaching them to ride a bike. He could see it now, Lola wobbling along without her stabilisers for the first time, careering off the path then getting her confidence and steadying into a straight line. You couldn't beat it. It was fashionable to sneer at the nuclear family, but Tessa, Max and Lola were all that mattered to him, they were all he ever wanted. This weekend they'd be together again, crashed out on the sofa most likely, watching a film. Maybe he'd take a quick look at Netflix now, see if there was something that might appeal to them all. *The Bourne Identity*, that would do, though not sure if it was up Tessa and Lola's street, they usually preferred something slow and French, but he really couldn't be doing with subtitles.

It was unfortunate that Richard stopped by his desk at that very moment.

'What's this, a bit of daytime browsing going on? I've just read through your latest version and I'm not entirely happy with your approach, can we have a word?'

As he followed Richard into his office, Matt saw Hayley smirking at him, horrid little girl.

Tessa shook out Lola's duvet and plumped up the pillows. Lola's bedroom was no longer a shrine to a departed child, but a living part of the house. She was so glad Lola was coming home, they would be a family again; a joint sense of purpose as they united for a birthday celebration. Another photo of candles on a cake to add to the archive, evidence of their happy togetherness.

It was a fine day and she decided to walk up through the park to Harriet's, where they were meeting for afternoon tea. Apparently her mother-in-law was feeling fragile and Harriet didn't want to leave her alone. Celia wouldn't join them, she said, but she just needed to know there was someone on hand. 'Don't know why you need to waste your money in a cafe, anyway,' she had said to Harriet, 'just get your friends to come here.'

Sandra's bike was already chained to the railings when Tessa arrived. Harriet ushered her in to join them in the unapologetically old-school drawing room. Osborne & Little striped wallpaper, gilt-framed paintings of soothing landscapes and wing-backed armchairs covered in dog hair. Scattered on the sofa were tapestry cushions featuring the Union Jack in muted colours and the sort of plaid blankets that posh people use for picnics. Sandra waved her greeting to Tessa and cast an appreciative arm round the room.

'Tessa, look how Harriet's become shabby chic without even trying! I'm tempted to go for it myself next time, I'm sick of clean lines. Maybe I'll try it out on a client first, if I manage to get another one after Megan, see how it turns out.'

'I've always felt comfortable at Harriet's house,' said Tessa, 'but the whole point is it doesn't have the faintest whiff of interior design. I don't see you getting to grips with shabby chic, you'd be dropping in oligarch-style statement pieces all over the place.'

'Wrong,' said Sandra. 'The secret of the best designed homes is that they don't look designed at all.'

Tessa settled into a chair with a cushion that had been embroidered with a stout piece of advice; plain white letters on a navy background urging the reader to Keep Calm and Carry On.

'How's Sam?' she asked. 'Is he keeping calm and carrying on?'

'He's in New York,' said Harriet. 'It's very exciting about your business, Sandra, but, more importantly, how is poor old Nigel getting on?'

Sandra discreetly kicked the pug that was dribbling over her suede shoe. She didn't like talking about Nigel's depression. It was bad enough putting up with it at home, she didn't see why it should seep into her convivial hours.

'Too many "shoulds" apparently. That's what the shrink is telling him now.'

Harriet gently pushed down the plunger of the cafetière, taking care not to make it spurt out hot water. It was a common middle-class injury, according to the A & E doctor who had once treated her scalded forearm.

'That will be his critical voice,' she said, 'he has to push aside those negative thoughts.'

'Yes, that's what Nigel told me,' said Sandra. 'Then he gave me this really depressing book called *Living with the Black Dog*, so I can share his pain. But honestly, what am I supposed to do about it? If anything, I'm the injured party here. If he claims his life is such a disappointment, what does that say about me?'

Tessa leaned forward to take a cup of coffee, chunky green and gold in the old French bistro style, a throwback to the confident

Conran years when everyone awoke to the idea that they could be bohemian and cook a chicken in a brick.

'You've just got to be patient,' she said, 'he'll get better.'

Harriet was less tolerant.

'It's not about you, Sandra, it's about him,' she said. 'We all know our husbands can be grumpy old men, but Nigel is genuinely unwell. I do think you could be a little more understanding.'

Sandra pushed aside the other pug which had jumped up beside her on the Chesterfield. It was funny how dogs always made a beeline for her even though she disliked them.

'Trust me, I've tried,' she said. 'But it's so draining being around someone who fails to embrace the glory of being alive. Anyway, I'm doing my best to keep cheerful, for Poppy's sake. She doesn't need both parents going around with a face like a smacked arse. Which is why I've started seeing Mariusz again. Yes I know, inappropriate. Condemn me now.'

She looked up at her two oldest friends, a glint of triumph in her eye. She'd still got it, could still pull a hot young man while they remained shipwrecked on the long, dull sandbank of middle age.

'When you say "seeing?" . . .' Harriet frowned.

'We had sex this morning. On the chaise, if you must know. Very satisfactory.'

'You never!' said Tessa, 'I thought you said it was all over, what made you change your mind?'

'Possibly Nigel's SAD box. But don't worry, this is purely therapeutic, we're both singing from the same song sheet.'

'How do you say that in Polish?' Tessa asked.

'*Please can I have small money?* Don't judge me, we're grown-ups, it's not hurting anyone. And it's helping me get through Nigel's depression.'

Harriet wasn't having it.

'I'm sorry to play the prude here, but hasn't he got a family back home in his own country?'

'Yes, that's what I mean about us both being on the same page, It's extra-curricular, nobody's falling in love or anything. Now, that's enough about me. What about you, Tessa? Have you heard about this, Harriet?'

Tessa made sure she was home by six, although she wasn't sure that John was serious about the Skype appointment. She was already regretting their exchange last night, begging him to show himself like that and sounding much too keen, silly of her to message at the end of an indulgent evening. Don't drunk text, she'd heard the children say it plenty of times, pity she didn't follow their advice. She shut herself in the office, cleared the desk and placed her laptop centre stage. It was like a gypsy's crystal ball, gaze inside and all will be revealed, past, present and future. Except it was flat and black, not round and sparkling. She opened the Skype app and waited.

Three minutes ahead of schedule, she heard the sound of the incoming call, a weird and extra-terrestrial wail, like being in a space ship. She clicked to answer.

'Hey, Tessa!'

She could see his profile picture in the corner of the black screen, no surprises there, the same baseball-capped portrait he used on Facebook. But his voice. Hearing those two words, she was back with him in his single bed, under the hot tent of the duvet, murmuring into the night about the things they were going to do together.

She leaned forward, unsure where the microphone was situated on the computer.

'This is spacey, isn't it?' she said. 'Ground Control to Major Tom!'

They grew up with dear departed David Bowie and she could still recite every single line, from 'Space Oddity' through 'Life on Mars' and 'Ziggy Stardust'.

'I should be taking my protein pills and putting my helmet on,' said John, in his warm, confident voice. He sounded familiar yet different, the estuary English she remembered overlaid with American ellipses. She could hear his emotion in the pause before he spoke again.

'It's so great to hear your voice,' he said eventually. 'You sound exactly the same.'

I am exactly the same, she thought. I'm seventeen, I'm all over the place and I don't know what I'm doing. She pulled herself together.

'And you sound fairly American,' she said.

'Over here they think I sound British, I'm a hybrid!'

'Like a Toyota.'

'Ha! Sure you don't want to switch the camera on?'

'I'm sure. It's enough to get used to hearing you, don't want to go into shock overload.'

'You're right, let's ease in gently. So, how've you been? Where do we start with this, Tessa?'

'I don't know. How about where we left off. The morning after your party, maybe.'

He said he couldn't bring himself to tell her he was leaving that morning. 'I'd finally made you see that we belonged together, we had just one night together, I couldn't bear to spoil the moment, you must understand.' Then when he arrived in Australia he had panicked, he wasn't going to spend the year pining for her, he was young, it was too soon. And when he returned to take his place at university, he hadn't dared to contact her, he was afraid she would be so angry. 'I was a coward,' he said, 'it was the biggest mistake of my life, I know that now.'

'I'm just so sorry I hurt you, Tessa. If I could have my time again, I'd do it all differently.'

Tessa couldn't speak for a moment, as she contemplated the other life she might have had. The path not taken, the unborn children they could have created. Wiping the slate clean to make way for another story, it made her head spin. They moved on to safer territory; John's subsequent move to the US and the misdemeanours of his ex-wife, who had made him wary of relationships, especially with American women. He liked British women because they were more relaxed, he said, they drank and swore, and he found that attractive. They'd talked for nearly two hours when Tessa suddenly noticed the time. Matt would be home any moment.

'I've got to go, do you realise how long we've been on this?'

'Not long enough! Let's do it again real soon. I love talking to you, it feels like you're sitting right here beside me.'

'Yes.'

'Tomorrow, same time?'

'I'm not sure, send me a message first.'

'Will do, you're the boss.'

'Bye then.'

'You go first.'

'No, you.'

'Let's go for simultaneous log-out.'

'Alright then, on the count of three.'

'Starting now! Goodbye, Tessa, take care.'

She wasn't so keen on the 'take care' platitude, but as she switched off her computer, Tessa admitted she was probably just looking for something to criticise, in an attempt to pour cold water on the unsettling feelings their conversation had provoked. She was already impatient for the next time.

Harriet was finding it hard to sleep. Sam had told her not to wait up, his flight was delayed, but she was listening out for him, wanting to hear about Alex and Nadia. They had been to the Polo Bar, it was *the* place apparently, where the waiters referred to themselves as Captains which sounded rather silly but she was glad her son was enjoying his glamorous life. And she wanted a full debrief on Nadia, who looked fabulous and a little bit terrifying in the photos.

There was no point stressing about insomnia. She had already done her breathing exercises and made a cup of Moroccan verbena tea, with no effect, but at least she could use these hours as an educational opportunity. She turned on the light and picked up *The Decline and Fall of the Roman Empire* to negotiate the Conquest of Trajan in the East.

When she heard Sam's key in the door downstairs, she changed her mind, it was too late to talk, better turn the light off and pretend to be asleep. Playing dead to avoid confrontation was a familiar old trick, which seemed to work for both of them. She heard him hanging up his coat, then filling a glass with water, the usual routine, before making his way up the stairs. In the bedroom, he undressed in the darkness, and put on the stripy pyjamas she always arranged, neatly folded, under his pillow.

'Harriet?'

She decided to answer.

'Hello.'

'Ah, you're awake. I was thinking of reading for a bit if you were already asleep, but it doesn't matter.'

'Read if you like, I've only just turned the light off.'

'Alright, if you're sure you don't mind.'

He leaned over and turned on the brass lamp. Beneath the velour brocaded shade, the ceramic base was decorated with fox-hunting scenes, though neither of them had ever been on a horse.

'Might as well join you,' said Harriet, pulling herself back against the pillows and picking up her book.

'Still on the Romans then,' said Sam, glancing at the cover.

'*Ita vero.*'

He nodded. They were both keen on Latin, it was one of their shared interests.

'I'm on Chapter One and there are six volumes. I might finish it before I'm sixty.'

'Herculean task,' said Sam. '*Labor onerosum.*'

'So how was Alex, did you have a nice time?'

'He was great.'

Sam opened his book.

'And Nadia?'

'Great. You'd like her.'

'Oh good. What did you talk about?'

Sam sighed.

'If you don't mind, I'd rather just read for a bit, it's been a long journey.'

Harriet tried unsuccessfully to bring her concentration back to the travails of Roman heroes conquering the world in their sensible leather sandals, defeating the barbarians at every turn. Instead, she thought about marital middle-aged beds like theirs, scattered across the globe. Husbands and wives lost in their respective reading matter, taking comfort in imaginary and bygone worlds when once, in the first flush of passion, they used to make their own.

Her sons were far away, it was just her and Sam now, and the dogs, and his ailing mother, two floors down. No wonder you needed the stimulus and release of literature.

Matt had dozed off in front of *Newsnight* so Tessa opened the laptop slumbering beside her on the sofa. There was a message.

> Tessa, my gorgeous astronaut space person, I loved our walky-talky talk earlier. Listen, this is very last-minute I know, but something's come up urgently with a client and I'm coming to London next week. Any chance we could meet up?

Meeting up? Just like that? Tessa stared at his words and tried to control her emotions. She pictured them running towards each other in slow motion like in a film, then reined herself in. They were old chums, it was perfectly natural for them to get together. You saw it all the time on Facebook, groups of middle-aged red-faced men and straight-from-the-hairdresser women holding in their stomachs as they smiled for the camera at the school reunion. She typed her reply.

> Yeah, sounds good. You must come to dinner.

The speed of his response was alarming, did he really have so little else to do?

> And meet your HUSBAND :-S ?

Not such an outrageous idea, was it?

Why not?

Not what I had in mind. Can we meet somewhere for lunch? I'm staying at The Ritz, let's have lunch there on Monday. Just the two of us, don't want to bore your husband with our talk of the good old days!!

The Ritz, he must be doing alright! She mentally flicked through her empty diary.

Puttin' on the Ritz! Sure thing, what time?

Fantastic! 1 p.m.

That night Tessa went to sleep dreaming of Fred Astaire in top hat and tails, leaping in the air and flashing his spats as he danced with a chorus of Fred Astaire lookalikes behind him, all of them looking exactly like Johnny Ormonde. She couldn't wait to see him again, and couldn't remember the last time she had felt so excited.

CHAPTER SEVEN

'Don't be jealous of your girl when she grows up because
you are afraid you will have to take a back seat.'
                    Blanche Ebbutt, *Don'ts for Wives*, 1913

The upside of an empty nest is the joy you feel when they
come home. Lola had turned up on the doorstep last night,
her petite frame swamped by an unflattering maroon university sweatshirt and Tessa had gathered her up in her arms,
familiarising herself with the small curve of her waist, the
smell of her hair. Then later, after dinner, cuddled up together
on the sofa watching some nonsense on television, Tessa knew
that this was happiness. If she could just keep her little girl
safely here beside her, there would never be anything to worry
about.

And now they were driving through the streets lined with
busy Saturday shoppers, on their way to have lunch with Tessa's parents. The familiar foursome, parents in front, children
behind, except the children were now adults, their lives played
out at a distance, their secrets safe from their parents' prying

eyes. Tessa had engaged in a bit of digging about Lola's new boyfriend, but so far had only ascertained that he was 'well hench' and the owner of her oversized sweatshirt. Hench as in henchman, Tessa wanted to know, is he somebody's sidekick? Lola had put her right, it meant 'very built', apparently, which was in itself a peculiar distortion of grammar.

'You alright in the back?'

She turned round to look at Max and Lola, squeezed into the shallow seat of their father's mid-life Maserati. How absurd of him to buy a smaller car when the children grew bigger, where was the logic in that? Both of them were plugged into their respective machines and staring vacantly out of opposing windows, heads nodding idiotically.

Lola turned and caught her mother's gaze. She pulled out her tiny earplugs and smiled benevolently, throwing a lock of silky brown hair back behind one ear. She was wearing a lace camisole with thin straps which offset her delicate beauty.

'Sorry?' she said, still only semi-engaged.

'Nothing,' said Tessa, blowing her a kiss, 'what you listening to?'

'Kings of Leon, reliving my school days.'

'Aah, I know them. Is your sex on fire?'

'Butters, Mum.' Lola pulled a face.

'What are you two talking about?' asked Matt.

'I wish I knew.'

He looked with satisfaction in the rear-view mirror at his daughter's fine nose and heart-shaped face. Lucky girl, she'd got his looks. She pulled a face at him in the mirror.

'Hey, girlfriend!' he said.

'Hey, Dad!'

She blew him a kiss and he beamed back at her, what a beauty she'd turned out to be, now she'd grown out of her awkward teenage phase.

'I don't want to sound too wholesome and Christian,' said Tessa, 'but when we were kids we used to sing along with our parents to the car radio, it was good fun. Whereas you two just stay locked in your little worlds, it's such a shame.'

'Bleak,' said Lola, making a gagging gesture. 'Where are we going for lunch again?'

'That Italian, where we went last time.'

'Good shout.' Lola put her earphones back in.

'We're having drinks at their flat first,' said Tessa, 'they want to show us their photos of Mexico on the computer.'

'Another bloody holiday,' said Matt. 'Alright for some.'

'You'd do the same in their position,' said Tessa, 'in fact, I hope we will.'

'Right. You'll be paying for it, will you?'

Tessa turned on the radio and sang along by herself until they reached their destination. Her parents had moved a few years ago into a retirement flat too small to accommodate any of their furniture. To adjust to their downsizing, they had ditched the three-piece suite and invested in two reclining chairs for themselves and a couple of hard stools for visitors, which had the desired effect of discouraging anyone from out-staying their welcome. It wasn't that they were inhospitable, but they realised their remaining time was too limited to waste stuck indoors at the mercy of people dropping in to make small-talk.

Matt parked in one of the visitor bays and they all piled out, uncreasing themselves from the journey. Lola clocked Tessa's outfit for the first time.

'Mum! You're wearing jeans!'

Tessa ran her hands defensively over her hips.

'Yes, so what?'

'You never wear jeans!'

'Which is why I thought I should. These are vintage actually. FUs. I used to wear them all the time when I was your age.'

She didn't mention that she had bought them on eBay after her first contact with John, to see if she really could still carry them off. The results were pretty credible, she thought, and so did he when she'd sent him a photo.

'You're too old,' said Lola. 'It's ridiculous.'

Matt sided with his daughter.

'I was going to say I was rather surprised to see you back in a pair of jeans,' he said, 'but I thought you'd probably bite my head off.'

'You thought correctly.'

'You can probably get away with it if you're thin like Sandra,' said Lola. 'Otherwise, no.'

'Well thanks for that!'

Max came to her defence.

'You look fine, Mum, take no notice,' he said.

They rang the intercom and passed into the disproportionately large lounge where a whiskery old lady was in her usual seat, checking out the new arrivals as she clacked away on her knitting needles. They piled into the lift which was fitted with a pull-down seat and the signature red emergency cord.

'One of those in every room,' said Tessa, 'but what's the betting you'll have your heart attack in no-man's land. Lying on the floor, mocked by the lifeline just out of reach.'

When they stepped out on the landing, June was waiting at her open door.

'There you are,' she said, putting her arms round Max. 'So handsome, you dishy boy. And my lovely Lola.'

She hugged her granddaughter. 'You must tell us all about uni, I've been looking through your photos on the Facebook, seems like you're having a whale of a time.'

She turned to her daughter.

'You look tired, Tessa, are you alright?'

'Yes, Mum, I'm fine.' Tessa felt the familiar flicker of irritation at her mother's scrutiny, but June had moved on to Matt.

'I'm so glad you could join us, Matthew, I know how precious weekends are when you're tied up in the office all week.'

Nobody else called him by his full name and Matt was sure she did it to annoy him.

They followed her in single file, crowding into the room where Donald sat with the crossword on his knee, cup of tea by his elbow. Tessa noticed he looked frailer than last time.

'There she is,' he said, smiling up at Tessa. 'Pansy Potter, The Strong Man's Daughter!'

'Don't get up, Dad,' said Tessa, bending down to give him a kiss, 'I'm not sure you should really be addressing me as the beefy one from the *Beano*, might give me a complex about my body image. Still, not as bad as Ten-Ton-Tessie.'

'Ten-Ton-Tessie, I love it!' said Lola. 'Was that your nickname, Mum?'

'Not exactly a nickname, just a term of affection, wouldn't you say, Dad?'

'She was always a lovely strong girl,' he said, squeezing her hand. 'Still is, look at her!'

'Well she looks worn out to me,' said June. 'You should look after yourself now you've got time on your hands, Tessa, you've got every opportunity. Now, sit down everyone, you're making the place look untidy.'

Max and Lola sat on the floor while Matt perched uncomfortably on a stool.

'Will everyone have a margarita?' asked June, moving into the kitchen. 'We're hooked on them after our marvellous time in Mexico, Don will show you the photos now before we go out.'

Donald picked up the album from the coffee table; he was the only person Tessa knew who still bothered to have his photos developed at Boots, instead of passing round the iPad.

'These are really cool,' said Max, turning the pages, 'I'd love to go to Mexico. I'm definitely going travelling once I graduate.'

'Oh, you are, are you?' said Matt. 'And how do you intend to pay for that? Also, can you tell me when it became the thing to refer to holidays as "travelling"?'

'Oh, don't be so stuffy, Matthew,' said June, coming through with a tray of salt-encrusted martini glasses, 'you've had plenty of lovely holidays yourself.'

Donald winked at Max.

'Your father's right, you know,' he said. 'Wait till you're old and retired like me.'

'That's not going to happen, though, is it?' said Max. 'We're going to have to work till we're eighty anyway, so we might as well do it now. Also while we're young enough to enjoy it. It's like Dad's Maserati, it's a much more appropriate car for me to drive than him.'

'Oh but your father has always been very interested in the appearance of things, haven't you, Matthew?' said June. 'It's important to him to be seen to drive the right sort of car. And why not, he's worked hard for it. Cheers, everyone!'

'Loving this drink, Grandma,' said Lola. 'Great hit with the salt and the lime, I'm going to start making margaritas for our pre's.'

'What is preeze?'

'Pre's. You know, pre-drinks. Before we go out.'

'Oh yes, that's what you all do now, isn't it? Whereas your mother always went to the pub with her friends, didn't you, Tessa, when you were young. With Sandra and Harriet and all the others.'

'We certainly did. No pre-drinks and nightclubs for us, just a half of lager and a packet of pork scratchings. Which reminds me, Mum, do you remember John Ormonde? He got in touch with me on Facebook the other day and we're having lunch next week.'

She might as well slip it in now, safety in numbers.

'John! Oh yes,' said June. 'Lovely boy, so enthusiastic. What happened to him?'

'He's living in America, been there for years.'

'He was always so cheerful and full of life,' said June. 'There was a time when I hoped you'd end up together . . . though of course we wouldn't want to be without dear Matthew,' she added quickly.

Matt frowned.

'You didn't tell me about this.'

'Didn't I mention it? I don't think you've met him, I would have invited him to our wedding but we'd lost touch by then. He went to school with Alan Doulton, we were all big buddies, with Sandra and Harriet and everyone.'

'He was very keen on Tessa,' said June. 'Often used to pop round on the off-chance of seeing her, then stayed to have a cup of tea with me instead, when she wasn't in.'

'Watch out, Dad,' said Lola, 'you might have a love rival.'

'Quaking in my boots,' said Matt.

'You shouldn't sound complacent,' said June. 'Tessa's a good-looking girl. And clever. She could have had her pick of men.'

'I know she could, and yet she chose me,' said Matt. 'Much to your surprise.'

'Nonsense,' said June. 'You've been a very good husband. I'm just saying you're a lucky man.'

'I realise that,' said Matt.

He watched Tessa sipping her her margarita, standing next to her father's chair. She looked alright in those jeans, once you got used to them.

'Then you wouldn't have had us, would you, Grandma?' said Max. 'If Mum had married someone else.'

'That's very true. Now drink up, everyone, and let's go for lunch. And, Lola, I want to hear all about this new boyfriend of yours.'

On the way home Tessa took the wheel while Matt entertained them by listing aloud the holidays his in-laws had taken since their retirement.

'Swimming with dolphins, treasures of Provence – Africa, of course, in the footsteps of Livingston. Then there was the Rhine Cruise. Oh, and not forgetting Machu Picchu, I rather thought the lack of oxygen up there might see them off, but no such luck.'

'Dad, don't be so horrible!' said Lola, 'just because they're not miserable like you. And Grandma says she can't wait to meet Ned, unlike you who shows zero interest.'

'Hmm,' said Matt.

'What do you mean, hmm?'

'What I mean is, there's plenty of time. You don't need to give yourself up to the first pimply youth who shows you a bit of attention.'

'Give myself up?! What century are you from!'

'I'm sure he's very nice,' said Tessa, 'and I hope you'll invite him home to meet us. Take no notice of Dad, he's just being grumpy.'

'I'm not grumpy, I just don't like seeing your inheritance frittered away. Oh, the annual winter jaunt to Antigua, how could I forget that one!'

'Anyone would think you married me for my money,' said Tessa. 'Anyway, they're slowing down now, the only thing they mentioned was a U3A coach trip to Yorkshire to watch rhubarb grow in the dark.'

'Well yes, that's more like it,' said Matt. 'That's exactly the sort of thing they should be doing. More in line with tending the allotment, which used to be the extent of retired people's ambition. A couple of years planting potatoes, then a swift demise.'

'Like your parents, you mean,' said Tessa. 'Who had the decency to die before they could enjoy the fruits of their labours.'

'Exactly.'

His mum had died first, and his dad a month later, glad to have done his duty and looked after his wife until the end. 'I can go now, Son,' he'd said to Matt in the hospital, his face the colour of parchment beside the bright freesias that Matt had brought in, knowing they were his mother's favourite flower. They never got to take the retirement cruise they had been planning for years, the brochures stacked neatly in the magazine rack, dog-eared from their enthusiastic browsing. Matt was damned if he was going to leave it too late.

He extended a conciliatory hand.

'Only joking, you know how fond I am of your parents. Very decent of Don to pay for lunch.'

Max spoke up from the back: 'And he's given me and Lola another load of dosh for the term. To fund our student lifestyle he said, what a legend.'

'Dear old dad,' said Tessa, 'he's very generous. And I'm glad Mum is having such a lovely time in her twilight years. When I think back to when she was my age, her life was quite boring, really.'

She stopped at the lights and looked at her children in the rear-view mirror. Max had opened his window, holding his face up to the breeze like he did when he was a little boy. Lola was listening to music, her turquoise-varnished fingernails resting lightly on her iPod. It had a cover that read 'you can't sit with us', a hangover from her *Mean Girls* phase.

It was true that June's life seemed incomparably better now than when she was bringing up her children, stuck on the treadmill of routine household tasks. Tessa remembered her once looking up from the ironing board, with her wonderful sparkling eyes and saying, 'I wish something exciting would happen.'

'Like what?' Tessa had wanted to know, the disdainful teenager, unable to imagine what kinds of desires you could possibly have when you got to that age.

'I don't know,' June had replied, 'just something. Anything.'

Beside her mother's bed had been books by D. H. Lawrence and the Jalna series by Mazo de la Roche, involving love in a southern plantation house, far removed from her own suburban semi. Had she dreamed of escape and romance? Would she have enjoyed reconnecting with a former admirer? More likely she would have dismissed such an idea as stuff and nonsense, she was, after all, a very practical woman. Then again, back in the pre-internet age, your options were more limited. You couldn't just whistle up a flirty conversation with an old flame, unleashing a tidal wave of memories and a flicker of desire with the click of a mouse. This time tomorrow, Tessa thought, we'll be together again. She could hardly believe it.

Later that evening, Sandra was preparing dinner, if you could call it that. Nigel had left earlier for a conference in Copenhagen, so it was just a few pea shoots and slices of beetroot for herself, though she had at least put a pizza in the oven for Poppy. Lucky Poppy, she could still afford to absorb the carbs.

As she often did in moments of boredom, Sandra called Tessa.

'Hey, how was your lunch?'

'Massive and delicious. I'm lying down to recover.'

'When's Lola going back?'

'Tomorrow. She's downstairs watching back-to-back episodes of *Made in Chelsea*.'

'Getting her London fix before heading back to the grisly north.'

'Yup. She's taking a load of fancy-dress outfits back with her, honestly, you'd think she was at primary school, not university.'

'She's alright, then?'

'Loving it, so that's OK. We're the comfy old sofa she comes home to flop out on, before going back to her exciting life.'

'Well don't be a cry-baby when she leaves. I don't want to spend the week telling you to man up. Anyway, I've got to go, we're having dinner.'

'You called me, remember! But wait, don't you want to hear my exciting news?'

'What?'

'I'm having lunch with John Ormonde tomorrow. At the Ritz, if you please.'

Sandra almost dropped the pizza tray she was pulling out of the oven.

'Get you! That was fast work! He's only just got in touch and now he's taking you to the bloody Ritz! He must be worth a bit, can we all come?'

'I wouldn't mind, but he seems set on a cosy twosome. I invited him to dinner at home, but he didn't sound that keen to meet Matt.'

'Course he didn't,' said Sandra, 'he wants to get it on with his teenage crush. No fun with the husband in tow.'

'Not at all,' said Tessa. 'He just thought it would be boring for Matt, to listen to us droning on about old times that didn't include him.'

'Yeah, yeah, very considerate of him, I want a full and frank debrief tomorrow. Maybe I'll meet you there afterwards, I could wait in the lobby and pretend to bump into you on your way out.'

'Please don't, it would look so obvious.'

'OK, OK. Enjoy and give me a ring, bye!'

'Bye!'

Sandra slid the pizza on to a plate, presenting it to her daughter who was sitting up on a high stool, tapping away at her phone.

'Here you are, darling. Phone away now, please.'

'You can talk,' said Poppy, 'you're always on yours. Who was that?'

'Only Tessa. She's had Lola home for the weekend.'

Poppy put her phone down next to her plate, where it continued to make intermittent beeping sounds.

'Lola's so cool,' she said, taking a bite of pizza and wiping a string of mozzarella from her chin. 'Mmm, delicious, why don't you have some?'

'You know why.'

Poppy looked critically at her mother's thin plate of salad.

'You're not a very good example, you could give me an eating disorder.'

'Nonsense, you're far too sensible. Anyway, it's only when you get to my age that you have to start being careful.'

'That's silly. When I get to your age, I won't care at all what I look like, what's the point?'

'You won't say that when you're middle-aged, you won't want to turn into a matron.'

'Like your bezzie Tessa, you mean?'

'No, of course not! Tessa's very comfortable with her curves, but I wouldn't be. It's a question of choice.'

'You mean she realises she might as well enjoy eating because she's had her life.'

'What do you mean, she's had her life?'

'I'm not being horrible,' said Poppy, 'but you're still going to be old even if you hardly eat anything. So you might as well be like Tessa. And she's a great cook, her brownies are sick.'

She reached across for her phone, smiled and tapped out a message.

'It's like your brain, that phone,' said Sandra. 'It's as if you keep your brain detached from your body and it sends you messages.'

'Funny,' said Poppy, not looking up.

She finished eating with the urgency of someone who had more important things to attend to.

'I'm just going out for a bit,' she announced.

'Where to?'

'Just for a walk.'

She went up to her room and returned a few minutes later, with a careful black line painted along each upper eyelid, flicking up at the ends.

'Nice eyeliner,' said Sandra.

'See you later, won't be long.'

She slammed the door behind her.

Sandra could always tell when it was Poppy coming home, she didn't close the door anxiously, the way Nigel did, as though there might be something frightening waiting for him on the other side. Poppy banged the door shut as if she knew exactly what she wanted.

Sandra slid the plates into the dishwasher and made herself a cup of pearl Chinese tea. You could only get it at Harrods, cost per pearl about £1.25, which but well worth it, to watch that flower unfold in a glass of hot water. It was as far as you could get from the Typhoo tea bags they had at home. After school, Tessa and Harriet would often come round and they'd sit there and talk about boys, dunking Garibaldi biscuits – dried fly biscuits, they called them – into sweet, milky mugs.

She took her cigarettes and went outside, to the discreet part of the garden where nobody could see. There was a missed call from Mariusz and she rang him back, wanting to hear his voice, but it went straight to voicemail. At least she could hear him delivering his answerphone message in a solemn tone that made her smile.

There was an autumn chill in the air now, and she warmed her hands over the glass of tea, blowing smoke rings into the night. Safe behind her garden wall, she could listen to people walking past the house, with varied pace: the important click of a pair of high heels, a rush of warm laughter and laddish banter, the squeaking of a jogging couple's trainers. Then she heard a low giggle, and someone speaking in a soft voice, and the sound of shuffling feet coming to a standstill just the other side of the wall. Sandra pushed her cigarette stub into the roots of a Japanese anemone and listened. The entreating tones of a boy, then silence, as they kissed, the timeless ritual. Feeling like an intruder, Sandra made her way quietly down the garden, and stood on a chair so she could see over the wall.

She recognised Poppy's coat, the grown-up trench she had chosen from Zara. The belt was loosened and the boy had his arms round her waist. As Sandra watched, he lifted her up, swung her round and kissed her again, pressing his face into hers. Her feet in their little ankle boots were dangling above the ground. The boy had short blonde hair, powerful shoulders. Sandra leaned over to try to see his face.

Suddenly, the chair tipped over, clattering noisily and sending Sandra crashing to the ground. Cursing, she picked herself up and stood still, waiting to hear if she'd been discovered.

The boy spoke first.

'Christ, what was that?'

At least he was well spoken.

'Nothing, probably our cat.' Poppy replied, in a new flirty voice that Sandra didn't recognise.

'Powerful cat! Sure it's not a burglar?'

'No! Unless, MUM? Is that you?'

Sandra pressed herself against the wall and closed her eyes tight, until she heard their voices move away. How mortifying, she'd have to leave the house to avoid facing Poppy when she came home. At least if they didn't see each other until breakfast it would be forgotten, or with any luck Poppy would think it was the cat or a fox, you could blame anything on the universal scapegoat that was the urban fox.

She quickly went in to collect her coat, then let herself out through the front door, turning away from the direction she imagined Poppy and the boy would be taking. I really should text her, she thought, let her know the house is all theirs, save them hanging around on street corners. She walked briskly down to Portobello Road, past the All Saints clothing store with its window display constructed from vintage sewing machines, which always made her think of her father. In retirement, he had volunteered at a workshop where they reconditioned old Singers, ready to send out to Africa for useful service. Dear old Dad, always so practical and keen to be of use, right up to the end. It was so sad he died before Poppy was born, he would have been a lovely grandpa.

She continued down Westbourne Grove, towards the cinema, maybe there'd be a film she could catch, to tide her safely beyond Poppy's bedtime. In her pocket, she felt her phone ringing and was pleased to see it was Mariusz returning her call.

'Hello, Huge Grant!'

But he wasn't in a joking mood.

'Sandra! Where are you? I am at your house, but no one is here. I need to see you now.'

'I'm just out for a walk ... What's the matter? And please don't come to the house in the evenings, supposing Nigel had been there.'

'I remember me, Nigel is in the Copenhagen. Where are you walking? I come meet you.'

'Portobello Road, by the sewing machine window at All Saints.'

'I come now, don't move.'

She waited on the corner, hoping that Poppy and her friend wouldn't walk past, that could be incredibly awkward. Five minutes later, Mariusz's van screeched to a halt beside her. She looked round quickly to make sure she hadn't been spotted, then let herself into the passenger seat.

'What's up?'

He had clearly been crying. She went to take his hand, but he leaned across the seat and wrapped his arms around her, pulling her towards him and holding her tightly.

'Sandra, I have terrible news,' he said, releasing her so he could look her in the face.

'What is it? You can tell me, whatever it is, I can help you.'

'Sandra, you are so kind, but you can't help me, nobody can help me to change this thing.'

'It can't be that bad,' she said gently, 'Just say what it is, then you'll feel better. Are you sick? Is it about that migraine you're always getting?'

He shook his head. 'No, I am not sick.'

Thank goodness, she thought, surprised at how relieved she felt. He was searching her face now as if she might be able to offer an explanation, then told his story.

'I always suspect maybe Katarzyna, she have another boyfriend, but always she tell me, no, you are Michal's father. And I believe her. But, last time back in my country, even though I think it is not possible, I take a small piece of his hair . . .'

She could see he was close to tears again. Poor Mariusz, she guessed what was coming.

'And you did a paternity test?'

He nodded.

'And today I have the results. Michal is not my son.'

He buried his head in her chest and wept like a baby. She cradled him in her arms, stroking his angelic blond hair, and it occurred to her that she couldn't remember the last time she had to comfort someone like this, not since Poppy was a little girl, devastated at some playground slight.

'Cry it out,' she said, 'it will be alright, you'll see.'

CHAPTER EIGHT

'Don't let breakfast be a "snatch" meal. Your husband often does the best part of his day's work on it, and the engine can't work if you don't stoke it properly.'

Blanche Ebbutt, *Don'ts for Wives*, 1913

Blueberry pancakes made with cottage cheese and oats, you couldn't get much healthier than that. Tessa sprayed the pan with a thin film of artery-friendly oil and listened to the oppressive tread of Matt coming down the stairs in his heavy office shoes.

'And so it begins,' he said, taking a seat at the table. 'We've got a meeting today to begin bottoming out our brand materials.'

'I wish you'd speak English,' said Tessa, flipping a pancake on to a plate and setting it in front of him. 'Have it with that yoghurt. And I really hate it when people say "and so it begins". So bloody portentous. Like you're God creating the world in seven days.'

Matt watched her as she moved to put the pan in the sink.

'Oh dear, bit menopausal, are we?'

She saw that he was looking at her in that cool appraising way that usually heralded an insult. He tugged at the bottom of his shirt that was fashionably untucked over his trousers.

'I think that T-shirt needs to be a bit longer. To glide over your love handles, rather than sit above them, if you see what I mean.'

'Thanks for the tip, but actually this is just my breakfast leisurewear. I'm getting changed later because I'm having lunch at the Ritz.'

He had clearly forgotten.

'Oh yes, so you are!'

He looked up from his pancakes.

'With that bloke you were telling your mum about.'

'That's the one.'

Matt took a sip of coffee while he processed this information.

'Who used to fancy you.' He gave an amused snort. 'Hope he's not too let down when he sees you.'

'Thanks.'

'Only joking, you still scrub up well. What are you going to wear, a little Chanel suit and a string of pearls?'

'Don't know, haven't decided yet.'

'So while I'm pushing the peanut forward, you'll be pushing a prawn round your plate and flirting with your former paramour.'

'He was never my paramour.'

'As long as he knows you're spoken for.'

'Of course.'

'Is he married?'

'Divorced.'

'Ooh, watch it, a predatory divorcee!'

'Hardly, I've seen his photo. You'd hate his clothes.'

'Well, I trust you to behave yourself. By the way, did I mention I've got an away-day think tank next Friday? We're booked into a country house hotel for a brainstorm, so you'll be rid of me for a night, I know how that upsets you.'

'Any excuse to whoop it up,' she said. 'Why can't you storm your brains in the office?'

'Offsite is always stimulating. And we get to shoot clay pigeons.'

'Poor birds, I hope you aren't attacked by animal rights activists.'

'Hello! CLAY pigeons, duh!' He made the moronic grunting sound they used when one of them was being obtuse. 'They're discs made of limestone and pitch, they're not living creatures.'

'Oh, really? I always thought they were a special breed, deliberately overfed to make big and slow-moving targets for big and slow-moving executives.'

'Well now you know.'

'Indeed. Rather you than me. Hang on, did you say Friday? I've invited Lily and Ian to dinner.'

'Sorry, you'll have to uninvite them. Anyway, I'm not exactly falling over myself to hear about Ian's latest promotion.'

'Don't be bitter.'

'I'm not. Right, got to go, is Lola ready?'

'I'm here.'

Lola appeared in the kitchen, her hair in a ponytail, pale-faced at the unaccustomed early hour.

'Here, darling, have a pancake,' said Tessa.

'Yuck, no thanks, I'll get something on the train.'

'There's my girl,' said Matt, catching her round the waist as she went to take some juice from the fridge. She kissed the top of his head.

'Thanks for taking me to the station, Dad. Saves me the 'mare of the rush-hour tube.'

'My pleasure, Euston's only down the road from the office and it means I get another hour of your company. We'd better leave now though.'

He stood up, a careful study in monochrome with his jacket and trousers – never a suit! – in slightly different shades of anthracite.

'Have you remembered your inhalers?' Tessa asked, following them up to the front door.

'Yup.'

'And just let me know if you want me to send anything on. You know I like nothing better than boxing up your bits and pieces and taking them down to the post office.'

She hugged her daughter, blinking back the tears. She mustn't be pathetic.

'See you at Christmas then,' said Lola, and Tessa heard the catch in her voice.

'Or maybe before,' she said. 'You might fancy another weekend at home, mightn't you?'

Lola shook her head.

'Doubt it, I've got a lot on.'

'Of course you have. Have a fantastic time.'

She waved them off, Lola lowering the window to blow her a kiss.

They drove off and she closed the door, taking a moment to readjust her focus. She was going to the Ritz to meet an old friend, she had cleared it with Matt, and now she must decide what to wear.

Upstairs, she rifled through her wardrobe, imagining herself through John's eyes, how would he like her to dress? The thought of it made her feel sick with excitement, she couldn't eat a thing at breakfast which was unlike her. She flicked through her dressier outfits. A Chanel suit, as suggested by Matt, was not an option, she had no such thing, but maybe her rather prim high-necked aubergine dress in a nod to Miss Jean Brodie. After all, today was in essence a trip back to her school days. The dress was belted and didn't entirely flatter the lumps and bumps Matt had so kindly pointed out, but the killer heels would help and she would conceal the damage with a fitted woollen jacket that was perfect for the chilly autumn weather. Pulling on her Secret Support seven-denier Bodyshapers, she remembered how it felt when you put on your school uniform for the first time after the summer holidays: sun-tanned legs concealed beneath regulation tights, flip-flops giving way to conker-shiny lace-up shoes, a sense of sadness mixed with anticipation of a new year. 'C'est la rentrée!' she would say, dancing round the kitchen in pretentious delight to entertain her mother. Re-entry into the system, onwards and upwards!

A final preen in the mirror, then she picked up her bag and set off for the bus stop. The tube was quicker but not nearly as much fun as the 14 bus which offered the best views of London from the prized front seat at the top and, before long,

she was at Hyde Park Corner, looking down at the cyclists ped-
alling between the sturdy legs of Admiralty Arch. She rang the
bell and picked her way carefully down the stairs, impeded
by the high heels which exacerbated her dodgy knees. Damn
her ageing body, and it was only going in one direction. No
matter how much time and money you threw at it, you were
never going to skip, loose-limbed, down the staircase, down a
sand dune, the way she'd done with John and Sandra and all of
them, in their post-exam elation, the future opening bright and
unfocused in front of them. School's out for ever, Alice Cooper
had declared as much, with his black eyeliner and vampire face,
which Lola had replicated during her pale Goth phase. There
was nothing new, ever, Tessa had told her daughter, we've all
been there.

She fastened her jacket, rather tighter than it used to be. There
was half an hour to kill but it was too cold to pass the time in a
deck chair so she headed for Fortnum and Mason. After admiring the window display, she slipped through the doors and wondered where to start in her sensory exploration. Chocolate was
the supposed magnet, but Tessa disliked the received wisdom
that all women were secret addicts, giggling over pralines when
they knew it was so naughty. Yet she was taken with the idea of
welcoming John back to his homeland with a gift of fine confec-
tionery, so different to the rubbish chocolate he'd be used to in
America. The assistant took a pistachio-green box and filled it
with a selection of rose and violet creams, you couldn't get more
English than that, though it did occur to her it was the sort of

thing you'd give to a maiden aunt rather than a hulking middle-aged almost-American who liked to slap a steak on a man-sized barbeque. Never mind. She dropped the daintily wrapped box into her handbag and decided she might as well be early. There was an advantage to being first, she could be safely seated at their table and watch the door for his arrival, rather than being the one to teeter in under his scrutiny, as he clocked the ravages of the last thirty years.

She walked past the Wolseley, the revamped car showroom that was now a successful restaurant full of fashionable people, then on to the Ritz which was resolutely unfashionable. As she was ushered through the revolving door by a uniformed lackey, Tessa half expected *Downton Abbey's* Carson to rush forward to take her coat. Instead, she was confronted by a corridor of elderly people sitting around in chairs. She continued down the hall, past the raised dais where blue-rinsed out-of-towners were already installed for afternoon tea. Carson would turn in his grave, who on earth took tea at one o'clock? Then she arrived at the dining room, a peculiar choice of venue for John, she couldn't quite imagine him here, in this gilded cage of frippery, with its pink floral carpet and rosy-hued frescoes like a Fragonard painting. The front of house welcomed her with the East European accent you heard everywhere in London's restaurants. She smiled at him graciously, looking forward to being shown to her table.

'Yes, thank you, I'm meeting John Ormonde, I think the table's booked in his name.'

He looked at his screen, an intruder from the modern world incongruously slipped into the eighteenth-century decor. He frowned and looked a little longer.

'I can't find anything here . . . Oh yes, I see there was a booking but it was cancelled this morning.'

'Oh.'

Tessa felt the flat grey of disappointment.

'Thank you, I can't have picked up the message, lines crossed somewhere. Thank you.'

She turned round and made her retreat.

On the bus home, she couldn't be bothered to go upstairs, not when she was wearing these ridiculous shoes. She chose a seat for the disabled, opened her handbag and helped herself to a violet cream chocolate.

Sandra was on her way back from her first planning meeting with Megan. She realised she had misjudged her client, Megan had shown herself to be open to ideas, and had immediately understood the concepts that Sandra had laid out before her. The apartment was full of possibilities, with the generous proportions you only found in purpose-built buildings, none of the boxed-up little rooms you found in conversions. She had forgotten her bike lights, so travelled home through the afternoon fog like a lawless amphibian, riding on the pavements when there were few pedestrians, reverting to the road to risk the consequences when there were too many people shouting at her.

It reminded her of when she took Poppy on a Duck Tour and the big yellow vehicle suddenly left the road to go crashing into the Thames, totally thrilling.

As soon as she got home, she spread her design sheets over the kitchen table, fuelled by enthusiasm at the task ahead. She was interrupted by a ring at the door. She hoped it might be Mariusz, she had told him to come round whenever he needed to, as long as he gave prior warning. It had been so difficult for him, she could see his pain and had tapped levels of tenderness she didn't believe she was capable of.

She jumped up to throw the door open, ready to play the angel of mercy to her distressed lover. Except it wasn't Mariusz, but her neighbour Lydia, an elegant widow who was looking very concerned.

'Oh, Sandra dear,' said Lydia. 'I just wondered, is your cat alright?'

Her cut-glass vowels and booming delivery spoke of years of landed gentry confidence.

'Hello, Lydia! I think so, last time I saw him, why do you ask?'

'Please, can you just check?'

She sounded serious.

After a few moments of searching, Sandra came back to the kitchen without Leo.

'Oh, Sandra, I'm so sorry,' said Lydia, her eyes filling up.

'I was talking to our road sweeper this morning, and he asked me if I knew anyone with a large grey cat so of course I thought of you. I'm afraid he may have found him on the side of the road . . .'

'Dead?' asked Sandra, thinking that was surely better than the alternative.

'I'm afraid so. It seems he may have been hit by a car, not that you could see any injury, he looked very peaceful.'

'Oh dear, poor Leo,' said Sandra, suddenly overwhelmed.

Lydia patted her shoulder.

'I am so sorry,' she said, 'it's dreadful, isn't it, with animals. I still miss my schnauzer so much. Would you like me to call the depot for you, I've got the number here, then you can decide what to do.'

Sandra composed herself, no point in going into meltdown, he was a cat for goodness sake.

'No, that's fine, I'll call them. Thank you for letting me know.'

She said goodbye to Lydia, then phoned the number she had been given. A kindly woman expressed sympathy for her loss and asked if she would like to collect Leo for a private burial.

What did she have in mind, Sandra wondered. A horse-drawn hearse moving through the streets past shuttered windows?

Poppy was due home soon, and Sandra spent an uncomfortable half hour rehearsing how she was going to break the news. This was a new life experience and not one she cared for.

'Oh hey,' said Poppy, when she came in. She had been a little offhand since the spying episode. Sandra watched her take off her shoes and put them neatly in the cupboard, she was so much her father's daughter.

'What's up, you look miserable.' said Poppy. 'Has someone died?'

'Not someone,' said Sandra slowly. She couldn't have anticipated the direct question, but at least it got it over with.

'Come and sit down, darling,' she said, patting the chaise beside her. Poppy did as she was told.

'You're freaking me out, Mum, what's happened?'

Sandra wrapped her arms around her.

'I'm so sorry, Poppy, it's Leo.'

As Poppy fell sobbing into her lap, Sandra thought how it was the second time this week that she had been the comforter. She wasn't much of a crier, herself, only when her father had died and she had spent a week in bed.

'He didn't suffer,' she said, stroking Poppy's hair, 'he would have died instantly.'

'You don't know that!'

She was right, but there was nothing to be gained from thinking otherwise.

'He's at peace, now, and at least he won't have to go through a horrible old age.'

'He was twenty-three in cat years, he had ages to go before he was old! We should have kept him indoors, I told you it was too dangerous to let him out.'

'No, that's so cruel, imagine if you weren't allowed to go out and had to spend your life like a prisoner, cowering indoors. It's only mad cat breeders who keep them in, because that's how they live their own wretched lives.'

'I suppose.' Poppy sniffed.

'And anyway,' Sandra said, 'it's better to live a day as a lion than a hundred years as a sheep.'

Poppy nodded at this grandiose sentiment.

'He's even called Leo, like a lion,' she said. '*Was* called Leo.'

'Exactly, it was well chosen for our magnificent beast,' said Sandra, wondering at how death had raised Leo's status from decorative introvert to fearless warrior.

'I spoke to the woman at Serco who asked if we wanted to bring him home for a private burial,' said Sandra, wiping away her daughter's tears with the hem of her cardigan, 'but I said I didn't think so.'

Poppy raised her head to look her mother in the face.

'I think that's a lovely idea,' she said, nodding bravely. 'I'd like to think of him resting in our garden.'

Tessa found John's message as soon as she got home and kicked off her shoes, rushing to her computer for an explanation. His flight had been cancelled due to fog, he was so sorry, he would have to reschedule his client meeting and let her know. 'Hang on in there, baby,' he said, referencing another song from their youth. He hadn't stood her up then. Her despondent mood lifted; it was a postponement not a cancellation, she could keep that spark of excitement going. She gave him her mobile number for next time. And now he was messaging her again.

You didn't get my message? Don't tell me you went to the Ritz and waited for me? I can't bear to think of you sitting there alone.

In my posh frock and everything.

No!

I didn't actually have the humiliation of sitting at an empty table. They told me you had cancelled.

Even so. I'm really sorry.

Not your fault. I need to get a smartphone.

She relaxed into easy online chat with him, describing the Rococo splendour of the Ritz, a far cry from their past meeting places; pubs with beer-stained carpets and scampi-in-a-basket.

We had lunch with my parents yesterday, who send their love by the way. Mum was saying how much she liked you.

Likewise! She was always gentle with me when I called round to see you and you were off with someone else.

Haha. You were never short of a girlfriend, I seem to remember. Jenny Colgate for one.

The toothpaste kid!

Perfect match for you with your Donny Osmond gleaming smile.

Not so white now! Yes, Jenny was a sweetheart.

You took her to see ELO I remember.

Mister Blue Sky!

I was quite jealous.

That makes me feel better.

And it made her feel powerful, knowing he was still having these feelings for her, after all these years. The ache of teenage rivalries, buried for decades, coming back hot and strong.

Only because I wanted to see them perform live.

I see, nothing to do with me then?

Nope.

That was a lie, it had cut like a knife when he'd started going out with Jenny Colgate.

Your parents are looking good. I saw the photos of you all in Thailand together.

That's a few years ago! Still checking out my photos then?

I liked them all. Except for your wedding pics, for obvious reasons.

I would have invited you if I'd had an address!

That's not why I don't like them.

Ah.

There was a pause, she knew exactly why he didn't like them.

I'm going to say goodbye for now. I'll let you know my new dates so you can put your posh frock on again, although I'd just as soon see you in a pair of jeans ☺

Bye then x

Tessa went up to her bedroom and changed her clothes, folding away the tights in her drawer in readiness for the next occasion. She tried to picture him in his home office. He had told her he had built a cabin in his garden, constructing it himself; he had always been good with his hands. It was 'real cosy,' he said, he had a heater for winter and a view over the plain so he could see the seasons change and there was an old couch where he could lie down with his computer and message her. She imagined lying down beside him, the way she lay down with him in his bed the last time she saw him. Or maybe outside in the fields, beneath the hot Midwest sun, where they could lay themselves down in the long grass . . .

Her dreaming was cut short by the arrival of Maria, reminding her that she was not romping in the hay fields of America, but in her London townhouse with a home help to instruct. She went down to exchange niceties with Maria, asking her to pay particular attention to the kitchen surfaces, then escaped to her usual game of dodge-the-cleaner which involved creeping from room to room and feeling guilty. Lying on her bed, she picked up *Don'ts for Wives*, and looked up the chapter on Household Management. It said that nothing was more annoying to a tired man that the sight of a half-finished laundry work and the remotest hint in your home of a 'washing day' is like a red rag to a bull. No worries there, Maria would have it all ironed and out of sight.

It wasn't the case in Tessa's childhood home, where laundry hung heavy, sheets and towels suspended from a ceiling-mounted clothes horse, drying in the heat from the kitchen stove. It was no wonder her mother was so keen on education. She loved the fact that Tessa was studying the metaphysical poets, her degree providing a door out of domesticity. 'Do something you can go back to after the children,' she would say to Tessa, wielding wooden tongs to heave wet clothes from the washing machine, feeding them through the wringer, then the double sink for rinsing, and into the spin drier. Don't worry, thought Tessa, as she dropped her dirty breakfast plate into the sink, there's no way I'm going to end up like you.

'You know you can get a machine now that does it all in one go,' she had told June. 'Why not get one and stop wasting your time?'

'But I've got the time,' June had said, her face flushed from the steam, 'It would just be a waste of money.'

That terrible frugality.

'Just work it out, Mum. You're paying yourself a pittance. Get an automatic machine and do something more productive with the time.'

'Like what?'

It was a good question. She could take in market research reports to collate at home like her friend Alison's mum. Neat piles on the dining room table, a bit of pin money, but still on hand to respond to her family's demands. Or she could work in a shop. Though it would have to be the right kind of shop. Tessa could see it was better to have your mother working through the steam of her own laundry than wearing a uniform and filling shelves.

'It'll be different for you,' June had told her, 'you can be whatever you want.'

Yes, she thought. Yes I can.

And here she was. Decades on and what had changed? Her mother's weekly treat had been sitting under a hairdryer for a shampoo and set, exchanging news with her friends as they waited for the rollers to take their crimping effect before emerging into the rain and crushing the results beneath an unflattering headscarf. Tessa's equivalent was a latte and almond croissant, or maybe a freshly squeezed kiwi juice and some edamame beans; she was trying to cut down.

Maria was coming up the stairs with the hoover so Tessa jumped off the bed to make her escape. She wasn't comfortable about employing domestic staff, it made her feel like a spoilt little madam.

Feeling hungry – she'd only eaten a few violet creams today – Tessa went into her sparkling clean kitchen and rummaged for some calorie-free radishes. She arranged them on a plate, and moved into the office, closing the door against the noise of the hoover.

She took a bite of radish and pulled the wire filing tray towards her, spilling out with bank statements and random correspondence. We were supposed to live in a paperless world but stuff still arrived through the letterbox, demanding attention. There were three missed calls from Sandra, obviously wanting to hear about her lunch, nothing to say there. She was filing away a discouraging summary of her pension expectations when the home phone rang.

Of course it was her mother, nobody else bothered with the landline.

'Hello, Mum.'

'Hello, darling, just ringing to hear about your lunch at the Ritz, it was today, wasn't it?'

'Supposed to be, but John's flight was cancelled.'

'What a shame! I thought it would give you a bit of boost after Lola had gone, did she get off alright?'

'Yes, Matt dropped her at the station. I was pathetic, as usual.'

'I knew you'd feel like that, which is why I rang.'

'Ah, thanks. I'll never get used to saying goodbye to them, it doesn't matter how old they are.'

'It never gets easier, believe me. But you need to find something else to focus on, a clever girl like you.'

'I know. As you would say, the Devil finds work for idle hands.'

'You're not idle! You've always got something on, and you've got that big house to run.'

'I just miss her so much, you must know what it's like.'

'Oh yes, whenever you went back to university, I'd go into the greenhouse and feed my seedlings to cheer myself up. And when Elaine moved to Canada, that was when your

SARAH LONG | 189

father and I decided to get into travelling. No point sitting at home moping.'

'Hmm, bit too soon for us, with Matt still working.'

'Of course, that's all to come. But in the meantime you should be able to get something, shouldn't you? You used to be such a high-flier.'

'Mum, I've explained this to you, there's no way I could go back at the same level, and I honestly don't fancy working in a shop or as someone's PA.'

'Nothing wrong with being a PA, I would have loved that. Or an air hostess, all that free travel in a smart pencil skirt.'

'You sound like the school careers adviser circa 1965. Women can do anything these days, didn't you hear? Unless they're fifty and out to grass.'

'Out to grass! Don't be ridiculous, you've taken a career break, that's all.'

'For two long decades. I've loved being at home, though, I don't regret giving up work for a moment. But now I just feel a bit redundant.'

'You were quite right to leave that job, such silly long hours and you've done a marvellous job bringing up the children. I can't bear this talk of women "having it all", it sounds so greedy. But the children are grown up now.'

'You're right, they really don't need me any more but I'm still pandering to them, doing their washing and everything. I know it's ridiculous.'

'All I'm saying is it would be good to have something else to think about, otherwise you just spend your time worrying about them.'

'Yes, I agree with you, I need to sort myself out.'

'I thought Lola seemed very happy, and I like the sound of that boyfriend.'

'She's bringing him home for inspection at the end of term, so we can see for ourselves.'

'Good-o, make sure you invite us over to meet him! Anyway, I've got to go, it's the weekly fish and chips residents' lunch, I just wanted to check you were alright.'

'I really am alright. Thanks, Mum, lovely to talk to you, speak soon.'

Tessa replaced the phone. Her mother was living proof that you never stop worrying about your children. Fast forward thirty years and it would be Tessa ringing a middle-aged Lola to check on her psychological wellbeing and work–life balance.

Returning to her filing, she climbed up the steps to reach the top shelf where she kept the archived papers. Hidden beneath a box of correspondence about their last house sale was a Freeman Hardy & Willis shoebox. Whatever happened to them, along with Lilley and Skinner? She pulled it out and brought it down to have a look. Inside were snapshots of her childhood: a contact sheet showing her four-year-old face in a hundred different poses; a school photo with gap-toothed classmates, she could almost taste the sour milk from the Tetra Pak pyramids, warm and sour from standing in the play-ground sun; a family holiday in Pembrokeshire, she's wearing turquoise shorts, standing with Elaine in front of the caravan, her mother's hair tied up in an orange headscarf.

There was correspondence, too, with postcards from Ibiza and Yugoslavia recalling the giddy early days of package holidays, and a bundle of letters from her mother, sent to her while she was away at university, soothing details of home life interspersed with health warnings hoping she wasn't smoking too much and was getting plenty of Vitamin C.

Right at the bottom of the box, she found a letter from John with a Lanzarote postmark. He was on holiday with his parents and wanted to know how her holiday job at the bakers was going. 'Hope they're not giving you any lip,' he'd written 'otherwise tell them you'll set your pet tiger on them.'

John Ormonde, her pet tiger. Her noble defender. She put the letter down and thought about an earlier birthday party at his house, when he was seventeen. He was mooning around after her but she was infatuated with Gavin Jones. She had bumped into John's parents on the doorstep as they were on the way out, leaving the coast clear for the teenagers, and John's dad had told her she looked like Joan Collins. 'Who's Joan Collins?' she'd asked. Fancy not knowing who Joan Collins was! It must have been in the lull between the old movies and *Dallas* and *The Bitch*. The way Tessa had been in the lull between childhood and grown-up life. Going to parties, casually trampling over people's feelings, unaware that thirty years later it would all come rushing back.

'So, how was your old friend?' Matt asked later, in the aftermath of their chicken cacciatore. 'I hope he paid for lunch.'

She was surprised he hadn't asked earlier. Perhaps he was secretly jealous and couldn't bring himself to mention it. More likely he'd just forgotten; she had changed back into her T-shirt and trackies after all. There was nothing to suggest she hadn't spent her entire day pottering round the house and preparing his dinner.

'Oh no,' Tessa said casually, 'his flight was cancelled because of the fog.'

As she cleared the plates, she was aware of a text vibrating through the pocket of her fleecy bottoms and had a feeling it was from John.

Matt grinned.

'Jilted Jane. It's true there were some cancellations at Heathrow. Unless he's making excuses, do you want me to sort him out for you?'

'Ha ha. Could you manage a slice of Nigel Slater's irresistible trifle?'

'Just a little piece . . .'

He watched her spoon out a modest serving.

'Little bit more . . . go on, one more spoonful, that's fine, stop!'

She passed the overflowing bowl to him.

'I came up with a great new expression today,' he said. 'How about this: "I'm not a digital native, I'm a digital anthropologist."'

Oh please, thought Tessa.

'Inspired,' she said. 'And did you succeed in bottoming out your brand materials?'

'We smashed it, thanks largely to me.'

'The hoary old anthropologist leading his young flock.'

'More democratic than that: I'm reaching out to my team, rather than leading them.'

'I can just picture you all sitting round in a circle, reaching out to each other.'

'You make it sound like an evangelical church!'

'That's what it is really. The corporation is the new church of Christ. With the late Steve Jobs as its prototype Messiah.'

'Now you're being silly.'

'Bill Gates and Mark Zuckerberg as the apostles,' Tessa continued, warming to her theme. 'With their sainted wives, of course, giving away their billions to make a better world. Then little Martin Sorrell and Stuart Rose at the far end of the table, who else could we have, who could be Judas?'

Matt pushed his plate away, and stood up.

'Glad you think it's funny,' he said. 'I've got work to do, unfortunately. I'm trying to get my presentation sorted for our away-day. Sorry about Ian and Lily, can we reschedule?'

'Of course we can. As long as you're feeling strong enough to cope with his promotion.'

'Strong as an ox. I was a bit tense this morning, but I'm back on top now! And I'm seeing my life coach tomorrow, that always gives me a lift. You should think about seeing her yourself, I think you'd find it helpful.'

He went out, leaving Tessa free to read the text that had been burning a hole in her pocket.

Sorted quicker than I thought. Flying to Holland next Weds, then heading to UK on Friday. Fancy having lunch or dinner some place? Promise not to stand you up x

Next Friday. When Matt would be talking hot air at his think-tank, droning on deep into the night at the bar with his fellow gas-bags.

Before she could change her mind, she texted back.

Friday dinner sounds great.

CHAPTER NINE

'Don't omit to fill your life with plenty of outside interests
. . . Nothing induces dullness, and even illness, so easily as
lack of congenial occupation.'

Blanche Ebbutt, *Don'ts for Wives*, 1913

The Hunterian Museum in Lincoln's Inn Fields was Harriet's
idea. 'We should take advantage,' she said, 'living in London.
We've got all these marvellous places to visit and yet we always
end up in the same cafe, and I want to feel I'm getting out
properly.'

'Reminds me of the old days, it's like coming into an office,'
said Tessa, as they signed in at the reception desk. 'I'm getting a
bit of a flashback.'

'God forbid it should come to that,' said Sandra. 'Parasites,
scroungers and bums, bring it on.'

'Dependents and spongers,' said Tessa.

'What?'

'You left that out. Helen Gurley Brown actually defined a
housewife as a parasite, a dependent, a scrounger, a sponger or
a bum.'

'Whatevs. Let's go straight to the syphilitic skulls.'

They took the lift and walked past the glass cases displaying floating human organs and medical horrors better suited to the back room of a teaching hospital than as light entertainment for casual visitors.

'Look at that,' said Sandra, when they arrived at their destination, 'literally pock-marked all over, as if worms have been eating into it.'

The three women gathered round to get a better look at the skull ravaged by sexually transmitted disease.

'Very Shakespearean,' said Harriet, 'reminding us that this is what's waiting for us all.'

'Not now, not with antibiotics,' said Sandra, 'the wages of sin aren't quite what they were. Let's move on to the foetuses.'

They gazed in silence at tiny, perfect human beings, pickled in homely looking jam jars. In a larger, rectangular display case, five foetuses were suspended together, as though in a dance routine, mouths gently open, hands dangling in front of their pelvises, as if to preserve their modesty. Tessa shared the thought that they'd make a lovely boy band. Harriet said it took her back to her own pregnancies, the time when her body had purposefully hosted the growing embryos who were now big people who occasionally came back to see her.

'That's enough weirdness,' said Sandra, 'let's just take in the Irish giant, then call it a day.'

The seven-and-a-half-foot-high skeleton of Charles Byrne stood in commanding position, looking even taller beside the doll-like bones of the Sicilian Fairy sharing the case with him.

'He died of the drink at twenty-two,' said Sandra. 'Too much stress, apparently, being in freak shows. I Googled him, there's a campaign to have him freed and buried at sea, like he wanted. It says if you press your ear to the glass, you can hear him whisper "let me go."'

'Poor thing,' said Harriet, briskly. 'Now, can we just squeeze in Churchill's dentures?'

By the time they made it out, they were all feeling a little queasy and ready to be revived in the cafe where they could get down to the proper business of the day, which was exchanging their personal news.

'So guess what!' said Tessa. 'I'm meeting John at the airport on Friday. We're going to drive out for dinner in Oxfordshire. I can't believe how excited I am!'

'That sounds dangerous,' said Harriet. 'Does Matt know? Dinner's not quite the same as lunch, is it? Especially when it's out of town. It sounds terribly illicit.'

'Harriet, your middle name is sensible!' said Sandra. I think it sounds great, where are you going?'

'Le Manoir aux Quat'Saisons.'

Her heart had leaped with excitement when John had suggested it. 'Sure will be fun to drive out together,' he'd said.

'Yes, very nice' said Sandra. 'People who aren't used to luxury hotels like it because it makes them feel at ease. Bit suburban, with slightly tacky statues in the garden. Lots of overweight women poured into taffeta when I was there. Good veg patch.'

'A hotel!' said Harriet. 'That sounds very compromising, how will you get home?'

'Who says she's coming home,' said Sandra. 'Maybe she'll make a night of it.'

'Actually, Matt's away on Friday,' said Tessa. 'He's got a brainstorming thing.'

'Well there you are!' said Sandra.

'But of course I'll come home, what do you think I am?' said Tessa, her indignation all the greater as the thought had crossed her mind.

'What the eye doesn't see, the heart doesn't grieve over,' said Sandra. 'But you haven't heard my story yet.'

She told them about Mariusz's drama.

'Oh dear,' said Harriet, 'she's been playing him at his own game. Still, he can't complain. Pot, kettle, black.'

'Not quite!' said Sandra. 'A discreet infidelity is not the same as pretending your partner's the father when he's not! He was so upset, understandably.'

'Did you minister comfort in a motherly way?' Tessa asked.

'I did. In fact, I've never felt closer to him.'

Harriet and Tessa exchanged a look.

'I'm feeling a bit left out here,' said Harriet. 'You two and your exciting lives. Whereas all I've got to look forward to is taking Celia for her chemo.'

'You're a saint,' said Sandra, hoping to be spared any further accounts of Harriet's hospital trips. As if life wasn't depressing enough, without evidence of disease and decay being thrust down your throat.

'Well I think you do a fantastic job,' said Tessa, 'I hope I get a daughter-in-law like you, one of these days.'

'So do I!' said Harriet, 'I mean, not like me, but someone caring. Wouldn't that be marvellous, to have a couple of lovely girls in the family? Sam met Alex's girlfriend in New York who seemed very nice, so fingers crossed.'

'Come on, girls, don't talk like this!' Sandra banged her coffee cup on the table. 'Living out your lives in service to your ageing parents and waiting for your children's weddings? That's no way to behave.'

'You're right,' said Harriet, 'but that's how it seems to me right now. I'm a 1960s stereotype, fussing about my family because I've nothing else to think about. Worst of all, it's self-inflicted; nobody forced me to give up my career. I'm a casualty of the feminine mystique, but I did it to myself.'

'Oh yawn, let's not hark back to Betty Friedan,' said Sandra. 'The problem that has no name actually isn't a problem at all. We're bloody lucky to be rich housewives. Who wants to go out there and do a boring job?'

Harriet didn't reply. She was thinking back to her time in chambers; the excitement of getting to grips with a new case, absorbing the facts, the adrenaline rush of getting her angle.

'Sandra, that is a passionate defence of laziness,' said Tessa, 'but you've actually got a job, if you can call it that. So of the three of us, you're the only one who's gainfully employed.'

'True, so I have! Megan turns out to be the ideal client, bags of cash and zero taste. In fact, I'm going to meet her right now, so I'll love you and leave you.'

She left the cafe and Tessa and Harriet watched out the window as she unlocked her bike and jumped on the saddle with the youthful ease of a schoolgirl, swinging her elegant bag across her shoulder.

'Look at her, she looks about twelve, doesn't it make you sick?' said Tessa, knowing that Harriet would understand it was a compliment.

'And actually got a job to do, lucky her,' said Harriet.

'Can't you go back to work in your chambers?' Tessa asked, 'wouldn't that be the just the thing for you?'

'Of course it would, but it's out of the question. Why would they have me when they've got hordes of bright young things they can choose from?'

'I understand completely,' said Tessa. 'I've got to find myself something to do. I spend so much time living in a bubble in my head, worrying about the kids and now fantasising about a boy I haven't seen for thirty years, honestly it's pathetic . . . Then there's Matt, I'm really starting to feel his resentment. And I resent his resentment, if I'm honest.'

'So you should! You had a deal, he was delighted to have you picking up the pieces at home when it suited him. He can't just move the goalposts later on when he decides he's fed up with it.'

'He's been seeing this life coach who's giving him all these airy-fairy ideas about the wonderful future he could be having. Whereas any fool can see his best bet is to carry on as he is.'

'You're not stopping him from doing anything though, are you?'

'Apparently I'm a dead weight. If I was out there earning my keep, he'd be free and happy.'

'Call no man happy until he is dead.'

'That's cheerful!'

'Aeschylus. I take great comfort from the Greek dramatists, don't you? When I'm folding Sam's underpants into his drawer and thinking how I got the top first in my year and now it's come to this, I find it helpful to remember that happiness is at best an illusion.'

'I like what Goethe says. "Happiness is a ball after which we run wherever it rolls. And we push it with our feet when it stops." In other words, we're programmed to think we haven't found happiness, and deliberately make it unobtainable.'

'The only ball I run after is the one I throw for my dogs. More of a stroll than a run. I'm sorry Matt's taking it out on you, I don't get that from Sam. He loves his work, especially the amount of time it takes him away from home, leaving me to look after his mother. So at least I don't get the guilt thing from him.'

'Never mind guilt, you don't really get anything from him, do you?'

'Separate lives,' Harriet sighed. 'We still get on, it's not like we don't have plenty to talk about, it's just a bit hurtful that he doesn't want to have sex with me. I know I've lost my looks, I'm fifty for God's sake, but all the same.'

'He's not exactly Adonis himself, is he?' said Tessa. 'And you're a fine-looking woman, so stop doing yourself down!'

'Thanks, Tessa. Right, enough of this gloomy talk,' she said, 'we've got our weekend in Gloucestershire coming up.'

'Of course. Looking forward to it. Haven't been for ages.'

Harriet had a village house in the Cotswolds where they often used to spend their weekends together. Bundling the children up in their pyjamas on the back seat of the car, ready for an easy transfer into bed after the Friday night drive. They would share the chores of bath time and tea time, enjoying the communal life before returning to London and their nuclear family units. Then the children grew up and became less amenable to spending time with the offspring of their parents' friends. Harriet had decided it was time to revive the tradition, without the 'children' who were now adults, and had invited Tessa and Sandra and their husbands for a weekend of fresh air and country pursuits.

'I feel bad I haven't invited you for so long,' she said, 'only Sam's been so anti-social, I knew he'd pour cold water on the idea if I suggested it.'

'It'll be great,' said Tessa, 'we're really looking forward to it.'

She knew Matt would enjoy trawling the estate agent's windows in the high street, calculating what kind of pile he could acquire by trading in their London house.

They said their goodbyes and Tessa walked slowly towards the tube, eavesdropping on the conversations of students as they flirted in small, self-conscious groups. Max's college was only up the road and she had the crazy idea that she should call in and surprise him, maybe they could have lunch together. When he started school as a painfully shy four-year-old, she had once driven up at lunch time and parked outside the playground. Like a private detective, she had sunk back in her seat and spied on him, watching out to see if he was playing with the others. She could still feel the stab of pain at the sight of him walking by himself, away from the fun and games, a small, lost soul. She needn't have worried, he was confident enough now, and far too busy for lunch with his underemployed mother. You give them life to set them free, and that was how it should be.

As she left the tube at South Kensington she found a voicemail from Matt, suggesting they meet at a restaurant that evening. He said he wanted to talk about the future. Or rather, The Future, she knew from his serious voice that he meant it in the capitalised sense because he must have just had his meeting with his Life Coach. Money for old rope in Tessa's opinion, but what did she know?

Harriet let herself into her house and was greeted by Celia calling to her up the stairs.

'Is that you?'

Who else did she think it was?

'Yes, it's me.'

'Can you come here?'

Harriet went down to Celia's bedroom. She was quite settled now and had arranged photographs and knick-knacks around the place, giving it the atmosphere of a room in an old people's home.

'I'm glad you're home at last,' said Celia, rising up from her chair with surprising alacrity and walking over to her wardrobe.

'I ordered these shirts from Uniqlo, but you'll have to send them back. These styles are no good for me, I don't know why they make them so tight.'

She threw them on to the bed.

Harriet took a breath. 'I'd better get going on lunch,' she said. 'Kedgeree?'

'Ooh, yes,' said Celia happily, 'but make sure you don't overdo the cayenne pepper, like you did last time.'

Be gracious, Harriet said to herself as she went back up the stairs, and just be grateful it's not you. She had been reading Philip Larkin's letters and recalled the one about widows living effortlessly on, cackling in their NHS specs and teeth and wigs, while their shadowy husbands lay effaced in dingy cemeteries. If only Sam's father were still alive, then he could be dealing with Celia and offering sartorial advice. But he had been absorbed by Alzheimer's, distilled into a sweeter version of himself – they said it intensified your true character – before dying and leaving Harriet to cope with the aftermath.

She put three eggs on to boil, filled the rice machine and pulled the haddock fillets out of their plastic wrapping. Her future as a carer flashed before her eyes: producing beige, digestible meals, making the bed with plastic under-sheets and efficient hospital corners, hosing down Celia when she could no longer manage herself. It wasn't pretty.

Matt had chosen his favourite Knightsbridge brasserie for them to meet. It was exactly how a French restaurant should be, as he liked to point out to Tessa, and all the better for being in London where people were livelier than in morose old Paris. She was seated first, facing the door, so was able to watch him arrive, appearing from behind the deep-crimson velvet curtain like a pantomime villain in his dark clothes.

He swung his man-bag, heavy with documents and God knows what, under the table, and looked at her, appraising her outfit.

'That top doesn't owe you a penny.'

'Joseph classic. Timeless, just like me.'

He glanced at the menu.

'I'm going to start with Jesus from the Pays Basque. What a sausage. You having your usual?'

'Of course. Warm garlic and saffron mousse with mussels.'

Matt turned his attention to the wine list. As he discussed it with the waiter, Tessa inspected the liver spots on the back of her hands. She should invest in some special hand cream that promised to make them go away, to banish these small brown reminders that she was getting on.

'Thanks for agreeing to come here at such short notice,' Matt said, as though he was opening a meeting.

Tessa laughed.

'I managed to clear my diary, thanks for inviting me. Why the formality? I get the impression this isn't just, let's go out to dinner for the hell of it.'

'No it isn't.'

Matt shook his head, and stared at her beneath the emphatic frames of his Prada glasses. Soho House twat, Tessa thought, but immediately banished the unkind thought.

'The thing is, I've been thinking a lot about The Future recently, as you know. And I had such a great meeting with

Trudi today, I wanted to share it with you immediately. Much better to be off-site when you're thinking outside the box. Look at this.'

He pulled a piece of paper out of his bag and pushed it across the table to show her. It was a diagram with arrows and half sentences written within loopy bubbles. 'Become an author/visionary' was the message in one of the bubbles, as though Matt could turn himself into Hemingway or Martin Luther King if he just put his mind to it. She looked across the page, where a different course was suggested. 'Start your own business', which sounded more achievable, if a little non-specific. 'Refine a go-to-market proposition', was written in another balloon, she wasn't sure what that meant.

Matt's eyes were gleaming at all the possibilities.

'So, what do you think? Really stimulating, wouldn't you say?'

Tessa stared again at the diagram, trying to make sense of it.

'Umm. Well, it's a bit . . . vague.'

'Of course it's vague, this is just the starting point! Next stage is to work out where to take it from here. I can't tell you how great it is to have someone show me the way ahead!'

Tessa wanted to share his enthusiasm but couldn't quite overcome her own common sense.

'It's easy for her to say that,' she said slowly, 'but not so easy to see where it leads. It's like a website I was looking at the other day, about how housewives can relaunch themselves in midlife. It's written by some crazed American homemaker, you know the sort, always making patchwork quilts. What was it she said? Ah yes, I remember now.'

She leaned forward and gave Matt an intense, psycho stare to deliver her line in a Californian accent.

'You are the president, CEO and star of your own life!'

In the old days, Matt would have laughed at her impersonation, but now he just looked cross.

'Well what's wrong with that? You've got to be positive about embracing change.'

'Not necessarily. I've never understood why change is always supposed to be a force for good.'

'Because otherwise you just go mad with boredom!'

He glared at her.

'Of course you should change if you want to,' she said. 'But on the other hand, you could just carry on as you are.'

Tessa had never quite got to the bottom of what Matt's job entailed, but he did seem enormously well paid for something it was hard to put your finger on. She had glanced though his PowerPoint presentations, beautifully laid out charts of abstract vocabulary which meant nothing to her.

Matt stared at her, unsmiling, through his silly glasses and she noticed a wiry grey hair curling out of his nostril.

'Carry on as I am?'

He had raised his voice and the woman at the next table glanced across at him, then at Tessa, then back to her menu.

'It's alright for you, faffing around all day doing God knows what! I tell you, if I had your life, I wouldn't need to see a life coach, I'd know I'd got it pretty cushy.'

Tessa looked down at her hands and noticed a new liver spot, one she hadn't seen before, just at the knuckle of her wedding

ring finger. Do stop complaining, she thought. We have a comfortable life, you never used to object, what is your problem?

'I'm sorry if you feel that way,' she said, 'I know it seems a bit
unfair, but you were more than happy for me to stop working
and, quite honestly, I don't know what sort of job I could get
now. Besides, it's not as if we're short of a bob or two.'

'If we're not short of a bob it's because I go out every day to
be humiliated in a job I hate.'

'You didn't use to hate it. I thought it was going really well,
with your digital anthropology and everything.'

'I make the best of it, but I'm not happy. And if I wasn't having to carry you and the kids, I'd be free to walk out tomorrow
and do something else. Something that employs my talents, that
gets to the essence of who I am.'

Good luck with that, Tessa thought.

'Oh look,' she said, 'here come our starters.'

She took comfort from the warm yellow of the saffron mousse,
the colour of crocuses. The softness melted into her mouth; texture in food was so important, it brought new levels to flavour.
Matt was slicing vigorously into his sausage.

'The thing is,' he said, 'when we agreed you'd take a career
break, I thought it was just while the kids were small, I didn't
realise it would be for twenty years!'

Neither did I, thought Tessa, I didn't really think about it at
all. I blithely walked away to a happy-ever-after fug of domestic
bliss, without a thought for the future. I didn't anticipate sitting
here decades later, listening to you bore on about what a drain
I am on your resources.

Neither of them wanted pudding, so Matt settled the bill and they stepped out into the night. He had calmed down once Tessa had apologised and shown more interest in the life coach. 'You only live once, it's true,' she said, 'YOLO as kids would put it, and of course you must explore your inner whatever.'

'Let's hail one, shall we?' said Matt, raising his arm at a black cab.

'Grim day at work, apart from my meeting with Trudi,' he said as they climbed in. 'I had to bite my tongue when one of my planners came in whinging about his stress. I said to him, I've got two words to say to you; heat and kitchen. He looked completely blank so I had to spell it out to him, "if you can't stand the heat get out of the kitchen, mate, this isn't a bloody nursery". Anyway, turns out he's just been signed off for a month in the Priory, so I'm bound to have HR all over me like a rash again but, honestly, couldn't we all do with a month's pampering on full pay? I certainly could have done when I had my bad patch a while back, but I just soldiered on because that's what I do.'

It was a few years ago when Matt had what they now referred to as his episode. One morning he had been unable to get out of bed. 'I just can't do it' he'd said, 'I can't get up, it's all going round in my head and I don't know what to do'. It was frightening to see him like that, Matt who was always so confident and definite, suddenly diminished by his intense anxiety. Tessa had helped him through it, he had refused to see the doctor, didn't want to blemish his record, he said, and she had so admired his courage in pulling himself back from it. At the time, she suggested he leave his job, they would sell the house, change their lives, go back to a flat in Brixton, it was all the same to her. All she wanted was for him to get well.

Back home now in the bedroom, she lay next to her husband in the darkness, holding hands in a post-coital truce. Sex was the currency of their deal, she thought. She didn't earn, but she still performed. The thought made her uneasy, for what did that make her? A provider of physical comfort in all its forms, the homemaker who acted as a warm sponge to her sponsor: meeting his needs, listening to his hopes for the future, reflecting him at twice his natural size, as Virginia Woolf put it.

She turned on her side and rolled away from him as his breathing settled into a slow heaviness. She wasn't sleepy, their discussion in the restaurant was going through her. Taking care not to wake Matt, she crept downstairs. It was deathly still in the office, in contrast to the lively images that tumbled on to the computer screen from Facebook friends in different time zones around the world. As she hoped, there was a message from John.

Having supper in Amsterdam. So looking forward to seeing you. Couldn't sleep last night!

It wasn't just her, then. She imagined him lying in his hotel bed, thinking about her, the same way she'd been thinking about him. He would be eating his dinner now; bread and sprinkles washed down by a pint of milk probably, that's what she remembered eating in Amsterdam; no wonder the Dutch were so tall and pale on that carb and dairy overload. She messaged back:

What you eating?

Steak, my lover.

Cheeky form of address, she thought as she pinged her reply:

Your WHAT?

He was quick to explain.

Say it with a West country accent, then it's nothing personal. Like saying my dear. Though of course I meant it personally ☺.

Of course he did.

Haha, I wonder what we'll eat on Friday. So excited, how long since we met?

She wasn't expecting the level of detail that followed:

Thirty-two years, four months and three days. Since I missed my chance with you. And buggered up my life forever.

He must have been drinking more than milk, this was getting maudlin. He quickly corrected himself.

Sorry! Didn't mean to press send!

She should play it down.

Oh well, all water under the bridge.

He wasn't having that.

Oh minimize, minimize! Gosh, look, I spell in American☹

What was this talk of minimising? It sounded like psycho jargon, but then again he was American and was bound to have had therapy, what with the divorce and everything. And having had his life buggered up forever – he claimed – by Tessa consistently turning him down: at their parties, in the sand dunes, and that time in her garden, when he was so desperate for her, as they canoodled up against the clematis.

She tried to picture him eating his steak.

Are you having room service or are you in the restaurant?

Restaurant. I'm saving room service for another time when I'll have company. The very best company ☺

She imagined them together in the unmade bed and someone is knocking at the door with a trolley, so they straighten themselves up to open the door and the waiter wheels in their dinner, then John flamboyantly removes the silver covers of the platters . . .

She cut short her fantasy and instead gave a business-like reply.

See you Friday. 4 p.m., terminal 5.

Two more days, counting them down xxx

If she wasn't able to sleep earlier, it was now completely out of the question. She crept back into the bedroom and slid between the covers, closing her eyes to dream. She hugged her secret to herself and drifted off to sleep.

CHAPTER TEN

'Don't give up all your men friends when you marry.'
Blanche Ebbutt, *Don'ts for Wives*, 1913

On Friday morning Matt was in ebullient form over breakfast, mentally preparing for his clay pigeon shoot.

'I've always been a good shot so this is the ideal opportunity to show them I've still got it. Life in the old dog yet!'

'Woof-woof!' said Tessa, suddenly light-hearted at the thought of her illicit rendezvous this afternoon. She kept picturing herself running towards John in slow motion, like the schmaltzy airport scene in *Love Actually*. She jumped up and cleared the plates with renewed energy.

'They're lucky to have you, as I keep saying.'

'I know, and I really appreciate it, Tessa, the way you big me up. It's a frail thing, the male ego.'

He grabbed her leg as she walked past.

'I'm sorry you had to cancel Lily and Ian this evening, will you be stuck at home pining for me?'

'Actually I might go out with the girls, see a film or something.'

Why did she say that? Why not tell him the truth?

'Good plan.' He nodded.

'And while I'm in apology mode, I'm sorry I've been a bit crotchety recently. I was over-the-top heavy with you in the restaurant the other night. Thank you for being so understanding.'

She put a hand on his shoulder.

'You're welcome.'

Lay your sleeping head, my love, human on my faithless arm. Faithless nothing, she wasn't faithless, nothing had happened. Meeting an old friend for a drink didn't exactly turn her into Madame Bovary.

'And I'm sorry if I was unreceptive to all that life coach bollocks,' she said. 'I'm probably wrong, but it just sounds like bullshit to me.'

'It's one of the things I like about you, your intolerance of bullshit. But you're wrong about Trudi. She's helping me to find myself.'

'Suppose you don't like what you find?'

'Oh stop it, you cynic!'

He stood up leave.

'Thing is, we're doing alright, aren't we?' he said. 'Not too much to complain about.'

'Nothing at all. Two lovely children, an almost-paid-for home. What more could you want?'

'Exactly!'

'Well, you've changed your tune.'

He was like a yo-yo, she thought, after he'd left for the office. One moment doom and gloom, the next he was Pollyanna, all sunshine and light and bringing his wonderful brand insights to another big fat corporation. And, in truth, they really didn't have anything to complain about, which was why she felt so little sympathy when he did.

Driving towards his day of country sports, Matt felt more positive than he had for a long time. It was only a job, after all, and when he was in good spirits like this, he could remind himself that what really mattered was his happy home life: the children he adored and his darling Tessa. Even if she did drive him mad sometimes. He let his mind wander back to their first meeting, a scene he often revisited when he was feeling well disposed towards her. It was after a cricket match on Hampstead Heath where he'd batted magnificently and he'd been celebrating with the team, sitting outside a pub with a pint of beer on a warm summer evening. She'd come up to him, brown legs beneath a green striped ra-ra skirt, hair tied up in a white chiffon scarf. 'I'm dying of thirst,' she'd said, 'do you mind if I have a sip, my friend's getting them in but there's such a crush at the bar.'

'Go ahead,' he'd said, then watched as she downed the whole glass. Afterwards they had wandered out onto the Heath until the early hours. The next day he rang his best friend to let him know he'd just met the girl he was going to marry.

Retirement might not be so awful, after all, provided they had enough to live on and one of his projects for this weekend was to fully assess his pension prospects. He remembered driving out to Suffolk one weekend to visit Tessa's uncle who had settled into village life after a career in the City. He had become the archetypal pub bore with cloth cap and pipe, joining a coterie of purple-faced old blokes who met up every night without fail in the local inn, or 'hostelry' as they preferred to call it. He had taken Matt and Tessa along that evening, after he'd been away for a few days. 'Where's your note?' one of them asked, merrily lapsing into schoolboy talk, demanding proof of permission to skive off games. He and Tessa had laughed about it, finding them completely ghastly. But now, a few years down the line, Matt could see the appeal.

Finally, the M4 was thinning out so he opened full throttle and put the Maserati through its paces, revving up in anticipation of his morning shoot.

Here I go, thought Tessa, it's the silver wedding weekend all over again. Her hair was whooshed up, potential outfits were laid out on the bed and she had packed an overnight sponge-bag, just in case. She had hesitated about the spongebag. If she left it out, there would be no question of her missing the last train home. But leaving it in implied she was potentially thinking of staying the night. In the end she told herself it was a precaution, imagine there was a problem on the railways and she'd just HAVE to spend the night and then she wouldn't have her contact lens solutions.

This was a lie and she knew it because she could always get a taxi home.

Matt wouldn't notice the expense, not with the amount that passed through their bank account, dribbling away on the fripperies that were supposed to bring pleasure if you were lucky enough to afford them. A case of Margaux grand cru, a hand-blown glass vase, a bespoke tailored shirt. It made her anxious thinking about it, the way they wasted money.

Not that it made you any happier. When they first lived together in Brixton, their idea of luxury was an occasional take-away from the local Indian, peshwari nan with its juicy sultanas and butter chicken, they'd get out the jar of mango chutney and chilled cans of lager and feel like kings, tucking into the feast set out on the tiny Habitat table they'd bought with a seventy-five percent discount in the sale.

She slipped a spare pair of knickers and the silver wedding silk pyjamas into her Birkin handbag, which was now looking a little dated if truth be told. After some considera-tion, she settled on a black waterfall cardigan, black trousers and black suede boots, enlivened only by a deep orange scarf. Colours were all very well, but she'd rather look thin than anything and for that there was no beating black. She put on her make up, making free use of concealer beneath her eyes, then added a nostalgic finishing touch – a spray of Rive

Gauche, she'd bought it from Boots in its bold silver, blue and black packaging, the smell of it taking her right back to when it was 'her' signature scent.

Packed and ready with hours to spare, she called Sandra.

'Don't tell me,' said Sandra. 'I bet you're wearing the waterfall black cardigan.'

'How did you know? Seriously, I'm turning into Shirley Valentine here, I'll be talking to the wall soon. I've got four hours to kill.'

'Your pathetically small life that will soon be over.'

'What?'

'Doesn't Pauline Collins say something like that in the film? Which is completely our story, by the way, we have now reached that age.'

'Stop it! Anyway John looks nothing like a Greek waiter. And certainly nothing like Tom Conti pretending to be a Greek waiter.'

'Well if you're bored, you could always come along and look at fabrics with me here at Chelsea Harbour. I've got to choose a cover for Megan's beloved old armchair. I've told her it would be cheaper to throw it away and start again, but she won't have it. She already knows it can't go in the living space, I'll only let her hide it away in the spare bedroom.'

'No thanks, I'll leave you to it. I might go a bit earlier to Heathrow, I actually love it; the atmosphere and all those people going to exciting places.'

'I agree. Treat yourself to a glass of champagne and a spot of people-watching. As you wait for your Tom Conti substitute.'

'You're right! I'm definitely going early now, I'm all excited.'

'Well you enjoy it,' said Sandra, 'you deserve a bit of fun, we all do.'

Do I though, thought Tessa as she hung up. Do I really deserve a bit of fun when my life is so privileged and unproductive? But then she remembered dining with an old friend was not exactly the last word in decadent self-indulgence, even if she couldn't actually think of anything she'd rather be doing tonight.

Standing behind the barrier in Arrivals, Tessa suddenly had cold feet. What if she took one look at him and realised this was all a horrible mistake, that their online flirting was absurd, that there was in fact no connection between them? Here she was, in prime position in front of the sliding-glass doors, offering an uninterrupted view of herself to the passengers coming through. Maybe he would take one look at her and think, oh dear, no thanks.

She quickly stood up, deciding to change tactics. She needed to see him before he saw her, you had to trust your instincts in these things, and if her heart actually sank at the sight of him, she could just slip away and pretend something had come up and she couldn't make it. With this in mind, she positioned herself half hidden behind a pillar. Plan A: move forward and greet and continue as planned; Plan B: slip back behind the pillar then make a swift retreat, texting an apology about unforeseen circumstances.

'Tessa!'

She jumped out of her skin. In spite of her precautions, he'd seen her first. She turned round and there he was. Big and reassuring in a leather coat, and with very little hair.

'Tessa!!' He said her name again and drew her into a strong hug. The embrace sent a shock through her which felt so familiar that Tessa was completely lost for words. The physical memory of him holding her was so clear, it was exactly how she remembered, but now he felt larger, stronger. It was normal, she rationalised, the boy had become a man.

'You smell like Tessa,' he said, breathing her in, then smoothing back her hair.

'Rive Gauche. I bought some specially.'

He was holding her by her upper arms now, pushing her away from him so he could get a better view.

'I can't believe it, you look exactly the same!!'

He looked her up and down, inspecting her as if she was a real piece of work.

'You look fantastic!!' he said. 'What are you doing behind this pillar, were you planning on doing a runner?'

His voice was familiar from their skype conversations. *Look atcher. Whaddya doin'*? He was transatlantic now, like an ocean-going liner.

She tried to think of something to say as she felt him looking at her. It was easy talking online, throwing out confidences from the safe place of your computer keyboard. Now, meeting him in the flesh, she felt shy.

He looked like his photo, older than his years, with no attempt to hide it. His hair was neatly cut, reminding her of the bald man they used to depict on a Daddies sauce bottle – not for him the fashionable shaved head. And a good, honest face that was still handsome.

'How was your flight?' she asked eventually. 'Sorry, really boring question . . .'

He looked at her with twinkly eyes, gently mocking her conventional enquiry.

'My flight was good, thanks. I sure was excited at the thought of you waiting for me. I kept telling myself you might not make it, you might, I dunno, disappear behind a pillar.'

There was an energy about him that she found hypnotic, and he stood a little too close.

'And now I'm here with you,' he said.

'I know. It's so weird—'

'I need a drink,' he said, 'but first things first. Shall we collect our motor car, m' dear?'

He offered his arm and she laughed at his Cary Grant impersonation. That was him now, of course, effortlessly straddling two continents.

Walking out of the hall, arm in arm, she remembered how he had always been the optimum height, just right for her to lean her head into his shoulder.

She looked straight ahead, but was aware of him giving her sideways glances, could feel his admiration burning into her.

They stood awkwardly at the car hire desk as he supplied information. Was he someone who would prefer to prepay petrol? Would he take the excess insurance? She'd known him all this time but she didn't know him at all.

'I didn't sleep last night,' he said, turning to her while the girl filled out the forms. 'I couldn't believe it, that I was going to see you again. You look exactly the same.'

'So you said, but you know it's not true.'

She watched him while he chatted to the car hire woman, charming her with his hybrid accent. The hulk of him was so different from the slim boy she remembered, but what had she expected, exactly? A pre-Raphaelite moment when her long-time admirer would step forward, unchanged, after thirty years of palely loitering? To pull her back through the decades to that age when time hung heavy, when you squandered sunny afternoons waiting for your life to start?

He picked up the key and turned to her.

'Come on, gorgeous, let's go.'

'You sounded quite American on Skype,' she said, settling into the passenger seat, 'but in the flesh you're much more English.'

'Nah, I practise every day,' he said, exaggerating the Cockney vowels, and Tessa had a glimpse of how he must play it in his adopted country, the Brit abroad, they all just *love* the way he talks.

They moved out on to the motorway; he was a confident driver, she remembered that, one hand casually on the wheel, the other free to stroke her hair when she used to sit beside him in his mother's run-around Mini.

As if reading her mind, he stretched out his arm and touched the back of her head.

'So soft, your hair. I'd know it anywhere. If you blindfolded me, I could still pick it out by touch. You're beautiful, Tessa.'

'No I'm not! Don't you remember, I'm a personality girl?'

She moved away from him slightly, but could still feel his hand in her hair.

'It's an interesting technique, apparently,' she said, trying to making light conversation. 'A friend of mine told me that to be successful with women, you need to tell the clever ones they're beautiful and the beautiful ones they're clever. Never fails, apparently.'

'What about if they're clever *and* beautiful? You were my dream girl, and you still are. You're gorgeous.'

I should stop him now, she thought. I should get him to drop me back at the airport and I'll just go straight back home and that's the end of it.

'I'm not sure this is such a good idea,' she said. 'I'm just wondering if the whole thing isn't a bit . . . weird.'

He turned and grinned at her.

'I know, it's crazy, isn't it? Like a beautiful gift that's just been dropped in our laps! Who'd ever have thought it?'

The car swerved slightly and Tessa gripped her seat.

'Keep your eyes on the road! And put both hands on the wheel.'

He withdrew his arm and did as he was told.

Just one drink, she thought. She'd go with him to the hotel and stay for just one drink, no harm in that.

'What do you drink these days?' he asked, as though reading her mind. 'I guess you've moved on from lager and lime? I bet you've grown up to be a white wine girl, now we've moved on from Liebfraumilch and Blue Nun. A crisp Sauvignon, I reckon, am I right?'

'That would go down very nicely.'

She wished she had a glass right there and then, just to calm her nerves. An ice-cold, goblet-sized glass to knock back and make her feel more normal.

'And you must be craving a pint of bitter,' she continued, 'because they can't make it in America, can they?'

'Tell me about it! Lousy beer and the food's not much better. I'm intending to really go for it tonight.'

'You can expect excellent food at Le Manoir.'

'Can't wait. And with my dream dinner date! I'm one happy man!!'

He turned to her again and she realised she would, of course, be staying for dinner.

They continued their journey out of London, familiar strangers. John tuned into Classic FM and Tessa recalled another journey they had made together, along with Sandra and Adam, skiving off school to drive through the night to camp by the Pembrokeshire coast. Watching the sun rise above the cliffs to the tune of Beethoven's pastoral symphony, there was no satnav in those days, you just had to follow the signs or read the map, or enjoy getting lost. Vignettes of their times together passed before her eyes like a slow-motion picture. Lying in the grass in the park throwing bread for the ducks while he takes her photograph; picking blackberries in the forest, their fingers stained purple and scratched. Sunday afternoon in the British Museum, he's whispering into her neck while the guide is speaking. You never think, when you're living these moments, that they're going to come back and revisit you thirty years later when you're driving along with a man who wants to convince you that you are the love of his life. Supposing he was right, what if he really was The One and her in-between life had merely been a prolonged interlude while she waited for his return?

Arriving at Le Manoir aux Quat'Saisons, Tessa was struck by how perfect a venue this was for a homecoming expatriate. The solid honey stone house, dominating the village with its long walled garden, fed the nostalgia for a country squire's blessed life that was rooted in every romantic English heart.

She studied the paintings on the wall while John checked in.

'I'm going to leave my case in my room before we head to the bar,' he said. 'Let's go.'

They were shown across a courtyard, to an outbuilding that might once have been a stable. The suite was on two levels, accessed by its own staircase, and the size of small house. A luxurious sofa and armchairs were arranged before an open fire, while a massive bed was on a raised dais beyond. The bathroom was a marble palace, where every form of ablution was awarded its own dedicated alcove.

'We've left a welcome basket for you,' said the bellboy, 'please let me know if you need anything, and enjoy your stay.'

When he left, Tessa slipped away to wash her hands and peer at herself in the mirror above the extravagant dressing table. She pulled her powder compact out and dabbed at her face. John couldn't mean it, could he, that she looked exactly the same? You could see the way the flesh hung differently, bags over and under the eyes, odd nodules of skin that developed for no apparent reason.

'Ridiculous bathroom,' she said, coming round the corner to the sitting area. 'I've never seen so many nooks and crannies. And all those toiletries! Whatever happened to the simple bar of soap?'

John was sitting on the sofa, opening the champagne. He handed her a glass.

'Here's to us,' he said.

She sat beside him and took the glass, very conscious of their intimate situation, alone together beneath the subtle lighting of this hotel suite. Over his shoulder, she could see the bed, shrouded by dark-green satin curtains.

'Nice room,' she said.

'Nice everything,' he said, putting his hand on her knee and leaning forward to study her face. 'You've reapplied your lipstick, is that for me? I'm flattered!'

She took a sip of champagne, leaving a smudge of Clarins Joli Rouge on the rim.

'It's a posh hotel,' she said. 'I thought I should rise to the occasion.'

'You've certainly done that,' he said. 'Although you don't need the warpaint, I can tell you could still get away without it.'

He brushed his fingers lightly down her cheek and she wished he would do it again.

'You were always a natural beauty,' he said. 'Not like my ex-wife. High maintenance doesn't even get near it. Always scrubbing and depilating and exfoliating, it's a miracle she didn't rub herself out of existence. Pity she didn't.'

'You've told me quite a bit about your ex-wife,' said Tessa, 'and now I know she's very clean.'

'Clean and mad. Not a winning combination. But then, of course, she didn't stand a chance, did she? I should never have married her.'

He moved closer so his leg was pressing into hers and topped up her glass. She wanted more of this. More champagne and more of him.

'Too many shoulds,' she said.

'What do you mean?'

'Nothing, it's just something a friend of mine's husband was told. By his therapist.'

'Oh. You get those here too then?'

'Oh yes. We're right up there with you yanks, now. Not me though, luckily.'

'Me neither. I tell them, I'm from England, we don't do depression.'

'We do now, we've caught up.'

John put his arm round her and squeezed her waist, which sent a thrill through her body.

'I don't know what the opposite is of depressed,' he said. 'But I can categorically say that I have never felt so un-depressed as I do right now.'

'Elated, maybe?'

'Yes! I'm elated!'

'Me too.'

He moved in and she was sure he was going to kiss her, but then he pulled back.

'Right, I'm going to take a shower then we can go down to the bar. Stay right there, honey, I won't be long.'

Honey. It was what he always used to call her. When she heard it now, it made her feel as though she had been handed back something she had lost. She watched him strip off his shirt on the way to the bathroom and noticed the no-nonsense breadth of his back.

'That's better,' he said, emerging two minutes later. Clearly he wasn't someone to waste time on male grooming.

Before going to the bar, she made him go outside with her to look at the vegetable garden. Long, hopeful rows of beetroot and chervil, spring cabbage, each marked by a handwritten label, it was the work of committed enthusiasts.

'I'd love that, wouldn't you?' said Tessa. 'A massive vegetable plot where you grow everything you need. Do you like gardening?'

It was like a first date, she had no idea what his hobbies were.

'Not really,' he said, 'I've got a yard but I don't grow stuff. No time. You could do it for me, though!'

He put his arm round her shoulder and guided her back to the hotel. For a mad moment, she imagined them living as a couple in his home. One of those sprawling American mansions with a kitchen like a spaceship. Sprinklers on lawns that looked like green carpets and the vegetable patch beyond, with a large glasshouse and tomato canes where he would play hide and seek with their grandchildren, like the Godfather before he collapsed of a heart attack.

In the bar, they sat by the window and John sipped his long-awaited pint of ale. He looked hearty and wholesome, as if he'd just come in from the fields and scrubbed up before changing into the sky-blue skirt and chinos which looked as though they had been bulk-ordered from a catalogue. She guessed they had been, as he'd always disliked shopping. She imagined he had a dozen identical models at home in his wardrobe, hanging above a row of big trainers. He looked quite different from the men at the next table, who were wearing sharp suits and expensive shiny shoes.

'This is great,' he said. 'Sitting here with you, shooting the breeze. It's like the last thirty years never happened.'

'I know.'

'Brought together by the miracle of the internet. Useful in many ways, but life-transforming in this particular instance.'

'Life-transforming, that's a bit strong!'

'It is, though. In the old days, I could never have tracked you down. I would have spent the rest of my life wondering what happened to you, regretting that I was too chicken to come back and claim you. Whereas, with a few clicks, here I am, back where I belong.'

He took a sip of beer and sat back in his chair, looking at her, his prize.

The waiter approached them.

'Are you ready for your table?'

They studied the menu in silence and Tessa guessed John would be looking for the most straightforward options. Whereas she and Matt always selected the most recherché dish on offer, then Matt got annoyed because he thought it was boring for them both to have the same thing.

Over confit of salmon and wild mushroom risotto, he explained the pleasure he took from running his own successful business. He was also voluble on the failings of his ex-wife.

'I should have known,' he said, 'the warning bell should have sounded when I found out she'd checked out my assets and credit rating before she agreed to marry me.'

'The American dream,' said Tessa. 'It's all about the money. Remember this is the country that had a collective nervous breakdown at the idea of universal health care.'

He shook his head.

'It's not that simple, you're speaking like a European socialist!'

'You do talk a lot about your ex-wife.'

'Sorry, I guess I'm still bitter, I'll shut up now.'

He folded his arms and sat back.

'What about the woman you said you were seeing? Or "sort of seeing", as you put it.'

'She's nice, I told you. But it's not the same when you meet someone off the internet. There's no history. You don't know how she looked when was seventeen, you haven't seen the evolution of the teenager into a woman. There's no price on that.'

Tessa nervously emptied her glass.

'You're right, we need more wine,' said John, 'where's our waiter?'

The sommelier appeared as if by magic.

'That burgundy was so good, we'd better have another glass each before the next course. Chassagne Montrachet Premier Cru, excuse my accent, I'm American!'

He winked at Tessa.

'The wine flight's a good idea, matching a glass to each course, but we really need double quantity!'

By the time they got on to dessert, Tessa was feeling quite lightheaded.

'This Sauternes, so delicious. Chateau d'Yquem, you see, I can even pronounce it. But not sure I can manage the second glass.'

She pushed it towards John, who knocked it back in one.

'Down the hatch,' Tessa giggled. 'Blimey, didn't even touch the sides.'

'I like the way you laugh,' he said.

She licked her spoon clean of the last drop of rhubarb coulis.

'You can tell we're not married,' she said. 'We haven't stopped talking.'

'I wish we were.'

He paused, and looked intently at her as the waiter cleared their plates then took their orders for coffee.

'As I was saying,' he said, 'I should have snapped you up when I had the chance, I was a bloody idiot.'

You're right, she thought. You are a bloody idiot, you should have stayed around and we would have got married like we were supposed to, and everything would be different. She was suddenly overcome by a sense of loss.

'The thing is, Tessa, as I may have mentioned before, you are my dream girl. You always were, and you still are.'

Tessa saw his face slide in and out of focus, she really wasn't used to this.

'Girl!' she said. 'In your dreams!'

'Exactly!'

The waiter arrived with their coffee and a plate of handmade chocolates.

'I'm stuffed,' said Tessa, trying to compose herself, 'do you think I could sneak those truffles out in my handbag?'

She checked nobody was watching, then deftly slid the contents of the plate into a crumpled Kleenex which she dropped into the bag by her feet.

'Nice manoeuvre,' said John. 'We could rob a bank next, Bonnie and Clyde.'

'It's a bit tacky, though, don't you think? Like going to an all-you-can-eat buffet and loading up some freezer bags.'

'Nothing you do could be tacky. Do you remember how we used to steal cigarettes from your dad's cigarette box?'

'Yes! He used to get so cross, but he didn't have a leg to stand on. Shouldn't have had them in the first place, filthy habit.'

'They're still alive and kicking, can't have done too much harm.'

'I told you how Mum always hoped we'd end up together.'

'Even after the fag theft?'

'Even then. You know what, I really fancy one.'

'A ciggie?'

'Yes! Don't you?'

'Wait there.'

John left the table and she saw him talking to their waiter. He then returned to the table and put two cigarettes on the table.

'Marlboro, he didn't have Camel. Also lent me his lighter. Shall we?'

He stood up and she followed him, unsteadily, out into the gardens, towards the lake, then into an enclosure where they were hidden from sight by a high hedge.

They sat down rather formally on the stone bench and he handed her one of the cigarettes, putting the other between his lips.

Tessa laughed.

'We're like a couple of addicts, sneaking out for a fix.'

He shook his head.

'You're the addict, I'm just the enabler.'

He flicked the lighter and their heads bowed together over the flame, just as she had recently imagined it.

Tessa felt the familiar kick, but the taste was sour.

'That takes me back,' she said.

'When was your last?'

'I stopped when I was pregnant with Max.'

'Your son. Who should have been mine.'

No, this was wrong, Max was Matt's son, he shouldn't say things like that. Tessa inched away from him.

'I told you, no more shoulds.'

'Alright then.'

They smoked in silence for a minute.

'Your husband's a lucky bastard,' said John. He was slurring his words and Tessa noticed for the first time that he was quite drunk.

'Thing about you, Tessa, you were always unavailable, always with someone else. And now you're bloody married to some bloke who doesn't deserve you.'

He could be right, she thought. The way Matt spoke to her, always seeking to undermine her. She drew on her cigarette and felt that anything was possible.

'But I'm not having it,' said John. 'I'm not giving you up now that I've found you again.'

He took the cigarette butt from her hand and threw it on the grass. Then grabbed her round the waist.

'Don't start a fire,' she said.

'Too late.'

And he kissed her, quite hard.

She thought, I'd like to stay here in this moment for ever.

'You'll stay, won't you,' he asked, eventually.

She extracted herself to look him in the eye.

'Yes.'

CHAPTER ELEVEN

'Don't be a household martyr. Some wives are never happy unless they are miserable, but their husbands don't appreciate this peculiar trait.'

Blanche Ebbutt, *Don'ts for Wives*, 1913

On Saturday morning, a grim little party was gathered in Sandra's garden, staring down into a hole that Mariusz had just excavated beside the rose that grew up around the study window.

'I think deep enough,' said Mariusz, dropping his spade into the space to demonstrate that it was sufficiently large to accommodate the macabre bundle that was lying on the ground, wrapped up in a black bin liner.

Poppy was standing next to Josh, leaning in to him and holding a single white carnation. To his credit he was being very supportive, thought Sandra, unlike her own husband who had stayed indoors to witness the scene from the warmth of his study. She looked up and saw his face at the window, staring out at the proceedings with no apparent emotion.

'Yes that looks right,' she said. 'Let's lift him in.'

Mariusz and Josh took one end each of Leo's concealed remains, and gently lowered him down. Poppy threw her flower into the grave and they all followed up with a handful of earth then Mariusz shovelled the remaining pile of soil, an astonishingly large quantity for one small animal.

'That was a lovely idea of yours, Poppy,' said Sandra, as they went indoors. 'We'll think of him every time the rose comes into flower.'

Poppy nodded and disappeared to her room with Josh to seek private solace, leaving Tessa to put the coffee on. Mariusz followed her to the machine and put his arm round her shoulder.

'I am sorry, Sandra. I know you say you don't have feelings for this cat, but I think you are sad.'

'Thanks.' Sandra said, leaning into him. 'It is sad, even though I am most certainly not an animal person.'

'I hate to interrupt this touching scene,' said Nigel, who had just come into the kitchen and was scowling at the sight of Mariusz's muddy feet, 'but would you mind taking your boots off?'

'Yes, of course,' said Mariusz, springing guiltily back from Sandra's side and busying himself untying his laces.

'I say to Sandra, I am very sad for you all.'

'Thank you, Mariusz, and please let me know what I owe you for this morning. I'm glad it wasn't me who had to do that digging, though if I'd had my way, I would have left the poor animal in the care of our council services.'

'Oh no, there is no charge for this, of course,' said Mariusz. 'I am happy to help.'

'Decent of you,' said Nigel, then turned to address Sandra.

'I'm out for the rest of the day. I've got an appointment with Paola then I've got that mindfulness class I signed up to. I've got a few things to attend to after that. Should be back in time for dinner.'

Perfect, thought Sandra. She saw him to the door then returned to the kitchen where Mariusz had pulled off his boots and was stretched out on the chaise. Eight hours at least, for them to console each other in the best way possible. Even more satisfactorily, Poppy and Josh emerged to announce they would be going round to Josh's house, so she would be quite alone with her personal gravedigger.

Tessa turned the key in her front door, pushed it open and listened, her senses on high alert like an animal. Good, Matt wasn't home yet. She went upstairs to the familiar privacy of her bedroom suite and ran a bath, taking off her clothes, then messing up the duvet to make it look as if she had slept there. It was the first time in twenty-five years that she had engaged in such deception, and she wondered whether Matt had ever done the same thing. He'd certainly had the opportunities, plenty of business travel, she never really knew where he was. There was a time when she would have been devastated to learn that he had betrayed her. When she was young and sexually jealous and her hormones were focused on protecting the family unit. Now she could consider the possibility with perfect equanimity. She actually wouldn't really mind that much.

She sank into the oval bath, enjoying her solitude. John had offered to drive her to the station, but she had preferred to slip out on her own, leaving him sleeping on his side of the massive bed, in a neat reversal of their first night together thirty-two years ago, when he had abandoned her. She didn't want the intimacy of shared early morning rituals. Fumbling in the dark for the complicated lighting controls, she had managed to turn up the dim wall lights just enough to guide her down the stairs and out into the crisp morning where her taxi was waiting.

Reaching for her phone, she re-read the message he had sent her when she was on the train.

Sorry. I put a lot of stuff on you last night. Too much wine!!!

What exactly did he mean by that? She had felt disappointed when she first read it, and rather ashamed. Was he trying to retract, was the whole shabby episode an embarrassing result of two middle-aged people getting tipsy and sentimental about the past? No. She knew that he was telling the truth when he said those things, she could feel it.

She sent her reply.

I think you meant it. In vino veritas.

The response came instantly.

Of course I meant it.

So why apologise?

Thought I'd better give you a get-out clause. In case you thought I was coercing you.

No. I liked it. I liked the stuff you put on me.

☺☺☺ xxx !!!

She was wrapping herself in a towel and considering her response when Sandra called.

'Hey, Sandra.'

'Hey? When do you ever say Hey? Already gone American then, clearly it was a success.'

'Yes. Well, you know, it was lovely seeing him. As I thought it would be.'

'So did you?'

'Of course not, I told you I wasn't going to.'

'You did not have sex with that man, Monica Lewinsky?'

'Not even in the Bill Clinton sense.'

'Really?'

Sandra sounded disappointed.

'It was lovely. We passed a chaste night of teenage intimacy. Reasonably chaste.'

'You'd better come over and tell me about it.'

Tessa dressed and went downstairs to leave a note for Matt. Her phone buzzed with a new message.

> So, dream girl, when do we meet again? Next weekend, after my meeting in Manchester? Please. In vino veritas. I had to look that up!

She took her coat and stepped out into the autumn air. It was a relief to be out of the house, she wasn't ready yet to slip back into her regular life, she wanted to hold on to the other, make-believe world of the past few hours. She walked down the Fulham Road where people were out doing their Saturday morning shopping, buying themselves little treats: a rack of lamb, each dainty bone decked out in a miniature chef's hat; an exquisite box of gourmandise from the French chocolatier, the dark, smooth surface of the ganache painted in fastidious gold detail; a dover sole prepared by a suave young man who looked like he'd just leaped off the boat in his fashion statement fisherman's boots. Here were the consolation prizes to make people happy if they had missed out on the big prize that no money could buy – the prize of unexpectedly finding the thrill of a lost love coming back into your life.

Thrill, that was the exactly the word for it, thought Tessa. Her Middle English lecturer, a harsh, unsmiling woman, had once explained that the word came from 'thirl', meaning to pierce or penetrate. How they had sniggered in the ranks, in the nasty arrogance of youth, believing Professor Thurston to be well beyond the age of penetration. She was probably a good decade younger than Tessa was now.

Sandra opened the door with a flourish and made a stage sign to look over her shoulder into the room, where Poppy and a well-built blonde boy were silently eating cereal at the breakfast bar. Mariusz was lying on the floor with a screwdriver, attending to a skirting board.

'We're all playing happy families here,' she said, ushering Tessa into the room.

Mariusz gave a cheerful wave.

'Hello, Tessa! You miss very sad thing, Leo now underground!'

'Of course,' said Tessa, 'I forgot that was happening today. Poor old Leo, are you alright, Poppy?'

She put a motherly arm round Poppy's shoulders and Poppy gave her a brave smile.

'This is Josh,' said Sandra. 'He stayed over last night, as he wanted to be here for the great interment, but don't worry, separate rooms.'

The boy blushed and nodded.

Sandra took Tessa's arm and led her into the garden. 'Let's go outside, shall we?'

They sat side by side on the solid wooden swing-seat that Sandra had bought after seeing it one year at the Chelsea Flower Show and deciding she just had to have it.

'It's alright,' said Sandra, pushing her foot against the ground to set them off on a gently rocking motion. 'I got over the spying incident, and now he's absolutely my new best friend. Quite a hottie, don't you think? I'm encouraging him to stay over. It's so dangerous for boys to travel around at night; they are much more likely to be attacked than girls, oddly.'

'Hello, Mrs Robinson,' said Tessa. 'As long as you don't end up in a mental institution while they run away and get married. Does Nigel mind him staying over?'

'Like I said, spare room, he can't object. And I must say I'm enjoying this new role, playing MILF at close quarters. Although they're going round to his house later, so Mariusz and I will have the house to ourselves. To my great delight.'

Tessa could see how happy she was.

'Are you sure about this?' she asked. 'I am worried about you, I'm not sure you appreciate what you're getting into.'

'Excuse me! I'm not the one who spent the night in a hotel room with a man who's not her husband.'

Tessa looked anxiously at the house, fearing someone would hear.

'Shhh . . . Anyway, as I said, it wasn't like that.'

'So you said.'

Sandra pulled her cigarettes out of her tight jeans pocket and lit up.

'What was it like, then?' she asked. 'I'm all ears.'

Tessa watched her exhaling,

'We smoked a cigarette, actually,' she said.

Sandra threw back her head and laughed.

'All the teenage sins! Don't tell me, you also engaged in heavy petting?'

And they were back in the classroom, exchanging details of their early forays into sex. Except they weren't. That was a stage you went through; once you were an adult it was no longer a suitable topic.

'I'd rather not discuss the detail,' she said, 'but it was so weird. In a good way. Remember what it was like when we were at school? So exciting, like you're really living every minute. Always anticipating the next stage. That's exactly how it felt.'

'You see! There's you getting all judgmental about me and Mariusz, and you're exactly the same. It's natural, isn't it, to want that feeling, rather than being stuck in your rutty old marriage?'

'Stop right there,' said Tessa. 'You can't compare my . . . meeting . . . with your outrageous affair with your builder!'

'Why not?'

'Well, for a start, we're not having an affair, and it goes much deeper than that.'

'So you're saying I'm a loose woman whereas you're operating on a more noble level?'

'Of course not!'

'But we're both keeping the information from our husbands . . .'

'Yes, I know . . . I don't know, I'm confused . . .'

'So are you seeing him again?'

'Possibly next weekend. I can't wait. I know it sounds ridiculous, but I just can't wait.'

She fiddled with her rings distractedly, and gestured towards Sandra's cigarettes.

'Can I have one?'

'If you're sure.' She passed her the packet. 'But as your friend, I've got to say it's a bad idea. Filthy habit.'

Sandra watched Tessa light up with practised ease. It was like riding a bike, you never forgot.

'Tell him that I send my love,' she said. 'Get him to look up my website, I've just posted some really good profile photos.'

'Why do you need photos of you? People are hiring you to decorate their rooms, they're not getting you as a permanent fixture, vamping it up on an armchair.'

'Of course they want a picture of me! It's an aspirational business, they want to entrust the design of their home to someone who looks the part. I'm the walking embodiment of William Morris's edict that everything in your home should be beautiful or useful. I'm both, obviously.'

Tessa laughed, then stopped as she heard her phone ringing. Maybe it was John, wanting to hear her voice. He'd only texted so far this morning, maybe he was calling to talk about next weekend. But it was Matt and he sounded grumpy.

'Where are you? I've just got home to find Barry on the door-step, he said you'd arranged for him to come over, but he left his phone at home so couldn't call you.'

'Oh God, sorry! I completely forgot, I'm just at Sandra's. I'll be right back. Make him a coffee or something.'

'Have you and Sandra got a thing going on? You were out with her last night as well, weren't you?'

'I won't be long, how was your think-tank thingy?'

'It was alright, but I'm not really in the mood for small talk with the builder, so please hurry up.'

*

After a few hours shopping for the rough-hewn slabs of stone that would be crafted into a bespoke designer surface for their guest bathroom, Barry dropped Tessa back home where she found Matt still frowning over his spreadsheets.

'All done?' he asked as she came in.

'Yes, I think it'll look really good.'

'That's alright then. So now I've just got to work out how to pay for it. I wish I could say the future looked bright, but it looks like I'll be working until I'm eighty at this rate. While you do sweet FA as usual.'

He looked at her over his glasses like a disapproving headmaster.

'Can't you just take your pension now?' Tessa asked.

'You're joking, aren't you?'

'We don't need much to live on. You could take up smoking to get a better rate on an annuity. I looked into it, it's the opposite of buying life insurance; they pay you more for having bad habits and poor health, in the hope that you'll die as soon as possible. We could enjoy a short but wild old age.'

'You're insane. Nobody buys an annuity any more, not at the rates they're offering. A few years ago, I would have been laughing, but it's all gone to shit, even worse than I thought. So, to answer your question, no I can't "just take my pension now". And what I really want is for you to start earning some money, never mind just helping yourself to mine.'

Money, he was obsessed with it, why couldn't he think of something else for a change, the loveless old miser? Dismissing the years she'd spent bringing up his children, doing everything for him, as if she was some kind of housekeeper who had out-lived her usefulness.

'OK, you win,' she snapped. 'I'll start a little business mak-ing overpriced knick-knacks and force my friends to buy them at pop up sales. I'll host those evenings where you offer wine and canapés and people feel too guilty to leave without spend-ing fifty quid. Let's see, maybe ethnic jewellery, or handmade soap. Or chutneys in jars with frilly little tops. I'll become one of those kitchen table CEOs and make a website with a photo of myself wearing a workmanlike apron.'

'Why not? At least you'd be contributing something.'

'Or else I'll get a humiliating job as a PA to some rich old entrepreneur who wants a mature lady to sort out his affairs.'

'What's humiliating about that?'

'Do you really need to ask? How would you like to take a job like that? Because that's all I could get, realistically.'

'Go back into the City then, get a proper job.'

'Hello! Fifty years old and out of the job market for half of them. Who'd hire me?'

'Sell your body?'

'Haha.'

If only he knew, she thought. There was someone who wanted to share everything with her, who was only waiting for her to agree then he would give himself and all he had to her, in a dazzling burst of warmth and generosity.

'Anyway, I really don't know what you're worried about,' she said. 'We've got loads of money sitting in the deposit account.'

'Oh, just sitting in the deposit account, is it? Wonder how it got there. Not by you sitting on your arse at home, that's for sure.'

'No, Matt, it got there through your hard work, well done. Now, if you'll excuse me, I'm going downstairs to get on with lunch.'

She escaped to the sanctuary of her kitchen, and opened the fridge to think about what to make. Then closed it again. It was of no interest to her what they should have for lunch. She texted John.

Next weekend then. Where?

He would be in the dining room, now, finishing his breakfast, or maybe back in the Jade suite, in front of the fire.

Fantastic news! I've booked this place for us, right after my Manchester meeting. Join me here on Friday.

There followed a series of photos of a hotel on the Yorkshire moors. A medieval manor, with interconnecting walled gardens, inviting you to step through riotous cottage planting to formal rose beds and box-edged planting inspired by Shakespeare, with fennel and columbines and rosemary for remembrance. It looked like the kind of place where you should arrive on horseback, sitting side-saddle in a velvet riding habit, to be greeted by a line-up of scrubbed-face servants as you came clattering into the courtyard. 'Welcome to Dursdale,' they'd say as they helped you dismount and showed you into the great hall hung with tapestries where a fire was burning in the oversized chimney.

His geography was a bit off, though, she ought to put him right.

Manchester is not in Yorkshire.

I know but not far. This is for R & R after my meeting.

So I'm your R & R?

You're my everything. As Barry White put it.

CHAPTER TWELVE

'Don't let him coop you up while he is away. You must live your life; you cannot vegetate.'

Blanche Ebbutt, Don'ts for Wives, 1913

'I've been thinking,' said Tessa in a voice that sounded artificially casual to her guilty ear, 'that I might go up and see Anne Davey this weekend.'

'Who?' Matt looked up from his granola.

'Remember, she came to our wedding. Tall girl with a mane of golden hair. Married a doctor and went to live in the Lake District.'

'Vaguely. Very English-looking. Sturdy ankles.'

'That sounds quite a precise recollection.'

'I remember looking at her and thinking I'm glad I went for something more exotic.'

'I haven't seen her for years, but she got in touch out of the blue. Her husband's left her and she's having a tough time.'

How easy it was to lie. She'd always thought of herself as a truthful person and was shocked by her own glibness.

'Oh dear,' said Matt, 'What was it, a midlife crisis?'

'Twenty-seven-year-old trampoline instructor, so yes, I would say so.'

'Lucky fellow. See how fortunate you are that I'm still here. When are you going?'

'Friday. Can I take your car?'

'Oh, I see. Not only are you leaving me on my own, you're also making sure I'm grounded for the weekend.'

'I could get the train, but it's in the middle of nowhere and I'd have to change and then get a taxi.'

'Can't she pick you up?'

'I wouldn't trust her behind the wheel. She sounded really upset.'

Tessa was surprised at her own inventiveness, and all the while Anne Davey was leading her calm Canadian life, unaware of the drama created in her name.

'Good old Tessa to the rescue,' said Matt, 'dropping everything to rush to the bedside of the bosom buddy she hasn't seen for twenty-five years.'

'I wouldn't put it quite like that. I'd like to see her. Anyway, you said yourself that we should both develop new interests and be more independent. We don't have to do everything together.'

'Maybe I should develop a new interest in a twenty-seven-year-old trampoline instructor.'

'Maybe you should.'

'Go on then, you can take the car. I'll plan a weekend of manly treats for myself. Trip to the Tate, take a look in Paul Smith, Thai takeaway for one.'

'Thanks.'

She cleared the plates, relieved at the excuse to end the conversation. That was it then, objective achieved.

'I might try and get tickets for the match on Saturday, see if Max wants to join me.'

'Good idea, he'd like that.'

Running the pans under the tap, she tried to push aside the image of Max and Matt in an imaginary future, keeping each other company as they tried to understand why Tessa had chosen to break up their happy home by running off with a bald American who wouldn't know a Paul Smith shirt if it hit him in the face.

'I'll take a cab to work on Friday then,' said Matt. 'You can play nursey to your friend and I'll amuse myself here, it will make a nice change for us both.'

But a nicer one for me, thought Tessa. All set then. She couldn't remember when she had ever planned something so deliciously selfish and wrong.

Naked in her superking bed, Sandra stretched out her legs and feet and wiggled her toes. She raised her arms above her head and held on to the top of the upholstered headboard. Mariusz propped himself up on one elbow and looked at her in amusement.

'What you doing?'

She glanced across at him, admiring the tone of his shoulders, the ginger blonde hairs on his arms.

'I'm practising mindfulness. Try it yourself.'

Mariusz kicked back the duvet and extended his full loveliness in imitation of her pose.

'Like this?'

'Exactly. It's supposed to reduce stress. Do you like it?'

'Often I have me big stress, Sandra. But not when I'm with you.'

He abandoned the position and pulled Sandra towards him. She rolled happily into him, enjoying the sensation of his skin against hers.

'Do you remember, Sandra, the first time in this bed? When I put towels up at the windows?'

'Of course I do.'

That was when they had the full team of workers in, scrambling around outside on the scaffolding, banging their tools and pots of paints while she and Mariusz were properly getting to know each other between the sheets. Now the towels had been replaced by sleek blinds and the walls were smoothly white, adorned only by a single painting by an emerging Russian artist.

Sandra felt happy and relaxed when she was with Mariusz. There was none of the treading on eggshells that went on around Nigel, when she was constantly on edge, in case she said the wrong thing and set him off. She detached herself from Mariusz' embrace and reached for her e-cigarette. Out of the question to smoke in the house but vaping was perfect. Like many smokers, she used it as a supplement to her regular habit, not as a substitute.

She inhaled the menthol hit and passed it on to Mariusz who looked at it suspiciously then did the same. He was wearing his favourite T-shirt, which had the legend 'High Performance' emblazoned across the chest. His body was made to be showcased in a T-shirt, she thought. He looked even better than Poppy's boyfriend did, with his biceps exposed by cap sleeves that could be unkind to lesser men. Poppy's boyfriend favoured clothes bearing beer slogans, which was a source of irritation for Nigel, who couldn't understand how any daughter of his could be attracted to such a sight.

'I might have some work for you,' Sandra said, running her hand possessively over his chest. 'My client wants her bathroom completely refurbished and asked me if I could recommend a builder. I told her about you.'

'Yes please, Sandra, I need me work,' said Mariusz. 'Always, I must find me more work.'

'That's the thing about you East Europeans,' said Sandra, 'you come over here with your work ethic and your skills and your excellent attitude . . .'

He nodded seriously, the joke was lost on him.

'Very hard worker. All my clients say I am very urgent person for them.'

She snuggled down again into the warmth of his muscular body and looked out the window at the weak afternoon sun. It would be fun to collaborate on a project with her choosing the designs and Mariusz bringing them to life; they made a good team. It was the most primeval interpretation of the man/woman dynamic, because what every woman really wanted was a man who could do practical stuff, unlike Nigel with his lofty disdain for anything that involved a screwdriver. Maybe they could set up a proper business together, offering a design-to-completion refurbishing service.

She inhaled on her e-cig and thought about the layout of their website; she'd take photos of Mariusz in his overalls to go alongside her own profile picture and artful shots of her recent projects. Better make that project, singular, but there would be others soon and she could always beef it up with pictures of her own house. Any woman in her right mind would want to have Mariusz as her builder once she'd seen the photos Sandra intended to take. She wondered if it would be over the top to have him strip to the waist for some of them.

'What was that?'

Mariusz sat up in the bed.

'Sandra, did you hear that? I hear the door, someone has come in!'

'No, it'll be something through the letterbox,' said Sandra. 'Nigel's away at a conference and Poppy's at school.'

'Hello? Mum?'

Poppy's voice floated up the stairs, and Sandra switched into emergency mode.

'Quick! Get into the bathroom!'

'*Corva!*'

Mariusz grabbed his trousers and did as he was told, as Sandra leaped out of bed and hastily pulled on her clothes, listening out for her daughter. She heard the fridge door open and the sound of the kettle being filled. Good, she still had time.

She stood by the bedroom door and practised her mindfulness breathing – three seconds breathing in, I am aware of my body. Breathing out, I release the tension in my body. Then walked casually down the stairs.

Poppy was sitting at the table with a cup of tea, her school books spread out in front of her.

'Hello, darling,' Sandra said, in as normal a voice as she could manage. 'I wasn't expecting you, did you get out early?'

'Yeah, English was cancelled, Mr Lamont was ill again.'

Poppy looked up and stared at her mother.

'What's happened to you? Your cardigan's done up all wrong.'

Sandra looked down at her front and saw that in her haste she had misaligned the buttons.

'Oh, yes, silly me, I can't have been concentrating this morning, too wrapped up in this project I'm doing for Megan.'

'Mm, Kim was telling me about that earlier. Says you've ordered some weird sculpture that her mum's not sure about.'

Sandra felt a flash of professional indignation.

'Oh, don't you worry, she'll love it once it's in place. That's what she's paying me for, a bit of imagination. You've got to go for a touch of drama here and there, otherwise the place will look like a furniture showroom. How was skating?'

'A bit rubbish, actually, the ice was melting. And I've only got a couple more practice sessions before the competition.'

'I'm sure you'll smash it. Megan can't believe how good you are. What did you have for lunch?'

Poppy looked at her in amusement.

'Why do you always ask me that? It's not as if you're interested in food in any way.'

'Don't know. Being a caring mum, I suppose.'

'Caring, sharing.'

'Exactly. Think I'll join you in a cup of tea.'

She dropped a pearl jasmine ball into a glass and topped it up
from the still-warm kettle.

'Are you working down here this afternoon, then?' she asked
nonchalantly. 'Not up in your bedroom?'

'Er, yes. I'm working here now obviously, and I may go up to
my room later. Does it make any difference to you?'

'Course not, just wondering.'

In reality, she was wondering how on earth she was going
to get Mariusz out of the house without her daughter noticing. Maybe she could tie bed sheets together and lower him
out of the window on a luxury linen rope. Poppy was a fiendish
worker, she could be sat there for hours. Possibly till dinner
time; she might still be keeping her vigil until whenever Nigel
came home.

'Actually, I think I'll take this up,' she said, 'leave you to it.'

''K.'

Upstairs, she closed the bedroom door behind her and went
to check out the bathroom.

Mariusz was sitting, fully dressed, on the bucket-shaped
toilet. His expression turned to relief when he saw it was her.

'Why she home, Sandra?' he whispered.

'Lesson cancelled. Thing is, I don't know how I'm going to get you out of here.'

Mariusz frowned. 'In my country, lessons never cancelled.'

'Maybe, but we're not in your country,' she hissed. 'And now we have to find a plan.'

He grinned at her. 'Lock the door,' he said, 'I have a plan.'

He stood up and unbuttoned his shirt, then peeled off his trousers and boxers and pulled her into the walk-in wet room.

'Very good Raindance shower, Sandra, dual function with thermostatic control.'

He turned the dial and ripped off her cardigan, with total disregard for the buttons, followed by the rest of her clothes, and pushed her up against the tiled wall. Tuscania by Fired Earth, replicating travertine, seventy-five pounds per square metre, if her memory served her well.

'No, we can't,' she giggled, 'this is crazy, YOU are crazy!' The water cascaded down through her hair, she closed her eyes and thought this was the most daring thing she had ever done in her life.

Twenty minutes later, cardigan now buttoned up correctly, she went downstairs again to check progress.

Poppy's glossy head was bent over her exercise book, her neat handwriting filling the pages. She looked up when her mother came in.

'Is Mariusz here?'

'Mariusz? Why? I don't think so!'

'Did he leave his boots behind then?'

She pointed to the front door where a sturdy pair of boots were neatly lined up, covered with a film of plaster dust. The evidence, massive and incontrovertible.

'Ah!' said Sandra, playing for time as her mind whirred through the options.

'Yes . . . that is, he was here earlier, then he had to go off to get some materials—'

'In his bare feet?'

'Obviously not. Maybe he came back then, without me noticing. He's still got a key. I'd better check. Mariusz! Are you here?'

She acted out her charade, going down to the basement to see if he might be fixing something in the media room, then walking back up the stairs, talking in an unnatural way, wondering aloud where he might possibly be.

'Maybe upstairs,' she said to Poppy, passing her on the way to the staircase and humming to herself as she threw open the bedroom door and retraced her steps back to the bathroom. Mariusz had resumed his position on the loo and was flicking through the pages of a builder's merchant catalogue he had picked up from Sandra's bedside table.

'Ah, *there* you are!' said Sandra, in a theatrical, found-you voice.

'Shh!' he frowned, 'Why you shout?'

She went back to shout down the stairs.

'Mystery solved, Poppy! He's in my bathroom, fixing that dripping tap at last!'

'Oh.' From a distance, at least, Poppy's usual flat tone did not suggest that this information was of any interest.

'But he's almost finished. Haven't you, Mariusz?'

Mariusz came towards her and put both hands round her waist.

'Finished for now, maybe, Sandra. But I come back soon, I believe me.'

At supper that night, Tessa couldn't believe how much noise Matt was making as he crunched his way through his fennel coleslaw. It was a recent phenomenon, probably an age thing, as the soft fleshy insulation of youth fell away, leaving only the creaking mechanism. Or maybe he'd always done it, but she was only now noticing.

'I'm not being horrible,' she said, 'but you do make a terrible noise when you eat.'

He stopped mid-crunch and looked at her coldly through his Prada glasses.

'I'm sorry?'

'You never used to, but now you do and I don't know why.'

He put down his fork.

'It that right? Tell me, have you listened to yourself lately? Because believe me, it's not pretty, what with the bits of food that get stuck to your face, not to mention the snoring.'

'I don't snore!'

'Do you want me to record it? You're a textbook case of sleep apnoea, I looked it up.'

'At least that sounds better than snoring.'

'Same thing. Either way it keeps me awake.'

'I suppose it's natural to find each other slightly disgusting,' said Tessa. 'In the old days, one of us would have died by now, probably me in childbirth, and the other would be left alone with their unappetising physical tics.'

'I wouldn't be left alone,' said Matt. 'I could get myself a hot new wife. Although, to be honest, I'm perfectly happy with the old model.'

He smiled at her in reconciliation, and brightened as he recalled his day at work.

'Had a great session today on customer experience. I was reminded of the power of threes. How do you like the idea that all brands fall into one of three categories: braves, blands or brants? Bloke called Tannenbaum came up with that. Brilliant, don't you think?'

What Tessa thought was: empty, trite, soundbite.

'Mmm, nifty,' she said.

Matt looked round appreciatively at the sparkling surfaces, enhanced by the cleaner's visit.

'House is looking lovely. What a marvellous little wifey you are.'

She lifted the glass dome off the cake stand.

'Do you want some gluten-free chocolate and hazelnut cake?'

'You spoil me.'

After a few glasses of Crozes Hermitage and a slice of cake, Matt's mood continued to improve as he gave a detailed account of his day's triumphs.

'Come on, old lady,' he said eventually, standing up and loosening his belt. 'Let's watch telly together and drown out our noises in boxset nirvana.'

Upstairs, they slumped side-by-side in companionable silence, legs outstretched on pouffes to take the strain off their legs, as if in rehearsal for their final laying out. They were lingering on a particularly graphic close-up of a pretty girl corpse when Tessa felt her phone buzzing in her pocket. She had taken to keeping it about her person, didn't want it to fall into the wrong hands. She glanced across at Matt, but he was asleep with his mouth hanging open, so she read the message.

Hey, gorgeous, what you up to tonight? Three days to go. Too excited to sleep AGAIN! Check out my photos of the Manoir!!xxx

Her laptop was beside her on the sofa, so she clicked on his time-line and found a series of beautifully atmospheric shots of the manor and gardens. He must have taken them on Saturday after she had left. The vegetable plot was featured, and the enclosure by the lake where they had kissed. He hadn't tagged her, thank goodness, but she knew the photos were for her benefit, although he had grouped them in an album with the non-committal title

'Back to Blighty!!!' Three exclamation marks, but she was able to forgive him.

Eager to share, she messaged Sandra.

> J put photos up on FB of Le Manoir. Check them out now you're FRIENDS.

Sandra replied quickly.

> Far too busy. Stop wasting your life on FB, you loser. But did check out photos of him. Disappointing weight gain and hair loss.

Tessa responded:

> Shallow.

She let herself think about her night with John, and the moment when he had first put a firm hand round her waist, as they were coming in from the garden before dinner. It felt exciting, but she had wished – vain woman – that it was the same waist she used to have, the one she used to cinch in with a wide leather belt, emphasising her hourglass figure, playing to her strengths. 'You pay for dressing,' her mother used to say, casting an appreciative eye on her when she was on her way out, just as Tessa now took pleasure from the sight of Lola in her finery. Each generation made way for the next, but you couldn't help feeling wistful for your own young body once the middle-aged spread set in. As if in sympathy, Matt suddenly emitted a loud snore, almost a death rattle. She prodded him awake.

'Up we go,' she said. 'Busy day tomorrow.'

Following him up the stairs, she sent John a quick message.

Me too. Excited I mean. I love your photos.

He replied:

This is just our beginning, Tessa.

CHAPTER THIRTEEN

'Don't get into the habit of staying indoors because there is nothing particular to go out for. Make an object if you have not got one: anything to prevent the stay-at-home habit from growing upon you.'

Blanche Ebbutt, *Don'ts for Wives*, 1913

Tessa spread a thick layer of butter on to her slice of bread and wished that she could be one of those women who sometimes forgot to eat. Or *claimed* they forgot to eat; she didn't buy it for a moment, they just wanted to stay thin while giving the impression they were too busy or cerebral for food. Whereas nothing seemed to impinge on the regularity of her own appetite, not even an illicit romance. Her bag was packed, she was ready to go, just as soon as she'd finished breakfast. She rang Sandra to discuss the curse of her healthy appetite.

'Why can't I just be like you, is what I want to know?'

'Priorities, that's what it comes down to,' said Sandra. 'I like food as much as you do but I would rather look thin than eat the most delicious thing in the world. As Kate Moss put it, nothing tastes as good as skinny feels. Remember our holy trinity.'

'Clever, rich and thin. And the greatest of these is thin.'

'What are you eating now?'

'Sourdough bread and sea salt butter.'

'Yuck. When I hear that, I'm thinking, bloating, ugly, the waistband of my jeans is digging in.'

'Whereas I'm thinking, the flow of my black dress will cover the damage.'

'Queen of carbs. What time are you setting off?'

'Very soon. I'm in a state of nervous anticipation, but I'm still stuffing my face.'

'Just Say No.'

'You're right. I'm binning it now.'

'I'm seriously impressed you're bunking off for a whole weekend, what did you tell Matt in the end?'

'I said I was going up north to see an old school friend.'

'That's true at least!'

'A female friend.'

'Ah. Anyone I know?'

'Anne Davey. She moved to the Lakes, so it's nearly true.'

'Netball captain, I remember her. Giraffe of a girl.'

'Except she emigrated to Canada ten years ago.'

'Well, well, you devious woman.'

'I hate lying but I've got no choice if I want to see John again.'

'I thought you and Matt were getting on better?'

'For about five minutes. Then he's back on his normal course of making me feel like a worthless encumbrance. Being gloomy about the future. Sometimes I look at him and all I see is a dried-up little grey man. I do wonder if it's his job that has done it to him, moulded him into someone he doesn't like very much.'

'Whereas John –'

'Can't wait to see me. Inundates me with messages. Makes me feel glad to be alive. I couldn't sleep last night, Sandra, and you know what a sound sleeper I am.'

'Sound to the point of intolerance, sleeplessness being the preserve of the weak and the guilty, in your book,' said Sandra. 'So obviously you're feeling guilty, which is ridiculous. You're a depreciating asset, we all are, and you should make the most of these last few years before you become completely invisible to men – as we were saying – and end up dribbling in an institution.'

'Nice thought, thanks for that.'

'You're welcome. And bagsy I get to sit next to you for bingo, once we're installed in the twilight home.'

Tessa entertained the idea of herself as an old woman, in a neighbouring armchair to Sandra, shouting at the bingo-caller.

'How is Mariusz, has he got over his shock?'

'Yes, he's coming to terms with it. He was so sweet on Saturday, digging that great big pit in the garden to bury Leo, while miserable Nigel peered out through the window.'

'You're very harsh, maybe he was too upset to come out.'

'He never liked the cat, anyway. Then he went off to service his mind, leaving Mariusz to comfort me.'

'Is that what you call it?'

'Yes, actually. I hate to sound slushy, but I think I really do love him.'

'That's a turnaround from your previous position.'

'But let's not talk about me. Have a great time and ring me when you get back.'

Tessa threw the bread away and went upstairs to tend to her make-up. She switched the lights on, to banish the gloom of the empty house, though she'd be out of it soon enough. On an adventure to meet the man who claimed to find her desirable exactly as she was.

The lamps on either side of the basin were set at chin height, as determined by her architect. It was how they were in actors' dressing rooms, he'd told her, the last thing you want is harsh overhead light. An online personality survey had recently declared her ESFP – extroverted sensing feeling perceiving, defined as The Performer, and therefore attuned to this Thespian bathroom. She shared the category with Marilyn Monroe; it meant she was a born entertainer. In which case, she wondered, why do I spend so much time daydreaming at home on my own with no audience?

Frowning into the mirror, she plucked out a single, freakishly long hair from her eyebrow. Mysteriously it was ginger; her face was full of surprises these days. Channelling her inner Monroe, she smeared a soft line of blusher to her cheekbones. Until recently she had been feeling that her world was shrinking but now she saw it was full of possibilities. The feeling stayed with her as she made a final check on the house, tidying the rooms, filing some paperwork, then she picked up her bag and closed the door behind her.

The traffic was fluid and soon she was driving up the Edgware Road, recalling personal fragments of knowledge as she passed significant sites on the long, straight route. There was the Turkish deli she had visited at the height of her Ottolenghi mania, sourcing pomegranate molasses before you could get it in Waitrose. Now she was driving by the stern mansion blocks of St John's Wood where she once attended a very grown-up cocktail party; then it was Kilburn, scruffy and Irish, you could almost hear the fiddle playing, and after that, murderous Cricklewood, where Dennis Nilsen lured back his young victims and buried them in his garden. Finally, she was on the M1, and beside her in spirit were Withnail and I, motoring out of the city to seek escape at Uncle Monty's bucolic wreck of a house, on the first-ever motorway with hardly any traffic, just a few half-timbered Morris Minors and friendly-looking trucks.

She tuned into Smooth Radio, what bliss, they were playing 'Radar Love'. She turned it up and sang along in loud and happy harmony.

She wasn't allowed to listen to that station when Matt was in the car; he preferred something more edgy. But for the next four hours, she could do exactly as she liked: gorge on The Carpenters and Elton John and all the other singers Matt considered so naff.

The last time she'd taken this route, Lola had been sitting in the back, surrounded by her books and possessions, waiting for her new life to begin. Tessa remembered again how bleak the return journey had been. She had hugged her daughter goodbye and held back her tears until they were on the M6, then cried solidly all the way home. Lola was probably at a lecture now, in a hall of hormonal young people eyeing each other up, the girls with careful make-up applied to flawless skin. In the seventies, it was a point of pride for university women to be careless of their appearance, but not these days where the number-one pressure was to look 'fit'. Nobody wanted to be fit when Tessa was at school, only plain girls played hockey.

It was a relief to come off the motorway and leave behind the industrial grimness. Arriving in north Yorkshire was the reward you earned for driving past the steaming funnels of Pontefract, the factories of Doncaster. Here was a different world of rich-green pastures and stone bridges and grand arrangements of autumnal trees. Tessa pulled over to study the map and educate her satnav into choosing a scenic route. She picked out a series of interim destinations to set along the way, ensuring her romantic weekend began on the right note.

They had agreed to meet late afternoon at the hotel, and Tessa certainly didn't want to get there first. Anyway, she was hungry. Lunch at a pub and an invigorating walk was just what she fancied. She stopped at a village a few miles away and parked outside a pub festooned with medals and promises of Theakston Old Peculier, the most peculiar thing about it being the spelling. A couple of local farmers eyed the car as she locked up, it was a definite consolation, having a decent set of wheels, at least something about you attracted attention once your looks were past their best. She smiled at them on her way in and they gave her a grudging nod. Respect for the woman with a flash car, even if it did belong to her husband.

Walking into the bar, she thought there was a lull in conversation, like in *American Werewolf* in London where the two hitch-hikers bring the pub to silence as they step in from the rain. Then she realised it wasn't a lull, it was just that the lunch crowd were unusually quiet, pensioners with their his 'n' hers short grey hair and maroon anoraks. Tessa ordered a Giant Yorkshire Pudding filled with sausage and onion gravy. It sounded filling, but she could pick at it, like in *Gone With The Wind* when the girls are obliged to eat before the party, so they can appear lady-like later by turning down the food. Her party for two with John; she mustn't seem to be too greedy.

She took a seat by the window and looked out at the arty wool shop across the road, dramatically framed by the sheep-grazed hills rising up behind it. She was drawn by a sweater displayed in the window, knitted in shades of purple, veering from deepest burgundy to delicate mauve. She imagined wearing it on the Hebridean island they had fantasised about moving to, during the sleepless night with John last week. 'Let's go to an island with a population of twenty-five,' he had said, sliding his hand between her legs. 'Live on a croft and have sheep and make love all day long.'

'It's too cold in Scotland,' she had protested.

'Not when you're in front of the fire on a sheepskin rug,' he said, 'and you can see how good I am at warming you up.' It was at that point that she had moved away from him, laughing, to the other side of the enormous bed. Now she entertained the idea again, maybe they would have chickens, and she would go out on a misty morning to bring in the eggs which they would eat for breakfast, poached on toast from a homemade loaf. She'd always fancied a bread machine, but it was pointless in London, where you were surrounded by excellent French bakeries. The Scottish wilderness was a different proposition, you'd have to get the ferry to the mainland, no chance of an Ocado van there.

'How was it?' asked the waitress at the end of her meal, looking doubtfully at the half-eaten remains.

'Lovely, thank you, sorry I just couldn't manage it all.'

No need to apologise for apologising, as Matt wasn't there. She ordered a coffee and asked for the bill. Taking out her card to pay, she then thought better of it, and put down cash instead, probably best to cover her tracks.

She checked her phone and saw a message from John, informing her that he was running ahead of schedule and would be arriving at the hotel in half an hour.

Tessa left a generous tip – they'd expect it, what with the Maserati – and nodded goodbye. It had started to rain and she hurried across the road to look at the jumper that had caught her eye. But there was no time for shopping now, and certainly not for the walk she had planned. Dursdale Hall was beckoning and, like a Georgette Heyer heroine, she must go and meet her bodice-ripping destiny.

As she swept past the stone gateposts, she realised the website had undersold the location. The manor was only distantly visible from the end of the long drive, surrounded by woods and moorland. Only when she pulled up outside did she see evidence of the walled gardens, beckoning you through an iron gate, still supporting the last of the summer roses.

Unwilling to present herself at Reception, she messaged John to announce her arrival. He could meet her at the car and escort her in, to avoid any awkwardness.

There was a tap on the window, making her jump.

'Classy motor,' said John as he opened the door and wrapped his arms around her. 'I see you went for the four litre.'

He was wearing a woollen beanie hat that gave him the look of a rugged mountaineer.

'Petrolhead,' she said, breathing in the scented warmth of his neck. 'You smell nice.'

'Aramis,' he murmured into her hair. 'Do you remember, it was one up from Brut if you wanted to impress a posh girl? I bought some specially.'

'Knicker disintegrator. That was how our next-door neighbour described Brut. He bought some for his son when he suspected he might be gay, so he could slay the ladies. The Great Smell of Brut, i.e. not for fairies.'

'Come on, gorgeous.'

He took her hands and pulled her out of the low-slung seat.

'You look fantastic. Wait till you see the room, you're going to love it.'

He took her bag from the boot and led her across the gravel to the entrance, the low solid arch leading into a panelled Jacobean hall. A woman wearing an old-fashioned lace cap and modern spectacles greeted them from behind the desk. It was a feature of the hotel that staff wore period costumes, but you couldn't really ban glasses on the grounds that they ruined the effect.

'Welcome to Dursdale, Mrs Ormonde.'

They went up the square staircase. A girl in a mob cap and floor-length dress nodded as she walked past, carrying a bucket.

'You told them I was your *wife*?' said Tessa, as he opened the heavy oak door. 'And why are all the staff dressed like Victorian maids? I hope we're not expected to use a commode.'

'Don't worry, full bathroom facilities. And yes, I said I was expecting my wife, it's only a matter of time after all, isn't it?'

'The room is gorgeous,' said Tessa, ignoring the question. He watched her eagerly as she looked around, taking in the intimate four-poster bed, designed for a shorter generation, and lime-washed walls hung with oil paintings of someone's ancestors. Leaded windows looked out on to the gardens, interconnecting through high hedges. Directly beneath them was a circular iron seat constructed around the thick trunk of a gnarly old tree.

'It's perfect, I completely love it.'

'Me too. Come here.'

He threw himself on to the bed, which looked comically small beneath his bulk.

Tessa removed her coat – Burberry equestrian style, in keeping with the premises – and hung it carefully in the Narnia wardrobe.

'No hurry, is there?' She wanted to prolong the moment. So much planning had gone into this, so many lies, she didn't want it to all be over in a trice.

'None at all,' said John, 'this is just the beginning.'

She walked slowly across the room and sat down on the edge of the bed. He took a tendril of hair that had come loose from her ponytail and tucked it behind her ear.

'I'm so happy you agreed to come. When I woke up and you were gone, I was worried I'd messed it up again.'

'You didn't mess it up. I'm here, aren't I?'

But as she said the words, all kinds of thoughts were spinning through her head. This was insane. She was insane.

'You are. And I can't quite believe it.'

He took her hand and she remembered the feel of it, rough and calloused, workman's hands. He had his own tech company but his real passion was carpentry he said, he loved nothing better than working with his hands.

He reached down her leg to unzip her boot and she pushed her doubts aside. This was enough. Live in the moment.

They were lying on the dishevelled sheets and John was gently stroking her back.

'I could spend the rest of my life in this bed with you,' he said.

Tessa ran her hand down the side of the mattress.

'Definitely pocket sprung in individual calico cases, with hand side-stitching. Did you know hotels like to have mattresses with extra firm edges, because guests spend a lot of time sitting on the side of the bed?'

'Is that a fact?' John asked, rolling her over onto the end of bed, from which vantage point she could see the wreckage of their dinner trolley: red wine stains on white linen, crumbs spilling onto the floor, gravy congealing on the silver cutlery.

'When do they come and get the trolley, do you think?' said Tessa.

'I could feel a bit insulted,' said John, 'with all this housekeeping talk, when you've just been given the sexual experience of your life. What are you, a hotel inspector?'

He turned his face away and she pretended not to notice that he was discreetly removing a hair from his mouth. He was more accustomed to smooth encounters with the neatly waxed.

'I read on the website that John Ruskin stayed in this hotel once,' she said.

'Who?'

'Victorian thinker. Now known mostly for the fact that he fainted on his wedding night at the sight of his wife's pubic hair.'

He looked at her in amusement.

'How appropriate.'

'As far as my interest in mattresses and trolley clearing is concerned, you must remember my life is largely dedicated to the home. My kids think it's hilarious that I'm a retro housewife. And I'm not complaining about the sex by the way. Not at all.'

She wrapped her arms round his chest and pressed her lips against the back of his neck. Different skin, a smooth head, unfamiliar contours. It had been twenty-five years since she had been to bed with anyone other than Matt, she had forgotten how it felt to take a leap into the unknown. It was like trying a different cocktail; an exciting and unexpected revelation.

'Yeah, I'm surprised that you stepped down from your career.' John turned round to look at her.

'You were always so bright. When I couldn't have you, I used to tell myself that maybe it was better that way, because you were way too clever for me. I knew I could never keep up with you.'

'Yet here I am, a redundant old housewife.'

'And I'm the bigshot. Relatively.'

'My relative bigshot. Well it wasn't really what I planned, it's just the way things worked out. I thought I'd stop work for a couple of years when I had the kids, then never quite got back in.'

It sounded feeble, but that was the truth. She was part of the washed-up tide of the comfortably unemployed, a foot soldier in the regiment of genteel non-earners.

'I'm glad, though,' said John. 'I'm glad if it means it gave you time to find me. Imagine, if you'd been Sheryl Sandberg or someone, you might have been too busy to bother with me.'

'The Facebook boss! If I were Sheryl Sandberg I suppose I'd have unlimited access to eligible men. Once I'd got over my husband's death, of course. Do you remember, he fell off the treadmill? Poor thing.'

She imagined Sheryl Sandberg in her plunge neckline business suit, leaning in and taking her pick from a sea of handsome profile pictures.

'Internet dating! I can't tell you how glad I am to put that behind me. You meet these women and you know there's nothing there, but you have to give it an hour and pretend you might see each other again. And now, from nowhere, you've come back into my life and given me this miraculous second chance.'

Tessa felt a cold blast of reality. He saw her as an angel of mercy, sent to rescue him from the hell of midlife dating? What the hell was she doing here?

'Which is why I was so happy when I saw you,' he continued. 'None of that usual disappointment. And finding now that you're beyond all my expectations. In every way.'

Tessa was determined to keep it light.

'I'm glad I'm not a let-down. Even if I am disappointingly post-pubescent in my lady garden.'

'No! Old school but nothing wrong with that!'

He extended a reassuring hand beneath the sheets.

'Don't deny it! I registered your surprise.'

'Alright, maybe it was a little unexpected. But I can get used to it. I'll get one of those "I'm a feminist" T-shirts while I'm about it.'

His hand felt warm and comforting.

'Good, because I'm not going to turn myself into a nine-year old, even for you.'

'Hey, stop making me sound like a pervert.'

'OK, sorry.'

'Anyway, as I said, you're beyond even my wildest expectations.'

'Please don't give me marks out of ten.'

'That's easy. Ten all the way. And I know you'd give me ten as well. Judging from the noise you were making. Or were you faking it?'

'Stop it! Inappropriate conversation.'

'OK, I'll become appropriate.'

He removed his hand and pulled the sheet up primly to his chin.

'That reminds me,' said Tessa. 'Do you remember that Carly Simon song we used to listen to? Or maybe it was just us girls. The one where she talks about moaning in bed, which we never understood in those innocent days. We thought it meant she was complaining.'

'Like that Jewish joke. Hymie says to his wife, I want you to moan in bed, so she looks up and says, that ceiling needs decorating.'

'Ha!'

They lie for a moment in complicit enjoyment of the humour from their youth, the heyday of ethnic jokes, when you could laugh about anything without being branded a bigot or a racist.

'No, Carly Simon was in the Janis Ian category for me,' he said. 'Girls slamming their bedroom doors and being moody.'

'While you boys sat around listening to Genesis. "I Know What I Like (In Your Wardrobe)". I've never met a woman who likes that song.'

'Gloria does, actually. She's the woman I've been seeing, the one in the photos? I met her on Tinder and she's a big Genesis fan, it was the stand-out feature on her dating profile.'

'Sounds like a match made in heaven.'

'Yeah, she's nice but something's missing, which I guess is why we never got round to the exclusivity chat. It's a bit like going out with your pal. Too mannish. I like a womanly woman. Like you.'

They remained silent for a while.

'So, where's your husband tonight?'

'He had a chemistry meeting.'

'I thought he worked in marketing?'

'He does. Personal chemistry, not test tubes.'

Matt had been so generous with her that morning, carrying her bag to the car, telling her to to drive carefully round those sharp bends in the Lake District.

John grabbed hold of her bottom and pulled her to him.

'Did I tell you, by the way, what a great bum you have?'

'I think you mean ass. Or arse, as we pronounce it.'

'That's why I said bum, to avoid the confusion. And don't for one minute think that I'm going to let you walk away again, now that I've found you. We're unfinished business, you and me.'

'Are we?'

'You know we are.'

There would be time for thinking, she knew that. But for now, it was enough to focus on the unfinished business that John was busily attending to.

The following morning, Tessa was stretching luxuriously between the sheets as she listened to John singing in the shower.

'One thing you're going to love in America is the showers,' he shouted through to her. 'None of this pathetic English dribble. Full overhead power.'

She chose to ignore the implicit assumption of their shared future.

'I prefer baths, actually,' she said. 'Old fashioned in that respect.'

'No problem, I've got a tub as well. All needs catered for.'

The water stopped and he came into the bedroom, huge in his white towelling robe.

'You're a bear,' she said, 'do you know that term? Irresistible to many gay men.'

He discarded the robe and slipped into bed beside her, enveloping her in a crushing embrace. She relaxed into his arms, surrendering to his overbearing maleness.

'They did a study to show how women are attracted to different male physiques according to their menstrual cycle,' she said. 'When they're ovulating, they look for big, hunky men to guarantee strong babies. Then, when they're feeling pre-menstrual and vulnerable, they go for sensitive, weedy types.'

He looked at her as if this was the most interesting thing he had ever heard.

'Fascinating. And where are you right now?'

'Oh, I'm well off the radar. My reproductive years are behind me, I'm glad to say.'

He propped himself up on his elbow and stroked her face.

'That's too bad. I would like to have had a child with you. Just think how that would have been.'

She conjured up their might-have-been offspring: big sporty sophomores, playing ice hockey in iron-barred masks.

'You never wanted them? With your wife, I mean.'

'We tried. She had a couple of miscarriages, then the moment was lost, really. She went on to have a son with her new husband. I guess I must have bad sperm.'

'Not necessarily, there can be lots of factors.'

'I bet we could have made loads of babies, you and me,' he said. 'A whole baseball team. And a super-brainy daughter just like her mom who'd be the first woman to Mars or some such.'

He brightened.

'Anyway, there are plenty of positives. No college fees for one. Better off spending that budget on our entertainment, don't you agree? So many places to go. We could buy a boat and sail round the world, what do you say? I can just see you wearing deck shoes, tasting of salt.'

He licked her shoulder.

'That's what they do in Africa, you know, they lick their children to check for salt, make sure they haven't been in the sea, because it's not allowed.'

She remembered the last time he had licked the salt off her, in Cornwall.

'Salty old sea dog. Do you know how to sail?'

'I could learn. The point is, we can do anything we like. That's the beauty of it.'

They lay together, contemplating their respective versions of an unmapped future. It was unfathomable, this blank page, Tessa couldn't imagine how to fill it. All she knew was this moment, lying here with a boy she knew from school who had become a man who wanted her on his journey, to use the ghastly modern expression. As if we were all pilgrims, forging our path to the Promised Land when, in reality, we are just helpless pawns, tossed around on a chaotic sea until we died.

'It's going to be a fun journey, however we choose to make it,' he said, as if reading her thoughts. There was no mistaking the 'we'.

'First class, or coach? To use your lingo.'

'First class, naturally. I'm planning to sell the company, you know.'

'You're jumping the gun,' she said, 'I haven't signed up for it yet.'

'Signed up for it? You make it sound like tennis lessons!'

He held her face in his hands.

'I just want to be with you, that's all. It's simple. Wait there.'

He slipped out of bed and walked, stark bollock naked, across the room to take something out of his khaki knapsack – ideal camouflage for his life journey.

He jumped back on to the bed and gave her an envelope.

'What's this?'

'Open it.'

Inside was a first-class one-way air ticket from Heathrow to Cheyenne.

'It's a flexible ticket,' he said, 'I chose a random date in January, figured you'd need a little time to make your arrangements, but you can change it, come any date you want. In time for Christmas, why not?'

Christmas, was he serious? Had he no idea how that word was enough to bring her slap bang back to reality? The box of decorations brought down from the attic, the smell of turkey permeating the house as Max and Lola mockingly unpacked the stockings they still insisted on.

'American Airlines, I don't think so,' she said lightly. 'Let's just see how we go, shall we?'

'No problem if you want me to change it to BA.'

'It's too soon,' she said, 'we hardly know each other. You didn't even know that I prefer a bath to a shower. You know nothing about me.'

'Know nothing about you!'

He leaned over her and pressed his hands on her shoulders.

'How can you say that? I know everything about you, I've known you since you were sweet sixteen for Christ's sake! Come on, Tessa, we're not kids! We don't have time to mess around, what do you want to do, wait till we're seventy years old and you're wheeling me to my doctor's appointments? Let's do it now, while we're still young and strong enough!'

'Had we but world enough and time, this coyness, lady, were no crime.'

'What?'

'Andrew Marvell, 'To His Coy Mistress'. Trying to talk her into bed.'

'I've already done that! And you've just proved to me one of the reasons I love you. You can open the door of poetry to let in my philistine soul, you know stuff I don't, you are the yin to my yang.'

He put his hands together in mock mystic supplication.

Tessa gently handed him back his ticket.

'Let's just enjoy the weekend, shall we? We've got plenty of more immediate decisions to make. Like, are we going to go for a long walk before lunch? I've brought my boots.'

He put the ticket on the bedside table, like a disappointed schoolboy who's failed to get full marks.

'OK, I'm not going to pressure you. By the way, I should let you know I'm listing you as my next of kin.'

'You're doing what!'

'On my passport. Person to be notified in the event of an emergency.'

'And you're putting *me*?'

'I'm changing it when I get home. I've already altered my will. I've made a few legacies, but most of my estate will come to you.'

'You can't do that. I couldn't possibly—'

'Why not? I'm serious, Tessa, we're going to be together soon, might as well get everything regularised. There'll be a couple of distant cousins who'll be disappointed, but I haven't seen them for years, so screw them. I thought you'd be pleased!'

'It's just weird, John. We don't know where this is heading, and you're already leaving me all your money—'

'What do you mean, we don't know where this is heading? It's perfectly obvious to me. We belong together, and you know that. Why else did you drive up here? Don't tell me it's because you were bored and fancied a change of scene, because I don't believe you.'

'No, of course it's not like that—'

'Good. Now, get your boots on and I'll race you to the top of that hill.'

It wasn't until they were back from their afternoon walk that Tessa decided to turn on her phone. There was a message from Matt.

> How you doing, Nursey? Bringing succour to your sad friend? Went to the match with Max. He's gone off with his mates and I've bought a Charlie Bigham TV dinner for two. Just about enough for one greedy lonely person. Missing you x

Liar, liar, pants on fire. She tapped out her reply.

> All OK, missing you too.

That sentiment, at least, was honest.

'Try again, Mum.'

Poppy leaned over from the passenger seat to look at the dashboard as Sandra pressed the fob into the ignition. Still nothing.

'Today of all days! I'm sick of these new-fangled things, what was wrong with a key that you just turned, tell me that!'

'Call a cab,' said Poppy.

'At six o'clock on a Sunday morning? I'd be lucky!'

'No! This is so stressful for me!' said Poppy. She was already fully made-up, the orange foundation making her look old beyond her years, her hair pinned into a bun that was rescued from severity by a gaudy pink hairpiece that matched the dress she would change into when they arrived at the rink.

'Why haven't you got Uber?' she said. 'Everyone else has.'

'I've explained before, I have no desire to get into a car with an unlicensed driver who doesn't speak English and doesn't know the streets of London.'

'But what can we do? We need to leave straight away!'

Poppy was panicking now, Sandra could feel it. Bad enough putting yourself out there, all alone on the ice, to be scrutinised and judged, the last thing you needed was a touch-and-go journey. The answer was simple, she thought.

'I'll call Mariusz, he'll take us.'

'Really? Why him?'

'Because I know he won't let us down.'

She wanted him there, it felt natural for her to ring him in her hour of need and he sounded unsurprised to hear from her.

'Thirty minutes, maximum, Sandra,' he promised. 'Sunday morning very beautiful time for the driving.'

'He'll get us there in no time, darling,' Sandra reassured Poppy. 'Let's get you changed into your dress now, then you'll be all ready.'

She took Poppy's bag out of the car and they hurried back into the house, where Poppy slipped into her sparkly over-boot tights and a pink dress liberally scattered with rhinestones and finished with a multi-layered floaty skirt. 'We're going to be fine,' Sandra said, 'we've got plenty of time.'

When she heard Mariusz's van draw up, Sandra threw open the door and ran out to greet him while Poppy was putting on her trainers. She gave him a devil-may-care big kiss, there was nobody up at this time to notice.

'Thank you so much, Mariusz, are you very cross?'

'Never cross with you Sandra,' he said, although he did look a bit bleary-eyed. 'I prefer you ring me for the drive, it is big risk to go with Muslim taxi driver.'

'How many more times must I tell you, you can't say things like that!'

When Poppy came out, Mariusz saw her flamingo-coloured skirt protruding beneath her short jacket and quickly unfolded a clean dustsheet over the front seat.

'Be very careful, Poppy,' he said, 'you no want plaster dust on your beautiful dress.'

'Three seats in the front, what bliss,' said Sandra, enjoying the novelty of sitting in the middle of the convivial bench, with all the tools of Mariusz's trade piled up behind them.

'It's cool,' Poppy agreed.

Sandra took her hand and squeezed it.

'Not too nervous?'

'No, It's alright. There's just one sequence in the routine I'm worried about, but it should be OK.'

'I'm proud of you,' said Sandra. 'I don't care if you fall over or forget the whole thing. It takes guts to get out there. You're a real trooper.'

'Super Trooper!' said Mariusz, 'Very good song by the Abba, I play him!'

He pressed a button on the CD control and beamed at them as the music struck up.

'Ah, thanks, Mum,' said Poppy. She looked sideways across at her mother. 'Pity Dad couldn't be bothered to come.'

Sandra hesitated before replying. Of course she thought it scandalous that Nigel was so involved in himself that he couldn't shake himself out of it to watch his only child perform in the competition she'd been working up to for months. He couldn't have driven them – they only had one car – but he could have come along to show his support. On the other hand, she refused to be one of those parents who badmouths their spouse in front of their children, that was very un-classy.

'It's complicated, Poppy,' she said. 'He's not well, as you know. We'll show him the video later, he'll be pleased to see it.'

They arrived in good time at the ice arena on the faceless outskirts of a town that Sandra would never visit outside these circumstances.

'I wait here,' said Mariusz, as Sandra and Poppy went into the changing rooms. Girls of all ages were limbering up with stretching exercises, pulling glittery dresses out of suitcases and applying garish make-up in an atmosphere that smelled of toilet cleaner and hairspray. It always made Sandra feel rather sick, but she gamely rummaged in Poppy's bags to find her zip-up jacket.

She turned to see Poppy looking aghast at the open suitcase.

'My skates!' she said. 'They're not there. I took them out when we went back into the house and I must have forgotten to put them back in.'

There was some sympathetic tut-tutting from the other mothers as Sandra took control.

'How long have we got?'

'An hour and a half before warm-up.'

'Right. We might just have time. Let me speak to Mariusz.'

On the way home, Poppy cradled the trophy in her lap, while Sandra looked through the photos on her phone. The action shots were a bit blurred but there was a good one of Poppy holding her cup, standing on the highest middle plinth, flanked by two rivals, all of them arranging their feet turned out like ballerinas, the blades of the skates sheathed in plastic covers.

'Mariusz, you're a total hero,' said Poppy. 'I can't believe the way you managed to get back so quickly.'

Mariusz flushed with pride. 'My van very fast, Poppy, and no cars on road, and to make me drive even more fast, I play "Wind Beneath My Wings", I like very much this song.' He began to sing it for them.

'Well I couldn't have done it without you, that's all,' said Poppy.

'And you win cup!' said Mariusz, interrupting his singing for a moment. 'I am urgent person!'

'Very urgent, Mariusz,' said Sandra, 'Will you come in for some coffee?'

Once they were indoors, Poppy went up to have a bath while Sandra prepared the coffee.

'You've got a fan for life there,' she said. 'Poppy thinks you're the bee's knees.'

It was possibly not the best expression to use as she then had to spend quite a long time explaining what it meant. In the easy laughter that followed, Mariusz's expression became more serious.

'Sandra, when I came back for the skates, I see your husband here.'

'Well yes, it is his home.'

'He very surprised to see me, but I explain.'

'He should be bloody grateful, it's his daughter!'

'But when I come in, he is talking on the phone and walking towards front door. And when I leave, very quickly, I see a woman going up steps to your house. And in mirror I see your husband open the door to her . . .'

He hesitated.

'Go on,' said Sandra.

'And he give woman a big kiss. Big, big kiss, not small kiss on cheek.'

Sandra had an intuitive feeling.

'What did she look like?'

'I could not see close, but she had black hair.'

'Would you say she looked South American?'

CHAPTER FOURTEEN

'Don't allow yourself to get into the habit of dressing carelessly when there is "only" your husband to see you. He is a man after all, and if his wife does not take the trouble to charm him, there are plenty of other women who will.'

Blanche Ebbutt, *Don'ts for Wives*, 1913

Tessa was dressed for the gym in a twenty-year-old pair of track suit bottoms and a baggy Frankie Says Relax T-shirt. She had never got round to investing in Lycra sportswear, couldn't see the interest when she had perfectly serviceable alternatives and her exercise pattern was so erratic. This morning, she needed something to do, anything to take her mind off the increasingly insistent messages that John was sending her. He had flown home last night and was already telling her how much he was missing her, how passionately he was waiting for her.

Matt gave her a disapproving once-over as he came into the kitchen.

'If you're shopping today, can you get me some Listerine? I don't want to breathe foul fumes over my colleagues. We've got to plan our strategy for an important dinner with a potential client at the Soho House tomorrow.'

'Get you!' she said.

'It could be a big one if we land it. I'll have to make sure I'm on form.'

'I'm sure you will be,' she said. The supportive wife, bolstering and reassuring.

'And while you're about it, why don't you get some styling mousse for your hair, to push it up a bit. I don't like it flopping all over your face.'

He really did know how to make a girl feel good.

'Put a paper bag over your head, then you won't have to see it,' she retorted.

'Oh dear! Your weekend away doesn't seem to have improved your spirit, sounds like your friend's misery has rubbed off on you.'

He swept off in his usual self-righteous rush of busyness, calling back to her over his shoulder, 'Shouldn't be late, see you this evening.'

Tessa cleared his plate, then put a sesame bagel in the toaster. She would comfort herself by finding out what Lola was up to, it already seemed ages since she had seen her.

She opened her laptop to find that help with rising funeral costs was on offer, alongside miracle menopause face cream. Never mind that she had long ago deleted her date of birth,

Facebook never forgot and would track her to her dying day. It would be Stannah stairlifts and Tena lady pads before too long. There was a photograph of Lola looking about thirty-five in a floor-length dress at a black-tie dinner, it was strange how these kids liked playing at being old, wearing stuffy formal clothes in a new kind of dressing-up game.

There was also a private message from John.

> I'm following up my declarations of love, which you must not doubt xxx. Now for the practical stuff. I've rearranged my closet. The drawers on the left are for you.

The photo was of an insanely tidy wardrobe interior. Hangers of identical chinos lined up beneath piles of ironed shirts like you found in shops, but never in houses, at least not in Tessa's chaotic experience. But what really caught her attention was the sock drawer. It was pulled out to display its neat partitions, each containing one pair of folded socks. She counted fourteen then sent her reply:

> What happens if you get more than 14 pairs of socks?

> I'd throw some away ☺ Same goes for you on your side.

She looked at the matching shelves and drawer compartments on the other side of the cupboard. He was already lining up storage for her underwear and telling her how many pairs of socks she was allowed?

He messaged again.

Your underpants and pantyhose can go in the bottom drawer.

She had to put him right there.

I have neither underpants nor pantyhose as I am British.

She logged off before he had time to reply and went upstairs to find her trainers.

'It's not good news, is it?'

Celia leaned back against the Keep Calm and Carry on cushion. She was wearing a green woollen suit, set off by a soft-pink chiffon scarf; as usual she had been the best-dressed woman in the hospital waiting room. Harriet tried to find a positive spin, then decided she couldn't.

'No, Celia, it's not. But you're getting the best care and you know we'll look after you. You're not facing this on your own.'

'I know, dear, and I appreciate it.'

'Let me go and make us a nice cup of tea.'

Harriet went into the kitchen and thought about the weekend ahead. She had arranged for a carer to move in while they were away in Chipping Campden, but the timing was unfortunate;

she would prefer to be looking after Celia herself, following the news she had received today.

When she carried the tray into the living room, Celia was looking more cheerful.

'They could be wrong,' she said. 'You hear it all the time. Let's accept that I'm not going to get better, but I could go on for years. Imagine, you could be bringing me cups of tea until I'm ninety-five!'

By which time I'll be seventy, thought Harriet. Give me strength.

'Now, you remember we're away this weekend, so I've arranged for a lovely young woman to come and look after you, she'll sleep in Alex's old room.'

'I don't know why you don't take me with you, I haven't been to your second home for years.'

She pronounced 'second home' as though it was an accusation: some people had all the luck and didn't know how well off they were.

'There aren't enough bedrooms,' said Harriet, 'I've invited Tessa and Sandra and their husbands.'

'That Sandra doesn't take up much space,' said Celia. 'Not much meat on her.'

'Even so. You can ring me any time, and I've told Mirela to do the same.'

'Mirela? Doesn't sound English.'

'She's Romanian.'

'Oh, I see, you're leaving me in the care of a gypsy.'

'She's very nice, you'll like her.'

Celia looked at Harriet with sad eyes.

'I'll be counting down the hours till you come back. Assuming I live that long.'

'What's this then?'

Matt stared at the unadorned piece of salmon on his plate, accompanied by five broccoli florets.

'We're on a diet,' said Tessa. 'You said we should be careful.'

She was doing her best to carry on as usual, to lead her normal life with Matt, ignoring the emotional drama unfolding with John. After the photo of the sock drawer, he had sent her pictures of the house, the wraparound veranda where they would have their evening drinks, the plain lawn at the back which was just waiting for her to break it up into flowerbeds. Part of her found the prospect so exciting that it stopped her breath. Another part of her was in a blind panic at the thought of such a life change.

'How depressing,' said Matt, 'and I suppose this carafe of water is all I'm allowed as well?'

'It's wrong to drink every day. Cirrhosis of the liver has increased eightfold amongst the middle-aged, I was reading a thread about it on Mumsnet.'

'Mumsnet brings out the misogynist in me.'

'I do agree. All that DH and DD nonsense.'

'So sexist. Does this diet fad also explain why you're wearing those clothes?'

'I went to the gym, yes. And, actually, they're really comfortable. Lola would describe them as "stash".'

'I thought that was drugs.'

'No, apparently it means sports clothes, though in my case without a university logo. I'll show you her latest pictures, once we've finished, so you can see some better examples.'

Their dinner was soon dispatched and Tessa brought her laptop to the table.

'Look, there she is, in her hockey stash.'

Matt peered at the screen, frowning.

'Ah yes, lovely athletic figure she's got.'

He scrolled down her timeline and stopped at a photo taken at a nightclub, Lola at the centre of a group of young people grinning at the camera, arms draped over each other.

'Why do they always have their mouths open?' Matt asked, 'pulling those awful gurning faces. And why is that one dressed like a rabbit?'

'They're living the dream,' said Tessa, 'and I'm glad she looks so happy.'

She had heard it said that as a parent, you are only ever as happy as your least happy child. If Max or Lola were suffering in some way, it was impossible for her to feel at ease. It was pretty obvious how they would react to the news that she was leaving their father to start a new life in America. And yet. Max and Lola were grown up, they would be making their own way in the world, leaving her behind in the empty nest with her hypercritical husband. She could walk away from this humdrum life of hers, fall in love and start all over again.

'Let's watch *University Challenge*,' she said. 'I recorded it for you.'

It was an average performance for them both, with three correct answers from Tessa and eight from Matt, who shouted his responses at the screen and made a celebratory chain-pulling gesture every time he got one right.

'How come they know so much stuff?' Tessa wanted to know. 'We're both well educated but it makes me realise we hardly know anything.'

'Excuse me, I think you'll find I know considerably more than you.'

'That's because you're a man and therefore disposed to store facts. Whereas I excel in emotional intelligence.'

'Whatever that is.'

'I think it means interpretation. Discarding irrelevant stuff like chemical formulae and dates.'

Later that evening, they stood before their his 'n' hers hand basins, engaged in their toilet rituals. Tessa wiped off her eye make-up and looked in the mirror at Matt who was flossing.

'Forgot to tell you,' he said, putting down the unappetising thread and picking up his toothbrush.

'There's this annoying new thing at work where we have meetings standing up.'

'Like a drinks party, you mean?'

'More like being in a tube train. It's supposed to save time.'

'Some truth in that, I suppose. Stops people dozing off over tea and biscuits.'

'They won't be doing it when the global CEO comes over next week. Napoleonic little fellow, he'll be the shortest man in the room, much better to disguise it sitting behind a desk!'

He paused to vigorously brush his teeth and spit into the basin.

'In fact I learned today that Napoleon was five foot six, the average height for a Frenchman in those days,' said Tessa. 'So not really a short arse at all.'

'Sounds like you've been gorging on Radio 4 all day,' said Matt, 'I wish I had the time.'

'Listening to the radio is compatible with many unchallenging household tasks. I do them so you don't have to.'

John had told her he didn't want her to lift a finger when she moved in with him. He had a daily maid because life was too short to waste it on cleaning. He could think of far more creative ways for them to spend their days together.

'That's nice of you. Anyway, back to the Napoleonic CEO. He's rich as Croesus, the bastard. So loaded he could afford to ditch his wife and get a second family.'

Tessa squeezed some youth eye serum out of a tube and applied it with her finger.

'You're not thinking of doing that, then?'

'Too poor, luckily for you,' said Matt. 'I can safely say you'll be the one accompanying me on the retirement cruise. There's something to look forward to.'

He turned off the tap and went into the bedroom.

Tessa rubbed night cream into her neck and thought about what it would be like on a cruise ship. Imagine if you were standing in front of your bathroom mirror and suddenly the cabin walls came down and you could just see a shipload of old people, flossing and cleaning their ears and taking their pills, all on the great voyage of no return.

She took her phone out of her dressing-gown pocket and checked the latest message from John.

I know you need time but don't leave it too long.
I need you.

CHAPTER FIFTEEN

'Don't vegetate as you grow older if you happen to live in
the country. Some women are like cows, but there is really
no need to stagnate.'

Blanche Ebbutt, *Don'ts for Wives*, 1913

Harriet struck a match and set fire to the scrunched-up newspaper
at the centre of the wigwam of kindling she had constructed in the
grate. The flame flickered and took hold and she sat back on her
heels, gratified that she still had the knack. There was a satisfaction
to be found in simple tasks in the country you just didn't get in the
city, it was one of the thrilling benefits of having a second home.
She wanted to welcome her friends with the reassuring warmth of
a log fire. They'd be here soon but there was just enough time for
the house to heat up.

She sat down on the Chesterfield sofa and looked round the
room, every detail rich in memories. The Laura Ashley curtains that she had run up on her old Singer, the distempered
walls they had painted together, the mahogany desk acquired
at an auction in Evesham along with the large wardrobes that

dominated the bedrooms upstairs. Like all the other yuppies, they'd been gripped by *Brideshead Revisited* fever, inspired by the grandiose fantasy that filled their TV screens on Monday nights. She had even knitted Sam an intricate Fair Isle tank top which he wore over pleated corduroy trousers, embracing his inner Sebastian Flyte as they arrived late on a Friday night with pots of paint and busy plans for a weekend of renovation.

They had bought the house with Sam's first bonus, back when he was still called a merchant banker, before the merchant bit was quietly dropped. Chipping Campden was an obvious choice, a heritage village in the heart of the sheep-filled Cotswolds, where would-be aristocrats could imagine putting down roots and founding dynasties. When the estate agent showed them round, Harriet had stood in this room and felt almost sick with longing, her stomach telling her that she had never wanted anything more than this house.

Sam said to her once, as they were rag-rolling the bedroom – earnestly soaking a bunched-up towel in a tray of paint, then pressing it on to the base coat – that having a second home was like being married, whereas renting a holiday cottage was like having an affair. You couldn't just walk away from a place you owned, you were in it for the long term. And like their marriage, the house was showing the strain, both of them in need of an overhaul.

She stood up and rattled the leads, bringing the dogs to attention.

'Come on Benson and Hedges, let's go for a walk.'

She checked her phone, no messages from the carer she had organised for Celia, that was good news. She clipped on the dogs' leads, closed the door behind her and set off down the high street.

They didn't have dogs when they were first married, it would have been too constraining with them both out at work all day, and on the weekends when they weren't here at the house, they would be off somewhere: The George V hotel in Paris, skiing in Verbier or drinking spritzers on a terrace in Cap d'Antibes. Sam always insisted on the best hotels, the most prestigious destinations, it was an upward arc of aspiration; the sky was the limit in this exciting new world of money. Sam was from an ordinary background, the same as her, elevated by his grammar school so he could aspire to Cambridge. The rewards of success were all the sweeter when you weren't born with a silver spoon in your mouth.

But you can't buy happiness, which was why she decided to abandon her career at chambers after they'd had Alex. A simple, old-fashioned life of bringing up her children would lead to proper serenity, and by the time you'd factored in the cost of a nanny, who would require her own car and flat – no son of Sam's was going to make do with a shared childminder or untrained au pair – she'd be breaking even at best. Standing in front of the stove on a Sunday evening, stirring a pan of homemade soup, she could still sharply recall the parallel emotions: relief that she didn't have to worry about Monday morning; and an uneasy sense that her life had been put on hold, that she was stagnating and somehow letting the side down. Homemade soup, who needed it? Greasy Joan doth keel the pot. Shakespeare. At least she had her education to sustain her.

They were almost at the post office, and Harriet quickened her step. It was all water under the bridge now, no point in thinking about what might have been. A colleague from her chambers had just become a high court judge; it could easily have been Harriet, who was the undisputed star pupil of her year. And now she was working as an unpaid carer for her mother-in-law.

She tied the dogs up outside the shop and went in to chat to the owner, a zealous ex-Londoner who had made a new life for himself and his partner in the country, selling all kinds of creative knick-knacks alongside the usual Sellotape and Tic-Tacs.

'Hello!' he said, with the slightly desperate enthusiasm of someone hungry for news from the smoke.

'It's been a while, are you here for the weekend?'

'Yes, I've got friends arriving this evening.'

'Oh good, that means I've got a reasonable chance of selling a few papers. I've noticed it seems a bit of a competition amongst weekenders, to see who can buy the most newspapers. Right across the spectrum, to prove how broadminded they are: the *Guardian*, of course, but never too snobby for the *Sun*.'

Harriet laughed.

'You're right there.'

She handed over her basket of groceries and let her eye wander over the till-side offerings.

'Oh, what a lovely keyring, with a hand-knitted dog attached. I'll take that, thanks, and that iron thing to pull your wellington boots off, that's just what I need outside the back door.'

'You're my favourite customer, Harriet. Just wish we saw you more often. Now, do you need some horseradish sauce? You usually do, for your Sunday roast.'

'Don't think so, one of my guests is on duty for that.'

'Good guest, the sort who sings for his supper.'

'Exactly.'

She unfastened the dogs and continued her walk, up to the church, set behind a stern row of yew trees speaking of death, and into the porch, where a rota of duties had been posted on the wall. That could be me, I suppose, she thought, if I lived here all the time. I could take my turn doing the flowers and making teas and whatever it was that good churchwomen got up to. Fading away in my tweed skirt until eventually securing a plot, possibly, in this pretty graveyard where future generations of weekenders would wander aimlessly around, reading the tombstones and speculating about the lives of those who lay beneath.

Back at the house, the dogs settled lazily in front of the fire while Harriet decanted her oxtail stew from its Tupperware box into a large Le Creuset, a wedding present from her aunt. It wasn't a fussy dinner, not like the creations she liked to whip up in the eighties when she subscribed to *A La Carte* magazine, arranging curried melon balls and tiny vegetable slivers on black plates. She didn't miss those days, really she didn't. And soon her friends would be here and everything would be lovely.

'I love that building,' Tessa said to Matt, as they drove past the art deco façade of the Hoover factory on the A40. 'I always associate it with escaping from London.'

In all her extra-marital excitement, she had quite forgotten about this weekend, which had been organised a while back, in the way that grown-ups like to plan things: diaries consulted, dates marked in, all spontaneity thrown aside.

'You and your landmarks,' said Matt. 'You have measured out your life in listed buildings.'

'You can talk. You're worse than P. D. James, the way you describe every architectural feature in excruciating detail. And nobody complains more loudly than you when a building offends you.'

'But I love complaining!' he said cheerfully, as the lights turned red. 'In fact, I enjoy it more and more with every year that passes. It really is one of the hidden benefits of middle age.'

'Every man needs a hobby,' said Tessa.

She looked across at him, smiling behind the wheel. Sandra had suggested they travel up together in their Audi Q7, but Matt wasn't going to lose the opportunity of parking his Maserati prominently on the high street where it could be admired.

'It's the absurd follow-up that's best of all. I complain because I've got no connection and they send me a message thanking me for getting in touch but that it's not possible to call me because my number isn't active. Duh. Then another email about how passionate they are about customer relations, and please can I give my feedback. I should let the office sort it out but I'm enjoying it too much.'

'It's not complaining that's making you happy, it's being without a phone,' said Tessa. 'Look at you, you're so relaxed.'

It was true that Tessa hadn't seen him this carefree for years. He seemed decades younger and, sitting beside him now, she could imagine they were back in the old days, before the children, taking off for a weekend on a whim. Except that her new phone was buzzing with a reminder of her recent encounter. She had finally joined the modern world this week and bought an iPhone.

'You've got friends,' said Matt. 'Aren't you going to see who it is? It could be Lola.'

'Doubt it. She'll be at some fancy-dress function. Downing double vodkas.'

She glanced at the phone, confirming it was another message from John, the fifth of the day, then turned it off.

'You've changed your tune,' said Matt. 'What's happened to the weepy mother in constant hope of news?'

'Let's just switch off and enjoy ourselves, shall we?'

'Well I've got no choice. As I'm un-connected. Did I tell you, by the way, how well the chemistry meeting went?'

'Several times.'

'I told them, you don't need revolution, you need evolution. They thought it was bloody brilliant!'

They drove on, wrapped in their separate thoughts, Matt buoyed up by the memory of his magnificent performance in front of the client and Tessa reliving her time in bed with John, dreaming of their escape to the Scottish wilds. She found it was easier to imagine them starting out together in a more familiar setting. A Hebridean island was less frightening than Wyoming, and it would be easier to see the children. The fantasy stumbled when she went too deeply into the detail. Where would she see the children? Would they even want to see her, and what would become of Matt?

The sun was setting when they arrived in Chipping Campden, casting a soft glow on the terraces of honey-coloured houses that lined the broad high street. There was something about the Cotswold stone that allowed it to retain its luminosity, even when the light was low. Sleek cars were already parked in a look-at-me line but Matt was able to manoeuvre into a spot not far from the converted inn that was their destination. He lifted their bag and a case of wine out of the boot while Tessa took charge of the cool-box and bags of vegetables. There were shops in the village, but it was more convenient to arrive with your supplies and you'd be hard pressed to source fresh tarragon in the local Spar.

'Do you remember the first time we came here?' said Matt. 'I'd just got my first Porsche. Not so many flash cars then.'

'You could still imagine it as a sheep market town. We were the pioneering yuppies.'

'Closely followed by the supermodels. In a sheep-like manner, money following the money.'

They knocked on the door and Tessa peered through the window into the dining room, a claustrophobically dark and narrow room, filled entirely with a long trestle table and benches, still rich with the atmosphere of the public bar it once had been.

Harriet opened the door to them and Tessa had a flashback to their first visit, Harriet flushed with excitement as she showed them round, wearing clothes not dissimilar to what she had on now – blouse, cardigan and baggy woollen trousers that were quite the thing in the 1980s, but not so much today.

'Here we are again, fantastic to be here,' said Tessa, hugging her friend and familiarising herself with the sloping floor of the long passage that ran straight down into the back garden. 'Shall I put the food away?'

The kitchen was three steps down, with two large fridges and open shelves of catering-size pots and pans.

'I love this kitchen, it's so no-nonsense, just like you.'

'I suppose I can take that as a compliment,' said Harriet, watching her friend unpack, 'Ooh, is that grouse?'

'Certainly is. Matt claims game is a middle-class conspiracy, but I like it, especially when it's sexed up with beetroot and blackcurrant sauce and served with quinoa.'

'You are marvellous. I've done a rather boring casserole for tonight.'

'Nothing wrong with that, Harriet,' Matt shouted through from the dining room, where he was lining up his bottles of wine. 'You can get a bit sick of Tessa's over-elaboration, I'm sure she won't mind me saying. Sam and I will enjoy a nice brown stew after a couple of pints down at the Red Lion.'

'Ah.' Harriet looked uncomfortable. 'I'm afraid he's not able to make it tonight. Something's come up at work, as usual. He's hoping to join us tomorrow, but he'll have to let us know.'

'Shame,' said Tessa.

She wasn't surprised, and nor was Harriet, judging from her stoic expression. Tessa felt a burst of frustration with her friend. You can change things, she wanted to say, you don't have go around with a permanent air of martyrdom. Mix it up; surprise him or leave him. It's your life.

'Too bad,' said Matt.

He'd been looking forward to a manly chat with Sam. Now he'd have to make do with Nigel, who wasn't exactly a barrel of laughs.

'So what is it then, Harriet?' he asked. 'A takeover crisis? Some merger or acquisition he's set to make a mint out of?'

'I don't know the details, but you know how it is. You men with your big jobs.'

'Let's take our stuff upstairs,' said Tessa. 'Which room are we in?'

'I've put you in the front bedroom. I'll take the attic room as I don't even know if Sam's going to make it. No point Matt knocking himself out on that beam.'

'Are you sure?' said Tessa. 'Hardly seems fair that we should take the master suite.'

'No, honestly. I like it right up at the top.'

Matt nudged Tessa to stop protesting.

'Well, if you insist. I'll take our bag up,' he said.

Tessa followed him up the stairs and into a room with sloping ceiling and mullioned windows that offered Matt an uninterrupted view of his Maserati. He threw himself on to the bed.

'Yes!' he said, 'We got the best room. Come here.'

He opened his arms and she flopped on to the pink candlewick bedspread beside him, closing her eyes and running her fingers over the covers.

'Reminds me of my childhood,' she said, 'blankets and hospital corners, before we got into duvets.'

'Continental quilts,' said Matt, 'Freeing the housewife from bed-making chores.'

'Please don't use that word.'

'Housewife, mousewife. I wonder if that posh cutlery shop is still here, I think I might treat you to some new knives.'

'You're all give.'

'Though come to think of it, we probably don't need any more. That's the thing about getting older, isn't it, you run out of things to need.'

'Maslow's hierarchy of needs. Air, water and food.'

'Closely followed by a set of Robert Welch knives, though I suppose he's been rather overtaken by the Japanese, and we've got the top of the range Global set already . . .'

His brow furrowed as he tried to think of something they might need, then he brightened.

'I know what we could do with! Cheese knives! We'll check it out in the morning. You need something to cheer you up.'

'Why do you say that?'

'You've been a right misery the last few days. It's like living with one of those depressed menopausal women you hear about. Those sad cases who go to pieces when the kids fly the nest. I don't know what's got into you!'

She didn't tell him that what had got into her was John Ormonde.

'You're supposed to be the cheerful one,' he continued. 'I'm the one who's prone to misery.'

'And a set of cheese knives will put that right, will it?'

'Worth a try! We must seek our consolations where we can. Speaking of which, I'm glad we got the en suite bathroom. I'm too old to share a toilet with people I don't sleep with.'

He jumped up from the bed and took his copy of *The Times* out of his bag, and went into the bathroom, leaving the door open.

'Can you remember,' he shouted through to her, 'how far into our relationship we were before we started sitting on the lav in front of each other?'

'Couldn't say,' said Tessa. 'But I'm happy to reverse it. To be honest, I'd really rather you closed the door.'

'Spoilsport. Did you know that a high percentage of people die on the bog? So there's a health benefit as well as a social advantage to leaving the door open. Imagine if I was dying on the toilet and you didn't realise, because you were sealed off in another room.'

'I'm tearing up at the thought.'

'Exactly!'

The bathroom at Dursdale Hall had offered towels hanging in rigid symmetry, soft tissues in a dispensing box and hand lotion that smelled of almonds. She had closed the door behind her and worn the bathrobe to preserve her modesty. As you did in the beginning.

Matt's voice again.

'Damn! Tessa?'

'What?'

'There's no toilet paper. Do you mind?'

'I'll go and find some.'

Downstairs, Harriet was reading in front of the fire, her feet tucked up beside her. She looked up as Tessa came in.

'Settled in alright?'

'Lovely. Just after some loo roll.'

'In the kitchen.'

'Thanks. You're looking very relaxed.'

Harriet put her book down.

'I can't tell you how good it feels, to know I can sit and read a book without any risk of Celia interrupting me.'

'Is the carer working out alright?'

'Apparently they've really hit it off. She's everything Celia disapproves of. Romanian single mother, prone to hysteria, but it's a love match. Sounds like she can counteract every one of Celia's endless stories with one of her own. Very chatty, which is the main thing.'

'You should get her to come regularly. Make more use of this place, you could try and spend more time here with Sam.'

'I will, though it's often difficult for Sam to get away. I hope Matt's not too disappointed.'

'He's quite happy with the ladies, and there's Nigel, of course. What time are they coming, do you know?'

'Couple of hours,' she said. 'Which just gives us time . . .'

She pulled out a Scrabble set from the pile of boxes on the coffee table.

'Shall we?'

'Oh yes!'

Tessa sat down on the opposite sofa as Harriet went through the ritual of opening the board and shaking the letters into the bag. They each took seven letters, then drew lots to see who should start.

'L,' said Harriet.

'T.'

They moved their tiles around in companionable silence, looking at possible word formations until Matt's voice carried down the stairs to disturb their concentration.

'TESSA!'

Tessa jumped up.

'Oh God, the bog roll! Back in two minutes, don't look at my letters.'

Upstairs, Matt was reading the paper, boxer shorts round his ankles, forming a little skirt above his Hogan shoes.

'Here's something to make you sick,' he said. 'This CEO who says he's retiring at fifty because he couldn't find an answer for his wife who asked, at the top of Kilimanjaro, when would be the right time for them to go travelling together. What a smug bastard. I tell you what, if I had thirty million in the bank, I'd do the same, but I wouldn't expect to be admired for my courage or held up as a role model. What are these people on?'

'I know, I saw that. They live in their own silly bubble, don't they, the very rich? Here, catch.'

She threw the toilet roll to him and laughed as he caught it with one hand.

'Thanks, wifey.'

'You're welcome. I'm going downstairs to play Scrabble with Harriet.'

'On your own. I'm waiting for Nigel to take me to the pub for a couple of pints. Something to numb the pain of Harriet's boring brown stew.'

'Hypocrite! You told her you were looking forward to it, Sick of my over-elaboration, I think you said.'

'Only being polite. Your sophistication in the kitchen is obviously the reason we're still married.'

Tessa left the room.

'One of them,' he shouted after her.

On her way down, she switched her phone on to read John's text.

Missing you like crazy. Can't wait for our new life together!!

A knot of anxiety twisted in her stomach. Not the missing you like crazy bit, that was fine, she missed him too, she longed to see him again. But the new life together bit was something else. As she was contemplating this, another text pinged in.

Have you got WhatsApp? Now you've finally got a proper phone?

That was easier to answer.

Yes, Lola installed it for me.

Let's move over to that. More versatile. I'll demonstrate now.

Tessa sat on the stairs, safely out of view, and stared at the screen of her iPhone, with its colourful display of childish icons, like modern hieroglyphics. A message was showing on WhatsApp and she clicked to open it.

See what I mean? This is how much I miss you.

But it wasn't his words that grabbed her attention, it was the photo that accompanied them. A close-up of what she could only bring herself to describe as his naked loins.

She stared at it in disbelief, then covered the phone with her hand and looked guiltily over her shoulder, half expecting to find Matt there, sharing her outrage at this pornographic intrusion. Mercifully, the staircase was empty, just her and her shame. Fumbling over the screen, she deleted the message then stood up, regained her composure and walked downstairs, back to normality and Scrabble and good old Harriet.

'You're going to hate me,' said Harriet, turning the board so Tessa could admire her triumph.

'Undergo. Seven letters. Seventy-two.'

'I hate you.'

'Still, that's Scrabble.'

'Indeed it is.'

They were nearing the end of the game when Nigel and Sandra arrived, clattering into the stone-flagged hallway with their luggage and stories of Friday-night travel hell.

'I swear we nearly ran over Samantha Cameron,' said Sandra. 'It smells of rich people out here. If we ever had to leave London, it would have to be the Cotswolds.'

'Orpington not good enough for you?' asked Matt with a grin. 'You're as bad as Tessa, jumped-up suburbanites the pair of you.'

'The three of us, actually,' said Harriet.

'I don't count you, Harriet, you've got a naturally patrician air,' said Matt. 'I'm sure you're from old Orpington stock, before it became common.'

'Leave it out, Matt,' said Sandra. 'You and your minor public school snobbery and your dreams of country squirearchy.'

'Not my fault I was given a scholarship. And I'm hardly dressed like a country squire!'

He ran his hands over his usual black and grey ensemble.

'No brown in town,' said Sandra, 'but you're such a chameleon, you'd soon settle into your modern tweeds. I can just see you out with the hounds and your guns, once you've given up the urban pretension thing.'

'You'll be wanting a pint then, Nigel,' said Matt, escorting him back out of the door, 'we'll leave you to it, girls.'

'What a monumental waste of time,' said Sandra, sitting down on the sofa and inspecting the board. 'Scrabble is about as pointless as Sudoku.'

'Keeps the brain working,' said Harriet.

'So does learning Cantonese, doesn't mean you're going to do it. Anyway, now the coast is clear, let's talk about the ONLY topic we're interested in right now.'

'World poverty?' asked Harriet, fiddling around with the letters on her rack. 'Global warming? The so-called Islamic State?'

'I refer, of course, to Tessa's weekend of shame with former teenage heart-throb Donny Ormonde.'

Harriet looked up, shocked.

'You didn't!'

'I did. I can't really believe it, but I did.'

It still seemed unreal to her. The four-poster bed where he'd kissed her like a teenager and ripped off her clothes like they do in the movies. She wanted to be the good wife, enjoying a weekend away with her old school friends where the extent of her bad behaviour would be an overly indulgent dinner. Instead of which, she had landed herself with a situation.

'I knew you were meeting him for lunch,' said Harriet, 'but I didn't realise it would go any further.'

'Neither did I. I didn't plan it, it just happened.'

Which wasn't exactly true.

Harriet raised an eyebrow.

'I can't explain. It was all so exciting. I'm used to Matt moaning about everything and letting me know what a disappointment I am. Then suddenly, John turns up and tells me I'm fantastic and gorgeous, and how we're made for each other . . .'

Her voice faltered and she paused to compose herself.

'You just don't expect that to happen at our age. You think you've made your life, that all the passionate stuff is in the past. Then this happens. And it's fantastically thrilling and he makes you believe we really can pick up where we left off and have the charmed life we should have started all those years ago . . .'

She picked up the bag of letters and worked them like worry beads.

'And then you realise it's not that easy, the complications come rushing in and my head's spinning with it all. I just want to play Scrabble and have life go back to normal.'

'Scrabble may be your normal, it's not mine,' said Sandra. 'But hats off for going for it, I honestly didn't think you'd have the balls.'

Harriet frowned at her.

'Can you stop using that terrible male language, you sound like you're in the locker room.'

'I'm just saying,' said Sandra, 'that she won't regret it when she's on her death bed. She had one final bite of the cherry before passing into an invisible and respectable old age.'

'But that's just it,' said Tessa. 'It's not the final bite of the cherry, not at all! If you believe John, it's the start of a new life together. We're going to walk off holding hands into the sunset in Wyoming, or wherever.'

'Please not Wyoming,' said Sandra, 'you needn't think I'll come and see you there.'

'Scotland, then. Or the Bahamas.'

'That's more like it,' said Sandra. 'Handy for winter sun visits.'

'So that's what *he* wants,' said Harriet, 'but what do *you* want? I'm still trying to get my head round this.'

'I don't know. I want to keep that excitement going. I'd forgotten what it's like to really look forward to something again. Remember when you were a child how you couldn't wait for Christmas; that pure joy of anticipation? He's coming back in a couple of weeks and I can put that in a box as my secret treat and count the days down. But it doesn't mean I want to leave my life behind, because I don't.'

'Well thank you for that,' said Sandra.

'But I couldn't bear the thought of never seeing him again.'

'Oh dear,' said Harriet, 'you poor thing, you've got yourself into a bit of a pickle.'

'Bit of a pickle? More like a juicy pot of jam if you ask me,' said Sandra. 'Keep your options open and enjoy it while you can. That's my philosophy.'

'Philosophy, is that what you call it?' said Harriet. 'You and the builder.'

'Don't judge me, Harriet,' said Sandra, 'we all do what we can to make sense of our lives.'

'And then there's Matt,' said Tessa. 'He's been so lovely the last few days, I feel like I've got the old version back, instead of the grumpy old bastard.'

'Can't say I've noticed the difference,' said Sandra. 'They're all the same, boring and miserable. It's like they reach a stage in their lives and a light goes off. Middle-aged and disappointed and incapable of waking up and smelling the roses.'

'It's been a Good Year for the Roses,' said Tessa.

Sandra was straight back.

'Elvis Costello and the Attractions. 1981.'

'You bloke. You even know the year.'

Sandra laughed but Harriet looked confused.

'Now you've lost me,' she said. 'Still, it's obvious to me, Tessa, that you've suffered some sort of midlife crisis. What you have to do is just keep calm and carry on.'

'Like it says on your bloody cushion,' said Tessa. 'Except we're not in the Blitz, are we? We're at the settled, comfortable time of our lives, on a weekend break in a country cottage, looking forward to growing old gracefully with our husbands and waiting for our grandchildren.'

'Bleak,' said Sandra. 'You'll be wanting us to join a golf club next. Finding hobbies for an active retirement.'

She reached into her bag and took out her iPad.

'Your problem, Tessa, is that you haven't got a focus. You need a brilliant career like mine, to keep things in perspective. I'm looking for something to cover a wall, money no object, three metres by two. Quite tempted by this Higgins Rondelay glass screen, classic mid mod, what do you think?'

She passed them the tablet to show a photo of coloured glass discs, strung together in a cheerful patchwork.

'Very nice,' said Tessa, 'reminds me of a crochet waistcoat I once made. But I fail to see how that helps me.'

'A thing of beauty is a joy for ever. I'll acquire this for my client and it will hang there, an unchanging source of comfort, no matter what traumas she has in her life. Like all of us, she's got a boring husband, but this is the payback for all those years of putting up with him. Plus, I get paid for finding it.'

'Good for you. So you think I could solve my dilemma by sourcing an artwork?'

'Why not? You'd have the thrill of the chase and then the reward of seeing it every day on your wall.'

'I'm not as aesthetic as you, though. I prefer people to things.'

'Especially John Ormonde. Let's look him up on Facebook, see what he's up to, apart from pining for you of course.'

'I checked, there's nothing there, except—'

She was interrupted by a scream of excitement from Sandra.

'YES! I've been waiting for this! Poppy's been using my iPad and has forgotten to log out of Facebook. At last I get to snoop!'

Harriet frowned.

'I really don't think you should do that, Sandra, it's a terrible invasion of privacy.'

'She's my daughter, it's my responsibility to check up on her, by any means I can.'

'It's like reading someone's diary, I don't think it's right.'

'That's the difference between us, I would read anyone's diary, given the chance. Especially one belonging to my child.'

'I thought I was bad enough,' said Tessa, 'I'm always stalking Lola's profile. But I'd never actually try to hack into her account.'

'Who's talking about hacking? She's left it wide open, obviously secretly wants me to look. Right, straight into the messages, I really can't believe my luck . . .'

She fell silent as she scrolled through the inbox, most of them were disappointingly banal, confirming arrangements or sending links to dreary songs performed by unsmiling young men. She didn't know what she had been hoping for exactly, but it wasn't this series of trite exchanges about who was going to wear what at the gathering hosted by whoever had a free house.

'Are you familiar with that term?' she asked her friends. '"Free house." Not a pub without affinity to a particular brewery, but a home where the parents are away, no doubt so they can get up to all kinds of . . .'

Then she came across what she had been subconsciously looking for.

'OH NO! Oh my God, look at that!'

She passed the tablet to Tessa, who recognised the blonde boy first, grinning into the camera. Poppy was beneath him, her face upside down, her bare limbs wrapped around her lover. Both of them were giving the thumbs-up sign.

'Naked selfie,' said Tessa.

'Disgusting!' said Sandra, taking the iPad back, 'I mean, I know they're having sex, but they don't need to rub it in my face!'

'They're not rubbing it in your face, that's a private message you just looked at,' said Tessa.

Sandra sat back on the sofa, still in shock.

'My little girl. It was only yesterday I was buying her vests and she was snuggling into bed with me. I can still smell her baby hair. And now she's making amateur porno flicks with that boy!'

'It's not a porno flick, it's a naked selfie,' said Tessa. 'They all do it.'

'Doesn't matter! You know how it works, it'll be up in the cloud and everyone will see it, just like with Jennifer Lawrence.'

'I think, in her case, there was no sexual intercourse involved,' said Harriet. 'She'd just taken a private picture of herself. Which then went viral.'

'You seem to be surprisingly well informed,' said Sandra, 'for someone so snooty about social media.'

'That's exactly why I am snooty about it, I can see where it leads. And I honestly can't imagine why anyone would want to take a photograph of their genitals, even for private use. Sorry if that makes me sound like a fuddy-duddy.'

'Which reminds me,' said Tessa. 'I haven't told you about the little shock I suffered on the stairs earlier.'

She explained to them about her surprising initiation into WhatsApp. As she told them about the inappropriate photo John had sent her, it seemed even more unbelievable. Harriet looked appalled but Sandra was delighted.

'He sent you a cock shot! Can't believe it! Show it to me!'

'Deleted, of course. You surely don't think I'd keep that on my phone.'

'Too late, it's bound to have gone viral already, in fact, it's probably pinging its way on to Matt's phone right now as they're sitting in the pub, and on to Nigel's phone, and everyone in there will be laughing at him, the massive cuckold whose wife's just been seduced by her childhood sweetheart—'

'Stop it!' said Tessa, 'It really isn't funny.'

'It is, though. When you think about it, it's like a little boy in the playground pulling down his pants to show you his thing.'

'Dear, oh dear,' said Harriet, 'I really can't believe this. Are you sure, Tessa, that this relationship is something you want to continue?'

'I don't feel so bad about Poppy now I know that my oldest friend is up to the same tricks,' said Sandra. 'Are you going to send one back?'

'I most certainly am not!' said Tessa.

'Was he wearing paisley pyjamas by the way?'

'Paisley pyjamas?'

'Like that MP who got trapped into sexting a tabloid journalist. Everyone was fixated on the pyjama detail, never mind the honourable member.'

'Poor fellow,' said Harriet. 'I felt so sorry for him. Right, I'm going to get the brown stew on. That should calm everybody down.'

Later that evening, under the pink candlewick bedspread, Tessa was sharing the details of Poppy's photo with Matt.

'Serves Sandra right for being nosy,' said Matt. 'I can categorically say I would never invade Lola's privacy like that.'

'That's because you might not like what you find.'

'Well that's true. The thought of seeing her entwined with that caveman—'

'We haven't even met him! I'm sure he's very nice.'

'Hmm. But anyway, the whole thing is sick, isn't it? Like those men who take a photo of their dick to send to someone, can you imagine why you would do such a thing? It's mental.'

'Mmm.'

'I mean, can you imagine if I sexted you a picture? I'm telling you now, if I ever do anything like that, you have my permission to have me banged up in a loony bin. Use your lasting power of attorney.'

'I believe it's very common these days,' said Tessa.

'Really? Not in my world. But don't worry, my moral code means I will never check your phone, so feel free to sext away to your heart's content!'

Tessa's phone was plugged in, charging on the bedside table, like a sleeping dragon. At any moment and without warning, it could wake up and spit lecherous fire into this sleepy Cotswold bedroom. She couldn't switch it off; she always kept it on overnight in case Lola or Max suffered some drama and couldn't get through. And although she believed Matt when he said that he'd never read her messages, supposing he went to the loo while she was asleep and he heard her phone, and just checked to make sure it wasn't an emergency . . .

In her mind, she scrolled back through her exchanges with John that evening. First, his apology.

Hey, hope you're not offended!

She'd crafted her reply:

Not what I'm used to. Untried in funny tricks of modern dating game.

Then she'd deleted the 'modern dating game' bit. Whatever they were up to, it wasn't a dating game.

Not what I'm used to. Untried in funny tricks.

He'd come straight back.

I like your funny tricks. I like everything about you.

He'd promised not to do it again, but she couldn't be sure. What if he was overtaken by the urge to 'share' again after a few drinks this evening? With the time difference, that could be four o'clock in the morning, just when Matt was likely to be on his way to the bathroom, in thrall to the demands of his ageing prostate.

Matt's voice cut through her reverie.

'So shall we do Broadway Tower tomorrow? Then we'll drop into the knife shop and you can prepare your quail while Nigel and I go for a couple of pints. Can't see Sam joining us, can you?'

'Unlikely. And yes to Broadway Tower. Bring a Pre-Raphaelite flavour to the weekend.'

Broadway Tower was a romantic folly, a fake Saxon castle commanding dramatic views over the Cotswold Way. It was where Rossetti had dallied with the wife of William Morris. That sort of behaviour was alright when you were part of an aesthetic movement. Cheating on your husband didn't seem at all shabby if you were a Bohemian. If she could only imagine that she was an artist's muse and John was a dashing poet, it wouldn't seem so bad.

'Maybe I'll drape myself in flowers and float down the river like Ophelia's corpse,' she said. 'Did you know that Millais's painting is the most popular pre-Raphaelite painting, according to Twitter?'

'I do now.'

'Beata Beatrix came second. By Dante Gabriel Rossetti, who was also a poet of course. He changed the order of his names to make Dante come first, so people would make the association.'

'Vain man.'

'Handsome though. Better-looking than William Morris.'

She curled into her side of the bed, thinking of Rossetti's dark and handsome face, the Victorian version of Russell Brand with his revolutionary ideas and louche morals.

'We can buy postcards tomorrow then you'll see what I mean. I couldn't be doing with Morris's big grey beard. Night then, sleep tight.'

Matt nudged up behind her.

'Don't you fancy a bit of married?'

'Married' was their term for sex in which she wasn't fully engaged. The dutiful sort, a throw-back to the days when wives were expected to lie back and think of England. In its most lackadaisical form, it could involve her reading the paper while Matt got on with it. Like a dog worrying a bone, as she sometimes thought. 'I've got my needs,' he would say, half-joking, and Tessa didn't object. Sex was the oil that kept the machine of marriage running and there was no denying it improved his mood.

'If you must.'

She tried not to think about the Tory MP in Paisley pyjamas as they launched into their well-trodden routine. To be fair, Matt wouldn't be seen dead in any form of pyjamas; he was more a T-shirt and boxers sort of person. She closed her eyes and tried to pretend that it was John who was running his hands and mouth all over her. If she really concentrated, maybe she would be able to replicate the excitement of that first night in Yorkshire. But her powers of imagination fell short of the task.

'How was it for you?' Matt asked in the humorous tone he always used after a bit of married.

'Earth-shattering.'

'Did the earth move for you, Nancy?'

'Oh yes.'

'Night then.'

He squeezed her hand in a matey, post-match way and settled down to sleep.

Tessa lay in the darkness, waiting for his snoring to kick in. She remembered the fairy tale where Jack hides in the corner until the giant falls asleep so he can steal the gold and escape back down the beanstalk. Once she was sure that Matt was asleep, the snorts subsiding into a steady rhythm, she picked up her phone, its light glowing in her hands, and ran back over the messages. She shouldn't encourage him, but she couldn't stop herself.

Keep thinking of our time in Dursdale Hall. Please don't reply. Night Night.

Of course he replied.

Plenty more of those to come. Good night, beautiful!!

CHAPTER SIXTEEN

'Three, or even two, meat meals a day tend to make the world look very black to the middle-aged.'

Blanche Ebbutt, *Don'ts for Wives*, 1913, p. 11

The next morning found Nigel engaged in preparing a killer breakfast. Fat sausages were frying alongside man-sized bacon rashers, a saucepan of scrambled eggs thickening on the stove. First up was the porridge, which he carried into the dining room, where a jug of cream and bowl of brown sugar were already set out on the table.

'Here you go, everyone,' he said ladling it out into bowls.

Matt pushed the papers aside. As the man in the post office predicted, he had bought them all. When *The Sunday Times* made him feel sick with envy, he could turn to the *Mirror* and feel better about himself. It was pretty obvious that everyone reading that rag earned less than him.

'Thanks, mate,' he said, pouring in a generous helping of cream, 'notch up those calories, might as well go for it.'

Nigel nodded and passed brimming bowls down the table to the others.

'Not for me,' said Sandra, 'I'm still full of stew.'

'It's amazing what you can put away, isn't it?' said Harriet. 'Imagine if we ate like this every weekend, we'd all be the size of a house.'

'Speaking as someone with a gourmet for a wife, you'll notice that we're already pretty house-sized,' said Matt. He knew it wasn't true. Tessa might be carrying a bit of extra weight, but he was in pretty good shape and was waiting for someone to point it out.

Sandra obliged him.

'Barratt Home rather than mansion,' she said, 'don't be too hard on yourself.'

Nigel sat down and stirred four teaspoons of sugar into his porridge. He had already lined up Sandra's bowl as seconds. She watched him work his way manically through the bowlful, as if his life depended on it. His ferocious appetite was a new thing. She'd read that it was a good sign, that it demonstrated the will to survive in those suffering from depression. Even so, the clinking of his spoon repeatedly against the china was driving her mad. She hadn't confronted him with her suspicions about Paola, though he made no secret of his increasingly frequent visits to her, on a professional basis of course.

'I think I'll leave you to it,' she said, picking up *The Times* magazine and slipping under the table to crawl back to the door, which was the only way of getting out of the narrow room without disturbing the others.

'Your loss,' said Harriet, 'this really is the best porridge I've ever had.'

'Toast the oatmeal first, then simmer for eight and three-quarter minutes, pinch of salt, with exactly two and a half times liquid to volume of oats,' said Nigel, with deadening precision. 'It's not complicated to get it right.'

After breakfast everyone set about preparing to go for A Walk. When they first started coming to this house, nobody bothered, you just went out in your normal shoes. Now they wouldn't dream of stepping out without their merino and Lycra socks beneath their North Face boots, as if they were taking on Everest rather than a few meadows.

Sandra announced she was staying behind to make muffins for tea.

'That's very mumsy of you,' said Tessa.

'I'm on a bit of a baking roll, and I've discovered this fab sugar substitute with zero calories. I'll leave you to do the townies-on-a-walk thing. You do realise that real country people never go for walks, don't you? They just drive everywhere and chop wood if they fancy some exercise.'

'We're driving first, it's too far to walk,' said Harriet. 'Let's take my car as I've got the dog cage in the back.'

Sandra waved them off, then closed the door, enjoying the silence. The muffins were just an excuse; she had no wish to go tramping across muddy fields, following the hunched shoulders of her husband, hands in pockets as he tried to march his way into feeling better about his life. It could wear you down, that relentless negativity. She didn't care how they medicalised it; as far as she was concerned, it was just a case of morbid self-pity.

Her mother would have no truck with it. 'Snap out of it!' she used to say if anyone was looking down in the mouth. 'There's plenty worse off than you and it'll all be the same in a hundred years' time.' Sandra had since learned that the ancient Egyptians considered light-heartedness a virtue. They should teach that at all these bloody management training courses instead of how to be a leader and a team player, which was of course a contradiction in terms, as she had pointed out to Matt last night. Oxymorons for morons.

Before starting on the muffins, she stepped out of the back door for a cigarette, and to phone Mariusz.

'Yes, Sandra,' he said, in his confident, manly tones. She wished he was with her now; she'd like him to arrive in his van and for all the others to melt away on their walk, leaving them alone together. They talked about the quote he had prepared for Sandra's client, and arranged to drive to a specialist tile shop together next week, to find something for the bathroom walls. He reminded her that he missed her person very much.

She pushed her cigarette butt into a flower pot and stepped back into the kitchen. It was a far cry from her own modernist style, with its sloping slate floors and Shaker-style cupboards. They'd all been mad for Shakers in the eighties, longing for Amish austerity and pink-cheeked wholesomeness, like Kelly McGillis in *Witness*. Functional, too, with proper handles on the cupboard doors, as opposed to the sleek surfaces of her Boffi wall of units at home. The architect had insisted on handle-free clean lines, but it was pretty much guesswork when it came to tapping on the correct part of the panel to see if it would open.

She took out the Valhrona chocolate and her new fetish ingredient, Xylitol. What could be better than something that tastes of sugar which doesn't make you fat? She couldn't believe it had taken someone so long to come up with it. Even so, she was using mini muffin cases; there was no need to go completely mad just because you were in the country where nobody would look at you. You must always remember that you were returning to the chic slimness of the city. Jack Sprat could eat no fat, his wife could eat no lean, the other way round in their case, since Nigel had entered his big eating phase and was getting her to fill the fridge with all kinds of carbohydrate stodge.

Once the muffins were safely in the oven, Sandra went into the living room and stretched out on the Chesterfield, gazing round the room to think about what she would do with it. It wasn't impossible that Harriet would hire her, Sam was pretty loaded and Harriet would be the first to admit that her understanding of decor was immutably rooted in the 1980s. Sandra could work with her, to bring her gently into an understanding of Modern Country that would harmonise with her traditional values. Think Project Burgundy, deep colours, maturing like a fine wine, lightened with amusing touches of prosecco, a playful chandelier, perhaps, or a line of ironic flying ducks, subverting the hunting-shooting-fishing stereotype. She could come down for weekends with Mariusz while they worked on the project together.

'You go ahead, I'm going to sit here for a bit. I'll meet you back at the car.'

Tessa threw her coat down on the grass behind Broadway Tower, then sat on the improvised groundsheet to take in the glorious view. Sixteen counties they said you could see from the top, rolling green countryside with ancient trees concealing houses where you might live happily ever after. Roses growing round the door which you would brush past as you returned from the vegetable garden, your trug filled with fresh peas for supper and sweet peas for the table, displayed in a simple jam jar.

She watched their retreating figures, Matt and Nigel looking out of place in their sharp urban monochrome, while Harriet blended into the landscape with her frumpy tweeds and dogs.

Once she was sure they were out of sight, she reached into her coat pocket for the packet of ten Silk Cut she had bought from the Spar earlier that morning, after taking a quick look round the shop to make sure there was nobody she knew. You couldn't get away with anything if you lived in a village, she'd realised;

there would always be someone to catch you buying something you shouldn't, tracking your every move, net curtains twitching as you left the house.

She inhaled and allowed the first hit of nicotine to conjure up the cigarette she had shared with John in the dark garden of the Manoir aux Quat'Saisons. Imagine if he suddenly turned up now, what would she do? If he came round that corner and said he'd come to fetch her, that they were destined to be together, that he'd waited all these years and now it was their time. Would she stand up and take his hand and walk away to romantic fulfilment and an exciting unknown future?

As if in response, her phone buzzed. It was early in the States, he must have been kept awake by their exchange last night, unable to sleep for thinking about her. But it was from Lola.

Got a boring essay to write. I really hate my course.

Tessa tensed up with the familiar mix of love and anxiety. Could she not for one moment be free of the umbilical link that channelled her children's unhappiness directly though to her core? It wasn't as if there was anything she could do about it, miles away and with no idea what the task involved. Her days of supervising homework were dead and buried.

She tapped out her reply.

Poor you, but that's life I'm afraid, it's not all fun and games.

And I've been really sick. I had to miss the fancy dress ball last night.

Oh dear, are you better now?

Yes, it was just a one-day thing. But I've got the hockey dinner tonight so I don't know when I'm going to get this essay done.

I'm sure you'll manage. I'm at Broadway Tower.

Awesome. Can't wait to turn into you and have nothing to worry about. X

Tessa put her phone back in her pocket. She couldn't very well tell Lola that actually she did have something to worry about, that she was wondering whether to leave her father and start again with somebody else. Somebody Lola didn't know and would never come to accept. Somebody who would rip the heart out of their family unit.

Just time for one more cigarette, then she would go back and meet them at the car. This time it tasted sour and the hit was less intense. She remembered how ultimately disappointing smoking was. You always wanted another one and it was never quite enough. And it made you smell. Luckily she had a packet of Tic-Tacs to neutralise the taste.

But nothing could get past Matt's overdeveloped senses.

'Have you been smoking?' he said as she slipped into the back seat beside him.

'Course not!'

'Don't lie, I can smell it.'

'Must have been Sandra when she borrowed my coat last night to go out for a fag.'

'You've got a very sensitive nose,' said Harriet, starting the engine, 'I hope you're not bothered by the dogs.'

'I've always thought I should have worked for a perfume house,' said Matt. 'I would have been a brilliant nose. Or a wine expert, I'm always the first to pick up the peaty undertones and heather notes. Don't you find that you're always wishing you'd done something else? I know I do, I'm constantly thinking I should have followed a different career path, keeps me awake at night that does.'

'Infinite regrets,' said Tessa. 'Do buck up.'

'Look on the bright side,' said Harriet, 'at least you're not an unemployable housewife.'

'I've got one of those as well. Bloody unfair, don't you think?'

Here we go again, thought Tessa.

'I'll be earning my keep tonight,' she said. 'De-boning that quail.'

'I sympathise, Matt,' said Nigel. 'But you have to remind yourself that there is no ideal job. You need to bundle up those negative thoughts and push them to one side. That's what my therapist Paola has taught me, I can't tell you how much she's helped me.'

*

Back at the house, it was agreed that lunch would be a mistake, but Sandra's home-made muffins with a cup of tea would be just the thing. They grouped round the fire with plates on their knees, making appreciative noises.

'Nice muffins,' said Tessa, 'can't think why you'd want to ruin the taste with tea.'

'You're a freak,' said Sandra, 'everyone loves tea in this country.'

'Not me. Pale and insipid. Not to mention the leaden jokes. Lesbian tea. Builders' tea. Could stand a spoon up in that! Ha bloody ha.'

'You're grumpy,' said Matt, looking up from his newspaper. 'I'm just reading here about how middle-aged women don't want to be married any more. Is that it, are you sick of me?'

Sandra intervened.

'I must say that, to my shame, I used to feel a bit sorry for wives who had been left by their husbands. Now I'm quite jealous.'

Nigel shot her a look.

'Thanks,' he said, 'that makes me feel good. Who wants to play Scrabble?'

He opened the box.

'It depends on the timing,' Sandra went on. 'It's one thing when you've got a young child, but once they've grown up, you've got to ask yourself what's the point in being married.'

'Companionship,' said Matt. 'Someone to blame when things go wrong. Regular sex.'

He had finished his muffin and had moved on to a bowl of crisps. Tessa was transfixed by the noise he was making as he made his way through them. She stared at him, busy jaws working like a greedy rabbit, chomp, chomp, chomp. One of the pugs was snaffling up the pieces as they fell to the floor, wheezing and salivating. He'd already worked his way round the room, cleaning up the muffin crumbs.

'I'll play, Nigel,' she said.

'And me,' said Harriet.

'Loads more muffins if anyone wants them,' said Sandra. 'I'm going to check out that antiques shop down the road. 'I'm determined to embrace vintage. It's so cheap, if I had a big barn I'd fill it with old brown furniture, it's bound to come back up.'

'What's the difference between vintage and antique?' asked Matt, between mouthfuls. 'Am I right in thinking vintage just means any old shit?'

'Pretty much,' said Sandra. 'Come with me, if you like.'

'OK.'

Matt jumped up and went over to Tessa, but stopped just as he reached her.

'Oh! I was about to kiss you, but then I noticed you've got a blueberry stuck between your teeth and I was slightly repulsed.'

He turned round and followed Sandra out into the street, then banged on the window.

Tessa looked up and saw him grinning through the leaded glass, pointing to his teeth.

She ignored him.

'You go first then, Nigel.'

They settled into a competitive rhythm. Nigel was a tactical player who appeared to have swallowed the entire Scrabble dictionary of obscure two-letter words. This sat badly with Harriet's sense of fair play.

'You can't have "jo"! And what is "za" supposed to mean?'

'Diminutive of pizza, trust me, it's in the book. And "jo" is Scottish for darling.'

'Well I'm not sure about this. In my opinion, you shouldn't be allowed any word that you don't use in normal conversation.'

'It's in the book,' said Nigel, 'you can't change the rules to suit yourself.'

He won by a safe margin, and Tessa left them arguing about opposing theories of the game while she attended to the subtle butchering of the quail: removing their frail bones to reduce their tender bodies to small parcels of flesh.

She no longer felt the intense pleasure she used to find in preparing food. It would be different in the wild; hunting and capturing your prey, tossing it on the fire to ensure your survival. Now it just seemed frivolous and decadent.

She knew she was facing a choice. To continue her role as nurturer, channelling her refined skills into feeding the one last baby still in her care, the resentful provider who found her plump and lazy. Or she could be brave and magnificent, walk out of this tired old marriage into the unknown with a man she barely knew, but who worshipped the ground she walked on.

She inserted the point of the Global blade (it was essential to bring your own knives, you couldn't trust other people's) into the breast of the bird and thought about sex with John. The intensity of it, the feeling that this was all that mattered, that everything else was peripheral compensation for those who weren't getting it.

'Do you need a hand?'

Harriet was in the doorway, concerned face, cashmere twinset with a double string of pearls, the walking embodiment of someone who wasn't getting it.

'No, I'm alright thanks.'

An American friend of hers had made her laugh once, recounting how she had offered her sexual services to an attractive estate agent. Or a realtor, if you wanted to make him sound more glamorous, and he was the MD, as the friend had pointed out, not a jobsworth in a shiny suit. 'I knew he'd say yes,' she said, 'because I'd met his wife and she had one of those handbags like the queen has, that sits on the table with hoop handles. You know that anyone married to a woman with a bag like that isn't getting any sex.'

Harriet had many such bags.

Tessa was woken the next morning by a piercing scream.

She nudged Matt.

'What was that?'

He grunted and rolled over.

'Didn't you hear it?'

She was out of bed in an instant, throwing on her dressing gown and running down the stairs.

She followed the sound of sobbing to the kitchen, to find Harriet crouched over one of her pugs, who was lying on the floor.

'Benson! Oh no, no . . .'

Tessa was no animal-lover but she could see this was a tragedy. The dog was panting noisily, his eyes glazed over, making no response to Harriet's increasingly distressed attempts to revive him.

'He's eaten something. I don't know what's happened, he's never been like this before . . .'

Beside him was an empty cake tin, the lid dislodged, crumbs scattered on the floor.

'The muffins,' said Tessa. 'Sandra put them on that low shelf, he must have got into the tin.'

She was always appalled by the way Harriet's dogs helped themselves to any food that was within reach. Like the pigs she'd seen in Thailand, cleaning up the floor beneath the huts, eating scraps of food and, worse, the effluent of the primitive lavatories.

'We need to get him to a vet,' said Harriet. 'The number's by the phone, can you fetch it for me?'

Tessa went through to the hall, where she found a list of useful numbers, neatly copied out in Harriet's careful script.

'Here you are,' she said, bringing in the phone and the list. 'Do you want me to call?'

'No, give it to me.'

Tessa listened to her describing the symptoms, and remembered when she had made a similar call. In the middle of the night when Lola was four years old and she'd been terrified it was meningitis. Shining a light into her eyes and seeing if she could move her chin down to her chest. Thankfully her fears had been ungrounded.

Harriet put the phone down and stood up.

'I'm taking him in now, they think it was the xylitol, that sugar substitute that Sandra used.'

Tessa put her arm round her friend.

'It'll be fine, they'll sort him out.'

'I hope so, but look at him, poor Benson.'

He didn't look good, lying completely motionless apart from the rise and fall of his difficult breathing. Tessa was less hopeful than she let on.

'They'll be able to do something. Come on, I'll go with you, let's get dressed.'

'Will you? You are kind.'

'Of course, let's go.'

'Emergency trip to the vet,' she said to Matt as she hastily pulled on her clothes in the bedroom. 'Looks like Sandra's killed the dog with her diet food.'

Matt raised his head from the pillow.

'Really? Which one?'

'Benson. Still breathing, but looking pretty comatose.'

'No change there, then.'

'Don't be horrible. I admit he's not my favourite animal, but poor Harriet.'

'You're taking her car, presumably?'

'Yes, don't panic. I'm not going to risk soiling the Mazza with death fluids.'

Two hours later, Tessa escorted Harriet back to the car. The vet said he'd keep him overnight for observation, and would call if there was any change. Tessa was still reeling from the costs involved.

'I'm not being funny, but you could check him into the Lygon Arms for that amount. Four-poster suite.'

'No, that's not funny,' said Harriet, 'but I know you're only trying to cheer me up.'

Tessa decided not to share her thoughts about how many children could be lifted out of poverty for the price of a critical care package for one domestic animal.

'There's nothing more you can do,' she said, 'you should try to get some rest. Do you want to ring Sam?'

'I already have, he's coming down later. So you won't need to stay the night.'

'If you're sure. Matt needs to get back for work, but you know I'll stay if you need me.'

'Thanks.'

Harriet squeezed her hand.

'I do appreciate it.'

She wiped her eyes.

'I know it's silly, but you get so attached . . .'

Having a pet was a recipe for heartbreak, thought Tessa as they drove back to the house. Cradling the dog on her lap on the way to the vet, she had given silent thanks for not caving in to Max and Lola; it could only ever end one way. Just do the maths; you were buying a ticking time bomb when you brought home that adorable little puppy with an average life expectancy of fourteen years. They said it was good for children, to give them an early experience of loss, a sort of bereavement lite, to rehearse the pain that was waiting down the line. Tessa didn't buy it, there was enough sadness in the world without voluntarily adding to it.

Sandra opened the door to them.

'Harriet, what can I say? I'm so, so sorry.'

Harriet shook her head.

'Don't be silly, how were you to know? I just don't understand how they're allowed to sell the stuff.'

'And there was me banging on about this great product with no calories. I feel terrible, really I do.'

'I said it's OK.'

'Just goes to prove, really, that I'm not cut out for baking. Poison-fingered witch.'

'If you'd just thought to close the lid on the box properly,' said Harriet, 'there's no way he could have knocked it off if it had been tightly fitted.'

'I know, I'm really sorry.'

'This isn't something I usually say,' said Tessa, 'but I think we could all do with a cup of tea.'

'Well, that was an unfortunate end to the weekend,' said Matt as they set off, 'a dead dog and service restored to my phone, with a load of messages I could do without.'

'He's not dead yet.'

'No, but I'm not optimistic for the prognosis. Liver failure can't be good news.'

'Poor Harriet, she's so upset. At least she's got the other one. Maybe she'll get a new one to go with it.'

'And so the cycle continues, the relentless bind of pet owner-ship. I've never understood why you'd want to saddle yourself like that. Especially retired people, they've got time to go any-where they want, instead of which they choose to walk to the end of the street twice a day to let the dog have a shit.'

'I suppose we're just not pet people.'

'One of our shared non-interests. Mind you, Colin at work recently got a dog and said it's the most amazing fanny-magnet. He's never had so many attractive women coming up to talk to him.'

He pulled into a garage.

'Might as well fill up before we reach the motorway.'

She watched him get out of the car and help himself to a pair of clear plastic gloves, carefully pulling them on before handling the pump. What a fastidious, feminine thing to do, she never bothered with them herself.

John wouldn't worry about his hands smelling of petrol. He was comfortable around machines; she could just imagine him wielding a chainsaw, starting the engine with an effortless flick of the cord, whereas it was always a performance when Matt decided to trim the hedge. Leafing through the instruction booklet with a frown, cursing the bloody thing for cutting out every time, muttering about the flooded engine and faulty chain. You should have married an oily rag, he'd said to her once when she was mocking his attempts, I never claimed to be a mechanic.

Matt knocked the nozzle against the tank, to ensure he'd got the last few drops, then replaced the handle and peeled off the gloves. As he went in to pay, Tessa noticed a customer on his way out casting admiring glances at their car, checking it out as he returned to his own ordinary vehicle. Men were such babies, with their envy of other boys' shiny toys.

She checked her phone. Nothing since the last message. She read it again.

Skype tonight, I've got news.

Matt was on his way back, so she slipped the phone into her bag.

'I've just come up with a brilliant thing for my client,' he said as he slid back into the driving seat. 'It's amazing how a change of scene can free you up creatively. And I do love a bit of alliteration. Listen to this: Reward, Relationship, Reassurance and Repetition. The four Rs.'

There's a coincidence, thought Tessa.

'Are you adding R & R to that?' she asked.

'What?'

'Rest and Recreation. Make it six Rs.'

He shook his head impatiently.

'Don't be silly. Anyway, what do you think?'

'Umm. Well, it's four words beginning with R.'

'As I said. Alliteration. And a list, always best to have a list of three or four things.'

'So what does it mean, exactly?'

'It's the four Rs. The guarantees they give their customers. Good, isn't it?'

'I guess. How much did they pay you for that?'

'What do you mean, how much did they pay me for that?'

He shot her an aggressive sideways look.

'Nothing,' she said. 'Just wondering, in an admiring way.'

'I get it, you're having one of your little digs, looking down your nose at what I do, as usual.'

'No I'm not!'

'Yes you are, and you know what, I'm sick of it! It's alright for you to sit there and sneer at my job, you don't have to go out and earn the money.'

Tessa closed her eyes and wished she could be somewhere else. The scented white garden of Dursdale Hall, for example.

'You and your supposed feminist views!' Matt continued. 'You're a fake feminist, that's what you are, living off me and doing bugger all. Why don't you get out there and fend for yourself, like most self-respecting women!'

They continued the journey in silence, through the villages that had looked so attractive on the way up and which now appeared stern and oppressive. Stone houses on market squares gazing out disapprovingly through mullioned windows over the queue of traffic that snaked its way along roads designed for horse-drawn carriages.

'You still not talking to me?' asked Matt, as the M4 channelled down to two lanes after Heathrow and crawled to a standstill.

The street lights were set lower here, in deference to the planes that came swooping in overhead. On either side of the motorway were boring expanses of houses and offices. Only when they were over the Hammersmith flyover and coming into the Earls Court turn-off did you feel you were properly in London. Was she a London person, the way John claimed he wasn't? She was inasmuch as she didn't belong anywhere else. It was probably too late now to put down roots in a cosy community where everyone knew everyone else and the neighbours would drop round, beaming goodwill and bearing trays of mince pies.

They emptied the car without speaking and Tessa opened the door to the empty house. A pair of Max's trainers discarded in the hall gave her false hope, but he'd been and gone, leaving only an empty biscuit packet on the table. It always amused her, the way they'd help themselves to food and forget to dispose of the evidence. If you're going to steal a packet of sweets, don't give yourself away by dropping the wrappers, she'd told him once when he was about seven, call yourself a thief! In a way it was reassuring that he hadn't changed at all.

Matt took his computer into the study.

'I've got some work to do, don't wait up.'

Max had left a note on the table, sorry to miss them, he'd done his washing, maybe he'd come over for dinner in the week. Tessa went into the laundry to find his clothes thrown haphazardly over the rack. She rearranged them to optimise drying, putting the shirts on hangers, marrying up the pairs of socks. It only seemed like yesterday that she was hanging out his babygrows, then his trousers, increasing in size over the years until they were longer than his father's. 'You lanky beanpole,' Matt had said in affectionate mock indignation, inspecting the label on a pair of Levis that Max had just bought. 'I wish my leg measurement was two inches longer than my waist!'

Tessa took her laptop upstairs into Lola's room to make the Skype call, where she wouldn't be disturbed by Matt. The bed was still covered with discarded clothes from Lola's last visit home, she'd have to tidy them up when she came home for Christmas.

John came through, his voice had its usual effect on her, and she closed her eyes to think herself back into the four-poster bed.

'Weekend in the country, then?' he was saying. 'How was the room service? I'm guessing it didn't match up to last time?'

He was coming back in two weeks, he said. They should go away somewhere to make plans for their future. He'd been giving it some thought; if she wasn't comfortable with America, they could go elsewhere. Once he sold his company he'd be free as air. They could just fly away like a couple of birds wherever she wanted. 'Don't look back,' he said, 'don't throw away this great chance for happiness. It doesn't happen to everyone, it is a gift to be cherished.'

CHAPTER SEVENTEEN

'Don't think you can each go your own way and be as happy as if you pulled in double harness.'

Blanche Ebbutt, *Don'ts for Wives*, 1913

'I suppose I'd better offer to make you a cup of tea,' said Sam, now they were back from the vets where Benson had died during the night. Painlessly and at peace according to the well-rehearsed animal nurse who had been recruited for her caring manner.

Harriet sat on the Chesterfield with Hedges on her lap, enjoying the privilege of being the only one.

'To be honest, I'd rather have something stronger. I've drunk enough tea for one morning.'

Sam didn't need encouraging, and went straight to the drinks cabinet to bring out the whisky.

'Remember bidding on his?' he said, patting the mahogany top of the handsome piece of furniture. 'It was over our budget, but we really wanted it because it was bow-fronted. Funny how your priorities change over the years.'

'Our hearts used to leap at the sight of anything burnished and Victorian,' said Harriet. 'I'm over it now, though, the decorating phase. You too, I think?'

It was an invitation to discuss how he was feeling. They had been getting on so well since last night, when he had changed his plans so he could come down and join her here in the house where they had always been happiest. Mirela had been willing to stay an extra night with Celia, who was quite enamoured of her new friend.

'God, yes,' he said, handing her a glass of whisky then sitting down in the armchair. 'I'd be happy never to choose another stick of furniture in my life.'

'Thank you for cancelling your meeting,' said Harriet. 'It would have been horrid to do it on my own. Though I'm glad we decided against the garden burial, it's much more sensible to have the canister of ashes.'

Sam twisted the glass in his hands, looked away from her for a moment, then turned back to face her.

'Harriet, we need to talk.'

She carefully lifted Hedges down on to the carpet and prepared herself for what he was going to say. This was it, he was going to suggest they put an end to the farce of their marriage, it was hardly unexpected. She faced him calmly.

'I'm listening.'

'I spoke to mum's doctor and, as he told her, it's not good news. He reckons six months, a year at best.'

Harriet felt a lifting of her spirits, he wasn't leaving her then.

'Oh dear, as quickly as that,' she said. 'I didn't get such a precise prognosis from the hospital, but I was with Celia and I suppose unless she was specifically asking . . .'

'Exactly, but now we know.'

'Poor Celia. We must make things as comfortable as we can for her.'

'You've already done so much for her, I'm very grateful. Harriet, what I want to ask you is, will you come to New York with me?'

'New York!'

He'd never invited her along on a business trip before, it was an attractive prospect.

'Yes, I'd like that, when were you thinking? I could try and get Mirela to cover for a weekend.'

'I don't mean a weekend,' said Sam. 'I'm looking at relocating permanently. And I'd like you to come with me, it would be a new beginning for us.'

She hadn't seen that coming! Completely and utterly out of the blue! She imagined herself walking in Central Park, attending intellectual salons; she had a friend who had moved there recently and said it was far more acceptable – even expected – to have serious conversations. It was an extraordinarily exciting prospect.

'But what about Celia?' she said.

'Obviously, we'll wait until . . .'

'Yes.'

'I've explained the position to Eric and we're looking at next October, possibly later.'

'The fall!' said Harriet, imagining them on a weekend in New England, kicking through the massive American-sized red leaves before repairing to a diner for pancakes.

'We'll only need a small apartment in Manhattan, then I thought a place up the Hudson River for weekends.'

'Oh yes!'

Harriet jumped up and went over to hug Sam.

'Alex can come and spend weekends with his glamorous girl-friend and James can visit us, it will be fantastic!'

'Good, so I'll take that as a yes, shall I?' said Sam.

'Yes indeed. A very definite yes.'

Sandra was not in the best mood when she arrived home, following an auction where she had made a schoolgirl error. By mistaking a lot number, she ended up buying an enormous stuffed bear instead of the chandelier she had her eye on as a centrepiece for Megan's dining room. She could hear the television and went downstairs to find Poppy catching up on *The X Factor*, eating a blueberry muffin.

'Mind those crumbs on my new ottoman.'

'How was your auction?' asked Poppy, without taking her eyes off the screen. 'Did you buy something fab for Kim's mum?'

'Actually, it was a bit of a disaster.'

She told Poppy about her mistake.

'So funny,' said Poppy. 'I must tell Kim.'

She switched off the television.

'Actually, please don't. It is a bit embarrassing when I'm trying to appear professional.'

'OK. Dad's gone out by the way, he told you not to wait up for him.'

'Did he say where?'

'Nope. But he seemed pretty happy.'

'Really?'

'Yes. Haven't seen him like that for a while. Kind of excited, running up the stairs and singing.'

'Oh. Do you want a cup of anything?'

'Tea please. I'll come up with you actually, I need to do some work.'

Poppy followed her up the stairs, then pulled out her school books and settled down at the kitchen table.

'By the way, Mum, I can't believe you added Josh.'

'Added him to what?'

'On Facebook. You sent him a friend request.'

'Oh that. Well he didn't have to accept, did he?'

'He didn't want to offend you.'

If he didn't want to offend me, thought Sandra, he shouldn't have posted a pornographic image of himself.

'Actually, Poppy, I've got a bit of a confession to make. You left your page open on my iPad, and I got to look at your photos.'

'Mum!'

'I know, it was wrong, but I'm just nosy, I can't help it.'

Poppy was looking at her, trying to assess the damage.

'Which ones did you see? You didn't go into my messages or anything, did you?'

'Not really. Only a bit.'

'You didn't! Honestly, Mum, that's so low!'

Poppy put her hands over eyes, as if that could somehow prevent Sandra from seeing the compromising photo. Sandra went up to her and gave her a hug.

'I'm sorry, darling, I know I shouldn't have looked, but I am your mum so of course I want to know what's going on in your life. And I didn't realise that you and Josh were actually, you know . . .'

'I'm not a little girl any more, Mum! I can't believe you'd go snooping on me like that!'

Poppy pushed her mother away.

'It was wrong, I know that,' said Sandra. 'But when you have a child of your own, you'll understand. I realise you're not a little girl any more, but you always will be, to me.'

Poppy relented and wrapped her arms round Sandra's waist.

'I know, Mum. I love you.'

'Love you too.'

'Yuck,' said Sandra and they both laughed.

They remained locked together for a while, then Sandra said:

'But the reason I had to tell you I'd seen the photo . . . I wanted to be absolutely sure, you are being careful, aren't you? I'd love to have a grandchild some day, but not too soon.'

'Chillax, Mum, I'm on the pill.'

Sandra felt a mixture of emotions. Relief that her daughter was being sensible, and disbelief that her little girl was grown up enough to consult a doctor for contraceptive advice. As a mother, she was through to the next stage. Adulthood beckoned, and Sandra would soon be free.

'I'm glad you are, thank you for telling me and I promise I won't do it again,' she said. 'The only photos of Josh that I'll look at from now on are the ones he puts on his wall. Fully clothed, more's the pity.'

'Mum!'

They sat in companionable silence, Poppy with her school-work while Sandra emailed Megan that there was disappointing news on the chandelier, but she was sure there would be other, even better examples out there. Then she saw she had a missed call from Mariusz and a voicemail. This was unusual, he didn't tend to leave messages, relying on her to simply return his call. She listened to what he had to say:

'Sandra, please, I realise we must be living together. When I see Gregor lying beside me I know this is mistake and it must be you. I love you. Yours, etc.'

She smiled at the last bit. Somehow he'd picked up the idea that this was how English gentlemen signed off, as if dictating to a secretary with a dismissive flap of the hand. There was work to be done on his language skills, but she knew she could help him with that. Watching Poppy's head bowed over her homework, she knew her competent daughter was going to be just fine. And she had a pretty good idea where Nigel was this evening.

Max had been rather coy about his appearance in a university play, but he had eventually mentioned it to his parents. He was playing the lead role in *Le Misanthrope* and would get them a couple of tickets if they were interested. 'Of course we're interested,' Tessa said, 'do you really need to ask?'

Walking out to catch the bus, she fantasised that she was at the Oscars and Max was on stage, modestly taking his gong, his marvellous hair flopping over his eyes, like a less-annoying Hugh Grant. She had no idea he was in the Drama Soc, he had always been rather dismissive of actors; they were boring beyond belief, he said, always talking about themselves.

John wanted them to meet out of town again. 'Anywhere with a four-poster bed,' he said, 'we know where we'll be spending our time.' She wished she could just press a button and be there with him, without the attendant complications. As if they were teenagers who could do exactly as they pleased, without the clutter of half a lifetime. She recalled a conversation she and Matt had shared about the definition of middle-age. It was the point, he said, when the future starts to look less appetising than the past. As you went through your thirties and forties, you always felt that you were on your way up, that things were getting better all the time. Then suddenly, bang, you're fifty and the upward curve hits a plateau. Then the descent. Tessa disagreed. She now knew it didn't have to be that way.

She smiled at the driver as she touched in her oyster card. It was such a depressing thought, that you were careering down-hill. There were plenty of cheerful people over fifty, just as there were misery-guts amongst the young. On the bus behind her right now, for instance, she could hear a girl outlining her gap year plans to her friend, in the bored, flat voice adopted by the beautiful rich.

'So I'm going to Thailand in January,' she said, as if the whole thing was a chore, 'then on to Cambodia.'

'Fantastic,' said her friend, without enthusiasm.

Silly little girls, thought Tessa. And I'm off to the Bloomsbury Theatre to watch my beautiful son, so stick that in your posh pipe and smoke it.

The girls got off at South Kensington, floating down the stairs in a cloud of ennui, and Tessa tuned in instead to the conver-sation of two elderly gentlemen sitting across from her. One was complaining about his health and how his insurance only allowed him occasional visits to the specialist, then they lapsed into incomprehensible public school banter. 'Was he a Wyke-hamist?' 'Ah yes, he was Scottish.' 'Not very Scottish, though.' 'No, he was a Rugbeian.' Not for the first time, Tessa thought how eavesdropping on the bus was one of London's greatest cheap pleasures.

The theatre was filling up when she arrived, a generous audi-ence of friends and family members who were predisposed to love whatever they were going to see. From her seat Tessa could see Matt arriving, dapper in his subdued shades of dark grey. She watched him make his way towards her and thought about how it would be if she told him she was leaving him.

CHAPTER EIGHTEEN

'Don't believe that marriage is a lottery over which you have no control.'

Blanche Ebbutt, *Don'ts For Wives*, 1913

'So let's get this right,' said Sandra. 'He wants to leave you all his money and you said no?'

She crashed her espresso cup on to its saucer and looked at her friend in mock disbelief.

'That was a good weekend's work. You obviously have some serious Wallis Simpson skills. I'm surprised you're only telling me this now!'

'He'd already altered his will, even before the weekend.'

'It must be love.'

They were in the Members' Lounge above the Hayward Gallery in the Southbank Centre. Through the plate-glass window, they could look down at the busy life of the river; boats ferrying workers and tourists against an architectural backdrop of monuments old and new, the Gherkin standing proudly beside St Paul's Cathedral.

'Obviously he'll change it, depending on what happens,' said Tessa. 'He's acting as if we're already an item, because that's how he sees it.'

'Pushing for an early resolution. Do you like my new club by the way?'

The tables around them were occupied by people earnestly studying their laptops. It was London's best-kept secret, Sandra explained, a hundred quid a year and the perfect place for entrepreneurs like her to meet their clients and impress them with views of the city.

'It's very you,' said Tessa.

'I think so,' said Sandra, catching the eye of a hipster on the next table who was giving her an admiring glance.

'So, what are you going to do? Walk out on us all and set up home in the distant reaches of Oklahoma?'

'Wyoming, actually.'

'I don't see it, myself. You in *The Little House on the Prairie*. In a gingham dress.'

'That's Wisconsin. Anyway, it wouldn't have to be Wyoming. He said we can go anywhere I like. He said the world is our oyster. In fact he wants to buy a boat and go sailing round the world.'

Sandra raised an eyebrow. 'Ambitious, I like that.'

'He said there were no limits. We can do whatever we want. Which is true, I suppose. Except he has no baggage. And I do. For twenty years I've defined myself as a mother, I don't know what I am if I'm not that.'

'You'll always be a mother. It doesn't mean you can't be other things as well.'

'I know. But I can't trash everything I've got just for the sake of that giddy excitement. Maybe if I was braver . . .'

Sandra watched her friend, could see she was close to tears.

'You are brave, Tessa,' she said gently. 'You could do it, if you really wanted to. But I'm not sure you do.'

Tessa shook her head.

'You're right, I just don't know. When I'm with him, he makes it sound so simple. Look at this.'

She passed her phone to Sandra, showing a photo of a boat.

'He's already researched the exact model for optimum comfort and seaworthiness. We're supposed to go on a crash course in sailing, then go off round the Pacific.'

Sandra pulled a face.

'And get shipwrecked on a desert island and eat insects for the rest of your miserable lives. Or else get captured by murderous Somalian pirates. Do you think Matt would pay the ransom?'

'It's not funny.'

'Sorry. Quite thrilling though. Makes my plans sound pedestrian by comparison.'

'Your plans?'

'I've decided to leave Nigel and move in with Mariusz.'

'No!'

Tessa saw that Sandra was sparkling with excitement.

'It's all agreed. Turns out I've done Nigel a favour as he's in love with his therapist. Totally unprofessional but there you go.'

'Don't believe it! When did this happen?'

'Been going on for a while, apparently. All that anxiety and manic eating has been to do with his reluctance to give in to his true feelings. Didn't want to let me down, he said. Patronising bastard.'

'That's a bit harsh, he was unwell before he met her – that's why he met her.'

'You should see him now, right as rain. He's got a real spring in his step. It's like a giant weight has been lifted from his shoulders. That weight being me, obviously.'

'And what about you?'

'I'm happy! I've got a real sense of purpose, I'm going into business with Mariusz, offering full service from design through execution. And I don't need to tell you how it feels to be having proper sex again. With a hot young man in my case, of course.'

'You've always been more interested in physical appearances than I have,' said Tessa.

'I know, you've got the moral high ground as usual. Oh no, hang on . . .'

Tessa frowned.

'But seriously, Sandra, I'm really happy for you. Does Poppy know?'

'We told her last night. She's surprisingly cool about it. I guess the atmosphere at home's been pretty poisonous lately and she can see it's better to have two happy parents living apart rather than sniping at each other. Although she's such a little snob she'd rather Mairusz wasn't a builder, she would have preferred a techie entrepreneur or something.'

'Well, good for you.'

Over a second cup of coffee, Sandra outlined her plans. They'd sell the house, she would buy an apartment, for her and Mariusz to renovate, she was thinking two bedrooms and an enormous living space, a lateral conversion. She was sick of stairs and who needed all those poky little up and down rooms? Poppy would divide her time between them, everything would be hunky-dory.

As she listened to Sandra explaining her plans in such precise, realisable detail, Tessa knew for sure she wasn't going to leave Matt. They went down in the lift to where Sandra had parked her bike and said their goodbyes.

'Think hard before you make your decision,' said Sandra. 'I know I'm doing the right thing, it just feels like where I should be. But I'm not sure your heart's really in it.'

Tessa watched her cycle off, then started walking slowly along the embankment. Tourists were taking photographs of themselves, excited family groups grinning in front of the giant wheel. A Thames Clipper boat steamed past, the chic way to travel to work. John had talked about bringing the boat up the Thames to a mooring in St Katharine's Dock. They could stay there for a few days and do London, he said, after they'd completed the transatlantic voyage and achieved the nautical miles necessary to join the Ocean Cruising Club. 'It's our kind of club', he'd told her, 'for people who've said "yes" to adventure!' They

could paint the town red, really live it up the way she deserved –
and she'd be able to see her kids while they were there, before he
whisked her off to sail round the Norwegian fjords.

It was the way he said it, so casually, as if spending time with
her children was a small detail in their grandiose plans. He
didn't seem to understand they weren't just a parenthesis, they
were, still, the centre of her world. Just as Matt, for all his failings, was still at the heart of her existence. They had made a life
together, you couldn't just walk away and make another one.
Or at least she couldn't.

She made her way up on to Westminster Bridge, the traffic
surging past her, Big Ben rising up, newly stripped of its scaffolding. She suddenly felt lonely and estranged in the bustle and
heaving activity of her own city.

Uber cabs were all very well, thought Matt, but you had to admit
that driving to work in your own car was the best possible start
to the day. For one thing, you didn't have to engage the driver in
polite conversation which always ended in them asking you to
give them five stars.

He pushed the seat back to its normal position. Tessa had left
her usual debris, a congealed coffee cup, a screwed-up empty
crisp wrapper. One thing you could say about her; she hadn't
shaped up into a tidy middle-aged woman, she was still the
messy girl he had met all those years ago.

Marriage is like a dull meal with the dessert at the beginning. That's what Toulouse Lautrec said in the old John Huston film he'd watched on Saturday night, when he was eating his solitary TV dinner.

Slowing down at a zebra to let a group of long-haired beauties cross the road, he let his mind wander lustfully back to some early highlights. The steamy hotel room in Istanbul where they'd broken the bed and had to do a runner; the Suffolk graveyard where they'd performed acts to make the dead blush; their first flat in Brixton with no furniture except a saggy mattress. The homes had become more luxurious over the years, without too disastrous a decline in the quality of their sex life. Until the chilliness that had recently crept into their marital bed, isolating them into mutual resentment.

By the time he reached Brompton Cross, the traffic had reached a standstill, then an ambulance came flashing up behind him, forging its way past on the wrong side of the road. Some poor cyclist, maybe, it was one a month on average, giving rise to the ghostly white bicycles propped up on roadsides through-out the city to remind motorists of the terrible consequences of a moment's inattention.

Damn, he had an important meeting this morning and it wasn't looking good. Satnav couldn't be trusted in London, but maybe it could pick up traffic updates to suggest an alternative route. He clicked on the memory button to bring up his office address. Scrolling down the list, there were lots of northern-sounding places, Tessa must have set destinations to take the scenic route. Appleby, Gillamoor, evocative names to feed his retirement fantasies, when he could give up this nonsense and start living again, planting raspberry canes behind the manor house they would buy on the fringes of a pretty village. He might even take up drinking bitter again, or craft beer, as you now had to call it, parking his pewter mug on a hook behind the local bar and becoming the old bore he pretended to despise but secretly aspired to be.

Running through the list, he stopped at a name that was familiar. Thirsk, he'd been there on a childhood holiday, staying on a working farm where he'd been allowed to stroke a sheep, he could still feel the wiry toughness of the wool and the oily trace it left on his hand, smelling of grass and something more metallic. It wasn't in the Lake District, though, it was in Yorkshire, he remembered buying a postcard from the post office with a cartoon of a simple-looking fellow in a flat cap and the caption 'Yorkshire born and Yorkshire bred, strong in the arm and weak in the head'. Navigation had never been Tessa's strong point, but that was a pretty circuitous route she had taken; she would have had to cut back across the Pennines, why would she have done that?

Forgetting his urgent appointment, he reached back to pick up the roadmap from the back seat, and flicked through the index to find the page for Thirsk. There were all the other places listed on the satnav – Helmsley, Kirbymoorside, Gillamoor, plotting a wiggly line running north-east, away from the Lake District.

An unfamiliar unease gripped him. Not the usual tension related to pressure of work and the nagging sense of disappointment and failure, he was used to that. This was more disturbing. Whatever else life threw at him, his one constant was Tessa, his source of comfort and support. His rock, if that didn't sound too Paul Burrell. Had she been lying to him?

Tessa tossed the butternut squash in olive oil and garlic then spread it out in a roasting tin and into the oven, forty minutes at 200 degrees. I have measured out my life in tray-baked vegetables, she thought. But then again, what else were you going to do. You had to eat, didn't you?

'I don't believe you', John had said to her when she called him earlier. 'You're not thinking clearly; I'm coming over to make you change your mind.' His determination had only made her more adamant, appalled at the thought of him turning up on her doorstep.

'Please don't', she'd said, 'I've made my decision.'

It was hard to believe she had provoked such strong feelings, at an age when you think that sort of nonsense is behind you. She'd come close to breaking up her family, just to chase that fluttering excitement, the butterflies, the feeling you can't speak for the excitement, the conviction that this was meant to be. Her head had been turned, like a silly girl she had been flattered into betraying her husband. To think she was ready to walk out on him just because someone had told her she had a great arse. Now she was determined; she'd put things right with Matt.

She started chopping a red onion on the board that had been a wedding present from her parsimonious Auntie May. You'd expect something more generous today, with weddings ever more extravagant and even the humblest bride encouraged to behave like a spoilt princess incapable of doing her own hair and make-up. Matt had already allocated a budget for Lola's big day. 'You never know,' he said, 'she might decide to get hitched and we want to make sure it's a party to remember.' Tessa was ashamed at how enthusiastically she had gone along with him. You would hope to have bigger ideas for your daughter than a Carole Middleton fantasy of her floating down the aisle in a pure white haze. Tessa's own wedding dress had been hastily bought from Next in her lunch hour. A purple mini – the very antithesis of a patriarchal sacrificial meringue, as she'd smugly pointed out to Matt at the time.

John had wanted them to honeymoon on a Caribbean island, once they'd sorted out the formalities. He knew this great hotel on a sugar plantation, where they couldn't do enough for you and he would take her swimming in the turquoise sea that was warm as bath water.

The onions were making her cry and she dabbed at her eyes with a piece of kitchen towel then slid the finely chopped vegetables into an old Le Creuset – another wedding gift, recently reinstated into her *batterie de cuisine* since orange had become fashionable again. Everything in this kitchen was infused with significance; she could tell you when each wooden spoon had been bought, her married life was represented in these things that had been carefully chosen to enhance her career as homemaker.

Sandra had been ruthless about dismissing her own household clutter. 'I don't care,' she'd explained, 'I want to start all over again, I feel like I've been given a whole new life, you only get fixated on stuff when everything else has died away.'

Tessa weighed out the rice and stirred it into the pan, watching it become opaque. In a separate pot, homemade chicken stock was heating, ready to be added a ladleful at a time, to give the creamy texture essential for a successful risotto.

She heard the front door open, the familiar jiggle of keys, then the tread of Matt's feet coming slowly down the stairs.

'Hi,' he said, looking at her more intently than she was used to. 'Shall we have a drink?'

He pulled a bottle out from the wine cooler.

'If you feel that's wise,' she said lightly, 'in view of the latest depressing research about middle-aged boozers.'

'Why did you lie to me?'

Her stomach froze.

'Sorry?' she said, playing the innocent.

'It's true then. You're a rotten liar, Tessa.'

He took a large sip of his wine.

'Kirbymoorside, Fadmoor, Gillamoor, the clue is in the names. Not exactly the Lake District, is it? They don't do moors there, do they, they have FELLS. You have to go to Yorkshire for moors. Although I suppose it's all in the north so there's a kernel of truth in there.'

What an idiot, she'd forgotten to delete her destinations.

'The satnav,' she said.

'Yes, *my* satnav, in *my* car. Which I let you take for the weekend so you could visit your old schoolfriend in her hour of need.

Except I checked her out and it appears she lives in Canada. What do you say to that?'

His anger cut through the muddle in her brain. She'd have to tell him the truth.

'You're right,' she said. 'I was lying.'

She wasn't a Catholic, but she could feel the release of the confession. Sitting in that dark booth, whispering your sins through the grill to the unseen priest or, in this case, her rather less-forgiving husband, who had now started to laugh.

'Don't tell me, you've got a fancy man!'

He was so amused at the impossibility of such a thing that she wanted to put him straight.

'Fancy isn't the word I'd use. But yes. I was seeing somebody and now it's over.'

That wiped the smile off his face.

He slammed his glass down.

'You! *Seeing* someone? You mean *screwing* someone?'

He was looking at her in total disbelief.

Tessa stirred the risotto.

'Well?'

'I don't know what to say. I'm sorry.'

She watched the dawning realisation, as the penny finally dropped.

'So while I've been working my arse off, you've been screwing someone behind my back,' he shouted. 'And now you think you can just stand there cooking supper in that passive aggressive way!'

She poured in a ladle of stock, locked on autopilot.

'Who was he? Where did you meet him? Was it that online dating service for married people? Discreet encounters for bored housewives and desperate old men? Will I find your name listed on the dark web alongside all those civil servants?'

'Of course not. I wasn't looking for it, was I?'

'I don't know. I don't know what you get up to while I'm at work providing for everyone! Who was it?'

He was leaning on the island now and Tessa squirmed beneath his interrogation.

'Someone I knew from school. You don't know him.'

'What a cliché! Friends Reunited, was it? Thinking you can turn the clock back and you're sixteen again? In your dreams! Look at yourself, you're fifty and overweight and you don't care what you wear. You're not exactly love's young dream, you know!'

She flinched at his accurate cruelty.

'Facebook actually. He got in touch with me.'

'Oh, that's OK then, you were just the victim, nothing to do with you! I tell you what, I wish I'd got time to fool around on Facebook, hooking up with all my old girlfriends.'

'I'm sorry.'

'You're *sorry!*'

Matt was thinking now, she could see him processing the information.

'Wait, I've got it. It was that bloke your mum was going on about, wasn't it? The one who stood you up for lunch!'

Tessa nodded miserably, stirring the risotto.

'And you gave him another chance. I don't believe it. How could you?"

'I don't know . . . I was flattered, I suppose.'

'Flattered!'

She threw the spoon down and squared up to him.

'Yes, flattered! You're always telling me how useless I am, how I'm too fat to wear trousers, how bloody lucky I am to have you. Then John comes along and tells me I'm gorgeous . . . He wanted me to move in with him, that's how much he thought of me. He loves me. Which is more than you do!'

She should have done it, she should have made the break. She could be off with John right now, exploring the world, walking over the cloak he was laying at her feet. Instead of stirring a bloody saucepan and justifying herself. She'd had her chance and she'd blown it.

'John, that's the name. I thought your mum said he lived in America?'

'He does.'

'But managed to fly over to screw my wife.'

'Don't say that.'

'Well how would you put it?'

'It wasn't like that. It was . . . romantic. Exciting.'

'Oh, that makes me feel much better!'

He turned round and headed for the stairs. 'I'm going out. By the way, there's something I've got to tell you while we're in sharing mode. I resigned today. The goose that lays the golden eggs has committed harakiri. Maybe you should have run off with lover boy because I'm no longer able to support you. Bye bye, gravy train!'

Tessa heard the door slam. She turned off the gas, dinner now seemed completely beside the point, then refilled her glass and sat down on the sofa with her phone. Force of habit compelled her to open her Facebook. John had already unfriended her and their messages had evaporated, disappearing into the ether. Gone were the days of love letters tied up in a ribbon, hidden in a drawer and discovered decades later by wondering grandchildren. She clicked on his timeline, he had a public profile – he was an open kind of guy! – and went through the photographs. The gardens of Le Manoir and Dursdale Hall were still there, he hadn't got round to deleting them. Maybe he would keep them, she hoped he would, so she could always look at them and remember.

As she was browsing through them, a text came through.

I guess I was your midlife crisis. I love you.

CHAPTER NINETEEN

'Don't cease to be lovers because you are married. There is no need for the honeymoon to come to an end while you live.'

Blanche Ebbutt, *Don'ts for Wives*, 1913, p.17

Tessa was woken by her ringing phone, but by the time she'd fumbled for it on the bedside table, it had gone to voicemail. A missed call from Lola, what was she doing up at this ungodly hour? Then she noticed the time and sat up in a panic.

'Matt, wake up, it's eleven o'clock!'

'So what?' he said groggily, from beneath the duvet.

He threw his leg across hers and pulled her towards him.

'Have you forgotten, I don't have to get up any more. I can stay in bed all day, just like you.'

'I never do that.'

'More fool you. I intend to never get up early again.'

She snuggled into him, and watched the sun shining out from the sides of the curtains. They'd thought about blackout blinds, but Tessa said it was too depressing to be entirely sealed against the outside world.

'Reminds me of the old days,' Matt said, 'when we never got up before midday if we could help it. Remember I used to call you the bed slug?'

She slowly pieced together the events of last night, when he'd staggered in and tripped over the blanket chest, before falling into bed and declaring his undying love. She had been lying awake, staring at the ceiling and wondering what on earth she was going to do when he'd climbed in beside her. 'It's all my fault,' he'd said, 'I've been a complete shit, I realise that. I didn't like myself so I took it out on you. Please forgive me, I literally don't know what I'd do without you.' They had then had the best make-up sex ever. His clothes were still scattered over the floor where he'd discarded them in a loutish litter trail.

'Coffee?'

She ran her fingers through his hair, still as thick as when she'd first seen him outside that pub on Hampstead Heath. It had been what caught her eye, a dark curtain hanging over his beer glass. That and his slim, strong hands.

'And some Nurofen,' he said.

'Bad as that?'

'Almost as bad as nearly losing my wife.'

He wrapped his arms round her.

'I had a horrible dream that you'd gone off with an American.'

'What a 'mare.'

'Totes.'

She went downstairs to make the coffee, the uneaten risotto was congealing on the hob, an unpleasant reminder of their conversation last night. She took a miniature bottle of champagne from the fridge – a legacy from Matt's recent business flight, there wouldn't be any more of those – and poured it into two glasses, topping up with orange juice.

'Hair of the dog,' she said, kicking open the bedroom door and placing the tray carefully on the chest beside the accumulated contents of Matt's trouser pockets – business cards, memory sticks, laminated labels on neck ribbons that proclaimed him a Visitor to various important companies.

'You spoil me,' said Matt, sitting up to take a glass. 'On the other hand, you do owe me. Big time. How big was he, actually?'

'I don't think we want to go down that route,' said Tessa. 'I've said I'm sorry and you've accepted my apology, let's leave it at that.'

She got into bed beside him and clinked her glass against his.

'The reason I decided to forgive you is based on chemistry,' said Matt.

'Sorry?'

'It was on my third pint, I think. I was trying to Google my way to understanding why you'd done it, and I found this really interesting piece of research. Apparently, when you're a teen-ager, your emotional receptors are super-responsive. So when you have a romantic encounter at that age, it leaves a chemical imprint on your brain. And if you get to meet the fucker later on when you're a sad middle-aged person, it triggers the same feelings.'

'So I was a victim of chemistry.'

'A hostage, I'd say. And that's why I've found it in my heart to forgive you. Also, I couldn't bear to give you all my money.

Do you know, there's a bloke at work – sorry, the place where I used to work – who's just got divorced and he had to give eighty per cent to his wife. And half his pension.'

'Too mean to get rid of me, then.'

'It's not just that. I love you, I always have, you must know that. It's why I couldn't bring myself to leave you that time—'

She spun round.

'What time?'

'You never guessed? A few years back, there was someone at the office. Quite a babe actually.'

'Christ, what is this, the *Jeremy Kyle* show? Who was she?'

'Amanda. Marvellous gerundive name, thing requiring to be loved. But in the end, she wasn't you, so what was the point. Plus she wanted children.'

Tessa was surprised how unmoved she was by this revelation.

'So we're quits then,' she said.

'I guess we are. Equal partners. Also, both unemployed.'

'Yes, I didn't see that coming.'

'Too busy with your own mucky business obviously, no time to worry about me.'

'I know you've not been enjoying it. And that life coach business—'

'Don't knock it, I'm going to be needing some more of that.'

Tessa had a fleeting unwelcome vision of flow charts and personal goals. With Matt at home full time to indulge himself in his pursuit of the perfect career, as if such a thing existed.

'Anyway, I was already in a bit of a state, I think, that satnav business, though I didn't know then the full extent of it. So,

I was in this meeting and they were all talking in that bullshitty language you hate so much – I know I've always gone along with it, but something inside me was just dying, and then Steve said that we should reach out to the client on this. And I suddenly thought, what a load of old bollocks! REACH OUT to the client, what the fuck does that actually mean if you're not in a Tamla Motown band? So I said to him, "are you a member of the Four Tops?"'

'Haha, I love that song, wish I'd been there!'

'I wish you'd been there too. As it was, half the room didn't know what I was on about as they're twelve years old and Richard just gave me this look, and I thought, sod it, I can't do this any more. So I walked out. Then handed in my resignation.'

'My hero, how very stylish!'

'And afterwards I came home to find my wife had been screwing around with her teenage heart-throb. What does he look like now by the way?'

'Burly. Nice eyes.'

'Show me his picture.'

'Why?'

'I just want to see.'

'No.'

'Go on.'

'Only if you show me what's her name, gerundive Amanda.'

'Deal.'

Tessa passed her phone to Matt.

'That's him? It can't be!'

'Give it back. What do you mean, it can't be?'

'Look at his clothes! And he's completely bald, he looks ancient!'

'Stop it, I'm taking it back.'

'How tragic! I mean I know it was a chemical reaction and all that but, honestly, you would never choose him off a dating site, would you?'

'I wouldn't ever *be* on a dating site so the question's irrelevant.'

'You don't know, I might die and then you'd need to find someone new, now you've burnt your boats with old lover boy there.'

'Don't be gloomy, I thought this was a new beginning for us, that's what you were saying last night in your cups. Or was it the drink talking?'

'Not at all, *in vino veritas.*'

Tessa thought back to when she'd last said those words, then dismissed the memory.

'In fact, I thought we should start our brave new world with a winter holiday,' he continued. 'Have you noticed how second-time-round couples are permanently going on holiday?'

'I know, they behave like fun-grabbing teenagers. Holding hands on side-by-side sun-loungers. As opposed to miserable first-time-round couples who are bound together by obligation.'

'Like us. Except now we're going to have fun together, aren't we? Spend the kids' inheritance like there's no tomorrow. How about Vietnam? We can climb down those tunnels.'

'I might get stuck.'

'I'll rescue you.'

'Thanks.'

She settled comfortably back on the pillows. It really was so easy to be happy, she thought.

'We'll need to have some kind of income though. And from what you've been saying you're not too optimistic about finding another job.'

'Correct, I'm what is referred to as an industry veteran. Bring on the trench foot. Nobody wants to hire one of us when you can get a cheap young person to do it instead.'

'Like Amanda. I thought you were going to show me her photo.'

'If you insist.'

He took his phone and brought up a photo of a good-looking young woman with the obligatory swinging hair, smiling beneath the caption announcing her promotion.

'Blimey, it says she revolutionised the onboarding process. What is this, the *Titanic*?'

'She's a high-achiever. Learned from the master.'

'Spare me the details. She would have left you behind, though, you're much better off sticking with the old model.'

He kissed her shoulder.

'You're so right.'

'And I've been thinking, it's just come to me. It's my turn now, to earn the money.'

'Can't argue with that.'

'And what I'm really good at is cooking. And being a hostess.'

'You've got the Girl Guide badge, as you've often reminded me.'

'And you're sick of London, or so you say.'

'Especially now. No point living here without a job, having my nose rubbed in the success of others.'

'And you don't want to retire to Spain, or somewhere, you've also said that.'

'No I don't, we'd drink ourselves to death with boredom. My friend Ian did that but he came back. He said there's only so many times you can paint your villa.'

'So let's sell the house and buy a place in the country. I'll do bed and breakfast with optional evening meal. You can fry the bacon.'

He propped himself up on his elbow.

'I'm liking the sound of this.'

'Somewhere in Sussex, maybe. We could target the Glyndebourne crowd. Offer luxury hampers, with my signature smoked eel mousse.'

'We'll need a sturdy local woman to do the rooms. You're a shit cleaner.'

'Of course. And Lola and Max can wait tables in their holidays.'

'Make them sing for their supper for a change. This is a fantastic idea, I'm going on Rightmove straight away.'

She snuggled into him as they scrolled through likely looking properties.

'We could be up and running for the summer, here, look at this one!'

'Gorgeous. Those Georgian windows.'

'And a walled rose garden. Eight en suite bedrooms, it's perfect.'

'Done.'

'I'll ring the agent right now. So exciting.'

He beamed at her.

'You know, I really don't mind about you and the yank. In a weird way, it's done us a favour. Shaken us out of our stagnant torpor.'

'Proved that I'm not invisible.'

'What?'

'Don't you remember? When we were in that hotel in Cornwall. We were reading about women over fifty being invisible, and you said there was more chance of me being hit by a bus than finding a new partner.'

'Did I?'

'Yes.'

'Well, I was right. You haven't found a new partner. You've rediscovered your existing one. In all his fabulousness.'

'I suppose so.'

'Of course you have. And we're going to have a fantastic time running the Rose Garden guest house, the first choice for Glyndebourne guests. I'm already thinking about the website, we need to get a proper market segmentation done, make sure we strike the right note.'

Tessa took his phone off him and put it on the bedside table.

'Here, what are you doing?'

'I'm initiating our first planning meeting. Blue sky thinking. Under the duvet.'

And with that, she pulled the covers over them, and launched their new joint venture in a prolonged session of joyful marital collaboration.

Want to read
NEW BOOKS
before anyone else?

Like getting
FREE BOOKS?

Enjoy sharing your
OPINIONS?

Discover

READERS FIRST

Read. Love. Share.

Get your first free book just by signing up at
readersfirst.co.uk